PEDO ISLAND BLOODBATH

DUNCAN RALSTON

SHADOW WORK PUBLISHING

SHADOW WORK
- publishing -

Cover art by Jorge Iracheta
NIGHTMARE PILLS by Herofonts
used by permission.

ISBN 978-1988819419

ALSO BY DUNCAN RALSTON

Gristle & Bone (Collection)
Salvage (Novel)
Wildfire (Novella)
Woom (Novella)
The Method (Novel)
Video Nasties (Collection)
Ebenezer (Novella)
Ghostland (Novel)
The Midwives (Novel
In Every Dark Corner (Collection)
Afterlife: Ghostland 2.0 (Novel)
Ghostland: Infinite (Novel)
Gross Out (Novel)
Skin Flicks (Collection)
Try Not to Die: at Ghostland
(Gamebook, w/ Mark Tullius)
Puzzle House (Novel)

For more, visit
www.duncanralston.com.

And the sea gave up her dead, which were in her, and death and hell delivered up the dead, which were in them: and they were judged every man according to their works.

Revelation 20:13

I'M A VAMPIRE! I'M A VAMPIRE! I'M A VAMPIRE!

Nicolas Cage, *Vampire's Kiss*

PART 1

LAST VOYAGE OF THE *CERES*

BON VOYAGE

WITH A JAUNTY blast of its airhorn, the superyacht *Ceres*, owned by jet-setting financier-philanthropist Emory Jackman, pulled away from the docks at Miami's Island Gardens Marina, heading southeast to Little Pearl in the U.S. Virgin Islands.

As the airhorn blasted, activities onboard were already well underway. On the main deck, the waitstaff served champagne mimosas and crudités to hungry passengers, from supermodels to CEOs. In the galley, kitchen staff sweated and shouted, chopped and flambéed, prepping lunch for more than a hundred guests and crew. In the cramped bathroom in his cabin on the lowest deck, young freelance journalist Sven Olsen ran the faucet while speaking hurriedly to his girlfriend on a burner phone, worried his room might be tapped. In another cabin, on the upper decks where the wealthiest guests stayed, celebrated film mogul Ernie Wallis ejaculated into the oral cavity of his companion, a woman much younger than his current wife, but still not quite as young as he preferred. Passengers gossiped and fawned and schmoozed wherever they found one another, many of them famous or fame-adjacent, most of them wealthy or wealth-adjacent. It was a who's who of the best and brightest, as well as the most vile and dimwitted. To be seen on the *Ceres*, especially in the company of one of their hosts, was to be recognized as a Very Important Person by those whose opinions mattered most.

On the bridge, leading a crew manifest of twelve competent seamen and Emory Jackman's idiot nephew, Captain Philips—no relation—was hard at work. Though he'd done this trip and back countless times, the path from Miami to Little Pearl was considered "thorny." The island was due southeast on the rhumb line route, which looked simple on a map yet in reality countless obstacles lay in their path. The Bahamas, Turks and Caicos, several cays and archipelagos had to be circumnavigated, and—weather depending—the voyage could get extremely hairy. He would've preferred to disembark from further up the coast, the Hamptons, even a port in Connecticut, but Emory demanded that his guests pack light. Northern ports during the colder months would require them to wear more layers: heavier jackets, boots, gloves, and to pack more outfits than they might already carry, which for many was far too much. Guests on the *Ceres* were limited to two pieces of luggage each plus a small carry-on, in order to leave more room in storage for the regular deliveries required on Little Pearl Island: crates of non-perishable and perishable food items, toiletries, tools and materials for upkeep and maintenance, medical and cleaning supplies, etcetera.

Down in the cargo hold, porters Raymond Digby and Gabe Zimmer marveled again at the heavy crates and luggage they'd loaded this morning. It was a larger shipment than usual, with at least a dozen more wooden crates than the last voyage. Heavier than normal, too, like they were filled with gold bricks—which considering the passengers wouldn't have surprised Digby, to be fair. He had a good twenty years on Gabe, age-wise, and his back still ached, despite the brace. This was Gabe's first year working for Mr. Jackman. The kid was barely twenty.

"Hey, you notice Mr. Coltrane's trunk says VH on it?" Digby asked, chewing on a toothpick. They were sitting in their small office in the cargo hold, playing Hearts. Digby was winning, as usual. The kid couldn't play cards for shit, which didn't make it very fun, but it passed the time, and time was one thing they had a lot of down here. He would've preferred to be up on deck, sipping a Corona in the sun by the pool, or putting in some time working on Marnie, a new line cook. But Jackman never allowed crew on the pool deck aside from the men and women in service, and Digby wasn't too keen on fraternizing with the kind of fancy folks who'd be invited to Little Pearl, anyway. Plus, the head chef didn't like outsiders in his kitchen. Digby wasn't too eager to get further on the man's bad side, seeing as he had a temper that would put Gordon Ramsey to shame.

Gabe peered out the office window, regarding the old-fashioned steamer trunk with the initials VH embroidered in fancy script among the crates and luggage in the dark hold. "Maybe it's designer?"

"Already looked it up. Got nothin."

The kid shrugged. "I dunno then, maybe it's his wife's?"

Digby recalled watching the old man totter up the ramp with one skeletal hand holding the railing. He'd looked ancient, frail, pathetic. Digby couldn't imagine any woman wanting his withered old body bumping up against her even if they were the same age, which hardly seemed possible. Mr. Coltrane looked to be at least a hundred, maybe older.

"Or maybe it's, like, secondhand," the kid suggested.

Digby shrugged. "Well, alls I know for sure is it ain't Eddie's."

The kid looked perplexed. "Who's Eddie?"

"Van Halen," Digby said. The confusion didn't leave the kid's face, causing Digby's mood to darken. "Look, I'm still in mourning so I'm gonna give that comment a pass but fuck's sake, kid, learn a little something about music, okay? I'm going up for a smoke, you comin up for some air?"

"Nah, I'm good."

Digby gave Gabe one last disappointed shake of his head as he took the pack of Pall Mall Reds out of his lapel pocket and packed it against the heel of his palm, then he headed for the stairs. The kid still had a lot to learn, but he'd gotten his sea legs quickly, so that was something. Some of these newbies ended up loading themselves up with scope patches and still spent the entire trip puking. The motion of the ocean hadn't seemed to bug Gabe at all.

"Back in a minute," Digby grunted, a smoke already perched between his lips as he opened the door to the stairs.

The door slammed shut behind him and Gabe looked over the crates again. A sudden chill ran through him, as if they'd passed through an artic wind. Being down here alone always gave him the creeps. The bulkheads and overhead lighting threw heavy shadows over the crates and luggage. He probably should've gone up with Digby just to keep the guy company.

Then again, he *could* take a peek at Digby's hand while he was up there having a butt.

Nope, cheatin ain't cool.

True, but he did have to wonder if Digby hadn t been stacking the deck in his own favor. The guy won every single game, no matter what they were playing, from gin rummy to blackjack. Was it likelier that Digby was false dealing or marking cards, or that Gabe himself really was *that bad* at cards?

That's a good point. Shit, I'm gonna look.

As Gabe reached for Digby's cards movement in his peripherals drew his gaze to the window just as a shadow slipped behind a stack of luggage and vanished.

Gabe shot up from his chair, causing it to topple. It slammed against the cabinets and he jumped in fright.

"Who's there?" he called out.

The only response was the creak of the hull, the swish of the ocean. He squinted out into the dim light of the hold.

Swear I saw something.

He supposed his eyes could have been playing tricks on him, but he thought he saw a dark shape emerge near the top of the luggage stack, then vanish again.

"Nobody's supposed to be down here!"

Again his voice was met by the only form of silence there ever was on the *Ceres*, creak and swish.

Gabe flipped off his ballcap and scratched his head in thought as he regarded the clock on the wall. Digby usually took a full ten minutes on his smoke breaks, powering down two, sometimes three butts in one sitting up there on the deck.

Gonna have to go out there….

He put his cap back on backwards and stepped around the table, not daring to take his eyes off the dimly lit cargo hold, causing him to bump his hip on the edge and wince. Out in the hold it was noticeably chilly. It was usually a little cooler down here in the hold, but never this bad. Gabe imagined this was how cold it would feel in a submarine, a thousand feet below the surface of the water.

A solid *thump* drew his attention away from where he'd seen the dark shape, toward the luggage piled closer to the large wooden crates. Again he startled, nearly jumping out of his skin.

Just about shit a brick, he thought.

"If someone's in here, just come out," he said, trying to project confidence, rather than display the fear prickling up his spine.

A figure rose from behind the luggage, not dark as he'd

imagined but pale as milk with shimmering golden curls. Gabe staggered back a step, not in fright but in shock: the girl was the most beautiful creature he'd ever laid eyes on.

"You're—" Gabe's voice squeaked and he cleared his throat as deeply as he could muster. "No one's supposed to be down here," he finished awkwardly.

"I'm here with my sister," the girl said. Her eyes were as black as the shadows, set amid puffy dark circles and dark arched eyebrows. She wore a flower-print dress that hung off her slender shoulders, clinging to her small breasts. She looked a bit younger than him, maybe by a couple of years, which would put her in her late teens.

"Y-your sister's on the ship with you?"

The girl glanced furtively over her shoulder, in the vague direction of the crates. When she turned back to him she nodded slowly, her dark eyes never leaving his.

Holy heck, I'm in love….

"Well, um, I'm sorry but Cap'n Philips doesn't let anybody down here but us. Prob'ly worried someone'll steal something from the luggage." Noticing a small downturn in her perfect pink lips, he quickly course corrected. "Not that *you'd* steal anything, I'm not saying that, I just—I mean…" He chuckled nervously. "Can we start over? It was dark out here and I was scared…" *Shit, why'd I admit that? Maybe she'll appreciate me bein vulnerable. Do chicks dig that? Don't they all want alpha males?* "My name's Gabe," he said, holding out a hand with faux confidence. "What's yours?"

"Clarissa," she said. She made no move to step away from the safety of the luggage pile, leaving her too far away to shake his hand. Gabe lowered his in disappointment, thinking he'd do anything to feel her milky skin, even just her delicate-looking fingers.

"Clarissa," he repeated. "That's a nice name."

Her smile seemed nervous. She glanced back at the crates once more. Something she saw there, or heard, made her dark eyes widen in fear.

"I have to go," she said suddenly, stepping out from behind the luggage.

As she approached him Gabe thought she might touch him, and his body responded with an electric tingle, like when he'd touched one of those plasma globe things at the science center when he was a kid. He almost expected his hair to stand up on his head, but it remained where it was, a rat's nest tucked under his cap, and the girl—*Clarissa*—moved past him so close he could smell the sweetness of her breath, the citrusy tang of her shampoo, and a bass note of sweat. It was a fragrance he decided he wanted to breathe in everyday for the rest of his life.

And then she was gone, disappearing up the stairs. Her feet didn't make a sound on the metal steps because, as he suddenly noticed, she was barefoot.

Gabe shivered.

The door slammed and Digby started thumping down the steps with a grin. When he spotted Gabe standing in the middle of the hold, his expression changed and the fresh toothpick hung loosely from his lips. "You look like someone just beat off on your grave."

Gabe let out a ragged breath. "That girl scared the shit outta me, to be honest."

Digby frowned and looked around the darkened hold. His cigarette stench caused the girl's scent to vanish like a ghost. "What girl?" he said.

"You didn't see her?"

"See who?"

"The girl," Gabe said, getting annoyed. "You musta just passed her on the stairs."

"I didn't see shit."

Digby returned to the office and sat back down in his chair. Gabe followed him, eager to get to the bottom of this mystery.

"You *had* to've seen her."

Digby ignored the comment, apparently done with the conversation. He blinked at his cards. "Did you look at my hand?"

"Nah, I—*what the heck?*"

Gabe had absently picked up his own cards but only now looked at them. Where he'd had a shit hand before he left the room, random faces and numbers in all suits, every card had become the queen of hearts.

He stared at his hand in disbelief. No one had been in the room since he'd left. He'd been standing *right outside the door*. Nobody could've crept in and swapped out the cards and snuck out again without him having noticed. It was impossible.

Not only that, they'd played with this deck *multiple times*. There was no way it had this many of the same card in it.

Gabe glanced around himself, searching for the hidden camera. "Is somebody effing with me? Am I on *Prank Channel* or something?"

Digby frowned at him again. "What the hell are you talking about?"

"Man, I'm seri—" He held out his cards, prepared to show them to Digby… but when he looked again it was the same shitty hand he'd been dealt earlier. He retracted his hand and set the cards face down on the table.

"You goin squirrely on me, kid?"

"I'm… fine," Gabe said, feeling far from it. "Maybe I shoulda got some air with you."

Digby held his gaze. "Maybe you should get some air now. Or some medication."

Gabe laughed anxiously. "Yeah, maybe… Actually, I think I might take a nap for like an hour, if you're good."

Digby sputtered. "Go for it. I had a shit hand, anyway." He slapped his cards down on the table.

"You and me both," Gabe said with another nervous chuckle, getting up. He glanced at his cards again, left face down on the table, and quickly left the office, hurrying past the dark heaps of luggage and crates that made the hairs on the back of his neck prickle so that he had to turn and make sure nothing was following him as he rushed up the stairs. As the ceiling obscured his view of the hold Gabe thought he heard a small voice whisper his name from the shadows.

Gaaaaaaaaaaaabe.

Frightened, he struggled with the doorhandle, glancing over his shoulder into the dark until he finally managed to heave it open and stumble out onto the deck, slamming it shut behind him.

The ship swayed and rocked on the choppy surface of the Caribbean, and Gabe staggered toward the rail, gripped it tightly, and hurled his lunch overboard in thick, slimy chunks. He puked until every bit of sludge ejected from his guts and his abs hurt like he'd just done fifty crunches.

Gabe blinked at the moving ocean. He'd never thrown up on the water before. Even that time the staff had eaten a batch of bad clams, he'd been the only one to come out of that meal unscathed.

"Bon voyage, lunch," came Charlie "Cheery" Lassard's soft voice. One of several deckhands, he stood between Gabe and the sundeck, holding a mophandle like a lover with the mop in the bucket, looking every bit the pirate with his eyepatch, his bronze skin and salt-and-pepper hair in a frizzy ponytail. "Thanks for feeding the fish and not messing up my clean deck, Gabriel."

Gabe wiped his lips, embarrassed that he'd been caught puking with his supposedly iron stomach. He nodded and returned to the cabin he shared with Digby, its floor littered with the older man's dirty socks. Digby didn't even try to hide the porn mags strewn amongst his ruffled bedding on the top bunk. Who even jerked off to magazines anymore when there was an entire internet full of porn? *Never know when you'll need a tug out here on the high seas, if you know what I mean, and the kinda shit I'm into you don't wanna look up on the corporate Wi-Fi*, was his excuse. Gabe regarded the selection of titles and didn't see anything *too* outlandish: *Mommy Milkers*, *Hot & Hairy*, something called *Giantess POV*, whose cover photo was a big-boned woman in spandex, holding a miniature man by his collar between her thumb and forefinger. With her mouth wide it looked like she was planning to eat him whole rather than pleasure him.

Gabe went to their small shared bathroom and eyed himself in the mirror, pulling at the bags under his eyes. The skin on his face was waxy, like a piece of processed cheese.

As he did, the voice he'd thought he heard whispering to him from the hold replayed in his mind, causing another shiver to pass through him. The voice had reminded him of playing hide-and-seek in a dark house a long time ago, and the little girl in his class whose name he couldn't recall whispering for him to find someplace else to hide.

Someone's hiding down there, Gabe thought.

Then: *Maybe I* am *going squirrely.*

Without another thought he flopped down on his thin mattress and fell asleep before his head hit the pillow.

BENEATH THE SURFACE

SVEN OLSEN TUCKED away his laptop and burner phone under his mattress and returned to the toilet to apply some sunscreen before hitting the deck.

He smeared the supposedly chemical-free white goop onto his face, covering his nose, cheeks, forehead and ears. The last thing he wanted on this trip was a sunburn. Sun stroke was inevitable in these warmer climes, regrettably. Ever since he'd left his homeland of Sweden at the age of twenty it seemed like he couldn't be out in direct spring-to-summer sunlight for much longer than half an hour without getting struck by dehydration and a cluster headache. Back home, there were months when the sun never set at all, but the temperature also rarely rose above twenty-three degrees Celsius. It was comparably cool, and the sun didn't seem to affect him much as it did in America. He suspected it would be far worse in the middle of the Caribbean, and even more so once they reached Little Pearl.

Sven checked his face to be certain he'd smudged all of the lotion into his skin and no white streaks remained. He'd been incredibly lucky to get an invitation to Emory's cruise, he would've hated to spoil it by embarrassing himself in front of the man's celebrity friends. Emory believed Sven was writing a puff piece about him for *Rolling Stone*. In truth this was meant to be an exposé. Rumors of Emory's sex parties had been circulating for months. Sven intended to get himself in deep with Emory and record every moment with his spy camera glasses. He'd gotten his optician to replace the fake lenses with his real ones, so that if anyone checked them their vision would be blurry. Wearing them made him feel like James Bond, though admittedly more like Peter Sellers rather than any subsequent portrayals.

Sven left his cabin, locked the door, started down the hall then returned to check that it was indeed locked. Then he went off again, passing an elderly couple, the husband dressed in white linen with a mop of gray hairs bulging from its neckline, the wife wearing rose-colored glasses and sipping a Mai Tai, the plunging neckline in her one-piece swimsuit exposing her wrinkled neck and the top half of her sagging breasts.

"*Guten tag*," the husband said briskly as they passed in the narrow hall, looking up from poking a single gnarled digit at the screen of his cell phone.

"Hello," Sven said, nodding and smiling to them both. The woman ignored him, choosing instead to look at her straw—real plastic, Sven noted—as she sipped the drink. He glanced back when he'd passed them and saw that they were staying in the cabin right across from him. He'd noticed their luggage outside the door as he was boarding. The husband was patting his many pockets for the door key and the wife muttered at him in German. Sven was not among the third of Swedes who claimed to understand the language, though he knew the basics.

Sven continued to the stairs. "Excuse me," a grizzled voice spoke as Sven reached for the door.

He turned to bear witness upon the oldest man he'd ever seen outside of a coffin. The man was hunched over with a humpback, his chin folds hanging like a turkey neck, skin so withered it was almost gray, his hair about the only aspect of him with any life, short and combed in a shiny white side part. He wore lightly tinted bifocals and a gray cardigan over a pin-striped shirt and midnight blue vest.

"Yes?" Sven said.

"Would you mind kindly helping me up the stairs?" He spoke with a vague Northwestern European accent, likely Dutch or Belgian, which made Sven begin to wonder if they'd stuck all of the European guests on the lower deck.

"Yes, of course," he said, tucking an arm delicately under the arm in which the old man held his cane. Sven imagined it was like picking up a bird. Surely the man's bones had to be hollow.

He opened the door and slowly the two of them began to ascend the steps. "Are you from—?"

"The Netherlands," the old man said, shakily reaching for the banister. "My name is Coltrane. Jeffrey Coltrane."

"I'm Sven," he said.

"Charmed, Sven, charmed. Swedish then, are you?"

"Is it that obvious?" Sven said, chuckling.

The old man smiled. "A little. How long have you been in America?"

"Ten years," Sven said, then quickly corrected himself. "Eleven, actually."

"Already so long you've forgotten?" Coltrane said with a sidelong grin.

Sven chuckled. "I forgot I just celebrated my thirty-first birthday. I arrived in America when I was twenty."

"They get harder and harder to remember, don't they?"

In truth, it was harder to remember since leaving home. His parents and sister used to wake him up early on the morning of his birthday to begin celebrating with breakfast in bed and a big slice of Jordgubbstårta, a strawberry cake with jam filling, as was his family's custom. His last spent with them, the year he'd turned twenty, had been a large event with friends and family who'd visited from all across the country. These days, he still celebrated with his mother, father and sister, but it wasn't as much of a production over Zoom, and often he'd be half in his work, texting with some source or publication.

A little tug on his arm brought Sven back to the present. He turned to his companion, considering asking how old the man was, then thought better of it. Let him reveal his age, if he intended it. "Have you lived here long?" he asked instead.

Again, that sidelong grin, almost as if the old man was harboring a great secret. Sven had learned how to gently tease things from people, in his years as a journalist. Often people were like a can of nuts with a coiled snake ready to burst forth from within. All they needed was a little coaxing and *POW!*

"Mm, you could say that," Coltrane said. "I've traveled all across the globe, but America is where I've made my home for…" He let the words hang as they reached the first riser. "…many, many years," he finished once he'd settled both feet on the ground.

"Already so long you've forgotten," Sven repeated with an amiable smile.

"Indeed." The word had barely escaped his lips before it devolved into a fit of coughing. They paused on the riser, the old man hacking up a lung. Sven thought about patting him on the back but he'd read it wasn't good to do if the person were choking on something. Instead, he stood there awkwardly as the old man dug a white handkerchief out of his pocket and placed it in front of his mouth.

Coltrane hacked and coughed, his humpback spasming, a wheezy, phlegmy sound emitted from his lungs. When he finally stopped, he removed the handkerchief from his lips. It was streaked and smeared with fresh blood, partly obscuring the initials monogrammed on it. He flapped the bloody thing out with a dramatic flair and tucked it back into the pocket of his vest before Sven could get a better look at it, but it had looked like a V and a B.

Could the old man be doing so poorly he's resorted to hand-me-down handkerchiefs? Sven wondered.

"My apologies," the old man said, his voice scratchy.

"Are you…?"

"Sick?"

Sven was going to say, "okay," but Coltrane tilted his head from side to side, shrugging his pointy shoulders. "In a manner of speaking, aren't we all?" With this he laughed heartily.

"I suppose," Sven said. Together they resumed their upward travel.

"What is it you do, my boy?"

"Oh, I'm a journalist." The admission used to bring pride. With how the profession was perceived by many today, he often worried for his safety just by mentioning it.

"A writer? I'd meant to ask if you were on vacation, but a writer never stops writing, does one?"

Sven chuckled. "Not technically."

"I suppose you're already imagining for what possible reason I could have been invited on this voyage. I don't look the part, do I?"

Sven wasn't sure what he meant by that. Did Coltrane know the rumors circling Jackman's cruises and Little Pearl like gulls searching for unattended food? "I did wonder, yes," he admitted.

"Because of the shoes?"

Sven glanced at the old man's tatty leather shoes. Did men who preferred the company of young girls share his taste in footwear?

"The shoes?" he asked, confused.

"They say a man's shoes speak to his status. If that's so, surely mine must whisper tales of solitary TV dinners in front of the boob tube in a cramped apartment."

Sven let out a relieved laugh. "Ah, yes. Mine too, I'm afraid."

Coltrane regarded Sven's sandals and hmphed. "Truth be told, I was invited to Little Pearl by a very old acquaintance. Mr. Jackman, I suspect, was *compelled* to comply."

Compelled, Sven thought. *There's that word again.*

"Ah, here we are," Coltrane said as they arrived on the riser in front of the exit. He uncoupled his arm from Sven's. "One would think, considering the antiquity of some of his guests, Mr. Jackman might consider adding a lift."

Sven chuckled. "Yes, that would be helpful, wouldn't it? Are you going to the pool?"

"To the dining hall," the old man said with that furtive grin. He patted his flat stomach. "Sea voyages tend to make me feel positively ravenous."

"Good day, then," Sven said. "Perhaps we'll meet again."

"Undoubtedly." With that, the old man shuffled off down the hall toward the dining area, leaning on his cane.

Sven marveled over the peculiar man for a moment, then opened the door on a wall of sunlight. He took his magnetic sunglasses from the breast pocket of his Hawaiian shirt and fixed them quickly to the spy glasses, the bright light brutalizing his retinas.

The scene before Sven played havoc on his mild ADHD. The pool and recreation decks area were already brimming with activity, the afternoon sun beating down on everything and everyone, surrounded on all sides by pure blue as far as the eye could see, dry land left far behind them. Models and their wealthy fiancés lay in loungers around the pool, among business magnates and their trophy wives. Influencers moved among the crowd recording themselves chatting with attendees. Introverted tech gurus and inventors covered from head to toe in sunscreen and full outfits to hide their lack of tans and chicken legs, stood perpetually on the outside looking in. Hedge fund bros held up the bar doing shots of tequila they'd regret tomorrow morning. A small group, mostly young women in cut-out and skimpy bikinis, stood fawning over mononymous celebrity chef Amor, who flipped some kind of meat with an extravagant flair from his barbecue station. Even as a self-professed vegan since his university days, Sven had to admit whatever the man was grilling smelled wonderful. Set up on the deck below, where Sven noticed the Lord and Lady of a landlocked European country among those on the dance floor, the turntablist DJ Safe-T spun familiar records, pumping a fist in the air and twirling in place to the beats thumping from speakers placed strategically over all three decks. His booth was decorated with yellow tape and orange traffic cones. Here in the pool area the music wasn't quite as loud as it would be on the dance floor, and in the guest lounges above it would be at the level of a hip New York City restaurant. A Cayman Islands flag flapped lazily in the light wind above the half-covered pool, indicating their host had registered his ship there to avoid high taxes and fees.

Of the fifty or so people on all the three decks, a group of three sat in the jacuzzi, and only four were actually *in* the decent-sized pool. An elderly woman wearing goggles and a sunhat treaded water, a lithe young woman swam laps, and a middle-aged schlub with a shiny pot belly, wearing thick gold chains around his neck and gold-framed sunglasses, drank a fruity drink seated in a floating pool chair. Another young woman, likely an Instagram model, kept popping out of the water and flipping her hair as her fiancé snapped pics for whatever her latest sponsor happened to be, splashing and disrupting the others.

"Excuse me," the elderly woman said finally. "Excuse me!"

The fiancé reacted by standing up and hugging his phone in what looked like muted embarrassment. The model sneered at the woman. "*What?*"

"Some of us are trying to *use* the pool."

"Well, *some* of us have flabby arms and need the exercise."

"Hey," the guy in the floating chair said in a New Jersey accent, holding up his gold chain like a talisman against evil. "Just, you know, you don't gotta keep splashin—I mean, do ya? I'm tryin to relax. You know, we're supposed to be on *vacation* here."

The model rolled her eyes. "*Some* of us don't have famous daddies to pay our way through life and need *actual jobs*. Don't stop, this is good," she told her fiancé, striking another pose with a hand on her hip. The fiancé dutifully resumed taking photos, a man clearly held hostage by his own penis.

Sven crossed alongside the pool, feeling embarrassingly out of place, and headed for the only empty lounger. When he got there and reached for the folded towel at its foot, the young woman doing laps said, "Hey, that's my chair!" Sven recognized her as Simone Howard, Hollywood's latest ingenue.

"My apologies," Sven said, thinking if it was hers she should have placed something other than a towel on it. He surveyed the deck for somewhere else to sit. The last thing he wanted to do was have to stand among the tech gurus, like a wallflower at a secondary school dance.

"Sven Olsen?"

The familiar husky voice came from directly behind him. Sven turned, startled, to face the silver-haired, square-jawed man with the gleaming smile he'd come to know quite well in the past month. He wasn't exactly handsome—more of a middle-aged, white Everyman—but his wealth and charm afforded him the social standing of a George Clooney, or the Arabian prince Sven saw surrounded by young women near the DJ booth. Oddly, Sven hadn't seen the man when he crossed the deck, and none of his usual sycophants stood within his orbit. It was as though he'd appeared beside him out of thin air.

"Yes, hello, Mr. Jackman," Sven said, awkwardly sticking out a hand. "A pleasure to finally meet you."

Emory Jackman took Sven's hand in both of his, hugging it warmly and shaking it vigorously. Already Sven felt himself getting sucked into the man's gravitational pull. He'd heard celebrities and hangers-on speak of Emory's ability to make you feel like you belonged, like you mattered, like when you were with him you were *home*. His shimmering gray eyes had a sort of calming, mesmerizing effect. The music and sounds melted away until it was as though just the two of them shared this space, a private voyage for two. Just one of the world's richest men and Sven Jansson Olsen.

Remember why you're here, he told himself, forcing his gaze away from Jackman's.

The rich man's hands slipped away from his, and the electric feeling, the feeling of being *home*—a home he'd left so long ago—vanished with the lack of skin contact. Breakbeats thudded into his eardrums like cannon fire. Splashes and squeals, the sizzle of the grill and shouts of "*Shots! Shots! Shots!*" pummeled his brain. Rather than trouble him, it was a relieving reminder of his own body's shortcomings and consciousness.

For a moment there, he'd lost himself.

He'd lost his *self.*

Jackman seemed to sense the sudden change in dynamic, a flash of disappointment in the man's expression, as if a mask had slipped. "It's nice to finally meet you in person, Sven," his host said then, his gleaming smile returning—although lacking its earlier charm. Sven saw it now for what it truly was: aggressive mimicry. Like the luminescent fin on an anglerfish or the colorful leaves of a Venus flytrap, it was meant to lure the unsuspecting victim—be they impressionable young woman or Fortune 500 financier—into the man's sphere and then *SNAP!* He'd lock his jaws around them.

"You as well," Sven said.

Jackman nodded. "You want the tour? Let's give you the grand tour—sound good?"

"That sounds wonderful, Mr. Jackman."

Jackman grinned. "Please. My dad is Mr. Jackman. Just call me plain old Emory."

Sven allowed himself to smile. "Plain old Emory, it is."

His host clapped him on the shoulder and led him toward the stairs to the lower guest lounge. "Are you a carnivore, Sven? Chef Amor is whipping up a mean batch of his world-famous wagyu beef burgers."

"No, thank you. I'm vegan."

The disappointment was more acute this time, but again only momentary. "Well, there are plenty of vegan-friendly options on my *Ceres*. We'll make sure you get plenty of sustenance, my friend. Have you seen my helicopter?"

"There's a helicopter?"

"There's a heli*pad*," Jackman said. "Come with me."

Several people tried to get Jackman's attention as he led Sven away. He waved and smiled at his admirers and friends but he kept his attention on the task. It was clear he intended to win Sven over no matter what it took, and Sven, who needed to make Jackman believe he was on his side, had to try and find a delicate balance between friendly openness and preventing himself from getting drawn into Jackman's hungry jaws.

SISTER STOWAWAY

CLARISSA SLIPPED OUT through the cargo hold door, creeping past the older of the two porters who stood powering down a cigarette with his tattooed elbows perched on the railing.

Barefoot, her feet made barely a whisper on the cool deck boards. The man turned around, facing the other way from her, toward the stern, and grabbed the door as it swung shut behind Clarissa. Pressed flat against the wall to be sure he didn't see her, she watched him enter the stairwell, apparently unconcerned by the already opened door, then she hurried toward the garage, where she'd first entered the boat.

She turned at the next entryway, into the darkened garage where several black SUVs, a small fleet of ATVs, a gardening truck and a hovercraft were parked—and slammed into a hard yet yielding white surface.

"*Whoa*, there, girl!" the man in front of her cried.

"I'm sorry," she said, her eyes downcast as she stepped back. She'd seen this man earlier, with his white t-shirt, frizzy grayish ponytail and pirate's eyepatch. He stood holding a mop in a small damp circle on the floor, the bucket off to the side.

"You ain't supposed to be in this area." He looked at her until she couldn't help but raise her eyes. "But you know that already, don't you, honey?"

She nodded guiltily.

"Well, shoot. " The man looked around conspiratorially. "I can keep a secret. Lord knows I've had to keep my share workin on this ship. But look, if you're in trouble… you can talk to me, okay? I'm not… I'm not like *them*, you know?" With the patch over his left eye, Clarissa couldn't tell if he was blinking forcefully with the right or winking. He grabbed the single golden hoop in his right ear and wiggled it. "My pop used to say, 'Real men wear it on the left. Wear it in the right, you're a homo. Wear em in both, you're a pirate.' You get me?" With this he grinned, showing off a surprisingly white smile with a large gap between the top front teeth, like Madonna.

Clarissa didn't know what to think of his statement, whether she should nod or laugh or sympathize, so she did nothing.

"Listen, my name's Charlie but everyone calls me Cheery, and not just 'cause I'm gay." He paused a moment, awaiting her reaction. When she didn't react, his face fell flat. "Right, I guess you're probably too young to get the connection. You see, back in the day—"

Clarissa peered skittishly around the man, squinting into the darkness of the garage.

"Riiiight," Cheery said. "I guess you should scurry on back to your cabin or whatever. Listen, like I said, you need to talk, you come find ol' Cheery. I'll be around."

Clarissa nodded and gave him a brief smile to let him know she appreciated it. She stepped around the wet spot and headed deeper into the garage.

"Mom's the word, hey?" the man called after her. "Anyone comes asking, I ain't seen you. You can count on Cheery, sister!"

Clarissa hurried away, worried the man's shouts would call attention to her. Running swiftly through the garage and down the steps, she felt like a child running from wolves in the forest. She reached the other side of the garage and skidded to a stop as an armed guard stomped past the opened doorway. Her bare feet made little squeaks on the floor. The sole of her right foot tore open on a nail or a rivet and she fell back against the wall, suppressing a pained wince with a hand clapped over her mouth.

As the massive guard's bootsteps thudded away down the exterior corridor, Clarissa raised her injured foot, planting the dirty heel against her thigh, and inspected the wound. It had slashed her pretty good, right up the middle of the transverse arch, but it didn't look too deep. A couple of gauze pads and a bandage would do the trick, although it wasn't the *healing* of the wound that worried her, as fat drops of blood pattered on the cool floor.

Will she smell it? Clarissa wondered. *Even from here?*

The fact that she'd been able to communicate to Clarissa from miles away made her believe Ava might, in fact, be able to *smell* from a long distance as well. She seemed especially able to smell bodily fluids, blood in particular.

Ava never used to be like this. When they were children, she'd loathed the sight of blood, just as Clarissa had. Clarissa was her twin, and the two of them had shared many similarities other than physical. Vomit and feces made them gag. Sweat made them plug their noses. Snot made their faces wrinkle in disgust. They'd been mirror images of each other.

Until ten years ago, when Ava disappeared.

The two of them had been strolling happily through the Galaxy Galleria with their father after supper. It was two days before Christmas and after watching *Frozen* at the cinema, they'd gone looking for presents for their mother while Mom got her hair done at one of the mid-priced salons near the atrium. Already beginning to annoy their father with songs from the movie, Clarissa and Ava had bought Mom a nice pair of coral earrings she'd pointed out strategically as they'd passed by the jewelry store earlier. Dad had gotten her the Miracle-Gro AeroGarden she'd been wanting for a few months. As they left the jewelers, he suggested they get ice cream while they wait for Mom to get done at the salon.

As they'd eaten their ice cream in the food court—Ava got her favorite, bubblegum, and Clarissa took big chomps out of her double-scoop cookies and cream even though each bite hurt her teeth—Clarissa noticed a man furtively watching her and her sister over their father's shoulders, causing her to stop singing along with Ava. The man wasn't eating like everyone else in the food court, aside from some big kids hanging out listening to music and laughing. He was glancing up at them over the top of his book, trying to be inconspicuous. Even at seven years old Clarissa had begun to notice particular attention from weird men. She'd get cutesy little waves that made her feel strange in her stomach. She'd get old men with curly Santa Claus mustaches wanting to pinch her cheeks. She'd get winked at by the photographer taking school photos.

This man was completely bald, his scalp shining under the mall lighting. He wore a heavy trench coat, even though it was a balmy Miami night and even warmer inside. His eyes were dark and beady, almost like an animal's, and he had no visible eyebrows. He kept running his tongue over his top teeth with his thin, purple lips closed as he watched them. He was only a few tables behind Dad so she could see that the book he was reading was that Will Smith movie Dad said they weren't allowed to watch until they were older, even though he let them watch the *Men in Black* movies with him when Mom wasn't home.

Clarissa forgot about the man momentarily as Mom returned with her hair done nicely. Clarissa and Ava raced to munch the bottoms of their cones, giggling as the melting ice cream dribbled down their hands. Dad told her it looked "real nice," and "someone's getting a special present under the tree tonight." Older Clarissa understood it as a slightly inappropriate comment to say in front her and Ava, which explained why Mom had blushed. Ava said her hair looked like Rihanna's and Mom wasn't sure who that was but thanked her anyway.

When Clarissa looked away from her mother, the strange man who'd been watching them was gone.

Parking lots had always made Clarissa anxious: the dim, sometimes flickering lighting, the large columns and parked cars where anyone could be hiding. It was no different that night, though the energy she'd gotten from the ice cream just made her more eager to get home and watch *Despicable Me 2* with Ava for the hundredth time.

Dad pressed the button on the key fob and their car made its funny little chirp. They'd parked between two pillars, and the shadows between the car and the back wall were deep and mysterious. Clarissa waited until her parents and Ava opened their doors and climbed in before leaving the safety of the overhead light, stopping in her tracks as a horrible sound arose from inside the car, like the growl of a raving, slobbering animal.

Her mother's scream was unlike anything Clarissa had ever heard before, high and tremulous. The sound of fabric tearing caused Clarissa to hug herself, quivering in fear. Something was happening to her mother and she wanted to help, but her feet refused to move. It was as if her shoes were stuck to the floor with crazy glue.

Her father shouted. Another slashing sound was followed by a gurgling choke. Dark, viscous liquid splashed against the driver's window. The back door was still open and her sister uttered a prolonged, high-hitched scream, but Ava made no move to escape whatever was happening inside the car. Clarissa willed her to flee, crying out in her mind, hoping she'd somehow be able to hear her. But either Ava couldn't or she was just as frozen as Clarissa herself, mirroring her reaction in their shared terror. Ava's scream echoed throughout the parking lot.

A moment later her voice was cut off. Clarissa had a moment to worry her sister had been harmed like her mother and father, but the man in the trench coat, now drenched in red, climbed out of the car with Ava hugged tightly in his arms, covering her mouth with one gnarled, claw-tipped hand. Blood smeared her face and covered her clothes but she was clearly still alive, kicking at the monster's thighs, her green eyes which mirrored her sister's wide with fear.

The creature opened its jaws wide, gore dripping from sharp fangs, and let loose a horrible, snakelike hiss that chilled Clarissa to the bone. Then the thing ran off with her sister, leaping with a wide gait, bounding over the roofs and hoods of cars, causing them to erupt in a cacophony of blaring alarms that smothered the sound of the scream which finally burst from Clarissa's throat.

The police, when they'd finally arrived, assured her that her parents must have been mauled by some kind of animal. "Probably a hungry coyote," the lady officer suggested. Her partner agreed that there had been sightings in the area. Neither officer could explain what had happened to her sister—did the coyote just *carry her away?* Nor could they convince her that what she'd seen wasn't "some kind of monster," as she'd tried to convince them.

Clarissa regretted telling them that later, when they'd placed her in a foster home and the psychiatrist they'd sent her to began asking prodding questions about the "strange bald man" who "looked like an animal."

In the following years, Clarissa never forgot that entirely hairless face, but over time she began to wonder if her memories hadn't gotten mixed up, as Dr. Grodin suggested. Maybe the bald man she thought she'd seen had sicced his dog on her parents before kidnapping her sister. Or maybe he'd used the coyote attack as an opportunity to run off with Ava.

None of this explained why no animal hairs were found in the car. No hairs were found *at all*, nor fingerprints, which matched

Clarissa's version of the truth more than that of the police, who'd had no leads and no suspects. None of the faces in the book they'd shown her were at all familiar, but she'd recognized a handful of them here, ten years later, on the *Ceres*.

What were convicted sex offenders doing on a rich man's superyacht?

In the time between then and now, Clarissa had lived in one foster home after another, never settling down, always seeming to fall into trouble and get shuffled off to the next home. She'd begun to hear her sister's voice in her head only a few weeks ago. When it first started to happen, she thought she was losing her mind. How could Ava possibly sound exactly the same as she had when they were little? Wouldn't her voice have changed, like her own had?

Help me, Clarissa. It's dark and smells like dirt. You have to find me. Help meeeeeeeee.

Clarissa dreaded her worst fears had come true. The monster had killed her and buried her in a shallow grave, possibly somewhere in the Everglades. It was her sister's ghost calling to her. She was hearing Ava's voice from beyond the grave.

Then, as quickly as the voice appeared, it went away again.

This had happened two more times since. Each time Ava would tell Clarissa she had to find her, that she was lost in the dark, in the dirt. The voice would start quiet, become louder, then fade away again, as if she were passing by on a slow-moving train. Whatever was happening, Clarissa refused to tell Dr. Grodin, afraid the woman would put her in an institution. No matter how she felt about the various foster homes she'd been in, she was smart enough to know that living in a padded white room in a mental hospital would be much, much worse.

Then last night, while Clarissa had been trying to do her math homework while her latest foster sisters bickered about who was hotter, Harry Styles or Timothée Chalamet, Ava's voice returned, far more urgent than any of the times before. More persistent. Loud.

Clarissa, help me! I'm in the DARK! I'm in the DIRT! YOU HAVE TO FIND ME! HELP MEEEEEEEEE.

This time, the voice wasn't just inside of her head like the times before. It seemed to be coming from somewhere outside of the house. She'd been staring at the window, watching the dark swaying branches of the gumbo-limbo tree, when her eldest foster sister snapped her fingers in her face.

"Helloooo. Earth to Rissa."

"I have to go," Clarissa said, slamming her math book shut.

She hurried down the stairs, creeping as she reached the bottom steps. Her latest foster parents, Juanita and Nan, were so absorbed in the latest episode of *The Great British Bake Off* they didn't hear her leave.

Clarissa was already a few blocks away when she realized she was barefoot. The pebbles and concrete hurt her feet but she couldn't turn back, not with Ava *so close*. She hurried as fast as her sore feet would let her. The smells of the inner city gave way to the rotten egg stench of Biscayne Bay at nearly low tide as she crossed Macarthur Causeway in the breakdown lane. Even the sustained honks of passing vehicles couldn't deter her, wouldn't smother the exigent call of her sister's voice. It was like she was sleepwalking, following a voice in a dream.

You have to help me, Clarissa. You're so close now.

It took her nearly four hours to walk barefoot from her foster home in East Hialeah to the spot where Ava's voice finally told her she was close. By the time she reached Watson Island it was nearly morning. She heard the clang of sails in the distance, the squawk of hungry gulls. She saw the silhouettes of ships against the midnight blue sky, some of them as tall as the smaller condos on the beach. When she finally reached Island Gardens Marina, her feet blistered and raw, she saw that a security gate prevented access. A guard was checking vehicles as they entered. Did she expect billionaires to leave their massive boats unguarded?

Hide, Clarissa. You have to hide now.

Clarissa obeyed, rushing into the dense foliage of a firebush. Only a few vehicles passed her, several work trucks, a cargo van and an oil tanker.

As time passed, and the sky brightened further, she watched the gate go up and down, wondering if she'd ever be able to sneak her way inside. When the rumble of another approaching vehicle startled her, she looked through the branches to see a white truck driving slowly toward her.

Go, Clarissa! Ava's voice insisted. *Jump on the back and hide!*

Clarissa had never jumped onto the back of a moving vehicle

before but she knew she'd never reach her sister if she didn't at least try. As the truck passed slowly, she leaped out of the shadows and grabbed the tailgate.

Hide! Quick, before they see you!

She pulled herself over the tailgate swiftly, pushing with her bare feet on the bumper, lifted the crinkly tarp and hid among the groundskeeping equipment smelling of fresh-cut grass and damp soil.

It's dark and smells like dirt, she thought, idly wondering if her sister had been murdered by groundskeepers.

The truck came to a jarring halt. She heard the driver speak to the guard, and the buzz as the gate lifting. This was it. She was almost there.

The truck began to move again. It drove for half a minute, long enough for Clarissa to realize she had no idea where she was going, nor what she'd do once she got there. Was her sister buried on Watson Island? Had her body been dropped into the bay, held down by cinder blocks? Was she on one of these boats?

The truck stopped again. Men shouted. She heard a loud grinding buzz, something mechanical and much louder than the arm at the gate. Then a booming *CLANG!*

After a moment of silence, she risked a peek out from under the tarp. A massive white ship stood in front of them, gray in the early morning light, towering over the truck's cab. The word *CERES* was painted on its hull. She didn't know what the word meant, only that it was likely the name of the ship.

Then the truck started moving again, bounding over a bump and rolling over corrugated metal.

Now, Clarissa! You have to get out now!

Clarissa lifted the tarp. She saw the dark shapes of men on the dock, within a rectangle of slightly brighter light. She leapt out as the truck kept rolling, landing hard on the cold metal floor.

Run and hide!

She scurried in a crouch and hid behind a pillar. Was it irony that her journey ended here, in another dark parking garage, after so many years had passed since that fateful night at the Galaxy Galleria when she'd lost everyone she'd ever cared about? Or was it fate that she'd find her sister here?

The truck parked. The doors opened and the men got out. They slammed the doors and walked past her without noticing, heading for the dock. The drawbridge thingy they'd driven over began to rise with its loud mechanical buzz and the men beyond it sauntered away, leaving her in pure darkness.

She imagined the bald man, the monster with claws and fangs who'd murdered her parents, climbing out of one of the vehicles she'd seen as she ran, rising up out of the shadows before her and flapping open his trench coat like a giant bat, like Dracula's cape.

But Dr. Grodin said there was no such thing as monsters, that the *real* monsters were human. Her Mall Monster was likely just as human as Clarissa was herself. Flesh and blood and nothing more. No sharp teeth. No clawed fingers.

A man.

The thought failed to comfort her.

You're so close now, sister.

Ava's voice comforted her. Her fear of the dark lot had held her in place, as it had that night two stories below the mall, but hearing her sister's voice once more drove her to her feet. She followed it to an exit on the other side of the ship. The light outside was purple like a bruise, the dark before dawn.

She ran along the side deck as her sister directed, and down a set of stairs. The door here was closed, but it opened easily with a squeal of metal and she winced at the sound, certain she'd be caught. She waited a moment in silence, then stepped into the cool dark beyond and pulled the door shut. This time it didn't make a sound.

I'm down here.

Clarissa crept down the metal stairs. As her eyes readjusted to the dark, she began to see shadows in the large space she'd entered. Stacks of boxes or crates.

In here, Ava whispered.

Clarissa followed her voice to a crate set apart from the others, placed directly on the floor. She regarded it, the final resting place of her sister. A square wooden box among dozens like it. Had she lost her mind? Had she really come this far on the whim of a voice in her head, the voice of someone who could've been dead for as long as ten years?

Open it, that voice said. *Release me.*

Clarissa pulled at the lid but quickly realized it would be

impossible to open with her hands. She looked around the dark space for something to pry it open with.

The office. There's a bent metal thingy in the office.

Clarissa entered the small office. There was a table and two chairs and a desk with drawers. Cards had been left mid-game on the table. Hanging from the wall were several tools: hammer, metal clippers, sledge, crowbar. She grabbed this last, feeling its cool metallic weight, and brought it back to the crate.

Here it is, she thought. *Are you sure you want to know the truth?*

Clarissa answered herself by jamming the bent claw of the tool under the lid and beginning to pry. She threw all of her weight down, and the top came up with a squawk of nails against wood. She pushed the lid away, unconcerned by the loud clatter on the floor, and peered down at the contents she'd revealed.

It was soil, just like Ava had told her—or her imagination had conjured up. Black, damp soil, rich and earthy and pungent in her nostrils.

Without another thought, she dug her hands into the black earth, clawing away heaps of it, digging and digging until her fingers touched something cold and yielding.

Flesh.

She wiped away the rest, delicate so as not to disturb the remains. With her eyes fully adjusted to the dark she finally understood why Ava's voice had never changed in her mind. There she stood, face to face with herself as a child. Ava's face was ghostly pale against the black earth she'd been buried in, her flesh perfectly unblemished, untouched by the rot of the grave. Here lay Ava Mackenzie Hurst, perfectly preserved, forever at age seven.

Clarissa studied her twin sister for a long moment, relief tinged with grief causing her to cry tears she thought had been expended years ago. She wept for her dead parents and sister, for the years she'd lost with them and the time she'd wasted wondering what might have happened to Ava. She cried for her crummy life and her family's sad death. She cried because she knew she'd never see justice, that the man who'd murdered her family would likely never be caught.

As she looked down again, vision blurry with tears, her seven-year-old sister's eyes sprang open.

"You found me!" the dead girl said.

Ava smiled, revealing fangs just like Mall Monster's, and she leaped out of the dirt like a jack-in-the-box into her living sister's arms. Clarissa staggered back in pure horror, Ava's hands as cold as ice water against her neck and shoulders. She stood as frozen as she had when the monster killed her family, while her little twin sister licked the tears and snot from her face, shaken by the realization that the man from the mall hadn't killed Ava.

He'd done *worse*.

He'd turned her into a monster, just like him.

UNDERCOVER

SVEN WALKED ALONGSIDE Emory Jackman during their tour through the great ship, though he didn't for a moment believe they were on equal footing. He'd told Jackman he was courting several major publications for the interview, and that was true. He'd had stories published in magazines and papers from around the world, from *Rolling Stone* to the *New York Times*. He'd been nominated for the Swedish Guldspaden award and the Norwegian Ossietzky Prize, but lost to Julian Assange and Edward Snowden respectively. Just his luck that he happened to be nominated in the same years as two of the most important and reviled journalists of the last twenty years.

Jackman had already taken him through the galley to meet the head chef and his staff as they prepared a wonderful smelling coq au vin for lunch. He'd shown Sven the helicopter near the ship's stern—an AW139, which was quite impressive, even to Sven who knew nothing of helicopters—and to the hangar where he showed off his fleet of jeeps and all-terrain vehicles. They'd met the ship's Bosun near the hangar, who'd been talking hurriedly to the *Ceres*'s Chief of Security, a man named Wilson. Both men looked like they didn't have clean flour in their bags, acting quite suspiciously until Jackman called the name of the security chief and introduced both men, then took the chief aside to speak to him privately. Sven had recorded it all with his spy glasses, hoping to be able to hear what the men were saying to each other when he played it back later in the safety of his cabin over the sound of crashing waves.

"Sven, meet our captain, Tom Philips," Jackman said as they entered the bridge.

"No relation," the bear of a captain said, sticking out a hand.

Sven shook it, his finger bones crushed against each other as he struggled to understand the reference. *Relation to whom?* he wondered.

Mercifully, the big man let him go. "Have you ever been on a bridge before?"

"I've only ever been on sailboats."

The captain smiled. "Well, then, this should be educational for you. You're lucky today, we have *most* hands on deck. This is Ibrahim, our OOW, Officer of the Watch." The OOW, a handsome Middle Eastern man, raised his eyes briefly from the large map he was looking over and nodded. "Aside from our Chief Engineer, who is unfortunately in the engine room at the moment, he plays one of the most important roles on our *Ceres*."

"Is there something wrong with the engine?" Sven asked.

Captain Philips's eyes widened, then he laughed heartily. "Not on my ship, Olsen. We make sure everything is running smoothly before we leave port. It's a thorny route, so we need her working at maximum efficiency if we want to keep our guests comfortable. Don't we, Ibrahim?"

The OOW looked up again briefly and said, "Yes, sir."

The captain then showed Sven the various instruments and implements used in piloting a ship, taking great pride in small details. When speaking of the possible inclement weather on this route, he again used a term Sven hadn't heard before.

"What does this mean, 'thorny'?"

Captain Philips ushered him toward the wide windows at the front of the bridge. "Between us and Little Pearl the waters can be treacherous, Olsen, particularly through the Bahamas, and Turks and Caicos."

"Is there a reason we go that way?"

"It's called the rhumb line. Crossing all meridians at the same angle from our port of departure. Going around would add too much time to the route, and our fearless leader insists on punctuality, don't you, Emory?"

Jackman smiled at this. "Being late is a pet peeve of mine."

"Hey, Uncle Emory," said a waving young doofus dressed in the same short-sleeved uniform the others on the bridge wore, aside from Captain Philips's long sleeves and hat.

Jackman turned away from his nephew without responding. "Well, if you don't have any more questions for our captain, Sven, perhaps we could conclude the tour in my quarters with a glass of my favorite scotch?"

"That sounds wonderful. Oh, if you don't mind, Captain, I'd like to speak with you again some time."

"Of course. When I'm not on the bridge or in my quarters you'll find me in the dining hall."

"Splendid. Thank you for the tour."

"A pleasure."

"Thank you, gentleman and lady," Jackman said, saluting his crew. They each returned the salute, although his nephew performed his halfheartedly, seemingly scorned by the rejection.

After the two of them left the bridge, Jackman led Sven down the corridor to the stairs leading up to his quarters at top of the ship. "So, what do you think, Sven?"

"The *Ceres* is quite impressive. Thank you immensely for the tour."

"It's my pleasure, Sven. I want to make sure you have a good time while you're with us."

"Yes, of course. I wonder…"

"Hmm?"

"I spoke earlier with a Mr. Coltrane."

Jackman stopped on the beige-carpeted steps and turned with a quizzical look. "Is there a question buried under your statement, Sven?"

"No. Only… he seems quite out of place among your other guests."

Jackman's blank expression gained a smile. "Right. Well, he's an old friend of my father's."

"That's interesting."

"Is it?"

"Well, yes. You see, Mr. Coltrane mentioned it was an old friend of *yours* who may have compelled you to invite him on this voyage."

"Am I being cross-examined here, Sven? I thought this was a friendly chat. *Mano a mano*."

"No, of course not, Emory. I'm merely curious as to who that old friend might be."

Jackman appeared to consider it. "I can only assume what he *meant* was an old friend of my father's, a family friend. He is awaiting us on the island, yes."

"And he is?"

"An old man very set in his ways," Jackman replied. "Much like our Mr. Coltrane. It's been… quite a long time since they've seen each other. I imagine they have much to discuss."

Sven nodded, then covered his embarrassment with a smile. "Sorry," he said. "I find it difficult sometimes to shut off my reporter's brain."

Again, Jackman clapped him on the back. "Everything has a story, Sven. But not every story is worth reporting, is it?" At this, the man winked.

"Quite right," Sven agreed.

Jackman opened the door to his quarters. "Shall we…?"

"Yes," Sven said. "Let's have that scotch."

The old man watched the young reporter and Mr. Jackman speak with the head chef and his staff, and once they'd left he shuffled over and knocked on the doorjamb to make his presence known.

Everyone was dressed in crisp white uniforms, the head chef sweating from head to toe over a lovely smelling pot. A young man peeled carrots. A young woman cracked eggs into a large tub. Another young man with his long hair in a net poured water from a jug on a hot grill and scrubbed the steaming area down, sleeves rolled up to the elbows. The head chef looked up as sweat from his brow dripped into the contents of the pot, though he apparently didn't notice. "Yes? Are you lost?"

"No, indeed." The old man smiled warmly. The chef didn't return it. "I'm curious. Will there be garlic in tonight's meal?"

The young kitchen staff standing at the butcher block gave each other knowing looks and resumed their cracking and peeling, as the head chef frowned and wiped his brow with the back of his forearm. "Mr. Jackman is allergic to garlic," he said, "therefore there is no garlic in our kitchen."

"No garlic," the old man repeated, disappointed but not entirely surprised. "That's a rather odd allergy, wouldn't you say?"

The young woman shrugged. "I'm allergic to latex."

"Yeah, me too," the young man peeling carrots said, clearly attempting to bond over it. The woman pulled a face as if she'd just sucked on a lemon. The young man resumed peeling into the bucket on the floor.

"My parents said I'm allergic to hard work," said the kid scrubbing the grill.

The chef and his underlings chuckled at this. "There used to be this Italian Prime Minister who tried to ban garlic because he was allergic to it," the chef said. "You think it's weird we don't have it on a ship with maybe a hundred people, mostly Americans. That guy tried to get *Italians* to stop eating garlic. Imagine how popular he must've been."

The old man nodded. "Yes, hmm. Tell me, Chef, I see that spaghetti alle vongole is on the menu for tonight, along with your lovely smelling coq au vin. How *does* one cook Italian food without the use of garlic? For that matter, does not coq au vin require garlic as well?"

The head chef waited patiently through the old man's query. He glanced back at his bubbling pot before replying. "We use garlic substitutes. Shallots. Scallions. Garlic chives. Green onions."

"Are garlic chives not garlic?"

"They're an herb. There's no bulb."

"They're a type of onion, I think," the woman cracking eggs added.

"Exactly," the head chef said. "It's the shoots from a type of onion."

"I see. So, they are garlic in name only."

"That's right," the head chef said, giving him an impatient look.

The old man smiled again, and once more the head chef didn't return it. "Thank you for your time, Chef."

"Sure. No problem."

The old man caught the chef's look to his underlings as he returned to his pot, insinuating their visitor likely suffered from dementia. Let them think it. He'd be prepared once they reached the island, with or without their help. He'd smuggled several dozen garlic pills in among his various medications. With the bottled water he'd had blessed by Father Ripley, he'd mix it into a thin paste and smear it over his entire body, covering himself from head to toe just as the chef appeared to be with sweat.

He would meet his nemesis on equal footing.

Finally, after so many countless years, he would have his

revenge.

Little over an hour later, Sven sauntered back to his cabin several decks below Jackman's, tipsy from one too many glasses of scotch. His host hadn't been kidding, it was the smoothest Sven had ever had in his life, though he didn't generally drink much outside of schnapps and the occasional light beer.

While they'd sipped from their glasses—Sven's with water, Jackman's straight up—the financier regaled him with tales of his early days in a British boarding school in India, where his father had been an American diplomat. He expressed his regret at having been involved in what used to be called "fagging," more commonly referred to as "hazing" in America, as both servant and master. He'd suffered his share of abuse at the hands of elder students as a freshman, yet claimed to have felt "poorly" about handing down the same "discipline" to those under him when it was his turn to hold the reigns. "But that was the culture," he told Sven with a shrug. "You either went along with it or you sat on the sidelines, a literal reject. A pariah."

From boarding school he'd gone directly into USC's Marshall School of Business, where he'd studied economics, psychology and decision theory. He'd met and become friends with several founders and current CEOs of major corporations. From there he'd attended swank parties and night club events in Beverly Hills, West Hollywood and Sherman Oaks, been invited to "hang out" with Hugh Hefner at the Playboy Bunny Ranch, met and connected with many big-name actors and musicians, some of whom became lifelong friends.

"I partied with the best of them, Sven. Believe me, if I named them, you'd be impressed."

Jackman seemed to be attempting to provide Sven with a "warts and all" account of his life, from his first fumbling attempts at losing his virginity to the breakdown of his first marriage, which he admitted was mostly his fault.

"I wasn't there." He offered his now familiar shrug. "And she wanted more from me than I was able to give. Not money, Sven. I mean emotionally. I'm very much like my father, in that regard. I can be distant. Too much time spent in my own head, I guess you could say. Fortunately, Tess understands I am who I am and I can't be everywhere at once."

"Is she with us now?" Sven asked, referring to Jackman's current wife, who'd been accused of "grooming" young girls for Jackman's parties on the island.

"She's been feeling under the weather lately and didn't want to worry the other guests with her illness."

The excuse seemed reasonable enough, considering what the world had been through during the past several years. Nobody wanted to infect anyone with any kind of illness. Sven had seen several guests wearing fashionable face masks during his tour of the ship. For a few, it was the only garment they'd worn other than their swimsuits.

Still, it did seem odd for Tess Jackman not to be here. She'd never missed an opportunity to be spotted at famous gatherings or her own, by the paparazzi or the entourage of hangers on she'd accumulated over the years, many of whom were on this voyage. Though she could merely have sequestered herself in their quarters until she'd felt better. Sven had to wonder if there wasn't some other reason for her absence on this trip.

Additionally, Jackman's "unvarnished truth" didn't align with many of the things Sven had heard about the man. He'd been told by several of Jackman's childhood friends that he'd participated "gleefully" in the hazing, both as victim and perpetrator. He'd heard stories of Jackman's "lecherous" behavior at the Playboy Mansion from the former Bunnies themselves. He'd been told that Jackman was nothing more than a "hanger on" from various rock stars and celebrities, who'd somehow made a name for himself as a "man of wealth and taste," as one had put it, despite having none of the latter. Sven had asked if he'd meant to quote the lyrics to the old Stones' song about the Devil, and the celebrity source had given him a dark look and said, "You heard the stories. You tell me."

Sven certainly didn't think Jackman was the Devil. But he did believe the man kept his cards much closer to his chest than he seemed to be indicating. He called himself an "open book," but steered away from questions concerning his current wife's background, of whom very little was known. He'd told Sven she was Hungarian and "of noble blood." Other than those facts and the occasional assurances of her "exquisite, youthful beauty"—

which Sven had witnessed in photos in all the usual tabloid rags speculating on possible plastic surgery and whether or not she'd discovered the "fountain of youth"—it was all he would divulge.

Over the course of this trip, Sven hoped to discover the answer to all of these queries and more. He had to be cautious, though. He had to play his cards as closely to his chest as Jackman himself, while sharing just enough details of his own personal life to make it appear as though he held no ace up his sleeve.

Back at his cabin, he slipped the laptop out from under his mattress and booted it up. He connected the spy glasses via USB and downloaded the few hours of footage he'd just recorded. While he waited, he went to the bathroom and looked at himself in the mirror. The alcohol had made him more relaxed but he hoped it hadn't made him careless, that he hadn't said the wrong thing at some point.

Bring your spikes down, he told himself. *You've done this before. Investigative journalism is in your blood. They won't suspect you unless you give your hand away.*

Sven sat down on his bed and unplugged the glasses, set them on the nightstand and swapping them out with his regular glasses, then scrubbed through the footage he'd recorded, quickly looking for what had concerned him earlier. It was as they'd left the hangar, after Jackman showed him the Jet Skis and hovercraft, when Jackman had pulled aside the security chief to speak with him briskly.

He played the footage. Most of their hushed conversation was washed away by the screech of gulls and the sound of waves crashing against the hull.

What he did manage to catch were the words "stowaway," "bloody footprints," and "lost her on the lower decks."

Whoever this mysterious stowaway was, the two men seemed to be deeply concerned by her presence on board.

The last thing Jackman said before turning back to Sven with a freshly polished smile was, "The *second* you find this kid, you bring her straight to me."

GABE WOKE SHORTLY before supper when Digby returned to the cabin, as loud as a hurricane. "Oh, shit, sorry, Little Buddy," Digby said loudly. "Didn't realize you were still out of it."

Gabe sat up and rubbed his eyes. He'd slept like the dead but didn't feel at all refreshed by his nap. Actually, he felt *worse*, like he'd been run over by a car. He had a screaming headache and his entire body felt sore, worse than he had during his ugliest hangover to date, when Digby had convinced him to drink moonshine on their first voyage together and he'd spent the entire following day asleep in their cabin, puking into a bucket. At least he wasn't vomiting this time. *Yet*.

"Yeah," he groaned, his mouth dry. "Must be some kinda bug."

"If you get me sick, I swear to God," Digby said. He entered the washroom and unzipped, pissing with the door open, as he most often did. Gabe had tried getting him to close the door, even going so far as to close it himself a few times, but Digby never seemed to learn or care. It sounded like horses playing polo.

"You gonna come to dinner then, or what?" Digby called from the bathroom, holding his gaze in the mirror as the torrent unleashed into the bowl.

"Don't think I can, Dig. I still feel like crap."

"I'll bring you back a doggy bag, sound good?"

Gabe nodded. "Yeah, man. That'd be good, thanks."

Digby closed the bathroom door as he started to undress for his shower. As the water splashed against the shower floor, Gabe's thoughts returned to the girl he'd met in the cargo hold. She was unlike anyone he'd ever seen before, so beautiful and mysterious, her eyes dark and haunted. He closed his eyes and imagined her, the strap of her dress slipping off her shoulder, the way her gaze rose from her bare feet to look up at him, her head tilted slightly forward. The way she shifted her feet awkwardly, seemingly eager to get away. Had she feared him? He didn't think so, at least not personally. More likely she'd feared getting caught at whatever she'd been doing down there in the hold.

That voice, he thought, no longer thinking of Clarissa but the other girl, the softer yet somehow more insistent voice that seemed to have spoken in his head, whispering his name.

Had he imagined it? Was there really someone hiding in the hold? Was that why Clarissa was down there? Was she harboring a stowaway?

Thinking this, Gabe fell asleep again.

He awoke to find the cabin full of what he'd first thought was smoke and sat up in alarm. Spotting Digby dressed in a fresh outfit, ready for dinner and buttoning up the silver satin sleeveless shirt he liked to wear on club night, he realized it was just steam from one of Digby's irrationally hot showers.

"You pass out again? Hope you didn't lose your sea legs, kid...."

Gabe didn't think that was likely, considering he'd grown up on the water. His headache had lessened a little, though. Maybe the steam had loosened up whatever had caused it. "I'll be fine. I'm just gonna take it easy tonight."

"Prolly a good idea." Digby turned and held out his arms like a welcoming game show host. "How do I look?"

"Like a hundred bucks," Gabe said, referencing their shared joke. Looking like a million bucks among the rich and famous wasn't likely with what Jackman was paying them.

Digby winked. "Think I'll get lucky tonight. Some talent in the new recruits this trip, huh? Might be a little old for you but they're right in my sweet spot."

Gabe shrugged and nodded.

Digby gave him a concerned look. "Kid, we're *both* gettin you laid this trip. No man left behind, ya hear me?"

Gabe tried to smile. "I'm good, thanks."

Digby regarded him more closely. "Look, if you met someone on shore and you're worried she's gonna find out about you gettin a little strange, what happens on Little Pearl stays on Little Pearl." He mimed zipping his lips shut. "My lips are sealed, Little Buddy.

You don't gotta worry about me."

"I don't have a girlfriend."

"You're not gay, are you? Not that it'd matter. Hell, probably got more options if you were. I wish I was into dick. I'd be the belle of the goddamn ball."

"Okay," Gabe said with an embarrassed chuckle.

"All right, well, gay, straight or somewhere in between, we are gettin you laid, kid, come Hell or high water."

Gabe chuckled again. He always felt awkward in these kinds of conversations. He'd only had one girlfriend throughout high school and while they'd messed around a bit, they'd never gotten around to the actual intercourse part of sex. She'd been religious and had wanted to save that for marriage, which they'd been planning for after she graduated from dental school. They'd broken up before his first trip on the *Ceres*, but Gabe still wore the crucifix she'd given him under his work shirts as a pledge of their commitment to abstinence.

Gabe had never been committed to God nor abstinence, but he had loved Ashley a fair bit and never had the heart to take off the necklace she'd given him, even after she'd dumped him for an older dental surgeon, and even though he didn't really believe in a higher power like she had.

All of this made talking about sex especially awkward and embarrassing for him.

Plus, now there was the addition of the girl he'd met in the hold. On the one hand, he wanted to tell Digby all about her. He couldn't think about anything *but* her—aside from that strange little girl's voice in his head—and he certainly didn't want to lose his virginity to some random crew member when all he'd be thinking about the whole time was Clarissa.

On the other hand, he didn't want to jinx anything by talking about her. He also didn't want to rat her out should she return to the hold to resume whatever she'd been doing down there. And he *wanted* her to return, even though it'd get both of them in trouble if she ever got caught.

"Sounds good," he said, forcing a smile.

"All right, kid. Get some more rest, you look like kaka. I'll bring you back some chow."

"Thanks, Skipper," he said.

Digby patted him on the shoulder. "You got it, Little Buddy."

As his roommate left the cabin, Gabe fell back against the pillow, his mind still swimming with thoughts of the girl in the hold. What was she doing down there? Why was she barefoot? Was she a passenger or a stowaway herself?

Gabe didn't know the answer to any of these questions, and he wasn't sure he *wanted* to know. If he could keep a picture of her perfect and unspoiled in his mind, all the better. He didn't want to think she was doing anything illegal down there, like stealing or messing with someone's luggage. Maybe she'd just left her Kindle or a hair brush in her trunk and came down to get it. Maybe she'd been barefoot because she'd been on the sundeck by the pool, although her feet had looked pretty dirty and worse for wear. She clearly hadn't been *swimming.*

Gaaaaaaaaaaabe.

The voice pierced his skull like a dagger between the eyes, and he thumped back against the pillow. He rubbed his temples, just glad he hadn't been standing when it hit him or he'd have fallen and probably knocked himself unconscious. This time the little girl's voice was far more persistent and intense. It almost sounded like she was screaming directly in his mind, like death metal blasted through headphones.

Woozily Gabe sat up, bumping his head on the bottom of the top bunk. While he rubbed the injury, sure there'd be a goose egg on it tomorrow, the girl spoke again.

Gaaaaaaaaaaaaaaaaaaaabe.

He was wrong. The voice wasn't coming from his head. It was coming from the ducts. The air vent beside the bathroom door, specifically.

He stood up carefully and staggered toward it.

Gaaaaaaaaaaabe. Release me.

"Release you?" he said aloud. "What d'you mean?"

REEEEELEEEEEEEEEEASE MEEEEEEEEEEEEE!

Gabe grabbed his temples, squeezing his head between his palms as the voice nearly shattered his mind. When the pain died down, when he was able to speak again, he stood on tiptoes and whispered into the grate, "Where are you?" He only hoped Digby wouldn't come back right now and see him talking to the vent like a madman.

You know where. Find me. Release me.

"Find you," he repeated, realizing he knew exactly where she'd be. "Release you."

He got down from his tiptoes, threw on his ballcap and went to the door. No one was in the hall when he peered out, otherwise he might've scurried back into his bed. He felt oddly clandestine about what he was doing, like masturbating or shooting heroin. He didn't want anyone to see him doing it.

Because it's wrong, he thought.

But was it? If there truly was a girl in the cargo hold, held captive there for some reason or another, how could it be wrong to set her free?

Maybe that's what Clarissa was doing when you caught her? Probably why she was actin so suspiciously.

He crept down the hall, telling himself if he ran into someone before he reached the stairs he'd turn right around and scurry back to his room. There was something *not right* about the little girl's voice. For one thing, if she really was in the cargo hold, how was she speaking to him through the vents?

She's not human, that's how.

Gabe shuddered at this, hugging himself with one arm as he opened the door at the end of the hall with his free hand, hoping to run into someone, *anyone*, to be able to convince himself to stop this craziness, to turn around *right now* and forget all about the voice in the vent, no matter who the little girl in the hold might be.

There was no one in the stairwell, so he continued, creeping up the stairs like a cat burglar.

What if Clarissa's back down in the hold? What would you do? Wouldn't you do anything to see her again? To see her RIGHT THIS MINUTE? Wouldn't you carve her name into your flesh merely to feel her gentle caress upon your cheek? Wouldn't you shout her name at the stars to fall under the spell of her dark, haunting gaze?

Gabe shook his head. These weren't his thoughts. They came from his mind and spoke in his voice but felt foreign, alien. They weren't words he would speak aloud let alone think. It was the girl. Somehow she could speak directly into his mind with his own voice, and anyone who could do that could not, *should* not, be trusted.

Gaaaaaaaaaaaaaaaaaaaaaaaaaaaaaaaaabe.

The voice had followed him, appearing to come from somewhere further up the stairwell. He obeyed, ascending again and opening the door and stepping out into sunlight that stabbed his eyes like nails made of ice.

He expected to see someone out here, but it was as if the entire ship was suddenly deserted, as if everyone had jumped overboard and left him alone on this ghost ship, a captainless voyage straight into the bowels of Hell. What was it Digby had said? *Come Hell or high water?* What did that mean, exactly? Whichever came first? Eternal damnation or sinking into the fathomless depths? Either option was a high possibility on a boat with no crew.

But no, he wasn't alone. It was late. Likely most of the guests and crew were at dinner. He could hear the thump of dance music and voices from the other decks. Surely Captain Philips and his crew were still on the bridge, Mr. Jackman in his quarters or somewhere holding court. Still, the way was clear somehow, almost as if she had known all he needed was to see someone else, someone *real*, to stop himself from doing what she wanted him to do. From *releasing* her. Like she'd made certain there would be no one in his way.

You're so close now, Gabe. Don't give up now.

"I'm coming," he answered under his breath.

In moments, he stood before the door to the cargo hold, a hand hovering over the handle.

This is wrong. Whatever's down there... it's not my business.

He lowered his hand and nearly turned away from the door. But if there was someone down in the hold, trapped in the dark, wouldn't he be considered a hero for saving her? Wouldn't he be damning himself to Hell if he knew a little girl was trapped in a box or a trunk down there and *didn't* help her? What if she suffocated to death? What if someone was abusing her?

He took off his cap and ran his hands through his hair, crippled by confusion. He wished Clarissa was here right now so she could ask her what to do. Even Cheery would be a welcome sight.

What now? he thought frantically. *Somebody tell me what to do!*

Come to me, the voice replied from down below.

Without another thought, Gabe reached for the door handle,

twisted it, and stepped into the cool dark of the hold. He pulled the door shut quietly behind him and stood at the top of the steps looking down for a very long time.

There you are, the voice said.

Gabe followed the voice, his shoes clanking on the metal steps, the echoes clanging in the darkness of the hold. When he reached the bottom, he stopped again. The hold was draped in shadow. He'd forgotten to turn on the light at the top of the stairs. The other light switch was all the way at the other end of the hold by the office door.

The ship groaned and creaked, rocking gently. Impossible to tell if the sounds were coming from the hull or from somewhere within the warren of black shapes stacked within the hold.

Commmmmmmme, the voice said.

He started forward into the gloom, his feet moving without instruction from his mind, of their own accord, like sleepwalking in a waking nightmare. His shin struck a hard-shell suitcase and he yelped in fear more than pain, but still his legs moved him onward, propelled by the will of the little girl who called to him from somewhere deeper within the maze of luggage and crates.

Commmmmmmmmmmmmme.

His feet stopped moving in front of a single crate, stood alone beside a stack of others.

Yesssssss, the voice said, apparently from inside the box.

He looked down. The crowbar from the office lay at his feet. He'd been looking for it, had assumed Digby had just misplaced it or left it on shore, and planned to borrow one from the dock crew once they got to Little Pearl.

But here it was, on the floor next to a crate that had been calling to him with the voice of a child all the way from his room.

Almost as though someone had left it here for him.

Almost like it was *meant to be*.

He bent and picked it up. It felt heavy and strangely cold in his hands, more like a potential murder weapon than a tool he'd used without malice hundreds of times in the past.

He wedged the bent claw under the first nail. It slipped in easily, and he pulled the nail up until it popped free of the crate and landed on the floor with a tiny *ping*. He did the same for the next, and the one after that, working in a daze, barely noticing that several of the nails were already partway up, as if whoever had packed it had been lazy with the hammer. *Ping*, *ping*, *ping*, they each struck the floor, like shell casings from a rifle, until the lid was free from the crate and slid off to the floor below with a loud *CRACK!*

Peering down into the crate, expecting to find a little girl huddled within, perhaps in chains, likely deprived of food and water for a day or more, he saw instead the crate at his feet was filled almost to the brim with dark, damp-looking soil.

A crate of earth.

Gabe stared at it for a long moment. Then he laughed. The laughter sounded insane even to his own ears, echoing off the walls. He considered the notion that he possibly was at least halfway there already. First the voice, then the hallucination with the playing cards, and now this, prying open a crate he wasn't supposed to handle beyond lifting it with Digby into the hold, all because a voice he'd heard in his mind had told him to, like a voice that commanded someone to murder.

"What are you doing?"

Clarissa's voice shook him from his mental fog. He turned to see her staring past him at the opened crate.

"*What have you done?*"

Behind him something thudded to the floor. Clarissa stepped forward and he caught her in his arms without meaning to as a skittering sound made the skin on the back of his neck crawl. The sound moved away, then rose, as if it was climbing the wall. It was followed by a metallic squeak.

Clarissa struggled in his arms. "Let me go, you idiot!" She slapped his face. His arms dropped instinctually and she raced past him.

Gabe turned to see the large grate near the ceiling fall closed with a clang as Clarissa skidded to a stop below it, her feet still bare. With horror on her face, she craned her neck to look up and whispered a single word: "*No.*"

"What *was* that?" Gabe asked, completely dumbfounded.

Rather than answer him, Clarissa whipped around with a fierce scowl that burned right through him and rushed toward him. For a split second he was sure she was about to deck him, then she blew past him, heading for the stairs.

"Wait!" he called, making to follow her. She was already halfway up the steps by the time he got going, his feet still working against him. The door above slammed as he reached the foot of the stairs and when he finally made it to the door at the top, stepping out onto the deck, Clarissa was gone.

Where'd she go?

Gabe didn't know. All he knew was that he'd screwed up big time, and now he needed to find Clarissa before the exotic reptile or whatever it was that had escaped from the crate found her.

He had a feeling their lives might depend on it.

MAN OVERBOARD

CLARISSA HURRIED UPSTAIRS, letting the door bang shut behind her, too worried about Ava getting caught outside of her crate to even consider her own safety on the ship.

It was almost as dark outside as it was down in the hold, and the ship appeared to be empty. The sun had sunk, both sky and sea the same shade of midnight blue, with a brighter haze at the flat horizon. Most of the passengers had been eating dinner in the dining hall when she'd crept past earlier, and the ship's crew were either on the bridge or wherever they happened to eat their meals.

Where did she go?

Clairissa ran toward the stern, hoping the boy with the backwards ballcap, narrow shoulders and peach fuzz above his girlish lips—she'd already forgotten his name—wouldn't follow her. She couldn't let him discover the truth about Ava. Bad enough the he'd let her out of her box. Ava was dangerous. She *had* smelled the blood from Clarissa's foot earlier, all the way from the garage, and once Clarissa had returned to the hold, Ava hadn't been able to stop herself from tasting the blood of her older twin. Like the voice that had drawn her to the ship from miles away, Clarissa had been *compelled* to feed her, though once she'd seen how hungrily Ava had slurped it up, she'd snapped out of her trance and pulled her wounded foot away.

"*No*," she'd said. "No more."

"Pleeeeeease," Ava had said. "*I'm so hungry*."

She *had* looked hungry. She looked wasted away and pale, aside from the black smears of dirt, climbed halfway out of the earth like a zombie who'd clawed its way out of the grave only to give up before it could even bother to hunt for brains. But the blood smeared on her lips and chin had given her life. Her hair, dead and frayed only moments earlier, seemed to almost shimmer despite the grime. Her skin, pallid and waxy like a bar of soap before her meal, acquired an almost sparkly glow.

"They know I'm on the boat," she told Ava. 'I shouldn't be here."

"Then let me out."

"I *can't*. They'll find us. They'll…" *What* would *they do if they found us?* she wondered. *Make us walk the plank?* "They'll arrest us," she said, though she realized that her sister's current predicament was far worse than being stuck in even the dingiest jail cell.

How did she live *like this?*

Easy, a dark voice spoke from deep inside her mind, a voice she'd first heard the day her parents were murdered and Ava was kidnapped, one she hadn't heard in years.

She's already dead, it told her.

And it was true, wasn't it? She wasn't a zombie, not truly. But she wasn't exactly *alive*, either. No living person could survive under a foot of damp soil for very long. There was also the indisputable fact that she wasn't breathing. If she wasn't alive and she wasn't dead, *what was she*?

You know what she is, the voice said. *You just can't say the word because then it will be true.*

"Get back in the dirt," she said. "I'll come back later, okay? I'll…" Much as she didn't want to use herself as bait, she also had no other way to convince her sister to listen to her otherwise. Ava could use her mind powers again if she wanted, and she'd be powerless against them. "I'll feed you again," Clarissa promised her.

As she'd said the word "feed," she could have sworn Ava's pupils glowed red for an instant, but the color in her eyes faded as soon as she'd noticed it. Then she'd left, back to the garage where she'd been hiding.

She had returned to the hold to give Ava another taste when she'd seen the stupid boy standing in front of the crate, holding the crowbar she herself had left on the floor beside it.

He'd stood there gawping at her while Ava's shadowy form had leaped out of the box and skittered across the floor, then—*impossibly*—climbed the wall like a fly and squeezed herself into the vent.

Clarissa hadn't meant to slap him as hard as she did. She understood he'd likely been compelled to help Ava the same way she'd been. But he wouldn't let go of her and she had to find her sister as soon as possible before—

Before what? she thought now.

You know what, the dark voice said.

And she did. She just couldn't bring herself to think that of her little twin.

Clarissa scurried down the side deck, crouching below the dining hall windows whose yellow glow bathed the shiny wooden boards beneath her feet. Her wounded foot hurt madly but the pain was secondary to her desire to stay hidden and find Ava before Ava found—

A victim? the dark voice suggested.

"No," she replied in a whisper.

Then why?

Because I don't want her to get caught.

But she's already caught. She told you what they did to her since they've had her. How could getting thrown off the ship or put in jail be any worse than that*? Let her do what she needs to do. Otherwise, she'll drain you like a dairy cow. How much blood do you think you've got in you? How long do you think you'll last? You think she would've stopped if you hadn't come to your senses just in time?*

The voice was right. She couldn't keep letting Ava drink her blood. But what other choice was there?

You know what.

In her distraction, Clarissa nearly got spotted by a man and woman ascending the steps arm in arm from the upper lounge to the dining hall. They wore the sort of outfits Clarissa had never even seen outside of a fashion show, the two of them swaying drunkenly. She pressed herself against the wall and waited for the sound of diners chatting and laughing inside to lessen as the doors swung shut behind them. Then she rose to a crouch and kept running toward the front of the boat.

That was too close, she thought.

And it'll get closer. How are you hoping to find her? She can literally walk through walls by climbing through the vents. She's gone, Clarissa. Let her do what needs to be done. You don't think these people deserve it for what they've put her through?

"Not all of them," she replied aloud. "They can't all be involved. It makes no sense."

But they know. *They* must *know. How could something like that be kept secret this long? It's just not possible.*

She knew that wasn't exactly the truth. The vast majority of people would be fine putting up with all kinds of atrocities behind the scenes if it meant they could keep on dancing like there was no tomorrow. And what better place to do that than on a Caribbean cruise filled with celebrities and the ultra-rich? Already she'd recognized at least half a dozen passengers from her place in the shadows: from social media influencers with followers in the tens of millions to famous actors and musicians. She'd seen at least one member of a royal family and a very familiar American politician. Clarissa didn't even follow these things much, so she imagined if she watched *TMZ* or read the tabloids on the regular, she'd recognize plenty more faces among the guests.

It wasn't likely all of them knew about what was going on below deck, nor what lay in store for Ava and her new friends in the other crates on Little Pearl Island. Was it possible? Sure. But not *likely*.

It was even less likely that all of them *participated* in the abuse. It did make Clarissa more curious who did. Those two wealthy friends sashaying drunkenly into the dining hall—did they know what was happening to young girls on Little Pearl? Did they join in themselves? What about the captain of the ship? What about the boy from the hold?

No, she thought. *He couldn't have. He was going to save Ava.*

Clarissa shook these thoughts from her mind for the time being. She had to find her sister before it was too late for Ava to turn back. Ava wasn't an abused animal escaped from the zoo on the run for its life. She was a tiger, prowling the ship for prey.

She was looking for a meal.

With a ship this big and a manifest likely in the triple digits, Ava would find plenty of choices on the menu: plump, thin or in between, from just about every ethnicity.

Unless Clarissa got to her first.

She hurried down the stairwell to the lower lounge. It was

empty aside from the furniture: comfy looking chairs and loveseats and low tables with recesses for small fires—rather than candles—which weren't currently lit. No one stood behind either the well-stocked bar nor the DJ booth, which still bore the yellow DANGER tape and several parking cones from the afternoon's performance. Clarissa thought her foster sisters would've gone wild raiding the liquor bottles if they'd been here with her. She'd never been a fan of alcohol herself. The last time she'd tried it, she'd projectile vomited all over Juanita's favorite rug and spent the entire next morning with a hangover, scrubbing it out.

She continued down the steps to the pool deck, certain Ava would be looking for a solitary victim. The lights in the jacuzzi and pool cast shimmering ripples over the ceiling. Spotting a young man and woman in the hot tub, she stopped in her tracks and hid against the wall, watching them. The woman wore a string bikini barely covering her fake boobs. The man wore shutter shades despite there being no sun and gold chains over his smooth, shaved chest.

Would Ava risk attacking a couple? Was she even strong enough? Clarissa doubted it. A weakened lion didn't go after a pair of gazelles. It went for the elderly and infirm. The ones that wandered away from the herd. But there was no one on the deck below, either.

I'll never find her.

She had to keep trying.

She turned around and headed for the front of the ship—the bow, she thought they called it—and kept running, peering deeply into every shadow and niche. She paused at the garage on the way, which appeared as empty as it had been when she'd left it maybe ten minutes earlier, and headed for where she'd seen the helicopter arrive that morning.

By the time she reached the helipad, the helicopter was no longer there. She hadn't heard it leave, so she supposed she must have been in the hold when it had.

A solitary man stood at the far end of the bow, looking out at the dark water. From the shape of his silhouette, he appeared to be one of several security guards she'd seen patrolling the ship. Clarissa crouched and tucked into a nearby bulkhead. The security guard appeared to be alone, which would theoretically make an easier target. But he was also armed with a large rifle, probably an automatic—though she knew next to nothing about weapons—and a Taser, as well as a collapsible baton and a pair of handcuffs.

Would Ava risk attacking him, knowing the sound of rifle fire would attract attention? Clarissa didn't suspect it would *kill* her, considering the seven-year-old girl was already dead, but it could certainly do plenty of damage. They'd already determined she had no pulse, and that wounds on her body would heal rapidly on their own. Ava's teeth had appeared normal, though. The things her body was capable of doing were impossible and she appeared to be nourished by blood but she couldn't possibly be—

What? the voice in her head asked. *You can say the word.*

She shook her head. *No.*

Another voice startled her, coming from nearby rather than inside her head. She'd heard it before. It belonged to the man who owned the boat, she guessed. Whoever he was he seemed to be in charge and constantly keeping tabs on things, the time's she'd heard and seen him from afar.

"Wilson!" he called.

Clarissa edged further into the shadows as the man himself marched out onto the helipad, about ten feet from where she crouched.

"Sir!" the security guard shouted back.

"Did you find her?"

Clarissa's heart beat faster. *They're talking about me.*

"Not yet, sir. My men are scouring the ship from bow to stern. If she's here we'll find her before too long."

"You sound confident."

"Very confident, sir."

The two men approached each other, their silhouettes only slightly darker than the horizon. It was harder to hear them from a distance, over the crashing waves. She had to strain to listen over the thud of her heartbeat and only made out what they were saying from the context of the words she did hear. "You were confident we were fine to disembark this morning," the yacht's owner said. "Next you tell me we have a stowaway. It's six hours later and still you say you're confident you'll find her."

"She's quite elusive, sir."

"Elusive."

"Yes, sir."

"Wilson, do you have any idea how precious the cargo in that hold is to our benefactor?"

"I do, sir."

"And do you have any idea how important that cargo is to my *special guests*?"

"Of course, sir. The cargo is not in any danger of—"

"Listen to me very carefully, Wilson, because I'm only going to say this once and I want these words to *really* sink in. Are you listening?"

"Yes, sir."

"You failed, Wilson. Get off my ship."

"Sir?"

"*GET THE FUCK OFF MY SHIP!*"

"But, sir…!"

The owner jabbed a finger toward the black sea. "You better fucking jump in that water or I'll make a call on the sat-phone and let our benefactor know exactly how you failed. You have three fucking seconds, Wilson. What'll be? *Three*."

"But, sir, I—"

"*Two*."

The security guard kicked off his boots. He bent down and laid his rifle on the floor.

"*One*."

The guard climbed the railing without hesitation. In the next moment, he jumped overboard.

Clarissa, who didn't think for a second the man would do it, flinched at the sight. Could he even survive a jump at this height, with the boat moving steadily forward? She wanted to run to the side and see if he'd made it but she'd be caught, and she couldn't even be sure which side he'd end up on, or if he'd been thrust under the hull and churned up in the propellers, chum for the sharks.

Instead, she slipped away hurriedly in the shadows and ran back the way she'd come as quickly and silently as she could, heart pounding in her chest.

It was clear she was in far more trouble than she'd ever imagined. Finding Ava could wait until morning. She had to keep moving, stay in the shadows. The last thing she wanted to find out was why a man with a machine gun would be more afraid of this mysterious "benefactor" than of jumping off a moving ship into likely shark-infested waters.

The sound of heavy footfalls arose behind her, clanking on the metal deck. Clarissa turned as a huge man in a black security uniform rounded the corner. His eyes widened just as she scurried away.

"Hey! Stop right there!"

She raced to the closest stairs, yanked open the door and hurried down the narrow steps two by two, ignoring the pain in her injured foot. The door slammed shut behind her but the guard tore it open again barely a second later, already on her heels.

Clarissa leaped down the last four steps and slammed into the door at the bottom of the stairs. As the guard's boots pounded down the stairs above her, she jerked on the handle, certain she'd reached a dead end, that the door was locked and she'd be caught in seconds.

"Stop running!"

The handle turned and the door swung open so suddenly she almost fell backwards. She quickly peered into the hallway to make sure the coast was clear, then vaulted down the carpeted hallway, past rooms with closed doors, hoping like hell no one would step out at just that moment and spot her dashing away barefoot and bleeding as yet another door slammed behind her.

As she reached the door at the far end of the hall, no idea where it led, it swung open, and before she could stop herself she ran right into the man who'd opened it, letting out a small yelp of fear as he caught her in his scrawny arms.

BODILY FLUIDS

MAGS O'KEEFE WAS so angry she could literally kill someone.

Taylor wasn't helping at all. Normally she'd be able to use him as a sounding board if not a punching bag. After dinner they'd returned to their room and he'd hurried straight to the toilet, making that all but impossible. He'd been harfing up coq au vin—what he'd jokingly called "cock soup" as dinner—for the past half hour while Mags doom-scrolled IG, looking at all the likes she was losing as her fiancé puked his guts out.

This afternoon's post—which Taylor *finally* got right after what felt like a hundred tries of her popping up from the pool in a cutout monokini and flipping her hair in what was supposed to be a sexy way, but ended up looking like a wet mop in about thirty-nine of the five-hundred fucking takes—wasn't doing very well. In fact, it was fair to say what Taylor was doing right this very second was an accurate representation of how well the post had faired, and the brands she'd worn—Spankini, a line of fitness and swimwear from Monte Carlo, and a diamond necklace from Tartovsky—were suffering for it.

PEDO! was the most liked comment, showing up right under the video, from some troll hiding behind the username @QStorm_1010 and a picture of a sad cartoon frog.

"What the fuck?" she muttered for the third time. "What the fucking *fuck*!"

She was so mad and confused she almost threw her phone. Cooler heads prevailed in the nick of time and she held it in both hands close to her chest, breathing in and out slowly through her nose and mouth the way her yoga instructor had taught her. "I am not my likes," she muttered, repeating the mantra she'd learned. "I am not my image on a screen. I am everything and nothing. I am stardust. I am a supernova. I have no beginning and I have no end. I am not my likes…."

She repeated this another several times before unlocking her phone again. The most liked comment popped up right below her video like a virtual slap in the face. She could almost picture the hunchbacked incel loser sitting at his computer in his mother's basement, cackling with glee as his likes went up and hers went down. Bad enough she'd started her period three days early, now she had to deal with this bullshit?

She stood up in a blind rage, gripping her phone so hard she could break it. "What the *fuck*, Taylor?"

"Huh?" Taylor groaned from the bathroom. It sounded like he was sitting on the floor.

"Why are they calling me that?"

"Why—? What?"

"They called me…" She couldn't bring herself to say it out loud. "P-E-D-O."

"Speedo? I thought you were repping Spankini?"

"*Not fucking Speedo*!" she screamed as loud as she could at the closed door. "*Pedo, you dickhead!*"

"Pedo? Why would they call—?" The sound of him retching again made Mags gag and she stepped away from the door. The vile word staring her in the face in capital letters brought her back. She turned the door handle, ready to fly into a rant.

"No, don't—!" Taylor cried, but it was already too late.

The door came open and there he sat, not on the floor but on the toilet, with his shorts and underwear around his ankles. The stench wafting up from the bowl was foul, melding with the splatters of vomit in the sink and on the countertop, chunks of undigested chicken and mushrooms and green bits amid the yellow-brown mess splattered over their toiletries, her makeup, her fucking *toothbrush*. His boxer briefs, bunched up within his shorts, were streaked brown with diarrhea. He looked up at her with sad puppy dog eyes and closed his legs so it looked like he had a well-trimmed mangina, and wiped away a runner of vomit from his chiseled chin, leaving a chunk still in the cleft.

"Ohmigawd, Taylor! That's *disgusting*!"

"Close the door!"

"Fuck!" she screamed and yanked the door shut. "I can't

believe you're *shitting*! You're shitting *and* puking!"

"Well, what the hell else was I supposed to do? It's not like I did it on purpose!"

Mags wanted to berate him some more but she suddenly found herself laughing uproariously.

"Are you crying?" Taylor asked timidly.

The question made her laugh even more. She thought she must've been broken. She'd never laughed at dick and fart jokes, even when she was a kid she'd been above that sort of thing. Now here she was laughing at the image of poor Taylor, puking and shitting his guts out all over the bathroom, looking up at her pathetically as if it was his fault she'd walked in on him, not hers.

Plenty of trolls and haters had called her fiancé a "simp" for taking all of her photos for her. It was practically a stereotype of the "Instagram boyfriend" that they put their girl on a pedestal, doing everything for them and asking nothing in return, aside from a little "something-something." Yet Taylor was practically model-hot himself, and he'd done some branding on his own before they met on Instagram.

She'd defended him to all her online haters. *Of course*, she had. But when she'd caught him sitting there on the toilet with his shit-stained boxers around his calves, the look he'd given her could've been the Wiki image for "simp," and it got her laughing so hard she actually forgot about the most liked comment on her reel for a minute.

Then everything she'd read on her post came flooding back and the laughter died in her throat.

"They called me a *pedo* on my reel," she said. "It's the top fucking comment. Why would someone *say* that? About *me*?"

"I don't know, Presh," he said, which was short for his pet name for her, 'Precious,' which she normally thought was cute but now found grating. "Do you think…?"

"What?" She waited half a second before asking again, much louder. "*What, Taylor?*"

"They couldn't *know*, right? About the NDA?"

The NDA. The fucking NDA. It was a little-known secret that the life of some Instagram models could be a little unsavory. Branding was a lot of the job, but if you wanted to make *real* money, there were people out there who could make it a reality very quickly. Many of those people lived in the Emirates, where the dark secret life of Instagram influencers unfolded behind closed doors with golden handles. There was also the world of "yatching," where wealthy people spent a lot of money to spend time in the company of beautiful women, and which, she'd been told, would culminate with sexual acts. Essentially a "girlfriend experience."

Mags had never been involved in yatching, nor had she ever travelled to Dubai. But when an ultra-wealthy member of a royal family reached out to her through her DMs with an offer of an insane amount of money, as well as a trip on Emory Jackman's cruise to Little Pearl, and a stay at the five-star hotel on the island, she'd conferred briefly with Taylor who'd agreed she should sign it immediately.

The deal was to take the virginity of the prince's young nephew. To "make it special." She and Taylor had... not exactly an *open* relationship, but what they called "loose boundaries." He was fine with her sleeping with other men as long as she didn't do it in their bed, and used protection.

The prince's nephew wasn't a *child*, though. He was eighteen years old, with a *birth certificate* to prove it. At least, that was what the prince's translator had told her. She couldn't actually *read* Arabic. She couldn't read anything other than American and a few words in Spanish.

"Mags?"

"What!" she spat back.

"They don't know about the NDA, do they?"

"No one *knows* about the NDA, Taylor. It wouldn't *be* an NDA if it was, like, public knowledge, would it?"

"No, I guess—" His acknowledgement was interrupted by a groan and a massive ripple of farts and splatter in the toilet water.

Mags let out an exasperated huff. She couldn't be in here a second longer with that noise and the stench wafting up from behind the door. She suddenly felt a deep urge for nicotine, and peered around the room, her mood darkening further the longer she looked.

"Where's my vape?"

"W-what?" Taylor groaned.

"Where's my fucking vape?"

"I… I don't know. When did you last have it?"

She pushed aside the curtains on the four-poster bed and lifted the pillows, the duvet. Not there. She checked on the vanity, the bedroom bench and the loveseat. Nothing.

Then she looked at the bathroom door.

"You don't fucking have it in there, do you?"

"What? Why would I bring your vape to the toilet?"

"I don't *know*, Taylor, that's why I'm asking! If you hit it last and maybe it's in your pock—" She felt the back pocket of her white Agolde jean shorts. "Oh."

"What?"

"Nothing!" she said, feeling a twinge of guilt.

"You found, didn't you?"

"*No*." She slipped the vape out of her pocket and perched it between her lips. "I'm going to get some air. It *stinks* in here."

Another bout of runny shits hit the bowl in reply.

"Jesus!" she said, nearly retching again as she opened the cabin door and hurried out into the hallway.

She made her way down the hall, so absorbed in her phone she nearly bumped into the British woman she'd seen at the pool, who had squeezed her hips into a glittering evening gown and wore a ridiculously large fascinator pinned to her silver updo. She was glamorous despite her flabby arms, where Mags was casual chic. The woman gave her a quick look up and down and dismissed her with a huff.

"Excuse you," Mags muttered as the woman entered her room. It was the same thing everywhere she went, no matter how famous she'd become. Old money always looked down on the nouveau riche.

Wait, that's French, isn't it? Guess I know some French, too. Café. Chic. Cannes. Voulez vous couchez avec moi, ce soir. Oui oui, monsiuer. Ooh la la, mon petit chêrie…

Merde.

Mags snorted a laugh. She hated when she did that, but it still felt good not to be thinking about the most liked comment on her reel for once, or that stupid fucking NDA.

Is he really underage?

She stepped into the stairwell and trudged up the stairs, her mind starting to wander. If he was underage, she could get into a lot of trouble for sleeping with him. The last thing Mags needed was to get MeToo'd while her star was still on the rise. She doubted her sponsors would appreciate branding posts from her cell in the women's detention center.

Hashtag-*cagedheat*.

Hashtag-*lovelaughlifesentence*.

But what could she do? It was way too late to back out. The prince wouldn't just get upset. He'd probably have her *killed*.

Mags stepped out onto the deck, crossing the pool area where she'd recorded her latest and currently most *dis*liked reel—though it looked like people were going back and trashing her previous reels and pics now, and the like counts were dropping there, too. She took the stairs down to the lower deck. There was a small railing here and steps down to the water, where she was told guests could swim from when the boat was stationary. It was dark out here but a full moon had just peeked out from the cloud and dappled the rippling water splashing and churning from the propellers.

For a second, she was sure the water had turned red, but she blinked again and realized she must have been mistaken. Unless the boat had run over a fucking orca or something, it wasn't very likely.

She leaned against the railing and took a hit off her vape, nicotine filling her lungs with an immediate calming effect. She vaped the menthol flavor, because there were only two options since the little bitches in Washington decided the mango she used to enjoy was too tempting for teenagers and took it off the market. For a while there she was able to get them shipped from a Canadian girlfriend but their friendship had imploded over a silly online misunderstanding, so now she was stuck vaping menthol. She'd heard the government wanted to get rid of that now too so eventually she'd have to switch to Virginia tobacco, which when that happened would be just about reason enough to quit for good.

Mags enjoyed the menthol well enough though, and for a moment she was able to stand there watching the swells trail off in the ship's wake and Zen out.

God, it's so peaceful, she thought. *I wish I could stay here forever. Fuck Insta. Fuck my brands. Double-fuck Miami Beach. Fuck Prince Whatsisname and his incel nephew. Wait... Ew, don't fuck him* that way. *Oh shit, I was just about calm there. I'm not a fucking pedo. That's such bullshit, why would they even say that? It's fucking crazy people can just, like, spread lies about you all over social media and nobody even takes a second to wonder if it's true. They just assume every sip of tea they read is straight facts. Like, do your research, bozos. Seriously.*

It was then that she noticed something moving within the water below. Dark shapes rising up from the water, moving in circles like vultures over the dying. She gripped the railing and leaned over, trying to get a closer look.

"Ohmigawd, is that—?"

She meant to say "sharks," but before she could finish someone grabbed her roughly by the shoulders, nearly scaring her right into the water. She spun around to confront Taylor or whoever it was but there was no one on the deck behind her and somehow the hands still held her tight. The vape fell from her lips as she reached back and grabbed the wrists, finding them slender and cold, like a child who'd been pulled from the water. For a fleeting moment she wondered if a little girl had leaped onto her back, hoping for a pony ride like Mags's dad used to give her when she was small, but then a sharp pain struck the side of her neck and she turned to see the black eyes of a little mud-streaked girl *biting her fucking neck.*

Mags struggled to shake the girl off of her shoulders but the child's grip was *so strong*, and a huge chunk of flesh came away from her throat with a terrible sound like someone ripping her favorite Agolde jean shorts, the pain worse than when she broke her ankle in gymnastics. As a gout of dark fluid she realized was her own blood spewed into the shark-infested water, Mags *swore* the girl's pupils glowed red.

Her scream upon the realization she was being *eaten by an actual monster* was lost to the sound of the sea churning in the propellers, and the horrifying image of those blazing red eyes and the tiny fang-filled mouth smeared with blood made her forget about likes and comments and eventually, everything else.

When the stupid boy let her out of her box, Ava scurried away and climbed through the metal door in the wall into the loud tunnels. Her senses were sharper than they'd been for as long as she could remember, guiding her toward her next meal. Usually she felt tired and slow, ever since the day she woke up in an old falling down house with a man called Lionel. His last name was de La Haye, which Ava thought was a funny name but Lionel said was French, like his accent.

Ava didn't know if she'd ever met a French person before but she didn't remember much at all about her life before waking up there, attached to a hospital stand with a needle in her arm. She remembered she'd been at the mall with Clarissa and Daddy, shopping for Mommy's Christmas present. She still couldn't remember what they'd gotten her to this day, and that was what bothered her the most, except for not having seen them in forever. She knew it was something Mommy wanted for a while, something small and shiny, but that was it. Like most of her life in the BEFORE, it was vague and unformed, like remembering a TV show she'd watched a long time ago. A mystery.

All she knew for certain was Lionel's undying love for her, because he told it to her all the time. He was the first face she saw when she woke up from the deepest sleep of her life in a hospital bed in a darkened smelly room with a needle dripping into her veins. He said she was suffering from a VERY RARE DISEASE with NO CURE and that her parents and sister and not even doctors could help her, and if she went back to them she would get them sick with it, too. Only he could help her, Lionel, because he had the same disease. Only about one in one million people in the whole world had it, which made them special. They needed each other. He told Ava her own blood was POISON, and it needed to be replaced with the SPECIAL MEDICINE, as Lionel called it, in the IV bag.

The disease made her forget important stuff like where she lived before and what school did she go to and what grade was she in and who was her bestest friends in the whole world (even though she remembered later on it was her twin sister, Clarissa). It stopped her from growing any bigger than she was and made sunlight into POISON. Even a little bit would make her skin burn and bubble.

Lionel gave her the SPECIAL MEDICINE and nursed her back to health. He gave her a wood box with dirt in it to sleep in, which was strange at first—*did he really expect her to sleep like a worm?*—but soon made her feel like she was home no matter where they went. He protected her from the sun, and from the bad men he said would want to hurt her because of their VERY RARE DISEASE.

For ten whole years she lived in that box beside Lionel, who slept in a bigger box. In the first beginning, Lionel taught her TRICKS to make men give her a different kind of medicine to make her less tired all the time. She didn't like to do it, had begged and pleaded for Lionel not to make her those first few times, but she always felt better once she'd gotten their "milk," as Lionel called it, even if it made her feel gross when she was doing it. Those weren't *fun* tricks, not like the ones she used to do with her sister Clarissa when they were little. They used to pretend they could read each other's minds, doing silly things like finishing each other's sentences or wearing the same clothes and pretending to be the other, but they'd really just practiced their lines so everything sounded just right. Still, people had been amazed by this simple trick, believing they truly shared a bond people without a twin didn't have. It was fun to be different. To feel special. When she thought about these times, she would reach out to Clarissa in her mind, praying their fun little game was real *just this once*, that Clarissa would come find her and save her. That she'd take away her disease and bring her back home to Mommy and Daddy, who loved her and weren't really dead like Lionel said.

Then just last night, after all this time, after all these *years*, it finally worked. Her sister found her. She'd *freed* her. Ava knew it was her even though they looked different—at least, Clarissa was *taller*. Ava hadn't seen her own face in a long time because Lionel said mirrors are BAD. The snot and tears she licked from her sister's face made her feel good, just like her TRICKS.

Clarissa had to leave quickly but when she returned, Ava smelled her SPECIAL MEDICINE coming from Clarissa's foot. It smelled even better though, and she begged her bigger twin to let her taste it. She'd used the SPECIAL VOICE Lionel taught her to use on the gross men and spoke directly into Clarissa's head the way she had to get her to find her, only stronger, and eventually Clarissa let her lick the dirty sole of her bare foot.

She wanted more immediately, wanted to drink it forever, but Clarissa fell over, and their mental connection broke. Her twin, who no longer looked very much like her at all, had pulled her foot from Ava's lips and told her *no more*. Then she'd promised to let her have some again later and hurried away with a scared look in her eyes.

Ava went back to sleep and woke up again a short time later, her stomach rumbling. She used her SPECIAL VOICE on the boy she sensed from inside her crate when he caught Clarissa before. She could tell he liked her sister and used it against him, tricking him into setting her free to roam what she found out was a very large boat. She spied on people through the ceiling tunnels, looking for someone who was alone and easy to trick. Lionel taught her a long time ago that men who were DRUNK or ON DRUGS were easier to trick than others, and she'd proven it on many occasions. But now she knew she could drink girls too, and probably even grown-up ladies.

Ava found a woman by the smell of her blood. Now that she knew what it was, she smelled it all over the ship. It was something she smelled all along without knowing what it was: a soft smell, like perfume, but somehow also rich and yummy, like the sweetest juice. Lionel either didn't know about this NEW MEDICINE or kept it secret from her. As she scurried through the tunnels she wondered if he kept it from her because he knew it would make her strong and fast and able to jump really high She could hear people's thoughts all over the boat and her head was LOUD but she figured out pretty quick how to make all the voices go away except the person she was close to, and now she heard this woman whose NEW MEDICINE smelled so good standing at the back of the boat. She was sucking on a thin plastic thingy that made her blow out minty smoke while she stared at her phone. She kept thinking a word Ava hadn't heard before, blazing brightly in her mind like the letters on a movie theater sign: *P-E-D-O*.

Ava ran on all fours across the deck, quiet as a cat, and jumped on the woman's back. The woman turned around but Ava held fast and plunged her teeth—suddenly long and sharp—into the place where the good smell came strongest. She didn't even mean to do it, it was just on instinct. She bit down hard and tore the flesh away, feeling the warm, lifegiving MEDICINE fill her mouth, spilling down her chin and splashing the deck as the woman screamed and screamed.

Ava spat the chunk of skin into the water and drank deeply as the woman's thoughts got quieter and quieter, fading along with her screams. She drank until her tummy felt sick. She drank as the flow of blood slowed down and the woman stopped thinking, then sucked until there was nothing left.

RUN, MY DAUGHTER.

The voice startled her. It came directly from her head like her SPECIAL VOICE and spoke with an accent like Lionel's, only different. His Rs sounded like the growls of a tiger: *RRRRUN.* Nobody except Lionel ever spoke in her head before. Whoever this was must be like them.

Ava rose from the woman as the sound of people nearby caught her attention. She scurried into the shadows like the voice commanded, waiting, listening.

"Imagine, like, being poor and never getting to go places like this," came a woman's voice.

"Ew, why would you bring that up right now?" said a deeper voice.

"I dunno. I'm high. Forget I said it."

Ava watched from the shadows, like a jungle cat in the low brush. Her tummy hurt but she could probably drink more if she wanted to. And she *did* want to. She wanted to drink until she was sick.

YOU COULD DESTROY THEM, the new voice told her, *THESE PREENED, SEQUINED INTERLOPERS—BUT YOU MUST NOT. REMAIN IN THE SHADOWS, MY DAUGHTER. YOU MUST NOT BE DISCOVERED. HEED MY WORDS. COME TO ME…*

The voice disappeared but Ava knew whoever it belonged to it was right. She needed to stay hidden. This ship was a VINEYARD filled with the FINEST VINTAGES IMAGINABLE. She wanted to try them all before they reached their destination, wherever that might be.

The tricks Lionel made her do wouldn't satisfy her anymore. From here on, she would drink blood and only blood. She would FEAST until there was no more blood left to drink, until the entire MANIFEST was sucked dry.

As Ava skittered away on all fours, keeping to the darkness, the higher of the two voices cried, "*Ohmigod!*" Clearly, they'd witnessed the mess she left behind.

"Are you *serious* right now?" the deeper voice asked. "Is this real or am I tripping? Okay, like, I know I'm for real tripping, but is this *actually fucking happening*?"

Ava was already back in the tunnels, leaving them to their dumbfounded horror, the metal thing shutting behind her with a clang muted by their sudden screams.

Back to her box then, to rest. When she awoke from her slumber tomorrow night, she would slip out once again and *feast*.

QUESTIONS

SVEN TYPED HURRIEDLY on his laptop, eager to write down all of his thoughts about the afternoon he'd spent with Emory Jackman before they flittered away into the ether. It was obvious his host was doing everything in his power to impress him, but there was clearly much he wasn't saying, and Sven intended to get to the bottom of it.

In addition to his main investigation, there were three major things about which he wanted to uncover the Five Ws—the Who, What, When, Where and Why—and he typed them up quickly in bullet points:

1- Tess (aka Emory's spouse): Who is she? (Emory's claim of Hungarian royal blood seems unlikely, considering nobility was abolished in 1947, at least directly, though still probable.) Where and when did they meet? Why is she not on the current voyage? (Illness excuse seems pat.) What if anything does she have to do with Emory's "extracurricular" activities on Little Pearl Island? Does she know? Is she a participant?

2- The stowaway: Who is she? Why has she "crashed the party," so to speak? What do they intend to do with her when they find her?

3- The "old man": Who is he? Why did he "compel" Mr. Jackman to invite Mr. Coltrane? For that matter, who is Coltrane? (His surname is Irish yet he himself claims to be Dutch.) Why did Coltrane agree to travel to Little Pearl? Are the two old men friends, or is there bad blood between them?

4- What happened to the filmmaker of the canceled Little Pearls *documentary whilst on Mr. Jackman's island?*

Perhaps the producer Mr. Wallis can enlighten me.

Believing this to be a good start for the time being, Sven closed the laptop and tucked it away again under his mattress. It was a lot of material to cover over the two-and-a-half-weeks he'd be on this trip. Along with everything else he'd come to uncover, he suspected he wouldn't have much time to relax and enjoy the voyage, nor the tropical paradise of Little Pearl.

He put on the glasses, which he'd charged while washing up for dinner, and left his cabin intending to go to the dining hall, locking the door behind him.

"What's he typing?" Emory asked Blitzen "Blitz" Wagner, the second-in-command on his security team. "Can you zoom in any further?"

The massive man shook his head. Emory was often surprised by the man's level of mobility, considering the hulking size of his muscles. Arnold Schwarzenegger would look puny standing side by side with Blitz, who was so large Emory had needed to get his black tactical uniform custom tailored.

Fortunately, Blitz wasn't just a massive block of hard muscle in a uniform. He was also highly intelligent, excelled at anything related to computers—hacking had been his specialty in high school, and had gotten him recruited to the Marines, where he'd been quickly promoted to FORECON—was highly proficient with various weaponry and had a brown belt in Krav Maga. He also played a pretty mean game of chess, which Tess appreciated, as Emory couldn't play for shit. In just about every aspect of the job, Blitz put Wilson to shame. Which was why Emory didn't feel too badly about what he planned to do about his security chief.

"Hang on," Blitz said. He toggled to the other camera and zoomed in on the mirror behind Sven, which showed a reflection of the laptop monitor. Emory could just make out the question written backwards: *Are they friends, or is there bad blood between the two men?* Unfortunately, it was at the start of a new page, and in the next moment Sven cracked his knuckles and closed the laptop before stowing it back under his mattress.

"Damn," Emory said, wondering who Sven had been curious about. He suspected it was in reference to Coltrane and the Old

Man. He'd been particularly pointed about that during their talk in his quarters. "All right. As soon as he leaves that room, I want you in there."

"What about the stowaway, sir?"

"Radio Wilson. Tell him to meet me on the helicopter pad in ten minutes."

"Yes, sir."

Emory clapped the big man on the shoulder. He felt the muscles ripple under the fabric. "How do you feel about a promotion, Blitz?"

The man craned his thick neck to look up at him. "What about Wilson, sir?"

"Wilson... might be going for a little swim."

Blitz nodded. If he had any feelings about it one way or another, they didn't reach his face. "I'd be honored, sir."

"Good man. Once you're done in that room, I want you back on finding that stowaway. Got it?"

"Got it, sir."

"Don't fail me, Blitz. You know what will happen if you do."

Blitz breathed out heavily through his nose. "I do, sir."

"This cargo *needs* to reach Little Pearl."

"Of course, sir. And when I find her?"

"Bring her directly to my quarters. Don't speak a word of it to anyone else, not even Tess when she gets here."

"Understood. When is she due?"

Emory glanced at his watch. It was nearing seven p.m. and he hadn't eaten anything since Amor's wagyu burgers at just past noon. "She should arrive before sunrise."

"That's good news, sir."

"It will be, if you find the stowaway. If not, it may be very bad news." He looked at the screen again as Sven left his cabin. "Very bad for all of us."

After Mr. Jackman left the security office, Blitz headed down to the rooms on the lower deck for Sven's cabin. He felt good about the promotion, though not quite the reason for it. Wilson may have disappointed Mr. Jackman but he'd always been a fair and honest leader. The truth was, the ship was humongous and even with cameras just about everywhere it was a lot of ground to cover. Blitz had poured through hours of footage and managed to find out when she'd arrived on board in the back of the gardener's truck from one of four cameras in the hangar. But after the initial entry, she'd been clever and stuck to the shadows, likely pressing herself up against walls to avoid being spotted. Wherever she was now, the girl seemed to bear a kind of supernatural knowledge of the ship. Either that or she was really damned lucky. Their security team of four armed men and women had covered the ship from bow to stern and found nothing more than a set of bloody footprints leaving the hangar a few hours after lunch.

She can't hide for much longer, Blitz thought. He swung his head from side to side, the joints popping, and left the security office.

Blitz had been working under Michael Wilson ever since he'd started on Mr. Jackman's personal security team. Wilson was a good man, and damn good at his job. It was a shame he had to go—and in such a pathetic manner—but Mr. Jackman ran a tight ship. Literally. You disobeyed his orders, you failed him, and you walked the plank. Simple as that.

Jumping overboard was better than the alternative. At least in the sea he had a chance of survival. Sure, he'd have to fight off hypothermia, jellyfish and possibly sharks. He'd have to tread water for hours or even days until he found something floating by—a log or some kind of discarded trash large enough to support his weight—and was able to reach it. There was a high possibility of being found by other cruise ships and sailboats on the rhumb line, even before he managed to wash ashore.

The alternative appeared to be a fate worse than death. Blitz had only witnessed the creature Mr. Jackman called "the Old Man" once, but once had been enough. He slept in a cave under Mt. Elsinore on the rotted remains of his victims. His face was so pallid it was almost blue, the skin pulled so thin and taut over his bones that every vein stood out like black highways on a roadmap. The eyes were glassy obsidian, sunken in fleshy pits of coal, with blood-red pupils sparkling like rubies. When Blitz had seen the creature, it had been feeding on what was once a man but had been so thoroughly drained of life he may as well have been dead. The creature, sitting naked against his heap of corpses, smeared with dirt and blood, hadn't even looked up from the meal in its lap when

Blitz and Jackman entered his chamber. His lips remained on one of hundreds of wounds on the man's body but still his voice spoke softly to Blitz, as if directly into his ear.

Wouldn't you like to join us, Blitzen? I'm so terribly hungry.

As horrible as the scene before him had been, for a moment he'd been convinced he wanted nothing more than to strip off his clothes and lie down in the wretched creature's lap. Fortunately, Mr. Jackman had clapped him on the shoulder before he could commit to the thought. "Shall we continue the tour?" he'd asked. Blitz, who'd been more terrified than ever before in his entire life, even on his first tour of duty, had nodded vehemently.

He would not fail Mr. Jackman.

But if the stowaway did manage to evade him before Tess arrived, he would gladly join Wilson in the water rather than have to see that face even *once* more.

He could still hear its voice calling to him on Little Pearl, usually as he rose from a dreamless sleep.

Wouldn't you like to join us, Blitzen?

Bathed in sweat, he'd think to himself, *No. That's the last thing I want to do.*

But he knew that if he returned to that cave, he'd be likely to answer in the affirmative. Especially if there was no one there to stop him.

He was still thinking about the Old Man when a dark shape flittered by him on the side deck. His first thought was that the Old Man had sensed him thinking about him and had come here to take him away. Then he grounded his thoughts. There was no way for him to travel here, was there? Besides, the shape was far too small to be the creature, which even in partial recline it had appeared to be at least seven feet tall.

The girl!

"Hey! Stop right there!" Blitz shouted, chasing after her.

The door to the stairs opened and the girl slipped inside. It slammed shut just as Blitz reached it, and he tore it open again. He hit the stairs already running and bounded down two at a time. He saw the top of her head a flight below him as she leaped down four steps and slammed into the door on the lower passenger deck.

"Stop running!" he said, pounding down the steps. The door below came open and the girl disappeared into the hall with a swish of golden curls and the hem of her flower-print frock.

Blitz grabbed the railing and leaped over it, landing with a heavy thud on the floor as the door in front of him closed. He ripped it open in time to see the girl just about to reach the door at the opposite end of the hall. The door came open and the girl tried to stop herself, but she was running too fast and slammed into the old man who'd opened it. He caught her in his fragile arms, dropping his cane.

"Hold her there," Blitz called out, out of breath as he stomped toward the two of them.

The old man's expression turned from shock to relief and a smile rose on his thin lips, wrinkling his face even further. He wore slightly tinted bifocals and peered through them at the girl in his arms.

"*There* you are," he said.

The girl looked up at him with frightened eyes.

"Sir, please let go of the girl."

"You misunderstand," the old man said. "I've been searching everywhere for my darling granddaughter and here she seems to have run right into my arms."

Blitz narrowed his gaze. "Your granddaughter."

"That's right." The old man looked down at the girl in his arms. "Isn't it, my dear?"

The confusion left the girl's face. She turned to face Blitz, the old man's left arm still draped around her, and nodded firmly.

"Why is she running around ship unsupervised? Blitz asked, not buying it for a second. "With no shoes on?"

The old man peered over the girl's shoulder and offered him an apologetic smile. "My granddaughter is... *special*, you see. What they once called a 'savant.' I suppose I must have fallen asleep while the two of us were at the pool, and she wandered off and left her sandals behind. The sun gets to me, at my age. You understand, yes?"

Blitz looked back and forth between the two. Either the old man was doing his best to sell the lie, or he was telling the truth. Still, he didn't buy it. The girl still looked frightened and guilty as hell. Unfortunately, there was protocol to be followed. Mr. Jackman only allowed physical contact with passengers if they were behaving out of line. He also couldn't ask for their tickets since tickets were never provided. ID was all that was required to board. The limit of what Blitz could do without provocation was ask their names and room numbers. He'd compare it with the ship's manifest back at the office. If they didn't match up, he'd return to their room and get the girl.

"All right," he said with a single nod. "It's late. You really should return to your room, Mister...."

"Eh, Coltrane." The old man nodded. "Jeffrey Coltrane."

"What's your granddaughter's name, Mr. Coltrane?"

"Wilhelmina," the old man said without pause.

"You two have a nice night," Blitz said, jaw clenched. "I'm glad you found your granddaughter."

"Thank you. Dear, would you mind terribly retrieving my cane?"

The girl snapped into action, holding the back of her frock to prevent it from giving them a show as she swiftly crouched, grabbing the cane and handing it to her supposed grandfather.

The old man switched it to his right hand and leaned against it, then offered his free arm for the girl. She slipped her own into it, though Blitz noticed the anxiety in her eyes as she did so. It made him think of a fakir grabbing the head of a snake to prevent it from striking.

The old man sighed and smiled. "Well, let us be on our way. Good night, sir."

"Good night," Blitz said, wanting nothing more than to grab the girl from the old man and fireman carry her back to Emory's door.

He stepped back as the old man shuffled the girl past him toward his room, tucked his cane under his arm and unlocked the door. Blitz made a mental note of everything: *Room 14. Jeffrey Coltrane. Wilhelmina.* What he could see of the room as the two of them entered was neat, the bed made, a few items placed on the dresser, an old leather satchel on the chair.

He caught Coltrane's eye as the old man closed the door and they exchanged a nod as the door closed. In her reflection in the vanity mirror, the fear in the girl's eyes was palpable.

As many times as he'd seen it, Blitz would never get used to that look. He'd seen it on the faces of dozens of young girls on Little Pearl. He'd seen it on the faces of women and girls in

Afghanistan, gang raped by Taliban scum. It was a look he'd promised himself he'd never abide when he returned to civilian life. But civilian life had different things in store for him. He'd thought the horrors of the Afghanistan War had been the worst he'd ever see. After he'd witnessed the Old Man feeding on his pile of corpses, his mind changed on both points.

Jackman had him by the short and curlies. That was why Jackman had introduced him to the Old Man on his first day on the job, and likely had for every member of his security team. If he betrayed Mr. Jackman, he was betraying that *thing*. So he followed orders, no matter how terrible he might feel about them. Because the last thing on Earth he wanted was to become a chew toy for that abomination.

He'd rather take his chances with the sharks.

"Well, that was a close call, wasn't it?" the old man said to Clarissa, turning from the door to face her.

His gray eyes widened when he saw what she'd picked up from his dresser: the straight razor from his shaving kit. He held out the hand not currently propping himself up with his cane and took a step forward. Clarissa jabbed the razor toward him. "Don't come any closer," she warned.

"My dear, I may have saved your life just now, and this is how you repay me? And might I remind you, the very burly gentleman outside my door is likely to hear us if we raise our voices."

She nearly yelled, before considering he was right. "I'm not playing any of your sick games," she said at a controlled volume, using a violent swish the razor to emphasize her point. "Just stay back."

"Sick games? Dear girl, I'm a very old man. The only games I have any interest in playing are backgammon and chess."

"Bullshit!" She caught herself and lowered her voice again. "Bullshit. I know what happens on this boat."

"My dear, whatever you think you know, I assure you I am not a party to. Surely you must have seen the other guests on this voyage. Do I appear as if I belong amongst them?"

Clarissa narrowed her eyes. Aside from the crew and staff she'd seen so far, the old man—Coltrane, he'd said his name was—looked to be one of a handful fit for a seniors' home. Even the other elderly guests she'd caught glimpses of looked either elegant or at least put together. With his dowdy, second-hand clothes he'd look more at home playing shuffleboard with the other retirees outside a hotel on Miami Beach.

"Why should I trust you?"

"Why should *I* trust *you*?"

She didn't reply. Was she supposed to answer that?

"Because, my dear," he explained, "we are the only ones keeping each other out of trouble at the moment. As soon as that mountain of a man checks with the ship's manifest, he will see that I of course did not arrive with my granddaughter. Now, either he will assume that I've kidnapped you for reasons I suspect might be rather unsavory, or he'll believe I am harboring you for some reason. Are you, perhaps, an unexpected guest?"

She saw no harm in telling him. He'd already protected her from capture. The least she could do was reward him with the truth. She nodded.

"I see. Then the two of us are in more trouble than I first thought. I suspect as my presence is required on the island they'll be lenient with me. You, on the other hand…" He clucked his tongue. "I would hate to think what they might do about you."

Again, she nodded. "I think I have some idea. Thank you. For sticking up for me. That was nice."

"You're welcome. Now, do you think you might return the razor to its case? I'd rather not have to sharpen it again so soon."

Clarissa looked at the blade in her hand. The old man was so fragile, she wondered why she'd even picked it up in the first place. Even if he did attempt what Ava had shown her, in her mind, the men had done to her over the years, she could easily fight him off bare handed. Besides, she doubted he'd be able to get it up no matter how badly he wanted to at his age.

She placed the blade back in the small wooden box she'd found it in.

"Thank you." The old man smiled, then groaned as he eased himself into a sitting position on the bed. "Forgive me, my legs are quite tired."

She nodded again. "That's okay."

"Feel free to sit, as well," he said, indicating the solitary chair beside the vanity.

She sat, glad to finally get off of her feet. Her injured foot throbbed. She lay her ankle over her knee to inspect the wound, peeling off the napkin she'd found in a trash bin. The wound had closed over but dribbles of blood and pus shone in the overhead light.

"Oh, my dear. You should be very careful with open wounds on this ship."

Clarissa looked up, suddenly suspicious. "What do you mean?" she asked pointedly.

The old man wobbled his head from side to side in a gesture of uncertainty. "Only… infection on the high seas can be difficult to heal. Particularly in your predicament."

Clarissa watched the old man. He was holding something back, she could tell. How could he know about Ava?

"Here, let me help you with that. I have antiseptic."

He pushed himself up with his cane and shuffled over to the vanity beside her, where he opened a drawer. "No," he said, rooting through whatever lay inside. "No. No. Ah, there it is." His withered hand came up holding a small, white plastic bottle which rattled as he held it out to her. "Would you mind very much unscrewing the cap for me? My arthritis is quite bad."

She took the bottle from him. It had no label. "What's in it?"

"Something to protect your wound." He took the bottle from her and shook a couple of little beige capsules into his palm, then plucked one out and put it back in the bottle, which he placed on the dresser. "We have to conserve," he said. He pinched open the remaining capsule and shook its contents into his hand.

Clarissa made a face. "It smells like garlic."

"It is. Garlic is very good for healing. Some ancient cultures used it as a poultice to protect from infection and expedite healing." He held out the palm filled with cream-colored granules toward her foot. "May I?"

She shrugged. "I guess."

"Now this may sting a little."

Without another word he cupped the hand over her foot. She winced and held her ankle in place as the potent spice infiltrated her wound. The old man rubbed it in, then removed his hand and inspected his work. With a gnarled finger he smeared it deep into the cut. It felt like he was burning her sole with a cigarette, a pain she knew from experience, unfortunately, having lived in several unpleasant foster homes before her current foster moms.

He unrolled a tensor bandage from the drawer and began to wrap it around her foot until it was encased like a mummy. When he was finished, he closed it off with the metal clip that had held the roll together.

"That should keep you protected," the old man said, pushing himself back to his feet with his cane.

Clarissa winced again and rolled her ankle. Eventually the burning sensation went away and it felt almost soothing, like balm on a muscle pull. "Thanks," she said, offering the old man a small smile. "I really should get back—"

"Back to where, exactly?"

"Why do you care?"

"Because, my dear, it is my *duty* to care. I've been charged with protecting everyone on this voyage."

"Charged? What do you mean?"

The old man smiled, easing himself back down on the edge of the bed. "Let us just say," he grunted, "you wouldn't believe me if I told you."

What does that mean? she thought. *Does he know about my sister? Are there others like her down there?*

Her blood turned cold as a terrible thought occurred to her.

"Are you all right, my dear?" the old man asked, concern in his tired eyes.

"I'm okay," she told him, but she was far from it. What if the Mall Monster was on the ship with them? She didn't think Ava would neglect to mention the man who'd murderer their parents was here, but she had said he'd taken her to dozens of cities with him, whoring her out for rich men in every dark corner of the world. Would her vampire freak of a pimp really have let her travel alone this time?

How many more girls are in those crates?

"Why wouldn't I believe you?" she asked the old man, praying he hadn't been exaggerating, eager to find a confidant.

He sighed. "What is your name, dear? I've told you mine, it's only right that I know yours."

"My name's Clarissa."

A smile brightened the old man's face and he gazed at her over the rims of his bifocals. "Well, Clarissa. Do you happen to believe in the supernatural?"

"May I sit here?" Sven asked the rotund, silver-haired man he recognized as Ernie Wallis, the multi-award-winning film producer.

Wallis was seated with a lithe young woman who was not his wife—Sven had seen pictures of Mrs. Wallis, and she looked quite similar to Ernie himself, both in their mid-sixties and quite plump. Wallis slurped up a spoonful of coq au vin and nodded for Sven to sit at one of two empty chairs at their table. "Have at it," he said, lips smacking as he chewed.

The young woman looked at Sven as if he'd urinated in her salad. He tried to ignore her sneer as he tucked in to his dinner.

"Say," he said. "You're Ernie Wallis, aren't you?"

The man chuckled. "Don't tell me. You're a screenwriter with a treatment you'd like me to read?"

The young woman laughed like a hyena. People dining at the tables surrounding them looked at her with obvious disdain.

"Actually, I *am* a writer," Sven said, carving into his portobella mushroom steak and taking a bite. It was soft, juicy and savory, with a slight tang of Merlot. He'd found it a rarity that the vegan options were any good in the restaurants he tended to frequent, but this was exquisite. He savored it and swallowed before adding, "A journalist, in fact."

Wallis sat up rigidly, banging his knees on the underside of the table and rattling the cutlery against his plate. The young woman saved her wine glass a split second before it toppled. Made anxious by the interruption and Wallis's discomfort, she glugged down its contents, then snapped her fingers toward a server.

Wallis composed himself, straightening his bow tie. "That right?" he said. "What kind? Tabloids?"

Sven smiled. "Quite the opposite. I have very little interest in films or television. No, what interests me, Mr. Wallis, is the human condition."

"The human condition?"

"Precisely. You see, in my opinion, the human condition is in a state of flux."

"Flux," Wallis repeated. He carved up a piece of chicken

floating in broth among potatoes and mushrooms, brought it to his lips and chewed.

"Yes. I believe we are in a transitory period, much like the Dark Ages led to the Renaissance, and further into modernity. Or, if you wish, as the Industrial Revolution led to contemporary history, analog to digital. We exist in an age in which human intelligence is beginning to struggle with the artificial. In which we have access to so much information at the tips of our fingers, it's become nigh impossible to decipher what is fact and what is fiction. I've come to think of this time in our collective history as a New Dark Age." He smiled at the term, though the thought of it didn't bring him much comfort. "You see, with access to such information comes the responsibility of absorbing and disseminating it. And, I'm afraid, we have been quite lax in our duties."

Wallis cleared his throat with a fist against his sternum. "You don't say."

"I do. As journalists, it is our responsibility to find the truth of a matter and expose it, no matter how ugly. Yet, we find ourselves at the mercy of a corporatocracy, whose only goal is to acquire vast amounts of wealth for its shareholders. They are not concerned with such trivialities as *truth*, Mr. Wallis. They are concerned, merely, with presenting a *version* they deem palatable to their audience. And so, as journalists, we find ourselves at a crossroads. Do we present to our readers the truth with a capital T, or merely an approximation of it? If we wish to publish, we are then tasked with editorializing that which needs no editorial. A fact is a fact, is that not correct, Mr. Wallis?"

The film mogul glanced at his companion. She gave him a sour smile and sipped from her refreshed glass of wine. "Sure," he said. "Yeah."

"Now, if I was to present the truth I see before me, I would perhaps say something like, 'Mr. Ernie Wallis was in attendance with a beautiful young woman who was not his wife nor either of his two daughters.' You see? *Facts*. If I were to editorialize, I would perhaps add that the young woman appeared to be the *same age* as his daughters, and further, one could assume the she may have been offered a prominent role in one of Mr. Wallis's many upcoming pictures, in exchange for her company on this voyage."

Wallis choked on his mouthful of food and held a napkin up to his mouth as he swallowed. "Now listen here, you little pipsqueak—"

"Mr. Wallis, allow me a moment," Sven said, holding up a hand in peace.

"I think we've heard just about enough. Haven't we, Greta?"

The young woman nodded enthusiastically, nibbling on the end of a breadstick.

"Then allow me to apologize, Mr. Wallis. I have no interest in writing about you. My piece is about Mr. Jackman and his rise to fame and power, such as it is. It is my understanding that he is a majority shareholder in Acumen Pictures. Is that correct?"

Wallis cupped his right ear toward Sven. "I didn't hear that apology."

"I am sorry, Mr. Wallis. Sincerely. I meant no disrespect to either of you."

"Fine," the film mogul grumbled. "Yeah, he's a majority shareholder. What's it to you?"

"It was my understanding there was to be a documentary about Little Pearl Island several years back, is that not true?"

Wallis took a casual sip from his lowball glass. "That was shelved."

"It was. I wonder, out of curiosity, whatever happened to the footage? For that matter, the director himself, quite prolific before his visit to the island, seems to have vanished entirely from public life quite shortly after *The Hollywood Reporter* announced his documentary film had been canceled. He's now raising alpacas, I understand, in Tucson, Arizona."

"Alpacas, huh?"

"Yes. Apparently their fleece is quite valuable. I wrote an article about it for *Quilting Quarterly*. Now, as an animal lover I can't say I fully approve of his current lifestyle, however we did have quite a lengthy conversation about his decision to leave the film industry."

"Oh yeah? And why was that?"

"What he said to me was that he was *compelled* to leave. I asked if he could elaborate and it appeared he could not. I asked if he'd signed a non-disclosure agreement, and again, he assured me no such document existed. I further asked if he recalled anything at all about his time on Little Pearl Island and he was unable to provide those details, as well. He remembered the voyage there, and the trip home, but everything he must surely have experienced on the island itself was a complete and utter mystery to him. A black hole, if you will."

"That's strange." Wallis turned to his companion. "Isn't that strange, Greta?"

The woman popped her eyes and nodded, feigning interest.

"I agree," Sven said. "And do you know what, Mr. Wallis?"

"What's that?"

He leaned over his unfinished dinner, fixing the film mogul with a pointed look. "*I believe he was telling the truth.*"

ANSWERS

CLARISSA LED THE old man out of his room, heading down the desolate halls, up to the higher decks, then back down toward the cargo hold. It was imperative, he'd said, to leave his room before the "burly gentleman" returned with the ship's manifest. She'd agreed, though walking at his sluggish pace in plain sight made her nearly as nervous as when she'd been in hiding.

The old man chattered the entire way, only pausing as they passed guests who appeared unconcerned by their pairing, caught up in their own business. Their conversation began in the room, and continued on their walk, with Coltrane asking her if she believed in the undead.

"You mean like zombies?" she'd asked.

"Eh… vampires, specifically, my dear."

There it was, the word she'd been avoiding. The word she'd *dreaded*. Could her sister really be a *vampire*? She'd sucked blood straight from Clarissa's foot—would a sane or healthy individual do that, outside of some strange perversion? It would also explain why she'd appeared not to age since they'd last seen each other, rather than her claim that she had an unknown "disease," and why she'd been able to survive under a foot of damp soil without suffocating.

Ava was undead. A *vampire*.

After everything Clarissa had been through over the past twenty-four hours, the truth of it was less shocking than she'd expected.

But what did it mean? Currently, Ava was scurrying around the ship somewhere, likely on the hunt for more blood. Was everyone in danger? What would happen if they didn't find her in time? Why did this old man believe in vampires? Had he seen one for himself?

"I believe in vampires," she'd said.

He'd nodded with a flat smile. "Good. That's very good."

"Why is that good?"

"It means you're more prepared than the rest of these fattened geese."

They'd left the cabin hurriedly. "How do *you* know about them? Vampires?"

Again, he'd smiled. "Perhaps it would be prudent to show you," he'd said, and from there he'd led her out of the room.

"Where are we going?"

"To the ship's hold."

"Why do you want to go there?" she asked suspiciously.

"Because, my dear, that is where my luggage lies."

Clarissa was reluctant to return to the hold, but the old man left her with little choice. Her best bet was to stick with him, at least until she was able to get out of sight again. The grandfather bit had worked for the time being. She had to hope it would work again if they happened to bump into another security officer on their way back to the hold.

"Juvenile vampires, you see," Coltrane said, "they are not *born* with a lust for blood. That is a common misconception. In fact, they can lead somewhat healthy lives, such as they are, by subsisting upon *other* bodily fluids."

"Like tears," Clarissa said, remembering how her sister had greeted her.

"Tears, phlegm, sweat, bile, saliva. Even scat and sexual fluids."

"Gross."

"Indeed. Yet to the young, or nascent, vampire they provide ample nourishment. For this reason, many young vampires are used as concubines, only provided blood intravenously so as not to *attune* their hunger to it. In a sense they are like addicts unaware of the substance to which they are addicted. Like a child born to a mother who used heroin. They believe themselves unable to leave their parental figure, whichever vile creature has turned them, due to their subsistence upon his nurturing and 'medicine'—or hers, for there are a great many vampires and familiars who are in fact women, as well."

They rounded a corner. Coltrane stopped speaking as the glamorous-looking man and woman Clarissa had seen entering the dining hall earlier sashayed drunkenly on their way toward the stern.

"Act cool," the woman said.

"I *am* cool, bish," the man said, to which they broke up laughing.

"As I was saying," Coltrane continued, "young vampires are often kept as concubines. They perform sexual acts in order to obtain the meager nutrition those acts provide. Their masters never teach them to consume blood. He won't *allow* them."

"Why not?"

"Because, my dear, it would make them too powerful. It would give them what I believe you young people like to call *agency*."

Clarissa glanced down at her injured foot as they walked. "What would happen if they *did* drink blood?"

"That is why I put the garlic on your wound. If a scroungling vampire were to smell it, she could find you in an instant. If you were experiencing your menses, I might also suggest applying some to your…" He glanced at her awkwardly.

"My period's not for another week." She counted back the days. "I think?"

"Excellent. Then you needn't worry, so long as you keep that wound of yours from reopening."

"So…" Clarissa began cautiously, "… let's say someone fed one of these young vampires blood. Would they be in danger?"

"Oh yes, very much so. The vampire's first taste of blood is much like a young person's first kiss, or more accurately, an addict's first hit. That memory is *etched* into their minds. They find themselves forever chasing the dragon, as the expression goes. They would bleed the pitiable fool dry."

"Oh."

Coltrane again gave her a sidelong glance. "Oh? My dear, please tell me you did not feed one of these creatures."

"I kinda… did. Yeah."

He gave her a mournful look over the rims of his glasses. "Oh, my dear, my dear. And where is that creature now?"

"She's not a creature," she snapped. "She's my sister."

"Your sister? I'm so sorry, my dear. " The old man's eyes became glassy, shimmering with moisture. "It is never easy losing a loved one to this scourge. Now we *must* find her. It's imperative to know where she is at this very moment."

"She was in the cargo hold. Then some idiot boy let her out."

"Likely not of his own volition," the old man said. "She's the reason you've stowed away on this voyage, is she not? She spoke in your mind? She *compelled* you to free her?"

Clarissa nodded. Tears spilled from the corners of her eyes as the guilt of her admission overwhelmed her.

"Oh, my dear." The old man wiped away her tears with a thumb. "You mustn't blame yourself, no. The call of the vampire is quite seductive. Precious few mortals are able to resist."

That must've been how she got the boy to let her go, she thought. *It wasn't his fault at all.* "How do you know all this stuff?" she asked.

The old man turned to her with a sad smile as they stopped in front of the cargo hold door. "I'm afraid I have a long and sordid history with their kind, my dear." He indicated the door with a nod. "Shall we?"

She opened the door. The lights were off downstairs, which likely meant the stupid boy had left, affording them the time they'd need to figure out what to do next. She led the old man down the stairs by the arm, one step at a time. "What do you mean by sordid?"

"Ah. Well, that perhaps is a story for another time. For the moment, we must try to determine how much damage has already been done, and if it is yet possible to reverse it."

"Reverse it?"

"Perhaps *undo* is a more accurate term. You see, when a vampire turns another into one of their kind, it is possible to undo those effects by piercing the heart of the one who turned them."

Clarissa stopped him, pressing a hand against his sallow ribcage. She felt his heartbeat under her palm, slow and sluggish. "Wait. We're not going to hurt her, are we?"

"Of course not. That would be incredibly reckless."

Clarissa sighed heavily. Something occurred to her as they reached the bottom of the stairs, how his eyes had glistened when she'd told him it was her sister who'd been turned. "Did you lose someone, too?" she asked.

"Indeed. I had a niece, long ago, as it happens. Her name was Wilhelmina."

Clarissa remembered that was the name he'd provided when the security guard asked. "A vampire took her, too?"

"The *king* of all vampires. Ah, here we are." He stopped in front of a large, old-fashioned leather trunk. Despite the dark, the initials on it stood out in the gloom: VH. "Help me with the clasps, my dear?"

Clarissa undid the belt buckle holding it closed on the right as the old man opened the left. When both were undone, he raised the lid. It wasn't possible for Clarissa to determine its contents as he bent with a groan to reach inside, only to see that it was filled with all kinds of objects, some of them shining in the semi-dark.

"My name is not Coltrane, you see…." He rose from his trunk, brandishing what her sleep-deprived brain first identified as a dildo, before recognizing it as a piece of wood sharpened to a fine point. "My name is Abraham Van Helsing," the old man said, his gray eyes gleaming as he admired the wooden stake, "and I am the first vampire hunter."

PART 2

HUNTED

THE FIRST VAMPIRE HUNTER

CLARISSA GRABBED ABRAHAM Van Helsing by his wrist. "You promised you wouldn't hurt her!"

The old man's look of astonishment crinkled into a warm smile. "I don't intend to *hurt* your sister, Clarissa. I do intend to protect myself should she or any of her blood kin attempt to hurt *us*."

Clarissa shook her head. "She wouldn't," she said, but her thoughts returned to the look of pleasure in Ava's eyes as she'd sucked the blood from the sole of her foot. "You said if we find the one that turned her, we can undo it. We can really bring her back?"

Abraham gave her a look that spoke more than words could possibly convey. "I've witnessed it myself."

"Then we *have* to find him. We have to find the Mall Monster."

"The… Mall Monster?"

Clarissa swallowed hard, holding back the pain of the past ten years of her life. All this time she'd thought no one could understand what she'd been through, what she'd witnessed. She'd thought she was alone, only to find out her sister had gotten it far worse than her. Now this old man, who'd called himself 'the first vampire hunter,' claimed to have lost his niece to the vampire 'scourge.' If anyone could sympathize with her it was him. "The man who killed my parents," she replied. It was the first time she'd spoken of the Mall Monster since the police and Dr. Grodin had dismissed her claims all those years ago. "He attacked us in the mall. The Galaxy Galleria. He killed them and kidnapped my sister."

"I'm sorry, my dear. Yes, if that vile creature of the night was the one to turn your sister, I believe we can reverse the effect and restore her life. But we *must* destroy its heart. There is no other way."

Clarissa exhaled a breath she felt like she'd been holding for a decade. The weight bearing down on her for as long as she could remember finally lessened, and for the first time in years, she allowed herself to feel a glimmer of hope.

"Now, my dear, which of these crates belongs to your… what was her name, please?"

"Ava. Her name is Ava."

"Yes, of course. Ava. And I believe I've found her place of slumber." The old man shuffled past her, toward Ava's crate. Dirty footprints and loose soil lay around its base, and the lid itself was somewhat crooked. "So, now we must determine in which of these your 'Mall Monster' resides."

"You think he's here? With her?"

The old man looked over the other dark shapes in the hold. "It is quite likely. An elder rarely abandons his progeny."

"What about my sister?"

"If she has not already, she will return to her box. Even nascent vampires know the dangers of sunlight."

That's right, Clarissa thought. *Sunlight hurts them. What else does? Wooden stakes. Crosses. Holy water. Garlic.* Clarissa had never been a horror fan but just about everyone knew how to kill or deter a vampire, so long as the legends were correct. According to the old man, stakes and garlic could harm them, though she had no idea why either should work, logically. If a vampire was dead, what good could piercing a heart which no longer pumps blood do? And why would a simple vegetable frighten a creature who'd survived death and subsisted on human blood?

None of this makes any sense, she thought. But she couldn't deny the fact that her sister was very clearly a creature of the night, as Abraham Van Helsing had called her.

Standing in front of her sister's box, Clarissa raised the lid. The earth was unsettled, a hole left where Ava would have slept. There were hand prints on the lip of the crate itself, from Ava pulling herself out of the dirt. Clarissa touched the soil, imagining what it must be like to sleep in this tight little space, a grave in a box. It was cool and damp. A fat worm squirmed its featureless head out of the earth and prodded her finger. She withdrew her hand in disgust.

This is how she's been living. And I thought my foster homes were bad.

"Why do they have her sleeping in the dirt?"

"Native soil," Abraham explained, as he wandered among the other crates toward the back of the cargo hold. "A vampire slumbers within or near its native soil. As little as a handful will do. Some leave a shovelful under their beds or carry it in a pouch on their person. It's an old superstition, mainly, and mostly adhered to by elders. I don't believe it's necessary for them to exist."

"How will we know which crate is his?" she asked.

"It could be any one of them. And we can't very well open them all. If your Mall Monster was prolific, he may have sired every one of these children of the night."

"Wait… there are *more* down here?"

Abraham waved his free hand in a wide arch, encompassing the entire cargo hold.

"*All of them?*" she asked, a chill passing through her.

"Oh, I suspect some contain provisions and the like. But the *Ceres*'s main traffic, from what I've been told, is girls and young women such as Ava and yourself. Still more await us on Little Pearl Island."

Clarissa staggered and grasped the side of a crate stacked on a second, her mind reeling. How many more vampire girls were in these crates of dirt? Was it possible to save them all? And what would happen if more got a taste of blood like Ava had?

Would any living person survive this trip?

"We have to lock her back up," she said. "We can't let her out again."

"No, I suspect not. Unless we manage to find her master and vanquish him, she'll be quite dangerous. Perhaps we should wait for her to—"

The overhead lights buzzed on all at once, causing the old man to fall quiet and Clarissa to cover her eyes.

This was it. They'd finally caught her.

"*Hide*," she whispered. The old man ducked with a pained groan behind a taller crate, only the hand holding his cane visible above it, which subsequently disappeared.

"Who's down here?" came a voice she recognized.

The boy, she thought. Her irritation almost caused her to call out to him just to get him to shut up. She heard his footfalls as he descended the steps. Knowing it was likely he'd head for Ava's crate, she crept in a crouch until she was hidden behind it. His shoes scraped the floor as he approached her.

"Hello?" he called. His voice echoed sharply.

Clarissa peered over the tops of the crates behind her. She couldn't see Abraham but she did spot two camera bubbles in the far corners of the ceiling. All she could do was hope they weren't able to see the old man or herself from the angles they were pointed. Otherwise, the massive security guard would be on his way, along with the others.

The boy stopped in front of Ava's crate. Clarissa crouched lower, desperate to remain out of sight. "*Who are you?*" he said. At first she thought he was talking to her, but when he continued without answer she realized he was talking to her sister. "How do you know so much about me? Are you and Clarissa friends or somethin? Dang, I really hope I didn't screw it all up. She was big mad. It's just she's so... she's so dang *cool*. I can tell just by lookin at her she's different than other girls, you know?"

Clarissa felt her cheeks turn red. The boy annoyed her, but being talked about in a nice way rather than the trash her foster sisters and schoolmates and previous foster families talked about her made her self-conscious.

A brittle snap like a broken twig came from behind her. "Ooh!" the old man cried.

"Who's there?" the boy said, sounding frightened.

Clarissa knew he'd find them if she didn't prevent him from searching the hold. If he did, they'd be caught on camera. She had to stall him. "It's me," Clarissa whispered. "Turn the lights out so we can talk?"

"Clarissa? Where are you?"

"Just shut up and turn out the lights!" she whispered harshly.

"All right, fine. Gimme a second."

She heard him move away. After a long moment the lights went out with a click.

"Oh, thank goodness," Abraham groaned. From the sound of his voice, he'd gotten to his feet.

"Who was that?" the boy asked anxiously.

"A friend." Clarissa said.

"A friend? Where are you?"

"I'm right behind the crate you opened."

There was a short pause before he replied. "Did you just hear me talkin about you?"

"I did."

"As did I," the old man said. "It was quite a lovely little pronouncement."

Clarissa's embarrassment deepened. She stood as the boy approached the crate.

"Thank you, sir. Whoever the heck you are.

"What are you doing back here?" she asked.

She saw him shake his head in the dim light. "She was callin to me again. But I guess she ain't here, is she? I'm sorry I let her out, whoever she is."

"It wasn't your fault," Clarissa admitted. "She called me here all the way from my house. I couldn't resist her, either."

"How?" the boy asked. "How can she talk in my head? How does she know things about me?"

"May I interject?" the old man asked.

"He won't believe you."

"We can try, can't we?"

"What's the point?"

"Who is this guy, Clarissa? He your dad?"

The old man rapped his cane on the ground, silencing them both. "I," he pronounced, "am Abraham Van Helsing."

"What?" the boy said, his tone doubtful. "Get the heck outta here."

"Then you've heard of me?"

"*Everyone's* heard of you. I've seen *Dracula*. Four different versions. But you're not real. Not *really* real."

"I assure you, my boy, I am as real as the air you breathe."

"So… what? You're sayin *Dracula* is a documentary? Wait a second, hold on a dang minute. Is the girl in the box… is she…?" Clarissa saw the whites of his eyes widen in the dark. "Oh, holy Hell! Well, that explains a lot, don't it? Heck, I really did screw up, huh? She's prolly out there somewhere lookin for someone to suck their blood right this second."

"You see?" Abraham said. "He believes."

"Well, I am a little skeptical but I'm willing to hear your side of the story," the boy said. He raised a hand in greeting. "My name's Gabe, by the way."

"A pleasure to meet you, Gabriel."

"So now what?" Clarissa asked, hoping to get them back on track.

"Now… we await your sister's return."

"Your *sister*?"

Clarissa huffed. "I'll tell you everything later, okay?"

"Okay, I guess. But we really shouldn't stay here too long. I ran into Blitz, the big-ass security dude, he's on his way down to the lower decks. He asked if I seen anyone lookin suspicious."

"What did you say?"

"I said I didn't see nothin outta the ordinary. I'm pretty sure he believed me but that guy's pretty sharp, even though he looks like a big dumb ape. If you find a good place to hide he might not find you, but he looked pretty serious when I seen him."

"He won't stop looking until he finds me," Clarissa said. "His boss made another one of the guards jump off the ship because they couldn't find me."

"Jump off—? *Mr. Jackman* did that?" Gabe sputtered. "No, that… He wouldn't do that."

"I saw it happen. He said if the guy didn't jump he'd make a phone call to their 'benefactor,' whoever that is, and tell them he failed. It scared the guy so much he climbed over the railing and jumped into the water."

"*Jeebus*." Gabe shook his head. "Oh, shoot… I wonder if he meant the Old Man?"

"Old Man?" Abraham asked.

"Yeah, there's s'posed to be this old guy livin on the island. I never met him but Digby, he's my partner and also my roomie, he said he heard stories about this old guy who lives in a cave on Little Pearl. He's friends with all the staff and guards and whatnot, Dig is, so he hears just about everything. I don't believe the stories, personally. I mean, why would anybody wanna live in a cave when they could live it up on the beach at Mr. Jackman's five-star resort?"

"The answer to that is quite obvious," Abraham said.

"It is?" The boy remained silent a moment before slapping his thigh. "Oh, shoot! The Old Man is *Dracula*, ain't he? Oh, wait. That's not good, is it?"

"No. It is very much not good."

"Wait a minute," Clarissa said. "Dracula? *The* Count Dracula? As in Vlad the Impaler?"

"Vlad Tepes," the boy added. "Vlad the Dragon. The Prince of Darkness. King of the Vampires. He's got a lotta names."

"Eh, technically this is true," Abraham said. "However, Vlad III was the inspiration for Dracula in name only. Mr. Stoker, the author of the book, was cautioned by his publisher to use the name of a famous dead person, rather than the name of the famous *living* person, or rather, *undead* person upon whom the character Dracula was based. You see, the *real* Count Dracula was a nobleman and libertine at the time of its publication, and Mr. Stoker's publisher wisely cautioned him against using the man's real name. It's known today that the British royal family is directly related by blood to Vlad III of Wallachia, and that in fact King Charles is fifteenth great-grandson to the maniac. However, this was not a well-known fact in 1897, when the book was published. Had it been, they certainly would have insisted he use the name of a *different* long-dead historical ruler. We might have had Count Alexander III. Or Count Khan."

"So, you're sayin Dracula isn't really Dracula," Gabe said.

"Correct. He is, in fact, Duke Ștefan of Moldavia. However, Moldavia and Wallachia became a part of Romania some ten years after his birth, leaving him a duke with no dukedom. He fell into drink, opium and debauchery. It is presumed that Mr. Stoker came upon The Duke's story as manager of the Lyceum Theatre. Duke Ștefan, you see, was an aspiring thespian and quite good friends with Oscar Wilde, of whom Mr. Stoker was also quite fond. It is believed that Duke Ștefan auditioned for Mr. Stoker during this period, and in this audition revealed the tale that became the basis for the novel."

"But wait," Gabe said. Clarissa's eyes had adjusted enough to the dark that she could see the confusion on his face. "If Dracula isn't Dracula, are you still Abraham Van Helsing?'

"None other. Mr. Stoker, you see, claimed that *his* Van Helsing was based on a rather famous physician—which he perhaps wisely preferred not to name—but in actuality, I had gotten wind that he'd been writing a book based on my and my niece's—and her very naïve fiancé's—confrontation with The Duke, and suggested he leave my name intact to spite the fiend. Duke Ștefan had perhaps bested me, but I would not let him win so easily."

Clarissa remembered something from the movie she'd seen with Keanu Reeves and voiced her concern. "Doesn't Dracula die at the end? Isn't that how they turn Wilhelmina back?"

The old man sighed heavily. "Indeed. However, Mr. Harper—his name was Harper, not Harker as it is in the book—he and I were not so fortunate. He was killed, and The Duke fled with Wilhelmina. I have never seen her since."

"Jeez," Gabe said. "Let me get this all clear in my head, 'cause it's past midnight and I feel like my brain is busted. We're on a ship full of vampires that we can't slay 'cause one of them's your sister… and we're on our way to an island with a whole lot *more* of em… where the *King* of the Vampires himself is waiting… for *you*."

"That is the long and the short of it, yes."

His shoulders slumped. "Well, great. So what do we do now?"

"Now, as I said, we wait."

"Until when?"

"Just before sunrise," Clarissa answered for Abraham.

"No," Gabe said, shaking his head. "You guys can't be here all night. Blitz is gonna search the ship from top to bottom. He'll find you here. You gotta hide in Abe's room, or something."

"He'll be expecting us to return to *my* room," Abraham said. "But… perhaps she could hide in *yours*."

Clarissa turned to Gabe as he faced her with a terrified look. He cleared his throat, opening and closing his mouth like a fish a couple of times before finally responding. "Um, yeah, I mean… except for the fact that I've got a roomie who's probably drunk off his ass by now, that's a g-good idea."

"Back in my university days," the old man said, "we would put a necktie on our doorknobs when we had company."

Again, Gabe looked mortified. "My, um, my roomie, he usually puts a sock on the door if he doesn't want to be, you know, disturbed. It usually stinks, too, so you wouldn't wanna touch it even if you *had* to go back in the room."

"Gross," Clarissa said.

"Yeah, that's what I told him." He shrugged. "But we don't got any ties, so…"

Clarissa nodded. As much as the thought of hiding out with Gabe didn't appeal to her, they were right that she couldn't stay with Abraham and she couldn't hide here all night. She'd already hidden from one of the other guards down here earlier in the day and been a hair's width from getting caught. And she'd hate to think what this Blitz would do to her if he found her. "Okay," she said with a firm nod. "Let's go."

"Okay, then. You gonna be all right down here by yourself, Abe?"

"I'll be fine, I'm sure. I've dealt with their kind many, many times before."

"Just don't hurt her," Clarissa said. "*Please.*"

"I shall do my utmost not to harm your sister whilst protecting myself. Be safe, the two of you. Let us reconvene, the three of us, in the daylight."

Clarissa approached the old man. He smiled awkwardly, seemingly unsure of what she intended to do, until she hugged him. After a moment, he delicately patted her back. "Thank you," she said. "You saved my life."

"It was my pleasure, Clarissa. Let's make it worth our while, hmm?"

She let him go and went to Gabe's side. "Let's get moving."

He nodded. "I'll scout ahead."

Hesitant to put her life in his hands, all things considered, but left without much choice, she followed him toward the stairs. With one final glance back at Abraham, worried she'd never see him again, she said, "Lead the way."

DESERT ISLAND DISC

GABE COULDN'T BELIEVE his luck. He'd finally found the love of his life and was currently leading her back to his room to *spend the night*—not that he had anything on his mind other than keeping her safe, although that other stuff was a constant worry teasing at the back of his mind—but it happened to coincide with the discovery that the boat they were on was full of vampires, and they would all probably be dead by sunrise.

Better make the best of it, he thought, glancing back at the shadows, where he sensed Clarissa hiding. He gestured forward with his head and she crept out of the shadows, running barefoot toward him.

"Not much further," he whispered. "Just down these steps."

She nodded but said nothing. She hadn't spoken since they'd left the hold. Gabe figured she was as scared as he was, probably worse. It was her sister running around the ship searching for blood. It had to be worse on her, knowing she was so close to being caught while her own sister was out there, hunting, likely to be captured herself. After she'd come so far.

And it was all his fault.

"He won't hurt her," he said, hoping to give Clarissa a little comfort. "Abe, I mean."

"You don't even know him."

"No. But I've read a lot about him and seen, like, all the movies, even the crappy one with Hugh Jackman. He's a good man, I can tell."

She nodded again but didn't reply. He figured she wasn't sure she could trust either of them, and Gabe didn't blame her.

He peered around the corner, looking out over the side deck and the dark water. The coast appeared to be clear. "I'll get the door open, then you follow me."

She gave him another nod, and he got moving.

The stairwell was empty, and Gabe waved her forward. He knew where most of the cameras were so it would be easy enough to avoid them. Going down this stairwell, as opposed to the one on the starboard side of the ship, would keep their backs facing the camera in the hall where his and Digby's room lay. As long as they were fast and no one happened to walk in, he could get the door opened and wave her over before anyone watching the feeds spotted her.

They trudged down the stairs, Clarissa right at his heels. Speaking of heels, he'd seen the bandage Abe must have given her and was once again glad she'd found the old man. Gabe doubted she'd had the time or inclination to pack anything when her sister had started calling to her, which explained why she was barefoot. It also meant she probably hadn't eaten since last night, either.

"I'm gonna go to the galley and get us some grub once you're safe inside."

She grabbed him by the shoulder. Her touch prickled his skin, even through his grubby work t-shirt, sending shivers down his spine.

Wouldn't you carve her name into your flesh merely to feel her gentle caress…?

"No," she said anxiously. "I can't be alone. Not now."

"Because of y-your sister?"

She didn't say anything, but her hand fell from his shoulder. He felt its absence like a wound. When he looked back to see if she'd heard him, she nodded gravely, looking at her feet like she had when he'd first met her.

"You think she'd hurt *you*?"

Her gaze rose to meet his eyes. "The way she looked at me when I—"

"When you what?" They stopped at the door.

"Let's just keep moving."

Gabe agreed with a nod and opened the hall door. Clarissa stepped behind him, shielded from the camera as he peered into the hall. "All clear. Wait here 'til I get inside. I'll hold the door."

Off her nod, he stepped out into the hall while she caught the door. As he neared his room, he worried he'd see one of Digby's tube socks, so dirty it was more gray than white, hanging from the doorknob, or that someone would step out of their room and catch them, or both. But the knob was free of obstruction and—at least for the moment—nobody left their room. Gabe muttered a prayer it would stay that way until he got Clarissa safely inside as he rummaged through his pocket for the key.

He unlocked the door, checked that Digby wasn't around—he was still out, for the time being—then stepped inside and held the door open. A moment later he heard footsteps thud briskly toward him as the stairwell door clicked shut. He muttered another prayer that it was Clarissa and not Blitz. In the next moment, she slipped through the doorway into his room, and he closed the door and locked it, sealing them in.

They stood by the door looking at each other, their chests heaving from fear and exertion, their eyes wide with excitement.

Gabe didn't know what to do so he smacked his forehead comically. "Almost forgot," he said. He bent and scooped up one of Digby's dirty socks, held it by the cuff pinched between his thumb and forefinger, then opened the door again and slipped it over the outer handle, hoping it would hold as he closed the door, and that Digby would respect the custom as he had himself over the course of the past year.

With the door locked and the two of them looking at each other again, Gabe remembered he hadn't had a girl in his room since high school, and had no clue what to do next.

"I think I have some granola if you're hungry," he said, just to break the silence.

Clarissa smiled slightly. "That'd be good." She turned to the bunk beds, looking at the lower bunk in distaste. "Which one is yours?"

"I'm up top. I'll sleep in Dig's bunk if you wanna stay in mine."

She nodded briskly. "Yes, please."

Again, they stood facing each other awkwardly. "I'll get the granola," he said.

"Okay." She turned and began climbing up the ladder. Gabe couldn't help sneaking a peek at her bare legs as she climbed. Just watching her made him feel like his heart might burst out of his chest.

Clarissa caught him looking as she climbed onto the bed and

narrowed her eyes. He averted his gaze, pretending like he was looking at the ladder. "This thing's gotten loose," he said, grabbing it by the rails and shaking it. "Yeah, better fix those… the sc-screws."

When he dared to look at her again, she was grinning slyly, sitting cross-legged by his pillows. "You forget about the granola?" she asked.

"Right. The, uh… I'll go get it."

He crossed to the set of drawers, crouched to reach the lower two—Digby had insisted on taking the top two, citing his bad back—and opened the bottom one. A couple of large clear plastic bags were tucked inside, one filled with dry granola and the other with Chex Mix, that Chef Bialczyk let him take from the galley. He'd told the man he was hypoglycemic, but really he just had a ravenous appetite, munching on them whenever he got hungry between meals, which was just about every day.

"Do you want salty or sweet?"

"Sweet," she said.

He picked up the granola, which was only vaguely sweet but the best he could do. He wished he had some chocolate—he'd read somewhere that girls liked chocolate—but this was the best he could do. He handed her the bag and sat on the edge of Digby's bunk as she began to munch on it. It sounded like she was really hungry, all he could hear was her breathing through her nose while chewing and moaning every once in a while.

"You believe that stuff?" he asked after her hungry moans subsided a little. "What Abe said about Dracula?"

"I don't know what I believe anymore," she said, talking with her mouth full. "This is really good but… do you have anything to drink?"

"Just tap water."

"That's good. This is just…" She smacked her lips as she chewed. "… really dry."

Gabe got up to get some. He had a cup on the bathroom sink he used to put his toothbrush and toothpaste in, even though Digby liked to empty it and use it to gargle. It drove Gabe nuts and he wondered why Digby wouldn't just get his own glass from the galley, but he never complained. He supposed he could just get another himself so they wouldn't have to share, but knowing Digby he'd just end up using both.

Gabe took out his brush and paste and rinsed out the glass thoroughly before filling it with cold water and returning to the bunks. Clarissa snatched the cup from him immediately, her cheeks full like a chipmunk's, and guzzled it down. She let out a satisfied gasp and handed it back.

"Want some more?"

"Uh-huh," she said, using her tongue to retrieve chewed-up bits of granola out of her cheek. Gabe thought it was about the most adorable thing he'd ever seen.

He returned to the bathroom and refilled the glass, drank it himself, realizing his throat was suddenly parched, then filled it again and brought it back to the bunk. She sipped it this time, which he was glad for. He wouldn't complain if he had to keep getting up to refill it over and over again if she wanted, but after the day he'd had, he'd definitely prefer be able to sit down.

"I just don't know," he said finally, sitting on Digby's dirty mattress, pulling up his legs and leaning back against the wall. "This mornin I didn't believe in any of that gunk, now I gotta contend with vampires and vampire hunters and fictional books being real and all that. I mean, is Frankenstein real now? What about the mummy? And werewolves?"

"Let's just stick to vampires for now," she said.

Gabe nodded. "Yeah, that's probably smart." He looked up at the coils holding up her mattress and imagined sitting with her, instead of on Digby's crusty bedsheets. He pictured her cherry red lips as she worked the granola around in her mouth. Sweat dripped down his ribcage from his armpits. "You think we should go to sleep or…?"

"Do you have anything we can do? I'm too wired to sleep right now,"

"Like what?" he asked, hoping she'd say something like *make out*, but fully aware that was likely the furthest thing from her mind, even if she hadn't been on the run.

"Like a board game, or cards…"

"Oh, sure!" he said, sitting up so quickly he bonked his head on the coils under the mattress. "Ow!" He rubbed the bump, hoping he wouldn't end up with a goose egg tomorrow.

"You okay?"

"Yeah, I just got up too fast. I got cards, if you wanna play?"

"Okay."

Gabe got up carefully and returned to his drawers. He pulled out a deck—not the same ones that had changed magically that morning, which were on the desk in the office—and when he stood again Clarissa was leaning over the edge of the bunk with her hands gripping the rail, watching him. He caught a glimpse down the front of her dress at the top of her beige bra and looked away quickly. The last thing he needed right now was to spring a woodie. He was already bad enough at cards without losing all the blood flow from his head.

"You wanna come down here, or…?"

"You come up."

Gabe swallowed hard. "O-okay."

He caught the grin slipping off her face as he reached for the ladder. *Chicks sure are weird*, he thought, climbing up the steps, and sat cross-legged at the foot of the bed. She'd propped up the pillow against the wall behind her, and sat with her knees and toes revealed under the hem of her dress.

"What d'you wanna play?" he asked, shuffling the cards expertly. It was the one thing he knew how to do well with them, similar to how he could roll a joint but never smoked himself.

"You're pretty good at that," she said. "I dunno, um… how 'bout Fish?"

"Go Fish?"

She nodded, then looked up at him slightly embarrassed. "It's the only game I know."

"It's the only game I'm any good at," Gabe admitted.

He dealt the cards, seven to the both of them, then put the deck down on the sheet between them and looked at his hand. "Aw, crap," he said.

Clarissa was already pairing off cards. "I bet you're great at poker."

"Haha," he said. Oddly enough the hand he had would have been a decent for poker, one card short of a straight flush of diamonds.

"I'll go first. Do you have any queens?"

"Shoot." He took the queen of diamonds out of his hand and passed it to her.

She tucked it in with the cards she'd already moved aside. "Do you have any… sixes?"

He grinned. "Go fish."

Clarissa frowned and picked up a card off the deck. "Got my wish," she said with a pleased smile, her wiggling toes just about crushing his heart with cuteness. She took the four cards from the outside of her hand and placed them face-up in front of her.

"Dang, you're on a roll. Got any eights?"

Another pleased smile crossed her lips. "Go fish."

He picked up the ace of clubs off the top of the deck. It didn't match with any of his cards. "Your mom and dad must be pretty worried about you an' your sister," he said, tucking the card into his hand.

"They're dead," she said, not looking up from her cards. "Do you have any twos?"

"I'm sorry, I didn't know."

She looked up and caught his gaze. "Twos?"

"Oh, uh, go fish."

Clarissa picked up the top card.

"I am, too," he said. "An orphan, I mean. I guess that's something we got in common, huh?"

She shrugged her right shoulder, not looking up from her cards. The strap of her dress slipped down and she tugged it back absently. "Your turn."

"Yeah, s-sorry. Got any eights?"

"You already asked that."

"Just hopin you picked one up."

"Nope."

"Okay then." He picked up a card. Through some stroke of luck, it was an eight. "Got my wish."

"Yippee," she said sarcastically. "Do you have any music?"

Gabe searched his cards for what she'd asked, then looked up in confusion. "Oh, *music*. Um… I don't have a phone or anything."

"*You don't have a phone?*"

"No. But hang on a second…" He set his cards face down on the mattress. "Don't peek."

She gave him a serious look. "I don't *need* to peek."

"Obviously." Gabe climbed down the ladder and returned to his drawers. He rummaged through clothes he'd heaped inside without folding, found what he was looking for, and brought it back to the top bunk.

"A CD player?" she asked, incredulous.

He shrugged. "All I got."

He set it down between them. She popped it open. Inside was the only CD Gabe had, with a plain white label and its title handwritten in large, black capital letters. "'Desert Island Disc,'" she read.

"It's, uh… my dad made it, I think. For my mom. One of them did, anyway. It's like a mixtape. Back in the day when all you had was CDs, people used to ask 'If you were stranded on a deserted island what songs would you take with you?'"

"I'd have my phone, so all of them," she said.

"Well, yeah, but I mean, you don't have your phone now, do ya?"

"Don't remind me," she said with a heavy sigh.

"Sorry. Anyways, you could pick eight songs, even though you can fit more than that on a CD, and that's all you'd have to listen to for the rest of your life."

"Or until you got rescued," Clarissa added.

"Yeah," he said, suddenly gloomy.

"So your parents left you this?"

"Sort of. We, uh…" He pondered whether or not he wanted to tell this story. He'd never told it to anyone before, but now that he'd tapped the vein, it seemed like he couldn't just stem the flow. Besides, after all she'd been through, it was only fair to share. "When I was three, my folks decided they wanted to sail around the world."

"Oh, wow."

"Yeah. Actually, I was born on the water. Somewhere in the Pacific Ocean. But anyways, they started out in Maine—that's where I'm legally from, Maine—and sailed south along the coast until they got to Florida, on their way down to Antarctica." He pronounced it like a woman's name: Anne Artica. "They hit bad weather somewhere in the Virgin Islands and beached the boat. I don't remember anything, but accordin to my grandma, God rest her soul, we were prolly on that island close to ten days. When the Coast Guard finally found us, my parents were already dead."

Clarissa stared at him long enough that he could no longer hold her gaze. "Wow," she said finally. "I'm sorry."

"Hey, every orphan's got a sob story, right?"

"Yeah, I guess so. Wait, so this is *literally* their desert island disc?"

"Yeah."

"Are you okay to play it?"

"I haven't listened to it in a long time, but I should be. I just bring it with me, you know, just in case."

"In case you get stranded on a desert island."

"Or somethin," he said with a nod, slightly embarrassed.

"You don't get worried? That you might end up stranded on Little Pearl?"

"You'll prolly think this is weird, but I just stay on the boat 'til it's time to leave."

Clarissa reached out and touched his knee lightly with the tips of her fingers, making him jump. "I don't think that's weird," she said. He so badly wanted to take her hand in his own and hold it, but his palms were sweaty, so he just stared until she took it away and laid it in her lap with her other hand.

"What island was it? Do you know?"

"I don't think it had a name back then. Whatever it was, they didn't tell me. There's fifty or so islands and cays in the U.S. and British Virgin Islands, some of them no bigger'n a sailboat. I 'member there were lots of trees on it, and some big rocks. That's about it."

"You never asked your grandmother?"

"She died when I was five. I lived in a few crummy foster homes 'fore I finally found a nice family who kept me 'til I was eighteen so I could finish school. Then I left and never looked back."

"It's tough, isn't it?"

Gabe shrugged. It had been tough but plenty of people had it tougher. "Yeah. Anyways…" He closed the CD player's lid and pressed play. After a moment, the first track, Weezer's "Island in the Sun," played from the built-in speaker. He knew all the tracks in order, and had grown to love every one of them. He actually liked these songs more than his own generation's music, but he'd always felt this track was a bit too obvious for a desert island disc, and would've chosen "Only in Dreams" from their first album.

After this was Kim Mitchell's "Patio Lanterns." Then Urge Overkill's cover of Neil Diamond's "Girl, You'll Be a Woman Soon," from the *Pulp Fiction* soundtrack. Then Heart's 1980's hit, "Alone." There were twelve tracks in all—even though it was only supposed to be eight—each one handpicked by parents whose faces he could no longer remember.

Clarissa leaned back against the pillow on the wall and closed her eyes. "My parents used to play this song, too."

He smiled. "It's a good one." Leaning back against the wall himself and closing his eyes, he imagined reaching over and taking her hand and just sitting there with her, holding hands, listening to the songs on his parents' favorite mixtape CD.

He fell asleep that way, not sure when exactly, but when he woke up the CD had ended and they were lying head to toe, Clarissa slept with the sheet pulled up over her. He watched her breathing softly for a short time, trying not to imagine kissing her while she slept like some pervy Prince Charming, then crept out of bed and down the ladder. He set the alarm clock for six-thirty A.M., then crawled into Digby's bunk and tried to sleep.

Wouldn't you carve her name into your flesh merely to feel her gentle caress...?

The voice in his memory froze his blood. He didn't know if he'd go that far, but he did know he'd do just about anything to protect her, even if it meant facing off against a bunch of bloodthirsty vampires.

In fact, he was pretty sure he'd die for her, even if she didn't feel the same way. After a long while of staring at the bottom of the mattress above him, trying not to imagine Clarissa curled up against the pillow under his covers but failing miserably, he finally drifted off to sleep.

TESS

THE HELICOPTER LANDED on the *Ceres*'s helipad at just past four A.M.

Emory Jackman had been in and out of sleep in the California king in their quarters, stressed beyond belief, waiting on the radio transmission from the pilot. He'd showered and changed into fresh clothes for the day before lying down, sleeping above the covers with his hands over his chest like some vampire in a movie. In truth, he knew that real-life vampires—though to many that word was derogatory, especially The Duke, who referred to himself and his offspring as *Moroi*, and to living humans like Emory himself who'd imbibed vampire blood as *Strigoi*, benefitting from their powers—slept however they felt most comfortable, often in the fetal position, sometimes amid their native soil. The whole coffin thing was a legend concocted by a long-dead Scottish writer over a century ago, perpetuated by Hollywood ever since.

Emory leaped out of bed the moment he'd gotten word that Tess had arrived on the ship, still tired but already feeling more energized by her proximity to him. Even in what she called her "waning phase," Tess was still able to invigorate him. Her ability to charge him like a battery was one of the things that had drawn him to her in the first place. That and the fact that when she was in "full bloom," as she called it, she could get him harder just by being in the same room than the erectile dysfunction wonder drug created by one of Little Pearl's only permanent residents.

Tess was deep into a waning phase, and why she hadn't boarded the previous morning. Typically, she'd have had Rufus drive her out to the ship in the early hours of the day, well before sunrise, and if she hadn't been projectile vomiting all night she would've been on the boat before anyone else. Emory still didn't quite understand how her body worked, particularly at her age. He only knew that certain adverse symptoms occurred when she was waning. According to their doctor, she'd finally managed to get several symptoms under control during the evening, and was ready to get in the air moments after sundown.

What she required to bring her back into full bloom was the blood of what she called a "rare beauty." The trouble was, among all of the people he'd invited on this trip there were only two Emory thought she'd be likely to consider: Hollywood's latest "It girl," Simone Howard, and social media influencer Mags O'Keefe. Tragically, it turned out that despite her online professions of a "clean lifestyle," Simone was a weekend heroin user, and she was currently incommunicado, passed out in her suite. Tess was very particular about who she'd consider as a candidate—or, more precisely, *her body* was very particular—and drugs, nicotine and alcohol were strictly forbidden.

"Do you have any idea how hard it is to find the kind of beautiful young woman that meets Tess's standards who doesn't drink, smoke or do drugs? In *Miami*?" he'd asked Wilson, back when the man had been first taken on as his head of security. "It's *exhausting*."

The rare beauty also had to be *pure*, that was the issue. Not *chaste*. Certainly, the two of them had fucked their fair share of these beautiful young women prior to the ritual. As long as they were STI-free and their blood was clean, they were fair game. He'd invited several other possibilities, but they'd each had prior obligations: modeling in Europe, filming in Canada, climbing in the Himalayas. They'd all *wanted* to come, of course—who in their right mind would decline an invite to an Emory Jackman cruise, if they didn't absolutely *have* to?—but the timing had been wrong.

Which left them with one potential candidate: Mags.

Unfortunately, it turned out that Mags was already dead.

"Mr. Jackman," Blitz said over the two-way radio about an hour after the two of them left the security office, heading in opposite directions. "We have a problem." The radio blipped, signaling he'd taken his thumb off the transmit button, but Emory preferred they stick with protocol, so he added: "Over."

"Oh, Christ, what now?" Emory paused a minute with the button still depressed, wondering if he actually wanted to know, then said, "Over."

"Mags O'Keefe is dead. Over."

"*Dead?*" Emory's pulse quickened. His mind returned to Simone tangled among the silk sheets in her queen bed, passed out and breathing shallowly, a hypo sticking out of the crook of her elbow and her heroin gear scattered around her. His first thought was that she might have OD'd. He wondered if Mags actually had. "What happened? Over."

"I think you're going to want to see this for yourself. Over."

"Where are you? Over."

"On the beach club deck. Over.

"Okay. I'll be right there. Over and out."

Emory had hurried straight from his quarters to the beach club deck at the stern of the ship, trying not to be rude as he passed friends and colleagues in the halls and on the decks. He practically had to forcibly remove himself from the company of Otto and Helga Fuchs, the elderly couple who ran an extremely prosperous watch manufacturer, who'd accosted him outside the dining hall and spoke to him in Swiss German, in which he was almost fluent. Once he made it to the stern, he spotted Blitz's mountainous form silhouetted against the moon-dappled water, the big man's head bowed. As Emory neared, he saw what Blitz was looking at, a corpse so pale it almost shimmered in the moonlight, her clothes covered in what at first looked like oil but was clearly blood. The deck boards were stained by a pool of it, in which she lay in a crumpled heap, her throat torn out. Emory checked her pulse, not expecting anything. She was cold to the touch, like a bar of soap in ice water. Her veins lay still.

"Jesus fuck," Emory said. In other circumstances her current state would have gotten him semi-hard. Now he simply felt sick. Judging by her grayish pallor, he doubted a single drop of blood remained inside her body. "What the fuck did this?"

Blitz gave him a serious look. "It looks like—"

Emory sneered. "I know what it *looks* like. But they're all still weaning. They have *no idea* they're capable of…" He glanced at the dead woman in distaste. Not because he was disgusted by the state of her—he'd seen far worse during his time spent with Tess—but because of what her death meant. Tess would have no recourse but to fall back on part-time addict Simone's blood, which might prevent her from turning into dust, or whatever would happen if she didn't perform the ritual soon, but wouldn't get her anywhere near full bloom. "*...this*," he finished, swallowing a hard lump.

"What about the stowaway, sir?"

"You checked the hold earlier in the day. The crates were all intact, were they not?"

"They were."

"Then can you explain to me how one of the girls could get in and out of their crate and nail the lids back down by herself?"

"Not by themselves, sir. But if the stowaway let one of them out *after* I checked the hold..."

Emory squinted off toward the upper decks. "Who found her?"

"The stowaway?"

"*Mags*, for fuck's sake!"

Blitz looked down at the dead woman between them. "Two guests. High as a kite. They started freaking out, alerted the staff. I was in Sven's room—I put the keylogger on his laptop, by the way—"

"Thank you," Emory said distractedly.

"Just doing my job. Anyway, I'd just left his room when one of the hostesses, Raylene, found me. She took them back to their rooms and I went straight here. I radioed you the second I saw her lying here."

"Good man." He clapped Blitz on his massive shoulder and squeezed. "Okay... I want you to go back to the hold. Check every goddamn crate and make sure they're properly sealed. If you see *anything* out of place, report back to me. I don't think it's likely any of them would be teething, but it's not like we've got any wild animals on the ship, is it?"

"Not to my knowledge, sir."

"That was rhetorical. Now, help me throw her in the water."

"In the water, sir?"

"Burial at sea. Or would you rather we let the other guests know what happened here? Have a little funeral for her?"

Blitz nodded. "No, I don't think that's wise."

"All right then," Emory said, deliberately smarmy. "Grab her fucking arms."

Blitz cracked his neck, then crouched to grab the girl's wrists. His massive fingers could have circled around both arms in one massive fist, but he used both hands. Emory bet the man had a hog like a donkey. He grabbed the girl's legs, his grip slipping in the blood on her ankles. Finally, the two of them got her hoisted in the air—she couldn't have weighed any more than a hundred pounds soaking wet—and Emory started to swing her back and forth.

"Should we say something?" Blitz asked, holding her steady.

"*Say* something?"

The big man shrugged. "A prayer, or something. I feel like it's probably bad luck not to say something."

"Fine. Do it quick."

Blitz nodded solemnly. "'We therefore commit this body to the deep,'" he said, "'to be turned into corruption, looking for the resurrection of the body, when the Sea shall give up her dead,' amen."

Emory chuckled bitterly. "That was lovely. Thank you, Blitzen."

"You're welcome, sir," Blitz said, either not getting the sarcasm or choosing to ignore it.

"Now on the count of three. One… two…"

On three they tossed the remains of Magdalene O'Keefe into the sea. Her body sank immediately, and the sharks swarmed, already following in their wake. Emory supposed he'd chummed the water with Wilson's voluntary "dismissal." Thinking of his former chief of security as human sushi made him smile.

"Sir?" Blitz asked.

"Yes, Blitzen?"

The big man looked sick to his stomach. "Am I dismissed?" he asked.

Emory thought his new security chief had wanted to ask something else, perhaps why he'd been smiling, but had thought better of it. Blitz knew the consequences of insubordination, if not meted out by Emory himself, then by Tess, who would be even more strict. She would feed his genitals to the sharks while his heart still beat in his chest.

Or worse, feed him to The Duke.

Emory dismissed the man, and the two of them went their separate ways, Blitz toward the hold, Emory back to his quarters.

No, Blitz would never betray them. He was a good boy. Ex-elite Marine. Commendations the length of his arm, which was as long as to be expected from a man his size. Not to mention, he was absolutely terrified of the Old Man.

Who wouldn't be? Emory thought on his way back to his quarters. *That's right. Tess. Only fucking person I've ever seen who didn't practically shit herself in the presence of The Duke. Stood her ground even when he threatened to tear her to pieces. Never met a stronger woman in my life. Never met a stronger* human being. *Christ, I hope she gets here safely. I've got a rod like a steel beam right now. That tight little thing back there... shame we had to throw her overboard. The things I could've done with all the blood drained out of her. Nothing quite like going balls deep in an ice-cold pussy. With the proper lubricant, of course.*

Emory smiled again, thinking about all the depraved things he'd done since he'd met Tess. Prior to her involvement in his life the worst he'd gotten up to were threesomes, foursomes and a handful of orgies, snorting cocaine off the ass cracks of strippers and models, sprinkling coke on the head of his cock and raw-dogging teen girls, drugging women in clubs and parties and forcing himself into their tight little balloon knots in the back of his limousine. He'd never dabbled in blood play, nor carving up flesh or fucking the literal warm, wet guts through holes cut in still warm bodies. Tess had introduced him to all kinds of bizarre and interesting new kinks. But once they'd met Duke Ștefan, all of that had to stop.

Drink this, for it is my blood, The Duke had said, tongue planted firmly in cheek. Emory had imbibed deeply, suckling on the wound the Duke had sliced into his own torso, which in another biblical reference, he'd opened in the same spot Pontius Pilate's spear had pierced Jesus. That first dose of The Duke's blood had rushed through Emory's circulatory system like freebased cocaine, awakening parts of himself he'd never known existed. The ability to read minds, albeit vaguely. The strength of a man twice Blitz's size. The power to seduce world leaders, wealthy elites and beautiful women—including a handful who fell into one or both prior categories, such as Lady Rose of Staffordshire, currently aboard the *Ceres* with her cuckold of a husband, Lord Southwood, which by his wife's account was an unfortunately apt surname—all without uttering a single word. With these previously untapped abilities, he'd been able to amass an even greater fortune, raising an empire out of nothing, upon the foundations built by men and women he'd stepped over in his rise to fame and power.

It was a house of cards, he knew. If The Duke wished, he could pull his ace at any time and topple the entire deck. Which was why they'd needed to supply him with as much blood as he'd required to keep his repulsive body from wasting away to dust, as well as many new "daughters." It was The Duke's idea to feed his blood to the girls whose own blood nourished Tess. Why waste a perfectly good body when it could be put to further use, serving as both a courtesan and a vessel for The Duke's great lineage? The Old Man had told Emory he'd thought up the idea during his time spent with the Marquis de Sade and de Sade's wife, Renée-Pélagie. While de Sade gave young women large and sometimes fatal doses of Spanish fly so he could bury his face in their ass cracks and smother himself in their farts and excretions, The Duke had drained the girls of their blood and fed them his own, creating a harem of nubile *Moroi* more than willing to trade sexual favors to lecherous men in exchange for the meager nourishment of their semen. It had taken Emory to perfect the technique, employing the pharmaceutical engineer Lewis Caspian to make a serum which cut out the need for consumption by mouth entirely, leaving them toothless. With extensive testing Caspian had been able to create a vampire who did not require the consumption of blood to live, given regular infusions, and whose reflection could be seen in a mirror—a side effect of vampirism, much like their aversion to garlic, that Emory had never quite understood. As the serum was perfected, Caspian had planned to remove the growth of fangs altogether, as well as the crippling allergies to garlic and sunlight, but now that the pharmaceutical engineer was lying in a hospital bed with third-degree burns all over his body, Emory would need to find someone else to continue his groundbreaking work in the field.

In his latest request, The Duke had asked for a young bride, not to drain her blood but to live eternally at his side. Emory couldn't imagine what that poor girl would have to endure, and was only glad he didn't have to suffer such a fate himself.

After meeting with Blitz, he returned to his quarters and took a quick shower. As he was toweling off, dragging the towel under his balls, there came a rapid knock at the door.

"Who is it?"

"It's Blitz, sir."

"Did you find anything?"

"I think I found the girl."

Emory wrapped the towel around his waist and opened the door. Blitz towered in the doorway, looking apologetic.

"Where the fuck is she?"

"I had to let her go, sir."

"*You let her go?*"

"Ship protocol states—"

"*Fuck protocol!*"

Blitz reacted as if he'd been slapped.

"Where is she now?"

"She was with an old guy. Coltrane. Told me she's his granddaughter. Only I checked the manifest and he boarded alone."

"Coltrane…" Emory knew the name. The Duke himself had extended a personal invite to this Jeffrey Coltrane. He'd been a difficult man to track down, but they'd finally found him living in a squalid two-bedroom apartment in Liberty City. 'Where are they now?"

"I returned to his room just before I came up. I've been calling you on the radio."

"And?"

"No one answered. I used the master key, but the room was empty."

"Fuck." Emory stood just inside the doorway, thinking for a moment, his wet hair dripping on the floor. "All right. Keep up the search. If she's with Coltrane, she can't have gone far."

"Yes, sir." Blitz nodded and began to move away from the door.

"Oh, Blitz?"

The big man turned back. "Yes?"

"This girl… would you say she's a rare beauty?"

The question appeared to take his new security chief aback, and it seemed to take a conscious effort to flatten his expression. "She's young. Maybe sixteen, seventeen."

"But is she attractive?"

"Sir?"

"Jesus Christ, I'm not asking if you want to *fuck her*, Blitz. Is she good looking? Would she make it as a model?"

The big man frowned. "I mean for a kid, sure. I guess."

"Thank you."

Blitz stayed a moment longer, assessing the situation, then nodded again and stalked away without waiting to be dismissed.

Emory closed the door behind him, already working out a new plan as he toweled off and dressed in fresh clothes. He tried to get some rest, but the thought of Coltrane harboring the stowaway, and one of his girls potentially teething on his ship, made sleep difficult to come by. When Chaz, the helicopter pilot, finally radioed that they were nearing the ship, Emory practically leaped out of bed, dabbed on some of Tess's favorite cologne, and rushed straight to the helicopter pad.

The propellors had already stopped by the time he arrived, and Chaz was hauling luggage out of the helicopter onto a trolley. He greeted Emory, who clapped him on the back in return, then went ahead with the bags. Emory peered inside the cabin, seeing the bowed shape in a black cloak hunched in the closest back seat, like an old crone from a fairy tale.

"Darling," it croaked.

"Tess," Emory said, holding out a hand to her. The crone reached out with a skeletal claw and grasped it, her flesh so thin he felt nothing but bone. She was in much worse shape than she'd been when he'd last been at the penthouse they shared in Sunny Isles a week ago. He was sure he'd never seen her this bad. She smelled like a musty closet beneath the copious perfume, and he was relatively certain the stench wasn't coming from the cloak.

Maybe she really will turn to dust.

Another thought arose then, as he helped her out of the helicopter: *Would it be so bad if she did?*

Thoughts like this often popped into his head when she was waning. He never would've considered being thankful for her death while she was in bloom. Her seductive powers were far too compelling to resist, despite his own. But when her flesh withered, and her strength weakened, he saw glimpses of the truth beneath the shiny veneer. The stunning creature the paparazzi photographed and the public fawned over was merely an illusion draped over this desiccating husk. She absorbed the youth and beauty from the girls whose blood she bathed in, trading the life of a stranger for immortality.

"Let us dispense with the pretense, now we're alone," she said.

"Very well, Erzsébet."

The old woman smiled as he assisted her decrepit shuffle along the deck. "Where is the girl? Shall we have her tonight?"

"About that..."

Her bony hand gripped him tighter, ancient eyes boring into his, glistening in the cold light of the moon. "Has something happened?"

"As it turns out, Simone Howard is a drug addict. And Mags O'Keefe..."

"Yes?" she demanded.

"Well, we can't seem to find her," he lied. Telling her they'd had her corpse in their grasp, even drained of blood, and tossed her overboard for the sharks, would only enrage her.

The grip tightened further. "Then you find her."

"My best men are scouring the ship."

"Perhaps you should send your best *women*," she quipped.

"If we don't find her—"

"*You must find her*," Erzsébet hissed.

"Of course. But on the off chance we don't... I may have found another girl."

The ancient eyes fell on him. "Is she... a *rare* beauty?"

"The rarest," he said, hoping the girl Coltrane harbored was at least nubile enough for Erzsébet to be convinced of her beauty.

"Well, then. Today, I sleep. Tonight..." Her withered hand cupped his genitals and squeezed. They hung there like fruit rotting on the vine, entirely devoid of life. "...tonight we *play*," she finished on a musty breath.

Emory forced a smile. "I can hardly wait, my love," he said, hoping in her waning state she wasn't able to sense the truth, that he'd never felt less turned on in his life.

VAN HELSING & THE LITTLE VAMPIRE

ABRAHAM VAN HELSING stood in the shadows of the cargo hold, listening to the groan and sway of the ship's hull, awaiting the return of the young vampire, Ava.

His thoughts traveled back to a time long ago when he and two men not much younger than he had been had stood waiting for The Duke to return to the crypt below his castle in the Highlands. They'd been duped, and he'd been much stronger and more agile than they'd expected. He'd played himself off as a decrepit old man but had been far more formidable an opponent. He'd incapacitated the two men guarding his beloved Wilhelmina's body—half concealed in soil, only her face and hands above the earth—and had struck Abraham upon the head roughly before he, Abraham, had even been able to lift the hands holding a crucifix and wooden stake respectively.

When he'd awakened, both The Duke and Wilhelmina were gone, and the men Abraham had come with were dead. Not just dead—they'd been *massacred*. The Texan was strung up by his innards, choked to death with the fetid tail end of his lower intestine, wrapped first around his neck and then a rafter. Jonathan Harper, Wilhelmina's betrothed, had lain nude and supine upon the soil in which his fiancée had been half buried, his throat torn out and his genitals removed. Likely, judging by the trail of blood The Duke had left in his wake as Abraham chased him across Europe, they had been eaten. One eyewitness had claimed The Duke found testicles, particularly those of young men, to be a delicacy.

In his grief, Abraham had set fire to the crypt. He'd lost his friends and his niece, his only remaining family member, all in the span of an hour before sunrise. He'd stood and watched the belly of the castle burn while the sun rose above the hilly terrain, wishing it had been The Duke instead who had turned to ash and been blown away on the cool morning breeze from the loch.

In the days following the murders of Harper and the Texan, Abraham had fallen violently ill. Though it was clearly some sort of bug, he'd considered it might have been the stress of the previous weeks leaving his body, or a vicious bodily response to the loss of the last of his lineage. In either case, he'd lain in bed nearly an entire week, feverish with chills, sweating, vomiting and shitting out whatever vile toxin or virus had invaded his system. By the evening of the seventh day, he'd felt almost his normal self and had ventured downstairs to the tavern above which he'd rested his head for the prior three-and-a-half weeks.

He'd plunked himself down in a dim corner, ordered a large mug of stout, and worked his way through the previous week's newspapers. Word of Blechney Castle having burned to the ground, and of the disappearance of solicitor Jonathan Harper, had been relegated to the second page due to war updates from the front in Sudan, whose authors voiced their unwaveringly patriotic support for British troops massacring the "Dervishes."

When the barmaid came round with his mug of beer, he'd happened to glance at the mirror behind the bar and caught a disturbing sight. He'd set the mug down heavily, startling the woman as she'd left the table, and hurried to the bar, gripping its edge in horror.

His reflection, wide-eyed and gaunt, was little more than a diaphanous blur.

He'd looked around himself in a tizzy at the tavern full of cavorting men and women, each of them reflected accurately in the mirror. Yet somehow his own reflection still appeared as a smudge on the glass.

He'd hurried from the tavern, leaving his newspapers and his glass full of beer, and back to his room. He'd picked up his shaving mirror from the vanity and peered at himself in wonder. If it had been some kind of parlor trick, it was impressive, his face barely visible as he'd twisted the mirror this way and that

Drink this, for it is my blood.

The words, spoken in The Duke's Moldavian-tinged hiss directly into his mind, returned with such suddenness that he dropped the shaving glass. It shattered at his feet, his reflection, what there was of it, blurred in multiple shards of silver-plated glass.

Drink this…

He'd been only half conscious, lying in The Duke's lap as Wilhelmina regarded him with a vicious smirk. The Duke had raised his hand above Abraham's lips and slashed his own wrist with a fingernail, gnarled as the bark of an old tree. Blood had poured from it, splashing Abraham's face. He'd spat and choked and drifted back into unconsciousness.

…for it is my blood.

Abraham stripped down to his underpants in front of the mirror, the full understanding of what the memory, half-formed like his reflection in the shards of glass on the floor, meant for him. The Duke's blood coursed through his own, yet he appeared to have no wounds on his body. He could not therefore be undead. The Duke had kept him alive, and over the years, as his body withered but refused to give up on life, he came to understand that it had not been a gift but a curse meant to make him suffer for what he'd tried to do that night so long ago. He was *Strigoi*—a half-human half-vampire abomination. He'd learned to control his disappearing act over the following weeks, during which The Duke sent letters meant to taunt him, assuring Abraham that Wilhelmina was still with him, and that no matter how hard he tried to find them, The Duke would forever be one step ahead of him.

Shortly after The Duke left for America with Wilhelmina, according to his last letter, they stopped coming altogether. For over a hundred years, The Duke remained silent, hidden away, unable to be found. Then suddenly, little over a decade ago, a letter arrived stamped by a post office in Miami Beach, where Abraham subsequently made his home. It was from a legal firm called Harper & Co. *Surely*, he'd thought, *it couldn't be the* same *Harper!*

Still, The Duke himself eluded him, had perhaps never been to Miami—certainly the solicitors had not seen him, had only forwarded an old envelope they'd found among their records during a move that had been addressed to him—and after several years spent chasing down a ghost, unsure whether he'd meant to destroy The Duke or allow the creature to take away the long life he'd been given, Abraham had finally given up. He'd fallen into a meaningless yet comfortable life, never quite putting down roots, ready to pack up and move the moment he received word of a sighting or another letter, but as settled as he'd been for the entirety of the twentieth century.

This meager, meaningless existence continued until late last week, when he'd received a phone call from a representative of Emory Jackson, extending a personal invitation to his private island in the Caribbean.

Abraham had balked at the notion. He had little interest in rubbing elbows with celebrities and royalty on a cruise, let alone fawning over them, as it appeared the general public did, according to tabloid magazines and television shows. A second call had come within the hour from Emory Jackson himself. He'd needed only to speak a single sentence for Abraham to accept the invitation, though he would have done so upon hearing the first two words:

"The Duke requests your presence on Little Pearl Island."

So Abraham had packed what he'd need into his old trunk, which had been gathering dust in the bedroom closet for twelve, maybe thirteen years, but was so ancient he'd already replaced the buckles three times in the hundred or so years he'd had it.

Two days later he waited in another darkened room for yet another vampire, or for the sun to rise—whichever came first. This time, he was much older, bowed over his cane, run down enough he worried he'd be unable to do the job even on a nascent vampire. If Ava failed to return before sunrise, he'd no longer need to worry. The sun's rays would take care of her for him. If she returned, the tools he'd brought would make short work of her should she attack, although he'd promised her sister she'd not be harmed. It was her master he was after, anyway. Or rather, her master's master.

Somewhere on Little Pearl Island, The Duke awaited.

After more than a century, Abraham would finally have his revenge… or die trying.

At the top of the stairs, the sound of the door alarmed him. Moonlight spilled down the stairwell, and suddenly all of the lights came on in the hold, nearly blinding Abraham. He tried to crouch behind the taller of the crates but his spine made a loud crack like a snapped branch, causing him to cry out in sharp pain. He leaned against his cane, holding his back, unable to move.

"Who's down there?" came a familiar baritone voice from above.

Trapped, with nowhere to hide, Abraham stood his ground, hoping whoever it was barreling down those steps could be easily swayed by magic.

The burly security guard who'd questioned him earlier, when Clarissa had run into his arms, stomped down the last few steps, looking in Abraham's direction. He squinted and came closer, perhaps twenty feet from where Abraham stood hunched over his cane.

"*Do not see me*," Abraham whispered.

The burly security guard frowned. He clomped across the room and stopped right in front of Abraham, mere feet from him, though his gaze lowered from the crate the old man stood before and peered down at the floor.

The big man bent swiftly and picked up a nail Abraham had missed when he'd cleaned up around Ava's crate. He'd rapped the others back into place on the off chance the man would come here looking for Clarissa before her sister returned, and had swept the loose dirt behind the crate.

The security guard rose again, studying the nail, which appeared not much larger than a thumbtack between his massive forefinger and thumb. He looked over the crates, his scowl deepening. Finding nothing out of the ordinary he turned again to where Abraham stood, holding in a pained breath. The big man's eyes went somewhat crossed as if he were looking at a fly on his nose, and his frown deepened. He let the nail fall to the floor and raised a massive arm, reaching out toward Abraham.

The old man held his breath, feeling the *glammer* begin to fade. He was far too old and out of practice. The guard was too close, or he would have attempted to speak it into being once more. He just had to hope—

The big man's brow relaxed and he chuffed a sharp breath. His head shook on his tree trunk neck as he turned away, heading deeper into the hold.

Abraham allowed himself to exhale.

The guard did a brief search of the rest of the crates, and finding nothing out of order, he stomped back to the stairs. His boots thudded heavily as he ascended. In a moment, the door opened and the lights flickered out, leaving only a small shaft of moonlight down the far wall. When the door closed behind him, the darkness returned.

Despite being perfectly safe in daylight, Abraham felt most comfortable in the dark. His vision was better in the dark, as yet another power bestowed upon him by a single taste of The Duke's blood, while his eyesight during the day began to wane as a symptom of old age and cataracts. Mainly, he'd spent so many years scouring after-hours haunts, loud clubs and seedy bars, for signs of his nemesis The Duke and his offspring, that sleeping during the day had become second nature.

High in the wall to his right, the vent came open with a metallic squeal, and a dark shape poked out from the duct, hair falling as it twisted back and forth before fully emerging. The little girl he'd been waiting for climbing vertically down the wall.

As many times as he'd seen it while hunting The Duke's spawn, the sight of what was once a live human being creeping up and down walls and along the ceiling like a spider never failed to bring a chill to Abraham's bones. He stood erect, grunting as another spasm struck his spine.

The skitter and scrape of her bare feet and fingernails upon the floor as she neared made him grip the stake tighter in his left hand. He was ready, should she choose to attack. It was rare that a vampire ever attempted to bite him. They might try to slash his throat, or gouge out his eyes, but they seemed to be aware the blood of their master coursed through his veins as it did theirs, even in as small a dose as he'd gotten. He was *Strigoi*, and the *Moroi* seemed to respect their similarities, to a point. Nor would less than their most powerful *glammers* work on him. And though they possessed strength far in excess of any mortal, throughout the years, Abraham had found himself on near-equal footing with each vampire he'd encountered.

Still, her nearness made him somewhat anxious. He hadn't encountered a vampire in the wild in several years, and his own powers and stamina had declined rapidly in the time since. He'd likely be able to fight her off, but he suspected her speed would be an advantage.

The skittering stopped abruptly.

Abraham couldn't see the girl despite his night vision, but the sound of her last movement placed her two crates behind her own. Unless she was somehow able to disguise her approach, the way he was able to hide himself from the eyes of susceptible mortals—

A blur of movement signaled her approach but she was upon him before he could raise the stake, her feet pressed against his hips and her small, cold hands gripping his shoulders. With her pallid face close to his, she *sniffed*... her wide eyes like onyx shimmering in moonlight.

"I mean you no harm," he said, his voice quavering as his hands trembled. "I've come with your sister. To help you."

The girl's lips parted, fangs protruding. She hissed—

Then her mouth closed. Her head tilted in curiosity and she sniffed the air once more. "You're like me," she said finally.

Abraham smiled. "Not quite." He studied her more closely. "There's blood on your face. Have you been up to something naughty, Ava?"

She frowned, letting go of his shoulders and dropping to the floor on her feet. "Nuh-uh," she said, wiping her chin with the back of a hand.

"Ava," he said in a cautioning tone. "I'm like you. You said it yourself. You can tell me the truth."

She gave him a sheepish look. "You won't tell nobody?"

"Your secret is safe with me."

"I hurted someone," she said, clearly ashamed. "Really bad, I think."

"You know you shouldn't do that, yes?"

She nodded, her gaze on the floor.

"But you didn't know any better, did you?"

The little girl shook her head.

"Excellent. Then you won't do it again, will you?"

She cocked her head, looking up at him questioningly.

"What is the matter, Ava?"

"I was so *hungry*," she said, her voice small. "But then... I wasn't hungry anymore."

"After you hurt the woman."

She nodded again.

"Ava, what did you eat before you hurt that woman? You must have eaten something, yes? Did your companion feed you any raw meat? Make you drink things that didn't look or smell nice but tasted very yummy?"

Again, she shook her head.

"Well then, what have you been eating? What made you feel like you did after you hurt the woman?"

"*Nothing*," she hissed. "Only…"

"Yes?"

"I'm not supposed to say."

"You can tell *me*, Ava. I'm like you, remember?"

"Not like me," she said. "You're like *them*."

"Them? Them who?"

"The men. They get undressed and give me their Milk."

"Their…" Abraham balked at speaking the next word. "Ava, do you mean cold milk from a glass? Cow's milk?"

"From their doodles," she said matter-of-factly. "Lionel said it was the only food I'd like, that it would make me feel good. And it did, even when the men were super gross." She scowled fiercely, her nose wrinkling. "But he was wrong. It didn't make me feel as good as what came from the woman when I did the Bad Thing. He was wrong, and I know it's bad what he made me do. My sister told me so."

"Yes," Abraham said, swallowing hard. He'd heard of it happening but had never met a child this young who'd been bred for the task. The very thought of it made him feel filthy, as if the repulsiveness of the act perpetuated by other men had sullied him by proxy. "It's *very* wrong, Ava. Unconscionable, what Lionel made you do. Perhaps even worse than what you did to that poor woman."

"Then what *can* I eat? *I'm so hungry all the time, mister*."

"Your companion, this Lionel, is he… like us?"

Ava nodded. "Like me," she said. "*Not* like you."

"That's good. Is he here with us now?"

When she shook her head, Abraham's heart sank. He'd hoped to free her from her curse but without her master aboard the ship there was little he could do to help. She would have to continue consuming blood to survive, or worse: the "milk" of these abhorrent men.

Is that why they're bringing her to the island? he wondered. He'd suspected The Duke might be calling home all of his children, perhaps for the same reason he'd summoned Abraham himself, but *now*… he couldn't be sure that was the reason at all. Was it possible this Little Pearl Island, where The Duke held court and the rich and powerful caroused, was no better than a common brothel? Much worse, in fact, if the men and women on this ship hoped to feed their "milk" to girls as young as Ava, trafficked as sex slaves.

"Ava, I believe I might be able to help you. Only…"

She looked up at him with her dark eyes wide. "What?"

"How long are you able to go without sustenance?" he asked.

A CHANGE OF WARDROBE

GABE WOKE UP to find Clarissa standing over him, bent down to peer below the top bunk. He startled, believing for a moment he was still dreaming, then rubbed his eyes and sat up. "How long you been standin there?"

"A few minutes," she said. "We should go."

"You can stay here all day if you want," Gabe said, eager to keep her around, to be certain she was safe. "I'll bring you food and stuff. Just hide under the covers up there when Digby comes back, you should be fine."

Clarissa smiled. "We have to meet Abraham. After that we can talk about where I'll stay."

"Okay." He slid out of the bunk. "You want some breakfast? There's still some of that granola left, I think…"

"I'll be fine."

Hungry himself, he grabbed the bag of Chex Mix, shoved a handful into his mouth, and chewed while putting on his shoes. "Oh, snap. I just had a great idea."

"What?" she asked, watching as he tied his shoes.

"You should wear some of my clothes."

She seemed wary of the idea.

"As a disguise," he elaborated, suddenly worried she might think it was some kind of kink. "I got an extra hat, you could tuck your hair under it. And I bet you could wear my pants if you used a belt."

She looked over the small pile of dirty clothes on the floor.

"Those are Dig's. My stuff's clean, I swear."

"Okay," she said. "But quickly."

Gabe rushed to the dresser. He picked out a large sweatshirt he used for cool nights on the deck while the rest of the passengers and crew slept on the island, and a pair of jeans. He grabbed his

Texas Rangers peak cap from a hook on the wall and brought them over. She took the pile of folded clothes from him. "I've got socks and a extra pair of shoes you could borrow, too. I bet you could fit in em."

She smiled, holding the clothing. "Thank you, Gabe."

"You're welcome. You can change in the bathroom if you want, or I can go out in the hall…"

"Stay. I'll use the washroom."

She stepped forward, then stopped abruptly and kissed him on the cheek. Gabe blushed, feeling his skin turning bright red under her sustained gaze. Then she continued to the bathroom and closed the door behind her.

Once she was out of sight, he let out the breath he'd been holding. He couldn't believe how lucky he'd been just to have spent a night in the same room with her, let alone the light brush of her soft lips on his cheek. He touched a hand to the spot she'd kissed and held it there, peering at the closed bathroom door. It was delusional to think she'd be interested in him, but just the possibility that she might become a close friend over time felt amazing—considering his lack of friends at home—even though he obviously would prefer her to be more.

He ate a couple more handfuls of Chex Mix waiting for her to finish getting changed. While he was picking bits of it out of his teeth a few minutes later, Clarissa emerged. The big sweater pretty much erased her chest, the baggy pants effectively hid her hips, and with her golden curls tucked up under the hat, she'd be unlikely to be noticed by Blitz or anyone looking for a female stowaway.

"What do you think?"

"It's like lookin in a mirror," he said. "I mean, you're obviously better lookin, I just…" He shrugged, feeling the sting of embarrassment yet again. "You know what I mean."

She grinned, then stuck out a hand holding her bunched up dress. "You should probably hide this."

Gabe's cheeks flushed further as he took it from her. Placing it in his bottom drawer alongside the bags of snacks, he promised himself he wouldn't take it out of the drawer to smell it once she was gone, already certain he'd break that vow.

He closed the drawer swiftly and stood. "Ready?"

She shrugged. "I guess so."

He went to the door, turned the handle and peered out into the hall. The coast was clear. "Okay," he whispered. "All good."

Clarissa followed him out. He removed Digby's dirty sock, tossed it into the room, and closed the door behind them.

As they began heading for the stairwell, the door to Cheery's room opened and Digby stepped out with the top buttons of his silver dress shirt undone. He turned without noticing them, leaning in to the doorway, surprising Gabe by kissing Cheery, who wore only a pair of tighty-whities, on the lips.

"Thanks for the great night, Puddin," Digby said.

Cheery reached around and squeezed Digby's left ass cheek. "Shake it for me, hot stuff!"

Digby started shaking his ass, turning in a half circle until he saw Gabe and Clarissa standing there, Gabe's mouth agape. Digby stopped his dance abruptly, clearing his throat with an awkward look. "How much did you see?"

"All-all of it, I guess?" Gabe said, equally awkward.

"Oh, hey, guys," Cheery said with a wave over Digby's shoulder. "Early birds get the worm, huh?"

"We should go," Gabe said.

"We'll talk later, okay, Little Buddy?" Digby gave him a desperate look he understood to mean, *Don't breathe a word of this to anyone, especially not Marnie*.

"O-okay. Sure."

"Later, boys," Clarissa said with a big smile.

Gabe took her arm and pulled her along. Once they entered the stairwell and started down, he said, "That was weird."

"I think it's cute."

"Sure. I'm good. I just mean, Digby's straight. He's always talking about plow—about *makin love* to women. Last time we went to Little Pearl, he told me he slept with at least three chi—*women* on the crew."

Clarissa shrugged. "Maybe he's expanding his horizons."

Gabe considered this and shrugged. "Yeah, maybe," he said, sure he'd find out all about it from Digby once they got to work.

A minute later the two of them reached the door to the cargo hold. Gabe opened it and let Clarissa go down first. A light was on downstairs but not the main ones, likely one of the office lamps. The lid to Ava's crate was nailed back down, the rest of the crates undisturbed.

Van Helsing was waiting for them behind the desk when they reached the office, playing Solitaire. He set down a two on the ace of spades and looked up from his game with a smile. "Here you are," he said. "I was beginning to worry. And you've worn a disguise." He tapped a gnarled finger against his temple. "Very clever."

"It was Gabe's idea," Clarissa said.

Gabe shrugged. "Just wish I had a fake beard or somethin to go with it."

"Well, you made due with what you had." Van Helsing pushed himself up with the help of his cane, uttering a small grunt. "First things first," he said. "Your sister has been safely returned to her crate."

"Did she—?"

"Yes, unfortunately. I'm not sure what has become of the young woman she feasted upon, but the two of us have come to an understanding. She will not ask to be released from her crate for the remainder of the voyage."

Gabe and Clarissa sighed in unison.

"You are aware what she's been forced to do over the years, yes?"

Gabe turned to Clarissa, curious what the old man meant. She nodded with a grave expression.

"Good. It's best you know. It is my belief that Ava and the others, however many more there are within those boxes, are being taken to Little Pearl Island to be employed as sex slaves."

"Sex—?" Gabe couldn't finish the question. He swallowed hard, disgusted by the mere thought of it.

"Yes. A horrendous deed, we all agree. I wonder…"

"What?" Clarissa said, quick and breathless.

"Your sister must feed within the next few days or she will wither away to nothing. I have spent the majority of my very long life hunting monsters. However, there exists another creature, more vile perhaps than the vampire scourge, which has gone as yet untouched by my blade and my stake. The pedophile who gives in to his or her urges and abuses young children is no better than a monster. Should I, as a hunter of them, permit these abominations to live whilst condemning vampires to ash and earth?"

Gabe didn't know what answer the old man was looking for, so he said nothing. Clarissa answered for him.

"Revenge," she said. "You're talking about killing people?"

The old man tilted his head in a shrug. "Think of it as thinning the herd. When there are more predators than prey, a cull must be administered. Your sister requires blood, therefore we require a victim. Would you prefer the victim were innocent, like the woman Ava attacked and drained last night? Unless either of you would be willing to supply the many pints she'll require over the next several days, perhaps longer..."

Clarissa shook her head with a frightened look. "But how do we decide who's bad and who's good?"

"Yeah," Gabe added, not sure he liked the idea of killing anyone at all. But if someone had to die, better that it was an evil man than someone with goodness in their heart. "Ain't like we can just go up to people an' ask if they're kiddie fiddlers."

The vampire hunter surprised Gabe by laughing. Clarissa startled and the old man held the hand not holding his cane palm out in a gesture of peace. "I do apologize. The idea of asking the sort of people on this ship such a question tickled me, imagining the shock on their faces!" He tittered again and covered his mouth with a hand, until the laughter died down. "I'm sorry. Where were we?"

"Talking about murdering people to feed my sister."

"Yes, of course. The easiest way to determine who is or isn't deserving of our wrath would be to employ you as a sort of bait and switch. You're seventeen, is that right?"

Gabe turned to Clarissa. Her nod made him feel like the world's biggest pervert. She was still a kid. Just seventeen. A grown man in love with a child. Sure, he was only three years older than her, maybe less depending on when her birthday was, but it was wrong. Wasn't it?

Clarissa caught his gaze and looked away quickly.

"Unfortunately, you're a wanted woman," Van Helsing said. "But perhaps..." He let the sentence trail off, looking her up and down in a way that made Gabe uncomfortable.

"What?" she asked, folding her arms across the front of Gabe's baggy sweatshirt.

"Yeah," Gabe said. "What?"

A grin formed on the old man's lips as he turned to Gabe. "What size are you?"

Clarissa snickered behind her hand, obviously hearing what Gabe wasn't quick enough to understand.

"What?" he asked. "Why?"

"Clarissa fits rather nicely into *your* clothing," Van Helsing said. "I wonder how *you* might fit in *hers*."

With a plan formulated, despite Gabe's protests, the three of them returned to Abraham's room. Gabe didn't speak a word until they reached the door, already troubled by what lay ahead for them. Before Clarissa and the vampire hunter entered the old man's room, Gabe gestured for her to step aside with him.

"I don't *wanna* put on your dress, if that's what you think," he whispered, his cheeks practically on fire.

Clarissa snorted laughter. "It's fine." She laid a hand on his shoulder. "I won't tell anyone if you don't."

"You better not."

"Who would I tell? I'm not even supposed to be here."

Gabe considered it a moment, then nodded. "Stay out of trouble, okay?"

"I will."

"You promise?"

She crossed her arms over her chest, obscuring his high school logo. "I promise," she said in a gruff, fake serious voice.

Gabe laughed with a shake of his head. Despite her being dressed in his clothes and their tragic age difference, he couldn't help still feeling deeply attracted to her. He waved at the old man. "Keep her safe, Abe."

"I shall do my utmost," Van Helsing said.

Clarissa gave him a small wave as the old man closed the door behind them.

Feeling pretty anxious about everything they'd been through the night before, and what was still to come—particularly about what he'd promised to do tonight—Gabe returned to his room in the crew wing. He heard water running before he unlocked the door. The bathroom door was open a crack, steam spilling out. Digby sang that "Could This Be Magic?" song he always sung poorly the morning after he got laid, while water splashed on the shower floor.

Gabe went to his drawers and opened the bottom one. He looked down at Clarissa's dress but didn't dare touch it, knowing if he pulled it out he'd want to smell it and be ensconced in the scent of her sweat and perfume. He would carry that smell in his mind all day anyhow, and there was no point in getting perverted about it.

Not to mention the fact that he'd have to actually *wear* the thing himself after dinner tonight.

He pushed the drawer shut with his foot, took two steps away from the dresser, then crouched and opened it again. This time he couldn't help himself. Like an addict trying to flush his drugs, he grabbed the crumpled dress and brought it immediately to his nose, breathing in deeply. The smell of her sweat was a little sharper than he'd remembered—she'd been wearing this for more than a day, and been on the run most of that time—but he tried to hold it in his memory as best he could before exhaling.

He had to convince himself it wasn't perverted. Women smelled their boyfriends' clothes all the time. Anyway, it wasn't like he was sniffing her underwear. The last time he'd done that, when he was too young to know any better, he'd realized too late they were period panties and the salty, metallic smell of his friend's big sister's discharge had stuck with him for days.

He let the dressed drape out in front of him and looked down at himself. Van Helsing was right, it was probably just loose enough around the waist that he could wear it comfortably. He bent a knee and twisted slightly, getting a better idea of how he'd look in it.

"Not sure it's your color," Digby said.

Gabe threw the dress into the drawer, mortified, unable to look his roomie in the eye. "That wasn't—I mean it's not what it looked like."

"Hey," Digby said placatingly, his tattooed torso glistening above the towel wrapped around his waist. "It's okay, Little Buddy. I ain't gonna judge you. It's fine to be curious about cross dressing."

"I wasn't—"

"You know, Cheery used to read to kids in drag before he started workin here," Digby said, gathering up his clothes.

"Why would he wanna do that?"

His roommate shrugged. "I guess maybe 'cause his mom used to read to him, and his teachers were mostly chicks, so it's kind of in honor of that."

With a complete lack of shame, his roommate threw his towel on the dresser and began to change into fresh clothes. Gabe turned away quickly, his blush deepening further. He'd always hated using the locker rooms at school, and the fact that Digby treated their room like his own personal change room had always bothered him. Gabe had always gotten dressed in the bathroom.

"Speakin of drag, who was that chick wearin your clothes? Finally get your dick wet?"

"She's… just a friend."

"Friend, huh? That why you put the sock on the door? Why you were prancin around in her dress."

"I wasn't prancin—" He shook his head, not wanting to get into it. He didn't have a clue where he'd start even if he wanted to start trying. "It's a long story, okay?"

"I'm just messin with ya." Digby put on a t-shirt, standing there in his tighty-whities and socks. "So you're really not gonna ask about me and Cheery, huh?"

"Hey, you guys are consentin adults, whatever happened is none of my business."

"Well, okay, twist my arm," Dig said, stepping into a dirty pair of jeans. "So, you know I was puttin in the work with Marnie, right? One of the new line cooks?"

"Sure," Gabe said.

"Well, she was givin me the cold shoulder all night. I dunno what was up with that, but you know me, I don't play games. Anyways, me an Cheery went back to his room to drink some of his homemade hooch, and he busted out his guitar and played my favorite Van Halen song—"

"What song's that?"

"'Could This Be Magic?'"

"Oh, *that's* Van Halen?"

"Jesus, kid, keep up. So he's pretty much serenadin my ass, and I got to thinkin 'bout what you said, if you were bi you'd have more options."

"*You* said that."

"Whatever, doesn't matter. So anyways, I figured why not give it a go? So just went for it, an' it turns out he was into me, or at least while we were a bit smashed, one thing led to another and we ended up…" He looked at a loss on how to describe it. "Well, you know."

"Makin love?"

Digby snorted laughter. "'Makin love.' Kid, you are funny as hell, you know that? Yeah, sure, we made mad, passionate love until our dicks chafed. Anyways, turns out he's a bottom, and you know I'm a service top."

"I don't really know what any of that means."

Digby laughed, zipping up his jeans. "Well, it doesn't matter. Needless to say, I unlocked a couple new fetishes last night."

"Well, I'm happy for you." As much as Gabe didn't want to think about Digby having sex with anyone, man or woman, he truly was happy for him. "Seriously," he added, just in case his partner thought he was being sarcastic.

"Well, thanks, Little Buddy."

"Welcome, Skip. You goin to breakfast?"

"Hell, yeah. I need carbs to soak up all this liquor sloshin around in my guts."

"Grab a table then, huh? Meet you down there?"

"Sure thing." Digby turned back in the hall with a wink. "And if you really are serious about putting that dress on, I bet I could get Cheery to give you some makeup tips."

Gabe said, "Haha," and shut the door on him.

Turning back to the dresser, where Clarissa's dress hid among his things, he considered Digby did have a point. If he wanted to play the role of a teenage girl tonight—or not *wanted* to so much as *had* to—then makeup and a wig would further the illusion. If Cheery happened to have either, or both, it might be smart to ask. As badly as he didn't want to do what Abraham and Clarissa had planned for him, he knew Clarissa's sister meant the world to her. She'd left her entire life behind to find her. If he wanted to get into Clarissa's good graces, he'd have to go through with it, no matter how embarrassing it might be.

He'd already told himself he'd do anything for Clarissa.

Tonight, he'd get a chance to prove it to her.

NO ESCAPE

CLARISSA SAT IN the chair in Abraham's small room, reading his journal while the man himself snored lightly in his bed, a white noise machine blaring and a sleep mask covering his eyes.

The journal was fascinating. It filled in details of what had happened to Abraham during his first encounter with Duke Ștefan of Moldavia up until the last moment he'd seen him, while semiconscious in the crypt beneath The Duke's castle. His niece had been seduced by the vampire. In Abraham's eyes, The Duke had lured Wilhelmina into a life of drink and debauchery. He'd seen no romance in the encounter, no charm. To him, it had been less like the charismatic vampires of the movies than a hypnotist using dark magic to lull his niece into submission.

After Abraham burned down the castle, The Duke had begun sending him letters, toying with him like Jack the Ripper allegedly taunted the police. In them, he'd referred to Abraham as "my child," which the old man soon began to realize had a far deeper and sinister meaning than a patronizing dig. He truly was The Duke's offspring—a bastard child, maybe, but a child nonetheless. He'd consumed The Duke's blood, and though he'd neither craved nor required a sacrifice of blood to survive himself, it had tainted him.

All the while, he knew very little of what had become of his beloved niece. The Duke's letters mentioned her by name but nothing else, meant to hurt him, to remind him she belonged to the vampire. Abraham knew the creature was resentful of having almost been bested. Just the fact that he'd seen through The Duke's "*glammers*," as the journal called it—which given the context, Clarissa understood to mean *magic*—was enough to enrage The Duke. That he'd trespassed in his home, *in his crypt* of all places—

his "*sanctum sanctorum*," Abraham called it, underlining the Latin phrase twice—was possibly the most unforgivable affront of all.

The Duke's final letter spoke of Wilhelmina's wish to visit America. Since the letter would've been posted several days or a week prior, Abraham had known they were likely already halfway across the pond. Still, he'd gone to the Port of London to watch for them every day for a week. He'd seen neither The Duke nor his Wilhelmina at all.

In the years since, he admitted to having attempted to take his own life several times. Whatever he'd tried, nothing worked. Gun, noose, knife, pills, his body would reject them, spitting out bullets, vomiting poison, healing wounds. He'd felt like there was no way out, that the only way he could die was if The Duke himself was destroyed, the entire evil bloodline wiped out. Maybe *nothing* could end his pain, he'd considered. Maybe he'd been cursed to eternal life, and even the end of the creature's vile existence on earth would fail to bring him peace.

As much as the vampire's curse, he suspected vengeance had kept him holding on to life, miserable as it had been. Perhaps more. His need for revenge was so ingrained and pure he could find escape. He half-doubted even his own death, eternally beyond his grasp, would end it.

Clarissa closed the journal, wishing Abraham had finally been able to discover what had happened to Wilhelmina. She wished she knew herself. As she considered this, something occurred to her from what she'd read in his earlier entries: he seemed to believe vampires had something he called "blood memory," which he compared to the idea of past lives. Only, in the case of vampires, the memories of their kin flowed through their blood. There were moments, sprinkled throughout the pages she'd read, where it seemed as though he'd seen through The Duke's eyes, or perhaps the fiend's ancestors—not in the present but in the past. He'd awaken feverishly from dreams of times long ago, what he called "bacchanalian festivities," in which the vampires walked and feasted among the living. They'd been *welcomed*, their bloodlust fulfilled by zealous volunteers.

If his theory of blood memory was true, and he hadn't just been experiencing hallucinations, then it was possible The Duke's memories of the past century would've been passed to Lionel de

La Haye, the Mall Monster. Meaning it was possible, even highly likely, that Ava would know what had become of Wilhelmina.

Thinking this, Clarissa tucked her hair back up under Gabe's hat and stood carefully and quietly. Abraham continued to snore, undisturbed by the small creak of the chair.

She went to the bathroom and changed the bandage on her foot, then put Gabe's socks and tatty sneakers back on. She crept as quietly as she could to the door, picked up Abraham's keycard, and tucked it into the front pocket of Gabe's jeans. She opened the door as quietly as she could, peering back at Abraham to be sure he hadn't heard. Satisfied he was still fast asleep, she slipped out into the hall and closed the door slowly behind her. The click was loud out in the hall, but she suspected Abraham's sound machine would be enough to prevent him from hearing it.

She felt safer wearing Gabe's clothes. Not just as a stowaway but in general. Men had always leered at her, and though several of her foster sisters and her foster mothers often wore baggy clothes, Clarissa had never felt comfortable wearing them, as if doing so would somehow make her less of a girl. It was silly, she knew, and being forced to wear Gabe's clothes she realized it wasn't just silly it was unfounded. Her dresses were comfortable but so were Gabe's jeans and sweatshirt. No wonder straight girls often wore their boyfriend's shirts. Not to mention, the lack of worry about crossing her legs a certain way or holding the hems down to prevent anyone from seeing her underwear.

Clarissa wandered down the hall. A door opened near the stairwell and she almost lowered the hat and turned back to Abraham's room but she forced herself to hold her head high. She recognized the guy stepping out of his room from YouTube but didn't expect to see him here. It was DJ Safe-T, the comedic musician.

He nodded at her. "Sup, li'l man?"

"Hey," Clarissa said back, with as deep a voice as she could muster.

They fell into step with one another, the DJ with a slight limp. "Yo, dude, whatchoo think bout these rooms?" he asked, affirming her suspicion she passed as a boy. Although she supposed it was still possible that he called everyone *dude* and *li'l man*. "I figured I'd be on a higher deck, you know? With my rep? Heard they got bidets in the fancy rooms an' shit. Just 'cause I ain't the son of a prince or some fuckin, I dunno, shippin company CEO, don't mean I don't deserve a clean asshole, you know?"

Clarissa laughed. "Seriously," she said in her deeper voice.

Safe-T gave her a sidelong look, then stuck out a hand. "I'm Richie," he said.

"Kyle," she said, shaking his hand firmly. A sudden thought struck her: what if he was one of the men on this trip going to Little Pearl to victimize young girls? What if he was an actual pedophile? "Good to meet you," she added finally.

"Yeah, you too," the DJ said, looking at the hand she tucked back into Gabe's sweater. "Yo, you ever do any hand modelin? My rep was tryna get me into it but I got them callouses, ya feel me?" He guffawed at this. Clarissa wasn't sure if he meant because of hard work or something far different. Judging by his laughter, she suspected the latter. Was this the "locker room talk" she'd heard so much about? Her own foster sisters got pretty filthy with each other, talking about which boys they'd "smash," and often described their sexual encounters in graphic detail. She figured the way guys talked had to be worse still, with the way it had been used to excuse some particularly horrible comments.

She laughed along. "I feel ya," she said.

"Yo, you seem pretty cool, li'l man. You heard me spinnin yesterday on the pool deck?"

"Sure," she said. She'd heard a bit of it, she thought, but it seemed like he'd just been playing old records. "That was cool."

"Mos def." He held out a fist for her to bump, which she did, awkwardly, despite not wanting the DJ to get another look at her hand, and tucked it right back into her pocket. He opened the door and gestured for her to go ahead. "Ladies first," he said with a smirk.

"Go ahead then," she said, hoping he'd meant it like guys in her school often did when they busted each other's balls.

Safe-T laughed, covering his mouth with a hand. "Oh, snap! Li'l dude claps *back*! Yo, sorry, I forget it ain't cool to say shit like that no more, you know? Gender equality and whatnot."

Clarissa wasn't sure it was ever cool, but she nodded and stepped into the hall. "No worries."

"Cool, cool." She began down to the next level.

"You ain't goin to breakfast? Eat your Wheaties?" Safe-T asked, looking suspicious. "You know what DJ Safe-T say: breakfast is the most important meal of the day, ya feel me?"

"Yeah, I just gotta, um, check on something in my luggage first," she said. "You know what I'm saying?"

The DJ stared at her a moment, blank-faced. Then a wide, metallic grin spread across his face as he nodded. "Shoot, I fuck with that, dawg. You bring enough to share with the class?"

Clarissa had no idea what he was talking about but she shook her head, eager to get rid of him. "Sorry. Just enough for me."

He tapped her shoulder with his fist. "Bet. You happen to come into some more, you let Safe-T know, a'ight? I'm lookin."

"Okay."

"Yo, peace out, homie." He held out a fist to bump. This time Clarissa bumped it, thinking she'd get off easy, but he turned it into a complicated handshake with finger wiggles and shoulder bumps. She got the rhythm of it quickly—many years spent playing Stella Elle Olla and other clapping games with her foster sisters paid off—and when it was finally over, he gave her an impressed nod. "You all right, li'l man. Don't OD or nothin. You know what DJ Safe-T say: everything in moderation, ya heard?"

"I won't," she said, finally understanding what he meant about sharing.

As the DJ headed up, Clarissa headed down, though she knew she'd have to go through the belly of the ship, past Gabe and Digby's room and the rest of the crew's, only to go back up and down again to get to the hold.

She was halfway down the first set of stairs, relieved to not have to fake civility anymore with someone who might be a sex criminal, when she heard footsteps coming up. Her first instinct was to hide, but with her disguise already proven she decided to keep going. She'd just about reached the lower riser when a hand shot out from below and grabbed her wrist.

Her heart leaped into her throat.

"Have you seen my girlfriend?" came a broken voice from below. The hand let go and the man worked his way up the stairs to get a look at her. He could've been a male model, with his chiseled face, broad shoulders and bedhead hairstyle. Her foster sisters might have called him a "beautiful" boy, comparing him to their favorites, Harry Styles and Timothée Chalamet. His piercing blue eyes stared into hers with deep distress.

"Your girlfriend?"

"Please, I've been looking for her everywhere. Mags Bunny on IG."

Clarissa frowned. She rarely if ever used Instagram and had definitely never heard of any Mags Bunny. "What does she look like?"

"She's five-eleven, drop-dead gorgeous, blonde hair, green eyes big enough to swim in, she could be a runway model but she's too curvy." It sounded like he'd been practicing this shpiel, possibly before he'd even lost her.

"Sorry, I haven't seen her."

The model's shoulders drooped, and Clarissa resisted the instinct to touch his shoulder in sympathy. Boys didn't do that. Instead, she said, "I'm sure you'll find her." The moment the words left her mouth she realized it was possible this Mags Bunny on IG was the young woman Abraham had said her sister had murdered.

The boyfriend must have seen the flash of dismay on her face and his own expression went slack. "No. Oh, no, no, you don't think…?"

"I think you should keep looking," she said. "Maybe she fell asleep at the pool and she's waiting for you at breakfast."

He nodded. "Yeah. Yeah, you're probably right. She prolly just didn't wanna stay in the room with me last night 'cause I was sick."

Clarissa forced a smile. She realized she probably could've made things a lot easier for herself if she'd told him to alert security, giving them a missing woman to search for as well as a stowaway. But she couldn't bring herself to make him feel worse, especially knowing she was pretty sure was right.

Mags Bunny was dead, and because of that Abraham wanted to kidnap a man and bleed him for Ava, on the basis that their victim *might* be a sexual predator. Clarissa knew her sister needed to feed, but she wondered how many victims they'd need to hunt for her until this was over. And what if no one took the bait? What then? What if the Mall Monster wasn't even on Little Pearl? What if The Duke was long gone, and they didn't get the opportunity to end his bloodline by piercing his heart?

There were so many What Ifs, she wondered if it was maybe

best for everyone to put Ava out of her misery herself.

No, she thought. *You can't think that way. She's your sister.* She's *the victim here. Not* them.

"I hope you find her!" she called after the boyfriend, who'd already started up the stairs in desperation while she'd stood there thinking. The door slammed above her in reply.

Clarissa continued onward herself. She paused at Gabe's door, considered knocking, then realized he was probably already at work down in the hold. She'd see him soon enough. He'd been hesitant about the plan, and with good reason. If she hadn't been on the run, Clarissa would've been anxious herself posing as bait to lure a pervert. All she'd been able to do was give them a description of the two men she'd seen yesterday, whose faces she remembered from the book the police had shown her after the Mall Monster murdered her parents and kidnapped her sister. For all she knew, she'd gotten them wrong and they were innocent men who merely looked similar to her ten-year-old memory of photos in a book.

That's not right, either. You remember them. You'd know those faces anywhere.

Whether that was true or not, they were about to kidnap one of them and use him as a human blood bag. It felt wrong.

More wrong than what they *did? To kids the same age as Ava? They* deserve *whatever happens to them. Good riddance.*

She'd thought the same when she'd seen them, while she'd been sneaking around the ship. Her first instinct was to break her cover, run up to them and throw accusations of their crimes in their faces. This was before she'd spoken to Abraham, before she'd learned this ship was likely *full* of men who preyed on girls as young as her sister.

Not all of them, though. The guy looking for his girlfriend probably isn't. Gabe and Digby and Abraham aren't. You can't go around assuming everyone's a rapist or you'll drive yourself crazy. You can't live your life assuming everyone's good either, or you'll get yourself killed one day. What's that called? Catch-something. Screwed if you do, screwed if you don't.

With these thoughts swirling in her mind, Clarissa stepped out into the sunshine on the breezeway, prepared to head for the cargo hold stairwell. As she turned to face it, she caught sight of a slim female security guard with box braids standing between her and the door. She was trapped. Her immediate instinct was to turn and run, but she would've had to head for the back of the ship, and it sounded like the festivities were already underway.

"Hey, kid," the guard said. "You see a girl in a dress around your age? Curly hair, no shoes?"

Clarissa shook her head, tilting it slightly downward so the hat brim would throw shade over her face.

"Okay, well if you see someone fitting that description, you come find—"

Before Clarissa could react, a gust of wind struck them both. It riffled the woman's uniform and Gabe's sweatshirt—and tore the hat right off Clarissa's head. Her curls sprung free in a golden spray and the woman's eyes went wide with recognition as Clarissa snatched the hat out of the air.

With ten paces between them, Clarissa turned and bolted.

"Hey!" the guard shouted, deepening her voice as Clarissa had earlier. "Get back here!"

Clarissa ran as fast as she could, the pain in her foot with every step a sharp and powerful motivator. She hit the stair railing over the pool deck and kept moving, not daring to look back, tucking her hair up under the hat as she took the steps. Dancers, swimmers, loungers filled the deck area. It was barely eleven but men and women in bikinis and shorts were already mingling, drinking fruity beverages. Funky jazz beats thumped from speakers on the deck above.

What now?

"Stop!" the guard shouted behind her.

Clarissa looked up, saw the desperate woman leaning over the balcony, and leaped into the moving crowd.

If she'd been wearing a bra, she might have stripped off the shirt and the hat and jumped into the pool. Her hair looked darker when it was wet. She might've been able to pass for one of the women already swimming. Even though there were a handful brave enough to go topless, Clarissa was reserved about even partial nudity, and didn't think it was worth the risk.

She weaved through the dancers and the minglers, hoping she could lose the security guard in the crowd of moving bodies. Glancing back as she hurried around the other side of the pool, she saw the woman hit the crowd and swing her head back and forth, clearly unable to find her. Clarissa kept moving. She was almost at the end of the deck, close to the far stairs.

"Get her!" she heard the woman shout. "In the hat!"

Clarissa glanced back, saw the guard on the other side of the pool, pointing at her. She half-turned and rushed forward, then struck an impenetrable wall that hadn't been in front of her a second earlier.

Looking up as large, powerful hands gripped her by the shoulders, Clarissa reeled at the face of her captor. Abraham's "burly gentleman" from the night before smiled down at her, his face cast in shadow.

She struggled, but the hands kept her firmly in place.

"So nice to see you again, Ms. Coltrane. If you'd kindly come with me, Mr. Jackman would like to meet you."

Without thinking, she kicked his shin as hard as she could. The big man didn't even flinch. She thrust the other knee upward, going for his balls, but he deflected it easily with his thigh. Her knee collided with the hardened muscle and she shuddered with pain.

"It would be much better if you came quietly," he said softly.

She was caught. With no way out, she did the only thing she thought might work in this situation.

"Rape!" she cried, as loud as she could.

Hands encircled her ankles and the two guards jerked her roughly into the air. "Nice try," the female guard said.

"*RAPE!*" she screamed at the top of her lungs.

As the two guards carried her wriggling and kicking through the parting crowd, people began to *laugh*.

"Don't minimize it, dear," an elderly woman called out from her lounger, half hidden behind a tanning reflector. "You'll sully it for the victims!"

But that was exactly what Clarissa worried about. On a ship potentially chock full of predators, what exactly would become of *her* once this Mr. Jackman got her in his clutches?

Would they throw her overboard, like the man last night?

Or worse?

Much worse?

LOST

ABRAHAM AWOKE WITH a start, heart pounding as he raised the sleep mask from his eyes and peered around the dark room blearily. He'd been dreaming of the last time he'd seen Wilhelmina, The Duke whisking her away into the night in his horse-drawn carriage, the lower half of the creature's pale visage spreading wide with a wicked smile while Abraham himself was unable to move, trapped in muck up to his knees. It was a recurring nightmare he hadn't had for quite some time, obviously triggered by his current situation with the young girls.

"Clarissa?"

She didn't answer. Abraham sat up abruptly. She wasn't in the bedroom, but perhaps she was in the toilet and the sound of the white noise machine had smothered her reply. He turned it off and called her name again, louder this time.

No response.

Abraham grabbed his cane which had been leaning against the bedside table, and eased himself over the edge of the bed, his heart palpitating. It was clear the girl had left the room, despite having promised not to do so. She'd left his journal, opened facedown upon the chair beside the dresser.

"Damn!" he muttered. Why would she leave when he'd strictly forbidden her, when she knew very well what these people were capable of, and the danger she'd face beyond these four walls?

She's a teenage girl, he thought. *Same as my poor Wilhelmina had been. May as well ask the wind why it blows, or why the dog must bark.*

Abraham stood and stretched his weary bones with the usual percussion of pops and cracks. He stepped into his slippers and donned his robe, then shuffled into the toilet.

Empty.

He couldn't fathom why she would have left. It was possible she'd gotten hungry, but he'd told her to wake him if she'd needed anything at all. He would have happily awakened for lunch, and gone to the galley to scrounge up some food for her to eat.

He glanced at his watch. It was a quarter of two. After all the activity and excitement of the night before, it wasn't any wonder he'd slept right through lunch. But Clarissa was a smart girl. She wouldn't have risked leaving the room for something as trivial as a snack.

Perhaps she attempted to wake you without luck.

No, it had to be more than that. She was in mortal danger, and not just herself. Her sister, whom she loved dearly enough to agree to assist in kidnapping and bloodletting a stranger tonight, needed her help.

His gaze fell upon the journal. He'd left it out unintentionally and Clarissa had clearly been reading it. Abraham bent to pick it up from the chair and turned it to face him. The pages before him discussed his theories of blood memory within the vampire population, sights and sounds and smells passed down through generations of immortals. He'd once said "knowledge is stronger than memory, and we should not trust the weaker," an adage which Stoker had used verbatim. But for the vampire, the memories his kin handed down were just as strong, if not stronger. It was something Abraham believed he'd experienced firsthand, though what little he'd gleaned from it still had not helped him find his Wilhelmina.

Oh, no. Could it be…?

Like being struck by a thunderbolt, he suddenly understood why and where Clarissa had gone, almost as if they'd shared blood themselves. She'd gone to speak with her sister, whose own blood—if the fiend who'd turned her was indeed related to The Duke—might contain the answers he sought.

Abraham dressed quickly and went on his way. This time, when he reached the door to the cargo hold, he found it locked. "Oh, dear. Dear, dear, dear." He rapped his fist on the door, hoping young Gabe might hear. Even having lived so many years, the wait was agony. After what seemed like forever, he pounded once more on the door.

No one answered his call.

Famished, he shuffled to the galley, hoping there might be some leftovers. The kitchen staff were busy cleaning up from lunch and preparing for supper. The chef greeted him coldly, though he was kind enough to give him a small plate of cold cuts, cheese, a sweet roll and a hard-boiled egg, reminding Abraham of breakfasts he'd had during his time in Austria.

"*Dánke*," Abraham said.

"Just don't make this a habit," the chef replied sternly.

After eating his breakfast and washing it down with a cup of coffee, Abraham decided it was wise to continue with their plan regardless of whether or not Clarissa had been found. Ava still required blood, with or without her sister. They'd agreed to reconvene at Abraham's room around eight, regardless.

He returned to his room to find Clarissa had not returned. He shook his head in despair, certain she'd been found, fearing what might be done to her. Whatever it was, it wouldn't be good.

"My dearest Clarissa," he muttered into the empty room. "I pray you'll soon return to me safely."

A knock came on the door, raising his hopes. His shoulders slumped when he recalled that Clarissa had taken his extra key.

"Who is it?" he called, hoping it wasn't the burly security guard from the night before, come around again to question his relationship to the girl.

Sven had been on his way back downstairs after lunch when he ran into the gentleman who'd lost his girlfriend. He'd seen the man at the pool the day before, taking photos of the missing woman rising from the pool repeatedly.

"Have you spoken to any of the staff?"

"You really think I should? What if she's just, like, mad at me and slept with some other guy? Emory's gonna think I'm a cuck."

"Think you're a what?"

"You know, simping for some thot. A thirst trap," the man said, as if that explained everything.

"You'll excuse me, I don't believe I know those words. But if you mean *cuckold*, might I suggest joining a wonderful online community that has sprung up around the subculture? I wrote an exposé for *Vice* not long ago. I'm sure you'll find them very supportive of your situation."

The man stared at him blankly. "What?"

"The cuckold community. Cucks and bulls. Doms and service subs. Penis shaming and the like."

"I'm not a fucking *cuck*, guy! I'm just looking for my girl."

Sven held out a hand placatingly. "Very well, calm down, my friend. No need to raise your voice. I am merely trying to help in any way I can."

"Look, have you seen my girlfriend or not?" The man turned his cell phone around for Sven to see. He'd opened an Instagram account to an attractive young blonde woman who called herself Mags Bunny. The man clicked the first post with his thumb, bringing up the looped video of her rising from the pool. It had quite a lot of hearts and shares. The first comment was simply the word "PEDO" in all capital letters. It had thousands of likes.

"Why has someone used this word?"

The man turned the phone around and scowled at the screen. "What word?"

"You did not notice this nasty word used to describe your significant other on her public platform?" Sven pointed to it.

The young man scowled. "Oh shit, she didn't *delete that*?"

"It would appear she did not."

"*Oh shit*," the man said again. He looked up and to the right, accessing his memory, perhaps of the night before. "There's *no way* she'd leave that comment up all night...."

"Judging by her profile, I suspect your Mags is an image-conscious woman. I would not imagine being compared to a pedophile would be very good for brand awareness."

"Fuck me," the man said, running his hands through his strategically messy hair.

"Peg," Sven said, eliciting a confused look from the man.

"*Huh?*"

"In the cuckold community," Sven explained, "subservient men are typically pegged, not fucked."

"I told you I'm not a *fucking cuck*!"

"There's no shame in it. Embrace your individuality. I'm sure you'll find sex positivity quite liberating."

"Jesus!" the man said, extricating himself from Sven's company. Sven watched him hurry down the hall, presumably to speak with guest services.

"What a strange fellow," he said with a shake of his head. He continued to the stairs and down to the hall where his room lay. Rather than enter, he chose instead to call upon Mr. Coltrane a few doors down. Late last night he'd witnessed through his peephole a brief altercation with the old man, his granddaughter and the large security guard Emory Jackman had introduced as "Blitz." The guard had left them and they'd entered the room, though it had been clear, even through the peephole, that the guard didn't believe what he'd heard.

Perhaps he believed she is this mysterious stowaway, Sven thought. Whoever she was to Coltrane, after his conversation with Emory, Sven had been meaning to speak again to the old man about his invitation to Little Pearl Island. Specifically, about his relationship to the supposed "old friend" of Emory's father, who allegedly awaited them on the island.

Sven knocked on the door.

After a moment, a small voice said, "Who is it?" from inside.

"Mr. Coltrane? It's Sven Olsen. We met yesterday? I walked you upstairs."

"Yes, of course. I'm, er… quite busy at the moment. Could you come back another time?"

"I promise I won't take up much of your time, Mr. Coltrane. Just a few brief questions and I'll be on my way."

After a pause, the old man said, "Very well."

With some shuffled footsteps, and the rattle of the security bar and lock, the door swung open. The old man peered out blearily from a darkened interior. "How may I help you, Sven?"

"Yes, well, I had an interesting chat with our host, Mr. Jackman, the other day and I was hoping you could fill in some details about a couple of things."

Coltrane glanced back into the dark room. "Would you like to come in?"

"That would be nice, thank you."

Abraham stepped aside to allow Sven entry.

"It's quite dark," Sven said, looking around at the tidy room.

"I'm afraid I was experiencing a migraine." He closed the door, locked and latched it, then flicked on the bedside lamps from one of two switches on the wall. "Have a seat," the old man said, directing Sven to the cuck chair. "Would you care for something to drink?"

"I'm fine, thank you." Sven sat in the chair while the old man shuffled to the bed and sat on its edge. As the old man got himself comfortable, Sven noticed a weathered leatherbound book on the table beside himself.

"Now, what was it you wanted to discuss?"

"Just to clarify something you said the last time we spoke. You told me you believed Mr. Jackman invited you to Little Pearl at the behest of someone you referred to as a 'very old acquaintance.' In point of fact, you used the word *compelled*."

"Did I?"

"Yes, you were quite clear about that."

Coltrane shrugged. "Well, I suppose if that's what you heard, I must have said it."

"Wonderful. Now, I asked Mr. Jackman about this, and it was his contention that your old acquaintance was in fact a friend of his family's."

"I suppose that's possible."

"What was interesting to me was that *at first* he mentioned that you, in fact, were an old friend of his father's."

"His father's?" The old man's brow furrowed. He took his glasses off and began rubbing them on his cardigan. "Well, that is odd indeed."

"Exactly my thought. It was only upon further questioning, using a bit of journalistic deception, that he told me you were a friend of a family acquaintance *instead*. So my question to you is, are you or were you friends with Mr. Jackman's father?

"Not to my knowledge, no."

"But you were invited to Little Pearl by an old acquaintance, correct?"

"Correct."

"Do you mind if I ask who?"

The old man smiled. Rather shrewdly, Sven thought. "My boy, if I were to tell you *who*, you'd think you were listening to the ramblings of a madman."

Sven smiled back. Friendly. Open. "Indulge me."

The old man's smile faded. He grasped the head of his cane in both hands and made himself more comfortable. "Does the name

Duke Ştefan of Moldavia mean anything to you?"

"Not a thing. Should it?"

"Perhaps not. Nonetheless, it is he who I am to meet on this Little Pearl Island."

Sven scowled. "But Moldavia hasn't been an independent country for over one hundred and fifty years. Surely, dukedoms are no longer a formal tradition."

"Indeed not. What brings you to Little Pearl, Sven? You never did tell me."

"I'm writing an article about Emory Jackman, our host."

The old man grinned. "A puff piece, is it?"

Sven grinned back. "I don't write puff pieces, Mr. Coltrane."

"Well, then: I believe I may have a scoop for you. The kind of scoop that only comes along once in a lifetime, you might say." With this, the old man raised his cane and pointed it toward the leatherbound book. Sven glanced at the book, then back to the old man.

"Do you mind if I record this?" he asked.

SURFACING DOUBTS

CLARISSA KEPT STRUGGLING all the way up to the security station, not giving the guards a single moment to relax. She'd given up any inklings of escape the moment she'd realized entire ship was against her. She wasn't supposed to be here, and the fact that she was despite the presence of security proved the ship wasn't quite as secure as they'd hoped. If she could get onboard with no one noticing, anyone could. Thieves, assassins, stalkers. *Anyone.* Still, it didn't mean she had to go without a fight.

The guards tossed her in a chair behind a desk in their small office, zip-tying her wrists and ankles to the arms and legs. Clarissa had seen porn that started like this, with a captive teenager caught shoplifting or vandalizing. Two of her foster sisters were obsessed with internet porn sites, but outside of her initial curiosity Clarissa had never been much interested. She suspected her sisters likely would've made an exception to their beautiful boy love for a giant like Abraham's "burly gentleman."

Granted, the videos were usually just the male security guard doing the capturing and all the rest. Although she supposed the woman could have been holding the camera, she doubted it was what either of them had in store for her.

"You've been a very difficult girl to track down," the giant said, sitting on the edge of the desk set up in front of the security monitors like a disappointed teacher after class. The plastic badge hanging from his left pocket, now that she was close enough to read it, said BLITZEN WAGNER. "Sticking to the shadows, somehow managing to avoid our cameras."

"She's slippery," the woman said. She leaned against the far wall. Her badge said JOURNEE TERRELL.

"Blitzen and Journee," Clarissa said, putting on a brave act.

The zip ties were too tight for her to move. "Sounds like an R&B group from the '70s."

"Funny," Journee said, turning to her partner. "She's a funny kid, Blitz."

Blitz gave Clarissa a hard look, widening his shoulders with a deep inhale through his nostrils. "Why are you on the *Ceres*?"

She shrugged. "Thought I'd get a tan."

Blitz and Journee shared an annoyed look. "What's your name? How 'bout we start with that?"

She saw no reason not to tell them that. "Clarissa."

Journey raised a microbladed eyebrow. "Got a last name?"

"Nunya."

"As in nunya business. We've heard that one before."

"Let's try this again," Blitz said. "Just tell us why you're here. Was it on a dare? Are you a fan of one of our guests? A jilted lover, maybe?"

"Yeah," Clarissa said with a sputter. "You guys know DJ Safe-T?"

The two guards looked at each other and shrugged.

"I'm his hype man." She made an irritating air horn sound: "*Pwa pwa pwaaaaaa! Ladies and gentlemen, put your hands together for the one, the only—*"

Blitz stood up, towering over her. She shut up immediately.

"All right. We're only trying to help you, Clarissa. If you don't want to talk to us, maybe you'll be more comfortable speaking with Mr. Jackman. Or his wife."

The way he said this seemed like a threat. "Who the fuck is Mr. Jackman?" she asked.

Again, the two guards shared a look. Journee stepped away from the wall to meet her partner, not quite towering over Clarissa, but crossing her arms over her chest in a posture of annoyance.

"You honestly don't know whose ship this is?"

"I don't. And honestly, I don't give a flying fuck."

Blitz twisted his head back and forth, his neck cracking. Clarissa expected a backhanded slap but the man was interrupted by a knock on the door.

Blitz and Journee looked at each other. Then Journee went to answer the door. Blitz placed his hands on his hips with a stern look—it seemed to be the only face he was capable of making—

and exhaled sharply through his nostrils like a bull about to charge.

"How can I help you, sir?"

"Yeah, hi, uh... this is gonna sound weird since we're all trapped here on a floating tin can, but, um... my girlfriend is missing."

Blitz's eyebrows rose in surprise. He glanced back over his shoulder, arms falling to his sides. Clarissa recognized the voice right away as the boyfriend she'd spoken to in the stairwell.

"Okay, and what's your girlfriend's name?"

"Your girlfriend's dead," Clarissa shouted past the boulder of a man before her.

"Wuh-what? Why would you say that?"

"Ask him to play the footage from last night after midnight."

Blitz scowled. The boyfriend's gaze shot toward him. "I need to see that footage."

"Sir, if there was a death on this ship, we would know about it. I'm sure your girlfriend will show up."

"So you *won't* show me?" The boyfriend took out his phone from the back pocket of his skinny jeans. "Hang on, let me get that on camera."

"Sir, please put down the phone," Journee said.

The tendons in Blitz's neck pulled taut. "Unfortunately, we can't allow you to see security camera footage without express permission of Mr. Jackman."

"*What?* If my girlfriend's... if she's *unalive*, I want to know." He pointed at the screens. "I should be allowed to see that footage!"

"No one is dead, sir," Journee said. "Now if you'd like to file a missing persons report I can happily assist you with that."

"*How can someone go missing on a boat? Huh?*" The desperate boyfriend's gaze shot back and forth between the two guards. "I've looked *everywhere!* What if..." His blue eyes popped with a sudden revelation. "What if she fell overboard? What if she's right," he said, pointing to Clarissa, "what if she is dead? We have to stop the boat! We have to turn around!"

"We can't just stop the boat, sir," Journee said, sounding bored.

"Well, we can't keep going! What if she's... what if she's *stranded* out there in the middle of nowhere all by herself?"

"Sir? Sir, look at me, please," Blitz said calmly. "What's your name?"

"T-Taylor."

"And your girlfriend?"

"Mags Bunny. I mean Mags O'Keefe."

"Okay. Taylor, I promise you, if you fill out one of these forms we will do everything in our power to find Mags. I'll comb through hours of footage on every single one of these cameras personally. But you have to go through the proper channels."

The boyfriend nodded.

"Good. Now, take the form, go back to your room and fill it out, then come back and we can discuss solutions. Maybe have something to eat first. A cup of coffee. I bet you're running on fumes right now, aren't you?"

"Uh-huh. Yeah."

"Okay. Will you do that for me then, Taylor?"

"Sure. Uh-huh."

Clarissa watched the man dejectedly shuffle away. Then both Blitz and Journee returned to where she sat, strapped to the chair.

"Why did you say that woman was dead?" Blitz asked her.

"She is, isn't she?"

Journee gave her partner a distressed look, as if she thought he might know a little more about what was going on than she did herself.

Blitz pointed at Clarissa sternly. He exhaled through his nostrils again, then lowered his hand, turning to his partner. "We need to take her to Jackman," he said.

"Why?" Journee asked, clearly dubious.

"Firstly, unless you're eager to throw a teenage girl in the brig with our resident alcoholic pervert, we don't have anywhere to keep her. We don't get to Little Pearl until tomorrow morning and it's not like we can keep her zip tied to that chair all day and night."

Journee considered this silently. "Isn't there a room free on the double-lux deck?"

"You think Mr. Jackman would allow that? Besides, Mrs. Jackman arrived early this morning by helicopter. She'll be in safe hands with the two of them."

"I don't like that woman." Journee's whole body shook as if she'd gotten the shivers. "She gives me the creeps."

Blitz gave her a stern look. "I don't want to hear any of that talk, you hear me? That might fly under Wilson's command, but not mine."

Journee rolled her eyes. "Yes, sir." She looked at Clarissa strangely. At the sound of Wilson's name, Clarissa had begun to laugh.

"What's so funny?" Blitz snapped.

"Oh, nothing. Just that I'm the reason you got promoted."

"What's that supposed to mean?" Journee asked, her thin eyebrows stitching together as her suspicion deepened.

"I watched Mr. Jackman make your former boss walk the plank last night," Clarissa said.

The woman reacted with shock, then made a visible attempt to hide it. "What do you mean, 'walk the plank'?"

"She's lying," Blitz said.

Clarissa ignored him, concentrating on sowing discord between the two. "He told him to jump overboard."

"And he did it? Just like that?"

"He said if Wilson didn't jump he'd tell your 'benefactor.' I don't know who that is, but Wilson just kicked off his boots and jumped. Whoever he is must've scared Wilson pretty bad, I guess." Clarissa shrugged indifferently, though the memory of the man just leaping off the deck to his likely death still made her shudder. "I'd rather take my chances with some rich asshole than a sea full of hungry sharks."

Journee turned to Blitz. "Is that true?"

"How would I know?"

"Well, let's check the tape."

"We're not checking the tape. She's stalling us. She knows she's in trouble and she's playing us against each other. Same with the alleged dead girlfriend. It's smoke and mirrors. If Wilson went anywhere, it was on the helicopter last night."

Journee raised a single eyebrow. "If it's 'smoke and mirrors,' you won't mind me checking the tapes, will you?"

Blitz exhaled sharply through his nostrils again. Clarissa was surprised not to see steam. "Fine. You want to check the recordings, go right ahead. I'm taking the girl upstairs."

Journee looked at the computer on the desk, then back to Clarissa. "Okay, but this doesn't end here. Soon as we get her upstairs, I'm coming back down here. I'm gonna check into that dead girlfriend thing, too."

"You do that," Blitz said. Then he crouched down, flicked open a folding knife and cut the zip ties one by one.

With her arms and legs free, she rolled and twisted her joints, loosening the numbness in her constricted limbs. 'While we're up there," she said, "why don't you ask him about the girls in crates down in the cargo hold?"

Journee gave her new boss a look of dismay. "What's she going on about now?"

"You really don't know what's happening on this ship, do you? I figured maybe you were okay turning a blind eye for the right amount of money, but that's even more impressive. A secret so well kept, even his own security team doesn't know."

"What's she saying, Blitz?"

Blitz wouldn't look at her. "It's bullshit. Bunch of right-wing conspiracy nonsense."

"Blitz, if there's something going on here—"

"*There's nothing going on!*" he bellowed. It was the first time Clarissa had seen him lose his cool, and his voice was as loud as the roar of a lion in the small room. Even Journee shied away from it.

"Okay, jeez," Journee said, still cringing. "You don't have to get mad, I'm just asking questions is all."

"You wanna ask questions, fine. But if it goes any further than the two of us, if I hear peep about girls in boxes—"

"Crates," she said.

"—or dead girlfriends, or Wilson walking the fucking plank, you'll be packing your bags and heading back home with the helicopter, understand?"

"*Okay*, I—"

"*Do you understand me?*" Spittle flew from his lips and struck her on the cheek, causing her to rear back even further.

"Yes," she said, anxious as a scolded child.

Blitz studied her face for a long moment. Then he puffed out another breath through his nostrils and allowed his chest to deflate. "Good," he said finally, and turned back to Clarissa.

Journee quickly wiped his spit off her face with the back of a hand and gave her a sympathetic look.

Clarissa looked up as Blitz sneered down at her. "All right, get up. We're going to see the big man upstairs."

She stood reluctantly. Journee zip tied her arms behind her back and the two guards led her out of the security station, toward her fate, whatever it might be. She'd played her last card, swung for the fences and missed. It was up to Abraham and Gabe to save Ava now, and any other girl who might be down there in the hold.

TRUE VAMPIRES

THEY BROUGHT CLARISSA to Emory Jackman's room, and sat her down roughly in one of the most comfortable chairs she'd ever sat in. "I'll be out in a moment," came a relaxed male voice from the darkened inner room across from her. A raspy breath accompanied it, followed by a dry, rattling cough. Someone was in the bedroom with him. His wife, Clarissa suspected. Before she'd set foot on this boat, she might've been concerned about catching a cold or the flu. She'd seen so much worse in the past thirty or forty hours, getting the sniffles seemed like nothing at all.

After a moment, a silver-haired man with a gleaming smile stepped out of the darkened room. He closed the door gently, and returned his attention to Clarissa. "My apologies. My wife is a tad… under the weather." He turned to the guards, who'd stepped to the side of the chair and stood awaiting orders. "Cut her free, would you? This is a cordial visit."

Blitz bent, flicked open his knife, and cut the zip tie. Clarissa couldn't help but wish the knife would nick a vein and put her out of her misery, dripping blood all over Jackman's Persian rug.

"Leave us," Jackman said.

"Yes, sir," the guards said in unison. Journee gave her a brief look of sympathy, and the two of them left the room. Jackman followed to the door, locking and bolting it shut behind them. "Now," he said, turning back to her. "What brings you to my ship, little girl?"

Clarissa clenched her jaw and said nothing.

"Don't wanna talk, huh? That's fine. Would you care for something to drink? A root beer? Apple juice?" He grinned, showing perfectly straight, pearly-white teeth. "Something with a little more kick?"

She was as thirsty as she'd ever been but she wouldn't give him the satisfaction of relenting. She blinked and said nothing.

"I'm going to have a scotch," he said, heading for the bar. "I always think better after a drink or two. Never *more* than two, mind you. That's a recipe for getting sloppy." He pulled the top off a crystal decanter and poured some into a lowball glass. "Do you always wear boy's clothes? I was told you were wearing a dress. Barefoot. Not pregnant, though. It's a good disguise. You tried your best, Clarissa, I'll give you that. You might've made it all the way to my island, and then we might *never* have found you. *If* you hadn't gotten cocky."

He sauntered over, sipping his drink. "Cocky. That's an interesting word, don't you think? When you think of someone who's cocky, you usually picture a man, don't you? Cunty, you think of a woman. But women can be cocky, and men can be cunts. Cocks and cunts, they make the world go round, God love em." He grinned, cocking his head slightly, and sipped his scotch, watching her over the rim of the glass.

"You know the term 'cocky' used to mean 'lecherous'? A pervert, in other words. Women can be lecherous, of course, but again, it's a term most often directed toward men. *Lecherous old man.* You hear that one a lot. Not often do you hear lecherous *young* man, although certainly there are a great deal of those out there in the world, aren't there? I bet you've experienced your fair share of that, and you're all of—what? Sixteen? Seventeen years old?"

He paused a moment, waiting for her to answer, though it seemed like he knew she wouldn't. "It's fine if you don't want to talk. As my wife is fond of saying, I'll talk until the cows crow. You see, that's my job. Talking. My father, rest his soul, he used to say I could talk an Eskimo into buying an icebox. Of course, you're not supposed to call them Eskimos anymore, are you? I think it's Inuit now. You know where this all started, don't you? When they said Pluto wasn't a planet anymore." He huffed out a single laugh. "After that, they wanted to change everything. Blackboards were chalkboards, up is down, left is right. Until you don't know your ass from a teakettle. That's another thing my wife says. She's fond of her malapropisms. I suspect it's because English is her… fourth language?" He nodded and sat in an identical chair across from Clarissa, placing his glass on a coaster. "Fourth, right. But that's something they don't tell you when you get married. Those little things you thought were cute, eventually they start to grate on you. Love gets old," he said wistfully, "just like people. Love dies. Just like people."

Jackman smiled and held her gaze. Clarissa found herself suddenly mesmerized by his eyes. Were they blue or gray, or somewhere in between? Whatever she'd expected, this man wasn't it. She'd pictured a hairy, sweaty pervert. A lecherous old man. What she got was a bland, banal middle-aged man in love with the sound of his own voice. He looked to be in decent shape despite the paunch, and his hairline had receded likely as far as it would until he was much older. He wore a lime green Polo shirt, pleated khakis and hiking sandals. His bare toes were neatly trimmed, with dark hair on the big toes almost as thick as eyebrows, which she found slightly repulsive.

The more she looked at him, the more she realized he wasn't the monster she'd thought. He was just a man trying to get by in a world full of sharks. Not prey but not a predator. He talked because he couldn't fight. His smile was trustworthy, neither cynical nor full of spite. His eyes were kind and gracious, not unforgiving and cruel.

What's happening? she thought suddenly, and tore her gaze away from him, looking instead at the closed door where his sick wife slept.

The longer she looked away from him, the more she realized he'd somehow been playing a trick on her. Had he *hypnotized* her somehow? This man *was* a monster. He'd made his head of security walk the plank barely twelve hours ago. He had crates filled with little girls on his boat, planning to turn them into sex slaves unaware they were vampires, shipping them to an island full of pedophiles and perverts.

He was the *real* vampire here. Not Ava and the others.

"Look at me, Clarissa."

She wouldn't look. She *couldn't* look. Not if she wanted to leave this room ever again. Not if she wanted to stay awake and alive. She tried to stand but her legs wouldn't allow her to move.

"*Look at me.*"

Clarissa looked up entirely against her will, her gaze zeroing in on his eyes, which were gray as the planet Mercury.

"'As flies to wanton boys are we to the gods,'" he said, quoting *King Lear*, a passage her English teacher had made her read aloud in class this year. "'They kill us for their sport.'" He smiled again. Innocently. Soothing. "My wife needs blood to keep her young, Clarissa."

"Wuh-what?" she said, her confusion and the muddy feeling in her mind causing her to finally break her silence. What did he mean, she *needs blood*? Was Mrs. Jackman a vampire?

"So I'm going to count to ten," he continued, without further explanation. "When I reach ten, you'll fall into a deep sleep from which you will never awake. I'm sorry, but it has to be this way. One…"

Don't listen to him, she thought, desperate to cling on to what little self-control she had remaining.

"Two…"

Look away…

"Three…"

You have to look away before it's too late!

"Four…"

The gray in his eyes began to swim and swirl. She felt herself drawn into them, not her body but her spirit, floating toward them like a shuttle through space, pulled into their atmosphere.

"Five…"

Abraham, Gabe, please HELP ME—

"Six-*ix-ix-ix…*"

His voice echoed in her mind as her vision shrank to pinpricks.

She wouldn't hear him count seven.

Sven pressed Stop and set down the tape recorder. "That's quite a tale, Mr. Coltrane," he said, refusing to use the name the man had claimed for himself. It was all so bizarre, yet so much of it lined up with what he knew about Emory Jackman's cruise and Little Pearl Island that it wasn't possible all of it was fiction.

"You don't believe," Coltrane said.

"My apologies." He gave the old man a sympathetic smile. "I am Swedish, and I am an investigative journalist. I grew up atheist, as did my mother and father. What is the expression? 'I don't have superstitious bone in my body'?"

"You require proof," the old man said. "Very well." He stood with the aid of his cane, grunting slightly. "What would prove it to you? A mind trick? A blood sacrifice?"

Sven smiled. "Surely you're pulling my leg?"

The old man sighed. Without another word, he pressed the withered forefinger of his right hand upon his left wrist. It was only then that Sven noticed how yellow and long his fingernails were, ridged like a tin roof. He drew the nail sharply upward, and the flesh parted cleanly. Sven sat up in shock as blood spilled from the fresh wound, pattering on the carpet.

"*Akta!*" he called out in his native tongue.

The old man smiled, blood dribbling from his wrist. Rather than shoot out in a geyser, the gore actually seemed to be slowing. Sven watched it happen in bewilderment bordering on terror. A moment later the wound sealed itself entirely, and he looked up at the old man in horrified wonder. If not for the dark, wet stain on the carpet, he might have assumed what he'd seen was an illusion, a trick of the mind. Even that would have been impressive enough. This was something *profound*, an earth-shattering occurrence. The old man had just *healed himself.* Sven had always been a skeptic, had always been taught to question everything. After seeing this, he would never be able to look at anything the same as he had before. He'd need to reevaluate everything he'd believed up until this very moment.

Vampires are real.

"How…?" was all he could manage to say.

The old man patted the wound dry with a handkerchief—monogrammed with the initials VH, not VB, as Sven had thought earlier.

Vampires are real, and I am in the presence of their greatest nemesis, a man who is more than one-hundred and fifty years old and whose flesh can heal itself.

"I must admit, Abraham," he said, using the man's given name finally, "I find myself at a loss for words."

"Understandably. I would feel the same, were I in your shoes."

Sven pressed Record on the tape recorder, swallowed hard, and spoke: "I have moral issues with vampirism, of course, not just as a fellow human being, but also as an ethical consumer. I believe so-called 'lesser animals' have as much a right to life as we ourselves. Therefore, I believe it a crime not solely against humanity to consume the blood of another human, but a crime against *nature itself*."

"I believe you and I are in full agreement there, Mr. Olsen."

Sven nodded absently, his mind already ahead of his mouth. "However, if a vampire *must* consume human blood in order to survive, we are presented with a moral dilemma… one that is not so easily solvable."

"Is that so?"

"Yes. You see, if their survival is determined by a lack or abundance of human victims, they are as animals in the wild. No one can damn the fox which sneaks into the chicken coop to eat, nor the mosquito for feeding on us at night. It is their very nature. On the other hand, it is morally abhorrent for a human to murder another human. This has been known for millennia, although there are a handful of extenuating circumstances in which it is deemed permittable. War, for instance. Or capital punishment—though naturally I believe that to be a crime, as well. In Sweden, we have not killed a man for his crimes, nor a woman, in over one hundred years."

Abraham made to interject, but Sven held up a hand to stop him. "Please, Mr. Van Helsing. If you interrupt my train of thought I shall never reach my point."

"My apologies," the old man said, thoroughly chastened.

"I'm sure you will agree there are crimes which are so heinous as to make a psychopath blush. Among them, I believe, is indulging in pedophilia. Pedophilia itself is not a crime. It is a curse I'm certain which no man, nor woman, would wish upon his own worst enemy. More than a mere fetish, Mr. Van Helsing, it is a *compulsion*. Perhaps as strong as a vampire's need to for blood, though one could argue a pedophile can survive quite fine without ever indulging in such obsessive fantasies. The father or sister or monk pledges his or her life to their god and lives a humble, meaningful life without the need for sexual intercourse, though I admit that is perhaps not the best example, given our current predicament. An asexual, let's say, may perhaps *fantasize* about sex but simply does not *desire* it. Likewise, many people suffering from pedophilia may have healthy sexual, *adult* relationships, at least on the surface. Some even have children and never attempt to harm them. It is an *attraction*, not an *action*."

"You seem to know quite a bit about this, Mr. Olsen."

"I wrote an exposé on a community of what they now call 'minor-attracted persons' for *Psychology Monthly*. It was quite illuminating. Did you know, according to psychologists, there are sexual predators *without* pedophilic tendencies who abuse children?"

"I didn't."

"Yes. Quite like how rape is not at all times about sex, despite it being an inherently sexual act. Often it is an act of aggression or dominance. A power play, if you will. Other times it occurs because the perpetrator cannot find a partner their own age. And yet, they are not *technically* pedophiles, even though they have indulged in pedophilic activities. Likewise, a teacher who engages in sexual intercourse with her teenage student is not a pedophile, not technically. He or she is an *ephebophile*, that being a person with an obsessive sexual interest in children in their mid- to late-adolescent development."

Abraham raised a hand. "May I ask where you're going with this?"

"Yes, I was just about reaching my point. I am sorry. We can agree, I'm sure, that the child predator is one of the most heinous individuals in society, and that the child trafficker is as much to blame as a drug dealer is to an addict. Metaphorically speaking, they are themselves the *true* vampires, Mr. Van Helsing. They suck young blood. They leave their victims hollow."

"On that, you and I agree."

"You believe the girls I've been told are being used as sexual slaves on Little Pearl Island, some as young as seven and eight years old, are themselves vampires, is that correct?"

Abraham seemed pleased to return to the subject. "*Nascent* vampires, yes. However, if they were to discover what they truly are… which is almost certain now that one of their number has become self-aware… it could be catastrophic for us all."

Sven considered this. "But also, for their captors, correct?"

"I suppose so, yes."

"I see. And you say there's no garlic on the ship? No holy man to bless the water? I believe I now understand the insistence on prohibiting outside food or drink."

"Correct. I've asked around. Many cruises employ a Catholic priest, however most merely have a crew member performing nondenominational services in the conference room or lounge. Mr. Jackman's ship is, conspicuously, lacking any crewman capable of performing such duties."

"This… this is not good."

"No," the old man agreed. "It most assuredly is not."

"What shall we do? How do we prepare ourselves?"

The old man gave him a cheerless smile. "We arm ourselves with wooden stakes. We befriend the crew in charge of the lifeboats. And we pray to whichever deity we believe in that our lives will be spared, and that the need for vengeance makes the blood of the wicked much sweeter than our own."

"In other words, let both brands of vampire duke it out themselves," Sven said, beginning to understand, "and pray to a deity I do not believe in that we do not find ourselves on the menu."

To this, Abraham chuckled. "I couldn't have put it better myself, Sven."

EMORY RAISED THE girl's arm. She was unconscious and extremely pliable, splayed out on the many pillows on his massive bed. He lifted her head and wiped the drool from the corner of her lips. She was an extraordinary creature. A thing of rare beauty, undoubtedly. He marveled at his luck while he undressed her, tugging the sweatshirt from some high school up over her head, revealing her perky little tits with nipples nearly an inch long and pointed toward the ceiling. He unbuttoned and unzipped the slightly baggy men's pants and boxer shorts. She was hairy beneath, on the lips as well as the mons pubis. He considered she was probably a virgin. If she was still conscious, he might have been able to draw that information out of her mind. Out cold as she was, he got nothing but a light hum from her, like white noise. He left the tube socks on, as it reminded him of porn from the '90s.

"I am going to enjoy this," he said.

He held both knees in place with one arm pressed against them, her calves slightly prickly from their last shave, unzipped his fly and pulled down his pants with his free hand. His cock sprung free, neatly trimmed and uncircumcised. He spat in his palm and worked it around the head and down the shaft. It throbbed pleasantly, already greased with precum mixed into a white froth with his spit, jouncing up and down like a dowsing rod having discovered water, making him dizzy.

He knew if he didn't put it in her soon, he'd shoot his load on her stomach. A waste of good seed, worse than a ruined orgasm. He wanted to believe some of his sperm would reach those young, fertile eggs of hers, that when she officially became one of The Duke's children she'd already be impregnated by his own seed. It was his dream to have children born of royal blood. Not just like himself, a half-breed, made this way by sheer determination and chutzpah. What he wanted more than anything was an immortal heir beholden to his *true father* more than The Duke. Someone to carry on his name and legacy for time immemorial. He wanted the eternal. He wanted *infinity*.

He wanted little Emory Jackman II.

The girl moaned under his weight. He was gentle on top of her but not inside of her. He thrust quickly and eagerly, shooting his meager load into her, crying out with every spurt, until he was spent. Then he sprawled over her, allowing her legs to fall to his sides.

In the silence following his orgasm, Emory raised his head, listening. Much like The Duke, only the scent of blood would wake Erzsébet. She wasn't like the creature in his lair on the island. She didn't *consume* blood, merely absorbed it through her skin through a ritual known only to a handful of people throughout the ages. But after more than four-hundred years spent bathing in the blood of the innocent and youthful, she'd become keenly attuned to its scent. The merest drop of it would alarm her.

Emory raised himself up on his hands and peered down. A smear of blood ringed his cock, like lipstick on a cigarette. The girl was a virgin. He *knew* he should've been gentler with her, but he hadn't been able to help himself.

The cold, sharp edge of a blade pressed against his throat. The blade inched closer to his jaw, Erzsébet's elbow pressed against his chest. He knew better than to fight against her. "*What have you done?*" came an ancient hiss in his ear.

"Erzsébet, please…"

"Erzsébet *nothing*!"

As she released the pressure of the blade against his throat, she nicked his Adam's apple. He pressed his fingers to the wound with a hiss of pain.

"You have *betrayed* me, my love."

Emory pulled himself out of the girl and rolled over, sitting half-naked on the leather sofa. Erzsébet stood above him. His dick shriveled at the betrayal in her cataract eyes. "We'll get rid of her. Once the ritual is over, we'll throw her overboard. Leave her to the sharks. No one has to know—"

"You *know* that is not possible," the ancient woman said. "The Duke will not have it."

"Fuck The Duke!" he blurted out. "There, I said it."

"Bring her to the bath."

"It's not night yet."

"*YOU WILL DO AS I ASK!*"

Emory startled. He'd never heard her use such a powerful voice when she was waning before. It made him wonder if she needed the blood to rejuvenate her at all anymore, or if it was merely habit. The withered body standing before him in her lacy white nightgown betrayed her. She stumbled, and grasped the arm of the sofa to hold herself upright.

Emory peeled himself off the couch and raced to her side. He held her up by the elbows, his limp, blood-streaked dick flopping pathetically. "Erzsébet, my love. I'm so sorry. We'll make this work."

She held him in her milky gaze. "Bring her to me. We must begin as soon as possible. Before your rotten seed sullies her innocence."

Emory winced at the insult but said nothing. He took the straight razor from her hand, folded it and laid it on a side table. Then he ushered her to the bathroom, removed her nightgown and helped her into the clawfoot tub. Her flesh was gray and withered, barely covering her frail bones. While she waited, glaring up at him, he left through the bedroom and stood for a moment in the sitting room, gathering his thoughts. Suddenly enraged, he pounded his thigh with a fist until it was numb. Then he crossed the room toward the girl, who was still unconscious, her blood and his semen oozing from her vagina.

He hoisted her up over his shoulder. She was light, though not quite as light as his wife, nor as light as she'd be after the ritual was complete, lacking blood. He carried her to the bath, where Erzsébet lay waiting.

"Turn her," the hag demanded.

Emory sat the girl on the toilet and turned her to face his spouse.

"She *is* quite an exquisite creature, isn't she?"

He forced a smile. "Not half as exquisite as you, my love."

"Save your lies. I know how I look."

You don't look a day over five-hundred, he thought but didn't say. Instead, he kissed her tenderly on the forehead, as dry as the carapace of an insect. "You always look perfect to me," he said.

To this the corners of her nearly lipless mouth curled up in what appeared to be a genuine smile. "Thank you, my love. Draw my bath now, please."

Emory started the water running, then returned to the bedroom for the length of rope to tie the girl, cursing himself inwardly for having transgressed their one explicit rule. He knew Erzsébet wouldn't sell him out to The Duke—doing so would get both of them killed—but he couldn't be sure she wouldn't retaliate. Now he'd need to be on guard at all times. Who knew what a raging psychopath like Erzsébet might do to him, after everything she'd taught him, after all the carnal carnage he'd enjoyed at her side?

He tied the girl's legs at the ankles and slung the rope over the sturdy shower curtain rod, then began to hoist her up, pulling the rope hand over hand. The girl fell off the toilet, moaning again as she thumped her head on the floor tiles.

"Gently," Erzsébet said.

Emory raised the girl more cautiously this time, her legs rising off the floor, then her bare ass, then her hair and arms falling as he hoisted her into the air. When she hung above the tub, Emory tied off the rope on the safety bar he'd installed beside the toilet for Erzsébet's waning periods. He returned to her side, gently smoothed her hair, dry and brittle as autumn leaves, and produced the straight razor he kept in the cabinet.

"May you live forever, my love," he said.

"With you by my side, dear one," the old woman said, as she always had.

With that, he drew the blade quickly and cleanly across the girl's throat, from jugular to jugular. Her pretty blue eyes opened wide and she sucked in a terrified gasp as twin geysers of blood poured out of her, spattering the insides of the porcelain tub and showering Erzsébet from head to toe. Her mouth opened as if to speak but nothing escaped her lips. Instead she began to struggle, weakly, pathetically, reaching for him with scrabbling hands as she swung back and forth from the rope until all of the strength left her body and the life left her eyes.

Then, as he always did, Emory stepped out of the room, leaving Erzsébet Báthory to her secrets.

Clarissa awoke in a moment of blinding pain to the most horrible nightmare imaginable.

She remembered very little of what had happened before she'd fallen asleep, only that she'd been brought to the room of the man they'd called Emory Jackman by the burly security guard and his dubious partner. He'd sat her down in a chair and asked the guards to cut the zip tie circling her wrists. After that was a black hole, as if she'd been drugged.

The first thing she saw upon waking was Jackman's shit-eating grin, except for some reason she was seeing him upside down. He was smiling and his face was spattered with red. The same-colored fluid washed down over her eyes, into her mouth and nostrils, choking her. She was hanging from her feet, swinging over a bathtub filling with red paint.

That's my blood, she thought in horrified awe.

She tried calling for help but the pain in her throat was so agonizing all she could do was utter a single weak, pathetic gasp.

He's killing me.

Clarissa reached out to her murderer, numb fingers fumbling weakly at the air. Blood poured into her eyes, temporarily blinding her. She blinked it away. Her strength dissipated, and her arms fell to her sides.

Finally, her killer turned and left the room.

Clarissa swung lazily from the rope. Blood dripped down her face and into her hair. She followed its descent with her eyes, which fell upon the creature in the tub. Her first thought was that it was long dead—an Egyptian mummy without its wrappings—but as the rope fell still, she realized the desiccated creature beneath her was whispering words Clarissa couldn't understand. It was a woman, that much was clear, with skin so wizened it looked like the leather of an ancient book, draped over frail bones, breasts shriveled against her ribcage like rotted fruit, and long, gray hair as dry as coconut husks. Clarissa's blood poured over her and strangely, as she watched, as the mummy whispered what seemed to be a single repeated phrase, the ancient woman's skin seemed to soak up the blood like a sponge. Her cataracts began to clear, becoming amber like a cat's. Her breasts and arms plumped, her sallow cheeks became full, her dry, brittle skin growing milky white beneath the curtain of blood. The ancient woman seemed to be growing younger by the moment, revitalized by blood, and whether this was really happening or a hallucination brought upon by Clarissa's nearness to death no longer mattered. She had no more blood to give.

As the lips of the woman below her cracked in a smile, white teeth pinked by her victim's blood, the world swam away from Clarissa.

"Thank you for your sacrifice," the woman said in a husky, healthy voice.

Her words followed Clarissa, echoing as she tumbled down into the abyss.

PART 3

HUNTERS

THE MENU

GABE LOOKED HIMSELF over in Cheery's full-length mirror, the embarrassment flushing his cheeks making it look like he was wearing rouge, though Cheery had only applied a little eye makeup and cherry-flavored pink lip gloss on him. "I can't do this," he said finally.

"Ain't no 'can't' in drag," Cheery said with his gap-toothed smile, sitting beside Digby on the edge of his bed. He raised his eyepatch and regarded Gabe with both eyes—the patch was for "esthetics," he'd earlier assured him. "You look *dusted*, girl!" He let the patch fall back over his perfectly healthy eye and snapped twice, throwing his hand back each time. The gesture might have worked in his drag persona but clashed with his pirate look.

Digby agreed with a nod. "Not bad, Little Buddy."

"Thanks," Gabe said glumly. He wore Clarissa's dress and a pair of sheer beige pantyhose. Cheery had slipped a pair of what he'd called "chicken cutlets" into a bra whose straps he'd pinned to fit Gabe, which had given him a little cleavage. The outfit was snug but actually looked kind of okay.

His concern at the moment was less about the outfit, and more that Abe hadn't seen Clarissa since shortly after they'd split up that morning. Which meant either she'd had to go deeper into hiding, which he *hoped*—or she'd been caught, which both he and Abe feared. The problem was he couldn't tell either Digby or Cheery that, otherwise he'd have to tell them Clarissa was the stowaway staff had all heard about, and fill them in on all they'd been through since the *Ceres* left port yesterday.

"We *must* move forward with our plan, whether Clarissa returns to us or not," Abe had insisted when Gabe met him after his shift. "If the young vampire feels she has been duped, she will surely break free of her bonds and hunt a victim of her own."

"You think she's strong enough to bust out of her crate?"

"If she'd succeeded in draining an adult, of that I have no doubt. But she'll need more blood, and soon. A teething vampire requires regular sustenance. We must lure one of these perverts into our web. You are the key to that. I will do the rest."

"You mean…?"

Gabe had swallowed hard, and Abe gave him a grim look. "Yes," the old man had said. "That is exactly what I mean."

Standing before Cheery's mirror, Gabe thought back to how he'd convinced Digby and Cheery to help get him ready for tonight by telling them he wanted to do drag for the crew talent show on the island. Digby had immediately asked him to do a duet—he'd been wanting to do "Islands in the Stream" for a while but couldn't find a willing partner, and Cheery assured them he sang "like a cat getting its tail stepped on." Gabe had promised he would, though he still had no intention of leaving the boat. The two older men had no idea what he and the others had planned, and he aimed to keep it that way.

"What do I do about this?" he asked, indicating the bulge below his waist to Cheery now.

"Tuck tape."

Digby winced. "That sounds painful."

"Takes a little gettin used to, but it ain't that bad." He held Gabe in a serious gaze. "Then you got a choice to tuck your sack in your crack, or push your jolly ranchers up into your belly like you just rode the big drop at the funfair, and just tuck the joystick."

Digby draped an arm around his new beau. "You sure got a way with words, Puddin."

"It's a gift." Cheery stood and sashayed surprisingly girlishly toward his chest of drawers. He opened one and removed what looked like a cake box. "Now, for the *pièce de résistance*." He set it on top of the dresser and opened it, pulling out what at first looked like a small furry dog. When he turned, Gabe saw it was a long auburn wig with curls. "Tada!" he said. "Boys, allow me to introduce: Mariah Marmalade!" He pronounced the surname "Marmalawd," like the old Christina Aguilera song.

"Aw, come on, guys," Gabe moaned. "I put on the dress, and the pantyhose, and the bra—"

"And the chicken cutlets," Digby added, unhelpfully.

"—but nobody said nothin bout a wig."

Cheery pouted. "You don't *have* to wear the wig. You're fabulous already, henny! But if you wanna complete the look, if you really wanna *slay*, these curls are the topper on the cake."

Gabe turned to Digby for backup. His partner betrayed him with a shrug. "Fine," Gabe sighed, holding out a hand.

"*Yassss*," Cheery said, and draped the wig over Gabe's head. He positioned it properly, letting the auburn waves fall over Gabe's shoulders, which he then grabbed, turning Gabe to face the mirror with a mock gasp. "*Quell surprise*. Looks like the fish outside have some fierce competition. Our li'l drag sister's a looker, ain't she, Dig?"

Digby nodded. "I'd hit that."

Gabe looked himself over. If he squinted and turned to the side, he too might have "hit that."

Cheery clucked his tongue. "Don't fall in love with yourself now, Narcissus."

"He won't," Digby said. "He's got a new girlfriend."

Gabe's blushing deepened. "She's just a friend."

"Who? That li'l stowaway girl? Does Gabriel have a crush?"

"No offense," Gabe said, "but I think I liked you more when you were a pirate."

Cheery guffawed and ruffled the hem of the dress. "I *thought* I recognized this. What's this really about, Gabriel? You ain't doin drag for the talent show, are you? You and her are gonna do a little switcheroo, try to get the heat off her tail."

"I guess," Gabe said.

"I figured it was something kinky," Digby said. "Reversing gender roles."

Cheery barked a laugh. "Your mind is always in the gutter, Raymond."

"Wait..." Digby's brow furrowed. "Does this mean you're *not* gonna be my Dolly Partner?"

"C'mon, Dig," Gabe said guiltily. "You know I never leave the boat."

His roomie huffed. "I shoulda known. Well, hell, I guess I can't stay mad. This is pretty damn noble, what you're doin."

Bet he wouldn't feel that way if he knew we're plannin to kill someone tonight, Gabe thought.

"Well, whatever you're up to," Cheery said, "you'll be doin it in style. This look boots the house down!"

Gabe looked back at them. "Is that good?"

Digby and Cheery shared a look. "Henny," Cheery said, "that is *all kinds* of good."

Emory closed the bathroom door and went to his laptop on the mahogany desk in his office. He hadn't realized it had gotten so late. The auction was about to start and he'd almost missed it in dealing with the new girl.

She'll fetch a pretty penny in the next auction, no doubt. Such a tight fit. Like a goddamn glove. And those lips... my god, I could spend a lifetime between those lips.

He fired up the laptop and used his passwords and biometric passkey to get the auction running. He was the first in the chat. After a moment, two more joined immediately. Their faces were not shown in the chat windows, just their room numbers, which were only visible to Emory. The auction was anonymous. Bids would be cast using the functions on their TV remote controls.

He suspected one of the other new girls—Lionel had gifted him several of his progeny—would do quite well tonight, as well. They'd never had anyone younger than ten before. This was his first time working with Lionel. To be truthful, Emory didn't trust the fiend. He was little more than a pimp, flying his girls from one shithole country to the next for other fiends to procure. But if tonight's offering did good business, Emory would put aside their differences and bring him along on the next trip to Little Pearl. Much as he didn't like competition when it came to "daddies" for these girls—once they belonged to him, they were his and his alone, despite what The Duke might believe—he really could use the connection. It was getting harder to find clean girls these days, particularly with all the news attention child trafficking was getting, with those Q-Crazies and that recent independent film getting backlash from Hollywood elites, some of whom were on this very ship.

Some of them are in this chat, Emory thought, as more black windows with white room numbers appeared around his own at the center of the screen.

Emory glanced at the clock on the taskbar again. The chat had almost thirty opened windows, nearly a full three-quarters of the paying guests on the *Ceres*. Those who didn't make it in time for the first item would lose out. He couldn't wait forever.

"Well, gentlemen and ladies," he said, though his voice would be modulated to prevent identification. "Shall we begin?"

Chef Amor, whose real name was Damien Evelyn Butler, turned on the television in his suite and sat on the foot of his queen bed.

"*Welcome to the Ceres's in-room entertainment system*," a pleasant female voice said. Crossfading shots of the ship on the open sea gave way to images and video of various common areas on the boat itself, the crew smiling in a row on the bridge, stewards serving tables with white table cloths in the galley—the meals had been quite good, Amor had to admit, though not quite up to the standard of his own Michelin three-star joints in New York, Vegas and Miami, and another set to open in Toronto later this year—guests lounging and swimming on the pool deck, others dancing at night to the unheard music of some DJ.

Amor studied the remote in his hand. "How do I skip this shit again?" There were so many buttons on it he doubted he'd find the right one in time. The auction was supposed to start in a few minutes. "Right," he said, "press Exit."

He found the button and pushed it. The video disappeared, along with its generic tinkling piano music, and was replaced by a selection of movies. It would've been easy enough for Jackman to hide the video chat link in the adult films section, but he'd hidden it elsewhere, perhaps as a sly jab to Amor himself. Amor navigated to the film *The Menu*, a wonderful satire about the food industry starring Ralph Fiennes and Amor's current favorite actress, and selected it.

He scrolled down to the Bonus Features option and selected it, causing a dialog box to pop up: *Enter Your Parental Control Password.*

Amor grinned and carefully entered the long and complex password he'd been provided. Emory had said to commit the password to memory because it was very sensitive information, but his dyslexia made that difficult, so he'd written it in the notes app on his phone. Even still it was slow going, and by the time he typed it out fully the auction was already well underway. He pressed the Enter button, hoping he'd gotten it right the first time and wouldn't have to do it again.

The screen went black.

"Shit," he said, standing up abruptly. "Did it work?"

A moment later the image of a girl, thirteen at the oldest, popped up amid dozens of black chat windows. Several had yellow borders to show they'd placed bids, though there were no indicators of who was who, for which Amor was glad. The box of the current highest bidder had a green border. The auctioneer's voice was scrambled, but Amor was relatively certain he recognized Emory Jackman's patter. The bid, according to the number below the girl's image, was already well past what Amor was willing to spend.

"Jesus Christ," he breathed. "Money talks, bullshit walks, Amor. You wanna play with the big boys—" *Playing with the little girls*, he thought but didn't add. "—looks like you gotta throw down some big cash."

Amor had always been a gambler. He'd gambled by sinking everything he made working as a sous chef fresh out of culinary arts school on video equipment and kitchen supplies to start his YouTube channel rather than make his student loan payments for those few months, and the gamble had paid off big time. Within six months of starting it, the monetization brought in one-hundred K a month. He was lucky, he knew that. Damien Evelyn Butler had always been a schmuck, but when he became Chef Amor, with his signature chopping technique and multiple catchphrases—"Amor means love, and food *is* love," "It's sushi time, baby," and "This puts the 'mmm' in 'mouthfeel,'" among several others—what he did was magic.

He was untouchable.

After his first year he'd started doing events. Small at first, then bigger. Not because he needed the money but because he needed the *fame*, the adulation. In college, Damien Evelyn Butler with his girl's middle name had one or two short-term girlfriends. Women *flocked* to Chef Amor. They watched his hands expertly handle various meats and veg and wondered what they could do to them. In the kitchen he was a guitar god, but he was a mediocre lover, despite the name. Women might've smashed Like and Subscribe buttons on his videos but his sexual performances received no

Michelin stars. He'd get no regular "subscribers" in his bed.

Amor's next gamble paid off even bigger: opening his first restaurant made him oodles of cash, and made it even easier to get laid, while the class of women he fucked only got higher. High-fashion models. Up and coming actresses. Incredibly flexible dancers. For a few years there, that and the Scarface levels of cocaine were enough for him.

When he met Shantelle, he made another gamble, this one potentially fatal. She was the young daughter of one of his regulars, the CEO of a prominent bank. She'd batted her eyelashes at him and he'd exchanged numbers with her, at her father's blessing, because she wanted to "be a chef like him someday." He'd told her father he could put her in contact with people in the industry. "Hard enough getting kids interested in anything these days that isn't the TikTok," the man had said, to which Amor had laughed and nodded while already imagining the filthy things he'd do to the man's daughter.

They'd messaged back and forth for a while on WhatsApp, stuff about the business at first, then vaguely flirty comments. He was wary of getting in too deep with her, but once she started flirting, he opened up quickly about what he wanted to do to her. He got her to send pictures of herself. Not nudes, since it was illegal, and already bad enough they were talking this way every night. Soon enough he was hooked. He spunked into the anal sleeve of his Fleshlight every night, imagining what it would feel like to shoot his load inside of her virginal—in his fantasies, anyway—pussy.

And then, everything changed. Shantelle ghosted him for weeks, and for a while there he was afraid her father had found out everything, since the CEO himself hadn't shown up for his regular Wednesday meal. When she finally messaged him again it was to threaten to go public and tell her father about everything he'd said and done. He'd Venmo'd her the price she'd asked—which was insane but worth it—in exchange for deleting all the screenshots and their messages. He only had her word that she would, and in retrospect the word of a blackmailer wasn't all that dependable. But what choice did he have? She could have ruined him. He'd built an empire from a few kitchen appliances and a thousand-bucks worth of camera and lighting equipment, and with a handful of compromising texts, Shantelle could've taken it all away.

The following week the CEO returned to the restaurant, telling Amor he'd been in Switzerland on a business trip. And while Shantelle hadn't messaged him in months, and the blackmailing appeared to be over, his fantasies about her only got more extreme, more violent. He'd foolishly deleted the chat, including the pics and videos, and the images he scraped from her Instagram before she went private were enough for a few months but eventually even that couldn't satisfy him.

He needed to *feel* her, needed to be inside of her. And if not her, someone very much like her. He considered trolling the dark web, or doing that commencement speech his former high school principal had been asking him to do, just to find someone to take her place in his fantasies.

Then, almost like magic, right when he was at his lowest point, Emory Jackman had showed up at his restaurant. Amor served the man one of the best meals he'd ever made, and when Emory was done and offered his compliments to the chef, he'd invited Amor to join him on his superyacht, the *Ceres*.

He'd said, "I'm sure you'll find everything your heart desires on Little Pearl Island."

Then he'd winked.

"*Our next girl*," Jackman's scrambled voice said, "*is a new face...*"

The image of a girl who could've been Shantelle's twin came up on the screen. Long, shimmering hair, big brown eyes and an elegant neck and shoulders. She was *exquisite*, and while Damien Evelyn Butler knew he'd reached a point of no return, that if he did this there would be no turning back, Chef Amor knew that he couldn't leave Little Pearl without having her.

"Mmm, fresh meat," Amor said, one of the first phrases to catch on from his YouTube channel. Then he gambled more than a hundred grand on his first bid of the night with a single push of a button.

THE NEW GIRL

GABE LEFT CHEERY'S room after the man finished doing his makeup, and headed for the lounge deck. It was after supper and people would be gathered there for the evening's events. Gabe felt deeply nervous, but less so than if he'd been wearing the high heels Cheery had offered. In his sneakers he wouldn't have to worry about stumbling and making more of an ass out of himself. When he reached the lower passenger deck, he ran into his first test: an elderly couple with their arms linked. The old man unlocking their door gave Gabe a serpent's smile. "*Guten abend, erdbeerchen*," he said, causing his wife to scowl and turn up her nose at Gabe.

"That was weird," Gabe muttered to himself as the couple closed the door behind them. He reached for the door to the stairwell at the same time someone opened it from the other side. When the guy caught sight of Gabe, his eyes popped before he put on a cool expression and opened the door wide, allowing him passage.

"Heyyyy, girl," DJ Safe-T said, looking Gabe up and down. "You lookin *good* tonight, ya feel me?"

It was only then that Gabe realized he hadn't practiced his girl voice. He cleared his throat. "Um, thanks," he said, as high-pitched as he was able, which actually wasn't that bad.

Safe-T sucked his teeth. "Yo, you got a voice like smooth velvet, you ever do any singin?"

"Um… only in the shower," Gabe said, thinking about Digby singing that Van Halen song that morning. He had to resist the urge not to adjust his crotch. The tape was chafing like a bastard and his balls felt like he'd sat on them.

The DJ smiled. "Well, shit, girl, I could listen to that voice all day long. But you know what DJ Safe-T say: don't stay in the water too long, you get all wrinkled. Bet!" At this, he hissed a laugh through his teeth while covering his mouth with a hand.

"I'll, uh, I'll keep that in mind."

"Okay, I ain't tryna keep you." Again, the DJ looked him up and down, licking his lips and stroking his chin. "Maybe I'll see you round tonight, uh? Come by my booth, I'll hook you up."

Gabe didn't know what DJ Safe-T intended to hook him up with, but he said that he would, then let the door close behind him. In the stairwell, he adjusted and scratched himself before turning back to the door, wondering if he should have tried his luck with the DJ. He was still anxious about the whole situation but he probably could've easily convinced Safe-T to go back to Abraham's room with him, considering they were only about ten paces from the door.

Nah, he thought with shake of his head. *They'll miss the DJ. He's gettin paid to play records or whatever he does. Gotta be smart about this, like Abe said. Find someone less high-profile. 'Sides, I didn't even tell him I'm s'posed to be underage.*

Gabe continued up the stairs. After a few more interactions on the way to the deck, each confirming he "passed," as Cheery had said, he began hearing sort of jazzy music thumping from the speakers. The voices of passengers grew louder as he reached the lower guest lounge. People chatted, either sitting around tables and in sofas or standing at the bar. Several women and a handful of men were on the dance floor, and Gabe hoped he wouldn't have to join them in order to catch his prey. He'd never been good on his feet, and had the hand eye coordination of an infant. Dancing was definitely not something he excelled at.

After some hunting, Gabe spotted a skinny guy slouched on a sofa by himself near the back of the lounge. He wore a Tilley hat and a loud Hawaiian shirt, with rectangular glasses that looked to be half-tinted. His silver goatee was trimmed thin and square above a sunburnt, almost froglike neck. His right hand, holding a fruity drink, was perched on his belly.

Gabe kind of felt bad for the man. He looked like a real loser, but he supposed he had to be at least semi-famous or rich to be on his way to Little Pearl Island. So he swallowed his pity and his nervousness and sashayed the way Cheery had taught him between the dancers and tables of guests to where the man sat.

Goosepimples sprang up on his arms, and he envied every single guy out here wearing t-shirts and sleeves.

Eyes followed his progress through the crowd, men glancing at his ass and chest. Even a couple of young women seemed to be interested, which was more than Gabe had ever gotten as a guy. One woman sneered at him, and he thought she might be seeing him as competition. He was almost to his prey when he passed one of the stewards serving horsie doovers to a couple of guests. They locked eyes for a moment and he felt certain he was done for, his heart racing. But Poppy just smiled at him and continued to the next table, holding out her tray. Gabe let out a sigh of relief and continued toward the man in the Tilley hat.

"Is, uh, is this seat taken?" he asked when he reached the lima bean-shaped table.

The man looked up, startled by the intrusion, then smiled awkwardly. "B-be my guest," he said, gesturing toward the empty space on the couch.

Gabe sat, holding back a wince as his balls crushed between his legs. He should've pushed his "jolly ranchers" up into his abdomen like Cheery suggested but it was too late to fix that now. He crossed his right ankle over his left knee, then realized it was the way a guy would do it and crossed them at the knees, smoothing down the hem of Clarissa's dress. His cheeks flushed again. This close to his potential victim, he felt a pang of guilt along with his embarrassment.

With no idea how to start, he thought back to what Abe had told him when he'd expressed his concerns that he'd be unable to do what was necessary. "Trust your instincts, Gabriel," the old man had said, patting his shoulder. "A good hunter trusts his instincts."

"You, uh… you ever been to Little Pearl before?" Gabe asked the man in the Tilley hat.

The man gave him a furtive glance and shook his head. His cheeks were as rosy as a cartoon pig's. "First time. You?"

Gabe nodded. "Same," he said.

The man fumbled with his straw and sipped his drink as casually as he could manage. The straw made a slurping sound. "Sorry," he said.

"That's okay," Gabe said. "I sound like a dog lickin from a bowl when I drink."

"Oh!" the man said, suddenly realizing Gabe was empty handed. "Uh, can I get you one? A d-drink?"

"Would you mind? I tried, but the guy at the bar wouldn't take my fake ID."

"Fake?" The man gave him another cautious, sidelong look. "How old are you?"

"My ID says I'm twenty-three."

The man stared straight ahead when he asked, "What does your b-birth certificate say?"

"Well," Gabe said, "I was born in 2007, so I guess that'd make me—"

"S-sixteen," the man said, his bulbous neck rising and falling with an anxious gulp, audible even over the music. "Are you, um, here with your parents?"

"Nope. I'm allllll alone," Gabe said, hoping he sounded suggestive.

The man's eyes bulged. "So you're… on the menu?"

"The menu?"

"One of Emory's girls?"

"Oh, right. I mean, I don't *belong* to him. But yeah." Gabe smiled, holding back a grimace. "I guess you could say I'm on the menu."

Without another word, the man shot out the hand out closest to Gabe and grabbed his thigh, striking like a cobra. He didn't even look at Gabe, as though he wouldn't have had the courage if he had. Any sympathy Gabe had left for the man evaporated, and he barely resisted the urge to grab the hand and throw it back in the guy's lap so hard it mashed the guy's grapes into wine. He thought about what he'd do if it had been Clarissa here instead of him. She was a year older than he was pretending to be, but still—if this man had put a hand on her he would've wanted to punch the guy in the face. He might've lost his job over it.

"Is this schmuck bothering you?" said a gruff voice nearby.

The hand left his thigh instantly as Gabe looked up to see a stout man with receding silver hair, dressed in a crisp black suit with his collar opened and no tie. He smiled wide with bristly cheeks at Gabe when they locked eyes.

"How ya doing, sugar? I'm Ernie Wallis."

Jeez, are these guys fightin over me? "Hi, Ernie," he said.

"Can I buy you a drink?"

"This, um, *nice gentleman* has already offered to buy me one." Gabe turned to the man in the Tilley hat, whose name he still didn't know. The man had shrunk into the couch, threatened by the competition. It made it easier, not knowing his name. But this new guy seemed like a hyena, sneaking in to steal another predator's meal. He thought he wouldn't feel as bad about letting Abe do what needed to be done to someone like him. *Maybe I should switch teams. At least this guy was sittin all by himself not botherin anyone. Gotta figure out if he's one a them first, though. Likin young women is gross but it ain't a crime unless they're too young.*

"You must be a new girl. I didn't see you on the menu."

"That's right," Gabe said. "I'm a… *house specialty.*"

The guy smiled wider. "Is that right? Say, you wouldn't happen to like movies, would you?"

Gabe laughed at the lame pickup. "C'mon. Who doesn't like movies?"

One of Ernie's bushy eyebrows rose suggestively. "You ever wanted to *star* in one?"

Gabe glowered. "What kind of movies?" he asked.

The man seemed to catch Gabe's meaning. "Legitimate stuff. I'm the head of Acumen Pictures. You know the *Arrowheart* movies?"

"Oh, sure, the, uh… lady Indiana Jones, right?"

The man grinned again. "That's our girl. At Acumen we're always on the lookout for new talent. Especially in the 'Strong Female Lead' department," he added with a lascivious wink.

Gabe stifled a laugh. "Is that how you see me? As a Strong Female Lead?"

"Well, I'd have to judge your acting abilities first. How 'bout you come on down to my room? We'll run some lines."

Gabe considered it. He looked at the man in the Tilley hat, who'd shrunken like a wilted rose. Would he have even followed Gabe to Abe's room if he'd been offered the chance? Still, the feel of the sweaty hand gripping his thigh made him shudder, and remembering how he'd felt thinking if it had been Clarissa sitting here instead of him… It was a pickle.

"Heck yeah," he said, standing up and smoothing the dress. "Who doesn't wanna be a movie star?" He looked down at the other man. "Sorry," he said. "Maybe next time."

The man in the Tilley hat glanced at him and nodded glumly.

"Sorry, pal. It's a dog-eat-dog world out here." Ernie flashed the other man a grin. "Maybe you'll find some scraps on the menu, if you're lucky."

Gabe thought that was unnecessarily mean, but didn't stick up for the other guy. Ernie had already won. He didn't need to rub it in. Then he remembered both of these men were predators, and focused on figuring out how to lure this one to Abe's room instead of Ernie's.

As they moved along the outside of the crowd, Ernie Wallis stuck out a small, fat-fingered hand. "I didn't get your name."

"Mariah," Gabe said, almost adding *Marmalade*. He stuck out his hand, intending to shake Ernie's despite not wanting to touch the man. Ernie surprised him by taking it gently by the knuckles and lifting it, bending slightly. The man's stubble prickled his fingers as he kissed him with dry lips. Then he frowned and let him go.

"Say, your hands are pretty calloused. They must've plucked you straight out of a farmer's field, sugar."

"I guess so," Gabe said, wishing he'd taken the cocoa butter Cheery had offered for his hands. "Would you mind if we go to my room instead?"

"Emory usually likes the girls to come to us," Ernie said with a seemingly suspicious frown. "Although I've never had one on the ship before. We usually do it at the manor."

"Yeah, but I'm new," Gabe told him. "The house specialty, remember?"

The man grinned and looked him up and down. "I'd sure like to nibble on your bones, I'll tell you that much." The man laughed, and Gabe wondered if he knew he sounded like a villain from one of his *Arrowheart* movies, or if he thought he was being cute.

Either way, Gabe played along with a friendly smile. "Well, let's run a few lines in my room first." He wasn't sure about his next line but he said it anyway. "I've still gotta decide if you're… right for the part."

The film mogul chuckled. "I like your moxie, kid," he said, offering his arm for Gabe to take. "Sure, let's go 'run those lines.'"

Feeling like he'd need to take the world's longest shower

before the night was over, Gabe looped his arm through the movie producer's and walked side by side with him away from the lounge.

HACKED

SVEN LOGGED IN to his laptop and used the decryption software he'd downloaded from his girlfriend's contact in cybersecurity to hack into the video feed for the night's silent auction.

He'd gotten a fair amount of information out of Ernie Wallis, who'd given him the details of how the auction worked in exchange for being left out of Sven's exposé. Sven found the way it was done peculiar, but somewhat clever. The likely intentional irony of disguising the login to join the anonymous video chat as the parental controls, requiring a complex password Wallis would not divulge, would make for a "fun fact" editors seemed to enjoy. The fact that Emory would take joy in the irony was telling, as well. Turning what under other circumstances would be an innocuous detail into something evil showed how much of a monster Emory Jackman truly was.

As Sven waited for the algorithm to do its magic, he considered one of Nietzsche's famous quotes: *He who fights with monsters might take care lest he thereby become a monster.* Though he loathed the dead philosopher's ethos, Sven wondered if in fighting monsters it was inevitable to become one himself. If he was in fact not *destined* to become one.

He'd tried to stay as impartial as possible while investigating Emory and the people on his ship. To stay a head above them. But Nietzsche also wrote, *And if you gaze for long into an abyss, the abyss gazes also into you.* Sven had gazed into many an abyss during his career. He'd gazed into the souls of his subjects—metaphorically, of course, for he did not believe in the soul—and had written down what he'd seen. How often had the people he'd written about looked into his own eyes and found ugliness or hatred? He'd always tried to be a good person. Conscientious.

Friendly. But often while investigating he'd had to pry his way into places his subjects did not want to allow entry. He'd reduced both women and men to tears. Children, on a handful of occasions. He'd exposed monsters for who they truly were, laying them bare for the world to see, while presenting the "lived truths" and humanity of those who'd been "othered." Was that not an inherently noble public service?

Perhaps that was true when working class writers made up the profession, he thought. *Now it's practically a requirement to have degrees from prestigious universities, and our inherent biases are perhaps beginning to rear their ugly heads.*

The algorithm flashed before his eyes, lines of code which reminded him of *The Matrix*, which of course made him think of the red and blue pills Morpheus offered to Neo, which brought to mind to the online discourse about being "red-pilled," which in turn reminded him that everything was political now, in large part due to his colleagues in this noble profession.

Child predators shouldn't be politicized. This is one thing, surely, we can all agree is wrong.

The code swept away, revealing a screen of anonymous chat windows, surrounding the picture of a pubescent girl—perhaps thirteen, maybe as old as fifteen—giving the camera what was likely meant to be a fetching smile. Sven saw beyond that to the victim beneath. Her face was pallid, her cheekbones speaking of malnourishment rather than high fashion, her large eyes sallow and haunted. This was not a girl here of her own volition, whether coerced or not. She was not an addict looking for her next fix. Nor was she a street kid desperately fighting starvation. This girl had been kidnapped and forced into sexual slavery. Her name, according to the legend beneath her photograph, was Yvette. The bidding was up to two hundred and ten thousand dollars.

Nearly all of the empty chat windows were highlighted in yellow, which Wallis had indicated meant that the user had placed a bid. The window highlighted in green held the current high bid, the bid displayed in their window. With a single girl fetching over two hundred thousand dollars and more than two dozen girls on "the menu"—the term Wallis had used, and also the film it was hidden behind—the Jackmans must have been making a killing.

"*Gentlemen and ladies*," the altered voice intoned, "*Yvette is fourteen years old and an absolute flyweight at four foot ten and ninety-six pounds. She's fluent in English, German, Arabic and Cantonese, a steal at two hundred and fifty grand. Which one of you will outbid our current high roller? Who wouldn't like to spend the night with her, in a true 'girlfriend experience' or simply an evening of wild debauchery the likes of which you've never dreamed possible?*"

The auctioneer—even disguised by the voice modulator, Sven recognized Jackman's patter—was almost comic book supervillain-level evil. Would anyone outside of QAnon believe it? Would any legitimate publication even *look at it*?

"*Usch*," Sven muttered, disgusted by the idea of having to go to independent or alternative media outlets with this story. Considering the similarities of this real-life conspiracy to the bizarre ravings of the "Q community," with their "children are being sold into sexual slavery but also to harvest the chemical compounds from their adrenal glands to keep the elite youthful," there was no way he'd be able to use the vampire aspect of the article without sounding like a complete and utter crackpot. And the quickest way for the average person to dismiss the truth as fiction was to bring it to YouTube or reddit, or worse, Truth Social.

The highest bidder won Yvette at two hundred and ninety thousand dollars. Sven wondered what had caused the bidding to end there, seemingly arbitrarily, just below three hundred. He wasn't able to interact with the chat through his computer. To the bidders and Emory, he was not even there. A fly on the wall. Unseen and unnoticed by all.

"*Folks, we're going to take a brief intermission before moving on to our next item. Please stand by.*"

The timing was great, as far as Sven was concerned. He switched to his word processor and began to type up what he felt would be the story of a lifetime.

If he could manage to sell it.

The two-way radio blipped at Emory's side as the latest bid ended. He glanced at it, annoyed that Blitz would interrupt him during the auction, announced a brief intermission to the bidders, then muted his microphone.

He picked it up. "This better be damned important," he said

with a sneer. "Over."

"Sir, he's gotten into your video call," Blitz said.

Emory's heartbeat quickened. "Is this the secure channel?"

"It is."

"Fucking A. Who are we talking about?"

"Olsen. The reporter. He hacked into it somehow."

Emory stood, his adrenal glands pouring hot rage through his body. "*What?* How?"

"I dunno. I must've missed the hacking software."

"Shit, that's a pretty big fuck up, Blitz!"

"He's typing now. Looks like he's back in that profile doc on you."

Emory paced the room. As he turned to face the bathroom, the door opened and The Countess stepped out, fully nude and as youthful and pale as Venus emerging from the clamshell. She'd washed away the blood from her skin and hair and he could smell her perfume, ancient and intoxicating, from all the way across the room.

"What troubles you, my love?" she asked.

He ignored the hard-on beginning to stretch his boxer shorts and let the hand holding the radio fall to his side. "The reporter I told you about… he's hacked into the auction."

"Sir?" Blitz interrupted.

"*GIVE ME A GODDAMN MINUTE TO THINK!*" Emory screamed into the radio. "*OVER!*"

"My goodness!" Erzsébet said, allowing a smirk to curve her lips. She crossed the room to him and placed a palm on his chest. "Your heart is racing like the hound chasing the turtle, my love." Her hand slid down his stomach and gripped his cock, squeezing it with a moan that sent literal shivers up Emory's spine. "This 'reporter'," she said with a sneer, "you mustn't let him vex you. Finish the auction and come to bed. Please me. Then we will deal with the rat in your belfry."

Emory nodded, his mouth hanging open, salivating at the thought of her. "Goddamn, you are perfect," he moaned.

"Yesssss," she whispered, holding his gaze as she slowly nodded. "Perhaps next time you will think twice before you consider playing with our toys without me."

"I will. I promise, I won't slip up again."

A smile touched her lips. "No. You won't."

When she let go of his throbbing prick, he gasped. He could barely stand it, being a moment without her touch.

"Get back to work, my love. I shall be waiting with our plaything in the bedchamber."

"We won't need her tonight," Emory assured her.

"You may not," Erzsébet said. "But I'm feeling quite… carnal. And I would very much like to watch my beloved husband fuck our toy tonight."

Emory grinned. He didn't need to be asked twice. His grin widened. So did his wife's.

Then she turned her body away from him, still holding his gaze, and sashayed toward the bedroom. She looked back in the doorway, displaying herself to him. With one hand holding the door she closed it, and Emory sucked in another gasped breath. He wanted nothing more than to chase her into bed, but there was business to take care of first. He knew she wouldn't let him come to bed and neglect the rest of the auction. They had an island and a superyacht to upkeep, hundreds of staff to pay, a penthouse in Sunny Isles Beach and another in Monaco. Each auction brought them one step closer to endless wealth, a legacy not for their children—which they could never have together—but to subsidize their own immortalities.

Emory sat behind the computer, his rock-hard cock a dull ache in his lap. He picked up the radio and thumbed the transmit button. "Blitz," he said.

After a moment, the new security chief came back: "Sir."

"Thank you for bringing the intruder to my attention. We'll deal with him tomorrow. Over."

"Sir?"

"Yes, Blitz? Over."

"Is there… something I should know about?"

Emory winced. So it had finally come to this. He'd shown Blitz the Old Man in the cave, as he had each member of his security team he'd been grooming for the top spot. He had never seen the big man so terrified before, and hadn't since. But the truth of their wealth was a secret even to the highest-ranking members of their staff. "Whatever do you mean, Blitz?" Emory said innocently. "Over."

He heard the security chief swallow over the radio. "Never mind. Over," he added hastily.

"Good. Now don't interrupt me again tonight, Blitz. Tess has awakened and I'll have my hands full. Over."

"Goodnight, sir. Over and out."

Emory set down the radio, expecting privacy for the rest of the evening. Then he turned the mic on his computer back on and addressed the auction: "Apologies for the interruption, gentlemen and ladies. Let's move on to our next girl, shall we?"

Ernie Wallis let the new girl walk him down to the lower decks, where the folks on the shallower end of the wealth and fame pool stayed, his dick harder than the Oscar statuettes on his mantel.

It was good that the girl had convinced him to go to her room instead of his suite. Greta was conked out on the master bed, drunk and high on prescription painkillers, and he likely could have fucked the girl on the couch without waking his latest ingenue, but it wasn't worth the risk. She'd get uppity, think he was tossing her aside for a new It Girl, and likely cause a stink. Maybe even take it to social media. He didn't need that sort of aggravation, so the girl's room would have to do.

Ernie could barely fathom his luck tonight. If that shitheel reporter hadn't swung by his table, he'd have been involved in tonight's auction and inevitably a part of the rat's exposé. He would've preferred to have the guy killed, which would be easy enough back in Tinseltown. But he couldn't exactly call in a hack job on Emory's watch. What could the guy do? Fly to Little Pearl on a helicopter?

If the snotnosed investigative journalist hadn't spoken to Wainwright, the director of that shitty little documentary Ernie had gotten shelved the moment he took over as studio head at Acumen, he wouldn't have given the kid the time of day. But he had, which meant Wainwright had spilled the beans. The footage itself and the computers he'd edited it on were buried in some landfill. Nobody would find a single clip of that shitty little documentary. But it didn't mean that Olsen kid or whatever his name was didn't still have dirt on Jackman and Little Pearl, corroborated or not.

And so Ernie had squealed like a stuck pig. He'd told the reporter all about the auction and how and where he could find it, but kept the password to himself. He had to keep some cards close to his chest. Then he'd skipped out on it altogether, just in case the kid was somehow able to hack into the TV cameras. The last thing he needed was to get caught with his dick in his hand, bidding on sexual encounters with underage girls, especially with all that #MeToo bullshit.

Then, like some miracle gift handed to him on a silver platter by the gods themselves, this beauty showed up in his life.

He'd had to cut in on that perverted little creep in the Tilley hat, but that was no bother. Where money didn't work the chance of fame usually did. He'd lured the girl—Mariah, she'd said her name was—into his web, and would have her on his casting couch soon enough. Even if the couch had to be the likely shitty single bed in whichever meager accommodations the Jackmans afforded the girls under their employ.

She took him down several stairwells, practically all the way to the subbasement, as Ernie snuck little glimpses at her small tits and boyish hips. On all his trips on Jackman's boat, he'd never been down here. It smelled musty, like how he imagined a poor person's closet might smell. Truthfully, he kind of felt a little bad for the girl, but it didn't stop him from wanting to fuck her so bad he was almost dizzy.

They didn't talk as she led him to the end of the hall, where she turned to him, stopped in front of the last door on the left. "This is my room," she said in her sexy country bumpkin accent, and unlocked the door. God, she was playing it coy now. This demure act after how eagerly she'd lured him in really got his motor running. Ernie undid another button on his shirt and smiled eagerly as she opened the door on her darkened room.

"After you, baby," he said, holding the door and gesturing for her to go ahead.

Mariah sashayed into the dark, her adolescent ass and narrow hips swaying nicely.

Ernie followed her inside.

It smelled like an old folks' home in here. A spicy cologne. Moth balls. More mustiness. The poor kid had to *sleep* here? The drapes were closed over the porthole even though it was already dark out.

She closed the door and locked it behind them. "Sit on the

bed," she said, pointing to it.

"You don't have a couch in here?"

The girl shook her head, barely visible in the gloom.

"Say, does Jackman approve of this? You know, you girls doing freebies?"

The girl hesitated a moment before answering. "What he doesn't know can't hurt him, can it?"

"No, I guess you're right," Ernie said, and sat on the edge of the bed.

"Take your shirt off," she said.

Ernie obliged, taking off his jacket first and laying it folded on the bed beside him, then unbuttoning the remaining buttons on his shirt. He always felt a little embarrassed by his saggy man tits and large, dark nipples, but the girl didn't seem to mind.

"Should I take off my pants?"

"Not yet. Are you ready?"

"Oh, I'm ready."

"Good. Then let's get started, I guess."

A floorboard creaked behind Ernie, startling him. *Someone's in the room with us!* his lizard brain screamed. *Some fuckin cuck peeping tom!* He turned quickly to see a specter of an old man standing in the gloom on the other side of the bed, and before he could defend himself the old man swung the baseball bat gripped in both gnarled hands. Fortunately, Ernie had a moment to duck just enough so that the bat struck him in the shoulder, shooting blinding pain down his arm, rather than a strikeout to the head. He cried out, "*You old fuck!*" Then he pushed the girl out of the way and rolled onto the floor, out of the old man's reach.

The girl kicked him hard in the stomach.

It's a sting! he thought frantically as great gust of breath expelled from his lungs. *That fuckin rat reporter busted me!*

He reached up blindly, grabbed a handful of fabric and yanked as hard as he could, not sure if he was trying to pull himself up or just tear off what he suspected was the girl's dress. He heard it rip.

"Get off me, ya sick pervert!" came a young guy's voice, with the same Southern accent as the girl, as another kick struck Ernie in the jaw, sending stars shooting across his vision like the Acumen Pictures vanity logo that came up before every one of his films.

Ernie's mind struggled to make sense of what he was hearing. The boy's voice had come from right where the girl had just been. He craned his neck and saw the girl with short hair slicked back, a mane of curly brown hair gripped in her hand at her side as she scowled down at him.

A wig! Fuck me, it's a guy!

"I'm not…" he gasped. "I'm not a f—"

The baseball bat came down hard and knocked his lights out.

HUNGER

GABE STOOD OVER the unconscious man, panting and angry. He hadn't wanted to hit the guy but Abe's first strike had struck the man's shoulder instead of his head, so he'd had to improvise. When Wallis had torn Clarissa's dress, Gabe saw red and kicked out as hard as he could, connecting with the pervert's jaw. The guy looked confused and disgusted when he'd seen Gabe standing above him, holding the wig. A far cry from the way he'd been ogling him only seconds earlier.

He was out cold now, snoring like a baby pig.

The first thing Gabe did was reach up Clarissa s torn dress into his boxers and peel the tape off his genitals. They were dripping with sweat, and he felt like he'd gotten hit with a soccer ball to the nuts. He sighed as he crumpled the tape and threw it in the trash. It was a relief to be freed, even if he now had to be self-conscious about the bulge showing through the dress.

"You're a natural hunter, it seems," Abe said with a dark grin.

Gabe huffed. "If you say so. Now what?"

Abe dropped the bat onto the bed. He looked exhausted, like he might drop dead at any minute. "Now," he said between breaths, "we take him to the bathroom."

Gabe looked toward the opened bathroom door, knowing exactly what awaited the unconscious Ernie Wallis in there. He'd nearly put out his back helping Abraham lug his trunk up here earlier in the day, and just knowing what lay within filled him with a creeping sense of dread, to the point that he'd almost freaked out when he opened Abe's door to darkness, thinking he'd find Abe dead and that thing wearing a little girl's skin like some malevolent cosplay waiting inside to pounce on them the second they stepped inside the room. He'd seen enough horror movies to know that plot twist by heart.

Gabe grabbed the pervert by his ankles and Abe took the wrists, and together they carried—but mostly dragged—him into the bathroom. The giant steamer trunk stood upright by the bathtub, with the monogrammed initials VH which Gabe now knew stood for Van Helsing and not Van Halen as Digby had suggested when they'd first seen it. They slid Wallis across the tiles and hoisted him into the tub on the count of three, where he landed with a hollow thud, striking his head on the wall and smearing it with blood.

More blood streaked the tiles.

The trunk shook, and Gabe practically leaped backwards out of the bathroom, so quickly that he thumped his hip on the doorjamb.

Abraham plunked down heavily on the toilet, gasping for breath. He reached for the sink and grabbed the stake he'd left there. "Get my cane, please."

Gabe looked around, unable to find it in the dim light spilling in from the bathroom. "Where is it?"

"By the nightstand."

He found the cane standing upright against the wall, picked it up and brought it back to Abe, who was still seated on the toilet, staring grimly at the snoring man in the tub.

"He's not worth your sympathy, you know." Abe tried to stand with the aid of the cane, groaning and plopping back on the toilet lid. "Men like him… men with enough money to skate through any legal troubles they may encounter… they don't learn their lessons easily."

"I know," Gabe said, still feeling guilty.

Something thumped against the inside of the trunk again. The old man nodded toward it. "Open it, please."

"I don't know if I can."

Abe held out a stake to him. Gabe stared at it but didn't take it. "I cannot do this myself."

Gabe understood. He accepted the stake and took a single hesitant step toward the trunk, knowing he'd likely be fine but worried she'd leap at the first thing she saw.

Last time I let her out she moved like a little spider monkey.

He took two hurried steps forward, flipped open the clasps and stepped quickly back.

The lid swung open immediately, hitting the wall behind it. The mound of earth inside parted and the little gray-skinned creature sprung from the trunk, rising into the air. At first Gabe didn't believe his eyes, but he blinked hard and confirmed it: she was *flying*. Her little bare feet hung a full two feet above the trunk.

He held the stake out like a boy wizard's wand. She hissed at him, baring fangs as sharp as a cat's, then again at the old man.

"I promised you I'd feed you," Abe told her. He gestured toward the tub. "There he is."

The little girl monster rotated her entire body in the air to face the man in the bathtub, like a puppet on strings.

Then she swooped down on him, her small red lips wrapping around his throat. The film mogul's eyes sprung open and he grabbed her around the waist but she tore out a chunk of stubbled flesh and his arms flailed, his eyes rolling back in his head as his blood painted the wall behind him, the tub, the ceiling.

Droplets spattered Gabe's face. He drew the curtain across and stepped back in horror.

"Help me up, boy," the old man said. "We needn't be here for this."

Gabe couldn't take his eyes off what was happening behind the semitranslucent shower curtain. The girl was drinking blood like juice straight from the carton, licking it, lapping it up from his face and chest, making awful slurping sounds like a dog eating its own vomit, uttering little moans of delight. Gabe took the hand Abe offered, then helped the old man to his feet. They both left the bathroom, and Gabe shut the door quickly behind them, then dragged a chair over from Abe's desk and wedged it under the door handle.

"What now?" he asked, grabbing a couple of tissues and using them to wipe the pervert's blood off his face.

"Now, we wait until she is sated."

"Is he… dead, you think?"

"If he's not, I'd very much suspect he wished he were."

Gabe considered he probably would too if he was in Ernie Wallis's situation. "You think they put Clarissa in the brig? I could ask around, I guess. But we're not supposed to know about her, I don't think, even though everybody does."

Abraham gave him a cold stare. "If she's lucky, that is where she'll be."

"What d'you mean, 'if she's lucky'?"

"There are monsters on this ship, far more dangerous to our friend than vampires, like the man in my bathroom. If she's lucky, she will not fall prey to one of their ilk."

Gabe thought about the man in the Tilley hat and shuddered. He thought about Mr. Jackman selling young girls to men twice their age and wanted to puke. To think he'd been on this ship with all of these sex offenders for almost a year and hadn't known a thing. He wondered if any of the rest of the crew knew anything, or if they were just as in the dark as he was. The security team had to know about it, at least. He was friendly with most of them, particularly Journee. He couldn't imagine her knowing there were actual pedos on the boat molesting young girls, and turning a blind eye to it.

Gabe winced. He'd been holding the stake in his hand so hard he got a splinter. While he tried to pluck it out, the two of them sat in contemplative silence, Abe's hands folded in his lap in the chair, Gabe sitting on the edge of the bed. After a while, there came a scratching on the other side of the bathroom door. Both men turned at the sound.

"I'll get it, I guess," Gabe said, standing up reluctantly.

Abe nodded.

Gabe crossed the room and removed the chair from under the door. He hesitated as he reached for the handle, and looked over his shoulder at the old man. Abe was holding another one of his array of stakes. "You sure about this?" Gabe asked.

"She should be quite full from our guest. If not..." The old man made a jabbing motion with his own stake.

Gabe wasn't sure he could stab a little girl, even if she was trying to eat him. But he turned the handle and quickly opened the door, stepping back and holding out the stake in the same movement.

The little girl monster lay sprawled on the floor by the door, drenched in blood. Even with the curtain pulled, the walls, ceiling, sink, toilet and tub were covered with it. The towels and toilet paper were soaked through. Ava vomited more of it, and Gabe wondered if much of the mess was from her overeating. The shower curtain was pulled open again and he got a glimpse of the man in the tub—or what had once been a man. Chunks of flesh hung in glistening flaps from his neck and face and belly, torn away from sinew and fat and bare white bone. Like the rest of the bathroom, he was covered in his own gore.

"My tummy hurts," Ava said, and let out a wet belch.

"Yeah, I can see that."

She raised herself up on an elbow and looked up at him with her big dark eyes. "Why are you wearing my sister's dress?"

"That's how we got your dinner," Gabe said, swallowing back the rising bile. "I dressed up like a girl so we'd know he was one of the bad ones."

"Oh." She turned to Abe. "I can't hear her anymore."

"Can't hear who?" the old man asked. "Your sister?"

Ava nodded slowly. "She's gone away again."

"What do you mean 'gone away'?" Gabe asked.

"I heard her thinking, like I hear you right now. It's sounds like flies buzzing in my ear. Only when she was close it was real loud. I could hear whole words and feel how much she loved me… and even how scared I made her. I heard her call me from the trunk right before you opened it and then… it's all gone. Did she go away?"

Gabe shuddered again. "They caught her," he said.

"The bad men?"

He nodded.

"Then they'll make her like me."

"Like you? You mean…?"

"A vampire. Clarissa told me that's what I am. I don't want to be like this but I can't help it. It's a disease."

"Yes, Ava," Abe said. "It's a disease. But we may be able to cure you."

"Lionel said there is no cure."

"That is because Lionel wants to keep you sick. He is a very bad man, Ava. One of the worst there are."

She pouted up at them. If she hadn't been covered in a dead man's blood, Gabe might have considered comforting her. "He made me do bad things," she said.

"Yes, he did."

"Now they'll make Clarissa do them, too."

The words sparked a volcanic explosion of rage to bubble up

from Gabe's guts. Without thinking, he slammed the stake into the wall beside the doorway as hard as he could, puncturing the plywood. He let his hand fall to his side, leaving the weapon buried in the wall and stalked back to the bed. As he slumped down on the mattress, he felt Ava and Abe's gaze on him. He couldn't meet their eyes, keeping his own downcast, waiting for someone to say something to make this all better.

"We should clean up this mess," was all Abraham said.

IMMUNITY

SVEN WATCHED THE entirety of the auction in silent awe, all the while beginning to type up what he'd begun to think of as the exposé of the decade, perhaps the century. With all of the high-level people on this ship, and the many foreign diplomats, dignitaries, politicians and royalty connected with Emory Jackman and his wife, this story could tear down the very fabric of the so-called Western world, and much of the rest of it. It was a Nobel Prize in the making, or at the very least the Right Livelihood Award from his own native land. Which was why Sven knew he needed to be extremely cautious from here on out. He could not allow anyone to become aware of what he was up to, and he could not allow this laptop to fall into the wrong hands. His meeting with Ernie Wallis may have been noticed, and certainly the film mogul would have been missed at the auction. Sven just had to hope his Faustian bargain with the *jävla pervers* wouldn't come back on him somehow.

He was typing up a great paragraph on the lack of morals in professions and positions most requiring it when a knock came on his door.

Sven lowered the laptop screen and peered at the locked and bolted door. The television was off. There was no worry about the visitor—the old man, perhaps—hearing the auction, as it had ended half an hour ago.

"Who is it?"

"Mr. Olsen," came a deep voice from the corridor. "It's ship security. Could we have a word with you?"

"Security?" He closed the laptop and stood. "Is there a problem?" He crossed the room to his bed and slowly, cautiously lifted the mattress.

"This would be best handled face to face, Mr. Olsen. Would

you open the door, please?"

"Just a moment," he said, slipping the laptop underneath and gently lowering the mattress. Then he hurried to the door, his mind racing. Could they possibly know already? Had the film mogul tattled on him?

Sven took a deep breath, unlocked and unlatched the door, then opened it, putting on a warm smile. The man who stood in the doorway was a giant with rippling muscles stretching the fabric of his uniform to its limits. His badge read BLITZEN WAGNER. Slightly behind him stood his petite female partner, a young woman with box braids. "To what do I owe the pleasure?"

"Mr. Olsen, we're going to have to detain you."

"*Detain* me? Whatever for?"

"A device in this room was found to be hacking into a secured network. That's a criminal offence and something we don't take lightly on the *Ceres*."

"That's preposterous. I'm a journalist, not a cyber criminal. I wouldn't have the first idea—"

"You can tell us all about it at the tribunal on the island. For now, please collect your laptop and come with us."

"Where?"

"To the brig."

"The brig? What about journalistic immunity?"

Blitzen gave him an impatient glower. "Even if that was such a thing, which it isn't, I don't believe it would fall under the purview of maritime law. Please get your laptop and come with us."

Sven caught the eye of the female guard, who gave him a somewhat sympathetic nod. "Fair enough," he said. "Just a moment, please." The massive guard held the door as Sven crossed the room for his secondary laptop in the shoulder bag hung from the desk chair.

"The *other* laptop, Mr. Olsen," the guard said.

Sven bristled. How could they possibly know? *Unless*... It took every ounce of willpower not to scan the room for hidden cameras. He should have known they would be suspicious of him, despite having been personally invited on the cruise by Mr. Jackman himself. Or perhaps it was *why* he'd been invited. Was it possible Jackman had known all along he intended to write an exposé on Little Pearl? Had the documentarian tipped him off after the interview?

"This is my only laptop," he said, not daring to turn and face his accuser.

"Under the mattress," came the baritone reply.

"There is no second laptop, I assure—"

Blitzen shouldered his way into the room like a tank through Poland.

"This is a *flagrant* violation of my civil rights," Sven announced, "and I *will* be demanding to speak to my lawyer the moment we reach the island!"

The big man stopped in front of Sven, towering over him with a sharp exhale through his nostrils. "As I said, you can take that up with the tribunal. Now, retrieve your laptop, Mr. Olsen. If I have to do it myself, my colleague will need to cuff you and escort you from the room."

Sven turned to the woman. She pursed her lips, no longer appearing sympathetic. "Very well," he said. He reached under the mattress, wishing he'd had a gun under there like some film noir detective, despite being an avowed pacifist, and pulled out the laptop. He stood and handed it to Blitzen.

"Thank you," the *jötunn* said. "Now please come with us peacefully. No need to put on a show for the guests, is there?"

"Very well," Sven said, stepping around the foot of the bed. He followed Blitz into the corridor, the woman—her name badge said JOURNEE TERRELL—walking behind him. Several people had gathered at their doors, gawping at them, including the old German husband and wife.

"Nothing to see here, folks," Blitzen said with a big phony smile. "Please return to your rooms."

As the gawkers began hiding behind their doors, Sven stared at the laptop in the giant mitt of the man detaining him and wondered how he'd get himself out of this one.

After Gabe and the old man returned the little vampire to the trunk full of cool earth they'd taken from her crate, Gabe changed into fresh clothes and left the room to get cleaning supplies from the janitor's closet, including bleach and industrial cleaner. He spent the next hour and a half cleaning out the sex offender's blood from the fabric and grout in Abe's bathroom. It was good, hard work that kept his mind off of what he imagined might be happening to Clarissa. By the time he was done, his fresh clothes were as sweaty as the bathroom had been bloody, even though Abe had turned up the air conditioning to slow the body's decomposition. All Gabe wanted to do now was go back to his own room and have a nice cold shower. Unfortunately, they still had the body to deal with.

"What are we gonna do with him?"

Abe had spent the last half hour or so nodding off in the chair, both hands gripping the cane resting between his knees. With his eyes still closed, he said, "We'll need to dispose of him before we reach land."

"Tomorrow morning," Gabe said. Having done this voyage a few times, he knew at cruising speed it would take two days and nights, plus half the following day to reach Little Pearl Island on the rhumb line.

He shuddered, glancing at the shower curtain to the dark shape slumped behind it. "You're in no shape to carry a body. I'm gonna need to get help. Will you be all right?" he asked, thinking of the girl in the trunk, how she'd levitated and pounced like a tiger onto her prey.

"Go," the old man said, smiling with his eyes still closed. "You needn't worry about *me*. I've dealt with situations deadlier than this more often than I care to admit."

"Okay then. What happens if you gotta take a leak, though?"

The old man opened one eye and nodded toward the stake on the table within reach beside him. "I'll bring a weapon with me. Besides, I reek of garlic. She'll think twice before attempting to make a meal out of me."

"Is that what that is? I thought you just had bad B.O."

Abe laughed. "Get some rest. You'll need it for tomorrow."

Gabe agreed and turned to leave. He stopped at the door. "You don't really think they're gonna turn her, do you? Into one of them?" he said, nodding toward the closed bathroom door.

"I will say I hope they do not. Or, that it is a process that can only be done upon the island, by The Duke himself, and that you and I manage to reach her before that happens."

"And if not?"

"Then we must pray we're able to reverse the change."

"By killing this Duke guy?"

Abraham opened his other eye and gave Gabe a look that chilled the sweat on his flesh. "That is my intent, yes. It is my *destiny.* Even if doing so brings me to the brink of death, I shall take my revenge for our Clarissa, and my poor Wilhelmina."

After methodically washing and drying both her hair and body, Emory carried the dead girl into the second bedroom and laid her gently on the bed, propping her up against the headboard with several goose down pillows. It was important to keep her head elevated during this procedure, in order for the Caspian serum to flow quickly and efficiently through her emptied veins.

He inserted the IV needle and ran some saline through to check the line before starting the drip. Then he brushed her slightly damp hair back from her forehead and stepped back, admiring her. She really was a rare beauty. Dark eyes. An elegantly sloped nose. High cheekbones. Dimpled chin. A long, graceful neck. *Clarissa...* with her dark eyes he thought she might have Latin blood—or lineage, at least, considering she no longer possessed any blood at all.

Why are you on my goddamn boat? he thought. It was much too late to ask her, even probing whatever synapses happened to be firing would be pointless. When she awoke again, the living dead, she would have no memory of what came before. She'd be a blank slate, shapeless clay he and Erzsébet would mold into an intelligent and refined courtesan. The perfect companion for their clients, and an unforgettable lover. They always awoke stupid and clumsy, like newborn children. The serum made them and kept them that way, derived from The Duke's blood but not pure like the blood The Vampire King fed to his direct progeny from fresh wounds in his flesh. Still, it was strong enough that the IV had to be covered with a paper bag and the tube was opaque to prevent light exposure. The serum would break down too quickly in sunlight, much like The Duke himself.

What do we need him for anymore? Why not just harvest the rest of his blood, make the serum and store it in a safe facility? We could create thousands of toys, unburdened by The Duke's old school bullshit.

He thought back to what Erzsébet had said to him, about her

needing him more than he needed her. This was true, but only because of her relationship with The Duke. With him out of the picture, Emory would be free to do whatever he liked with their girls. He could even try to impregnate one of them before they turned without worry of reprisal.

That's settled then. The Duke has to go. We'll incapacitate him. Contain him somehow. Hell, we can tour him around New York City like the 8th Wonder of the World.

But first, he had Olsen to deal with. He thought he might just have a plan that wouldn't involved killing him and hiding the body, and bring less attention to Little Pearl than the reporter's disappearance inevitably would.

Sven sat in one of two cells in the ship's brig. In the next cell, the stout man he'd seen in the pool the other day lay snoring on the bed with one arm draped over his eyes. His tan had turned to a deep red sunburn. Wearing a bright green tracksuit with white stripes, it made him look like he was doing an impression of a candy cane. A plastic bucket lay at the head of the bed, with vomit splashed around it on the floor, the stench occasionally wafting unpleasantly in Sven's direction. He presumed the man suffered from heat stroke as much as alcohol poisoning, causing Sven to wonder if they'd locked him up for being drunk and disorderly like a town drunk in a television program about small-town America, or if he'd committed a legitimate crime. Sven wasn't sure he wanted to know what sort of crime might be frowned upon on a ship whose owners condoned auctions for sexual relations with underage girls.

Whatever the reason, his snoring made it impossible to think clearly.

Sven had talked himself out of some sticky jams before, but this time he appeared to be in serious trouble. He wished he'd researched a little about maritime law to defend himself against whatever charges these people intended to throw at him. Unless they intended to throw him directly into the sea, which he supposed was a distinct possibility.

The man in the next cell snorted loudly, waking himself. He sat up bleary-eyed and look around himself. "What the fuck happened?" He caught Sven's eye through the bars. "Hey, dude, where are we?"

"We are in the brig on Emory Jackman's superyacht, my friend."

"How the fuck did I get here?"

"At a guess… you were causing a disturbance which Mr. Jackman did not appreciate."

The guy rubbed his head. "I musta blacked out. I can't remember a damn thing."

"What is the last thing you remember?'

"I think I remember running into a guy who looked like a brick wall."

"I believe we may have met the same man. Blitz, they call him."

"The security guard?" The drunk ran his tongue across his top teeth, seemed to taste something unpleasant, and grimaced. "Yeah, that sounds about right."

"Not a man you want to have on your bad side."

The guy sputtered. "You're telling me." He leaned over and glanced inside the bucket, then reared back with a sour face. "Jesus! Is that all from me?"

"You were the only one in the cell at the time I was detained. I'd think it unlikely they'd have left someone else's vomit for us to endure."

"Yeah, good point, I guess. Hey, where you from, my guy? Germany?"

"Sweden."

The man nodded sagely. "Land of Ikea and tiny meatballs." He pointed at himself. "I'm a Jersey boy, born and raised. Atlantic City, Bon Jovi and a whole lotta cows."

Sven smiled. "Let us not forget Sinatra, Springsteen, Queen Latifah and Whitney Houston, among many others."

"My pops worked with Sinatra back in the '60s, you know."

"Your father… worked with Frank Sinatra?"

"Yeah. He was a sound engineer back then. Owns a record label now. Y'ever heard of Tiny Music?"

"Of course, I've heard of Tiny Music."

"I'm Tino Bravo Jr. My dad's Augustino Sr., but they used to call him Tiny. That's why he called it Tiny Music."

"Yes, I'm aware. I wrote an article about the New Jersey music scene for *Stereophile*."

"Oh, cool. Hey, what'd they get you for? What landed you in the hoosegow?"

Sven smiled at the colloquialism. "I was detained for writing an article about our host."

"About Emory Jagoff? Why the hell would he lock you up for that?"

"It was… rather unflattering, let's say."

"For that you get stuck in the slammer?" Tino shrugged up his shoulders. "I guess they can do what they want out here though, huh? Maritime law."

"There seems to be quite a lot of mystique surrounding maritime law. Unfortunately, I do not know its intricacies, but I assume one can be arrested as justly for cyber crimes on the open sea as on land."

"Cyber crimes?" The guy looked impressed. "What are you, a hacker or somethin?"

"Not myself. A friend of my girlfriend's."

Tino looked surprised. "Oh, you got a lady back home? Hey, what happens on Little Pearl stays on Little Pearl, am I right?"

Sven sighed heavily. He'd thought he might have found the one innocent person on the *Ceres* outside of the old man, but apparently he was wrong. Although he supposed the man might just mean it in the Las Vegas sense. There was quite a lot to do in Vegas that didn't involve accidentally murdering prostitutes. "In what way?" he asked, just to be sure.

"Aw, you know. Getting shitfaced and havin a blast on the beach. Maybe doin a little—" He mimed snorting cocaine—or some other narcotic—off a thumb. "You know, stuff the gal pal might be better off not knowin about. That or the prostitots, but I don't touch kids. I'm just here for the party."

"The… prostitots?" Sven had never heard the term before.

"That's what your article's about, right? Jackman's 'Little Pearls?" The man used air quotes around the last phrase to indicate sarcasm.

"Ah, yes. Well, Tino, I don't use drugs, I rarely drink, I am not an ephebophile, nor do I do well in the sun. Might I ask, if you're not interested in the… *pearls*, as you said, why do you consort with people who harvest them? To continue with the metaphor," he added with a dour smile.

Tino grinned as if he thought he was being punk'd. "You really don't know? Jagoff's got dirt on all of us. We're here to make the *real* bad guys look squeaky clean."

"Is this true?"

"Hey, if I'm lyin I'm dyin. That's why Jagoff invites so many people, I figure. And once you know, and you don't say anything because your reputation's on the line, you're even deeper in the hole, you know what I mean?"

"Yes, I believe I do, Tino. It would seem that what happens on Little Pearl only stays on Little Pearl until Emory Jackman decides you are no longer of use to him."

Tino blew out an extended breath. "Shit. That's heavy, man."

"Yes," Sven agreed. "It is quite *heavy*."

The girl awoke.

At first her vision was blurry, but it cleared after several hard blinks and she was able to take in her surroundings. It appeared she was in a very large—she couldn't remember the word for a space with walls and a ceiling—lying half seated in a pillowy bed. Images hung on the dark wooden walls in frames. The—*Room, that's the word*—looked fancy, and so did its furnishings. A metal stand stood beside the bed. Something hung from it, covered in a paper bag. Whatever it was, a long black tube snaked down from it to her wrist, which felt bruised under the tape. She wore a blue-green thing that looked like an ugly smock-type dress with ties in the front, and plain white socks on her feet.

Gown, she thought, remembering the term for it. Thinking this brought another word to mind: *hospital*. But this wasn't like the image of a hospital she got when she thought about it. There was the stand—*IV drip*, she thought—but where were the other machines? The monitors to make sure she was still alive, that her heart was still beating?

"Where am I?" she tried to say, but the words came out as a croaked groan, like some monster from a movie. Whatever her mouth uttered, it definitely wasn't words. She wiggled her toes beneath the socks and lifted her arms. At least she could still move her body, even if her tongue didn't quite work the way she'd hoped.

What is this? she thought, regarding the paper bag hung over the IV. *Am I sick?*

She felt empty. Hollow. Like the insides of her bones had been scooped out and tossed in the trash. Her tongue was dry as a rattler's tail. Her brain felt like it was on fire. She tried to think back to how she'd gotten here—*An accident? An illness?*—but she realized she couldn't remember anything at all.

A horrific thought occurred to her then, one which made her sit up straight as a rod and grab fistfuls of her hair.

WHO AM I?

She couldn't remember her name. Not her first name or her family name. Worse, she couldn't remember her sister's name nor why it seemed she might be in very deep trouble, why she felt she had to save her. She knew she must have parents—*Everyone has parents, right?*—but she couldn't remember their names either, nor what they looked like. She saw only a vast, empty room where her memories should be. Dark and terrifying, she hurried from the room and slammed the door shut behind her.

Maybe this is a dream and I'll wake up in my own bed. I'll get up and hurry to my sister's room and she'll be okay, then I'll go to my parents' room and hug them so tight my arms hurt.

No matter how badly she wanted to believe it, she couldn't convince herself it was true. Wherever she was, it was far from home. The round window—*porthole*—across the room made her think she was on a ship of some kind. Maybe her parents had taken them on a cruise and she'd gotten sick from eating bad clams?

No. That wouldn't explain why I can't remember anything.

But what if I fell overboard? I fell overboard and they had to pull me out of the ocean and hooked me up to the IV because I'm still too sick to eat. I've got amnesia from hitting my head, or maybe I was in a coma because I drowned, and that's why I can't remember anything.

This seemed to make sense. More so than all of this being a nightmare. But if she did have amnesia and this was a sort of hospital room, someone would have to be looking after her, wouldn't they?

She tried to speak again. This time, her croak sounded almost like the word, "Hello?"

She smiled, proud for having accomplished it. When she tried again, her voice was louder and clearer. The croak was gone. She sounded almost like herself again, whoever she was.

Across the room, framed between her wiggling toes, a door opened, and the most radiant woman she'd ever seen stepped into the room. She had skin like ivory, dark eyes, and her chestnut hair pinned in a luxurious updo. She wore an elegant, sleeved gown with black veins running through the shimmering, slightly translucent fabric, and a black choker with a carved cameo the girl couldn't make out from where she sat.

"Mom?" she asked.

The woman smiled. "No, my dear. I am not your mother." She spoke with a thick accent the girl thought might be Eastern European.

"Do you… do you know my name?" she asked, hoping the question didn't sound silly.

The woman closed the door gently behind her, then took a few decisive steps toward the bed. "Your name is Clarissa."

"Clarissa," she repeated. The name felt foreign on her tongue, as if she'd never spoken it before.

The woman smiled again. "You are aboard the *Ceres*, a ship on its way to Little Pearl Island. My name is Erzsébet, but you may call me Tess."

"Tess?" she asked after a long moment of silence, during which the woman studied her as if she were an exhibit in a museum.

"Yes, Clarissa?"

"How did I get here? Am I sick?"

"I'm afraid you are, my darling. You are quite ill. Happily, my husband and I are privy to…" She seemed to search for the right word. "…secrets of the old country, let us say. You will soon find yourself feeling much sturdier as the medicine begins to take hold. It will not make you immune to the disease, however it will keep its most pernicious symptoms at bay."

"What disease?"

The woman hesitated. "It has many similarities to porphyria, a rare blood disorder, but it has not yet been given a name. It is characterized by ennui, confusion, lethargy and severe iron deficiency. You… must stay out of the sunlight, so it is best to sleep during the day. The sun is very dangerous for you and will cause severe burns on your skin. You must also avoid the consumption of garlic—"

"Garlic?"

"Yes. It will cause severe stomach cramps and…" She shrugged. "…let us say, unfortunate intestinal issues. Although this should not be difficult to avoid, as the consumption of food will be quite… *unpleasant*, to say the least."

Clarissa frowned. "Can I see my family?"

"Your family?"

"My mom and dad. My sister."

"We were told you were an orphan. You do not remember? My husband Emory and I adopted you. We rescued you from your foster family and you have been with us aboard the *Ceres* ever since. We are bringing you to your new home on the island. However, you became suddenly and violently ill yesterday evening."

"Why can't I remember any of this?"

"It is a symptom of the disease, I am afraid. You may never recover your memories—"

Clarissa surprised herself by weeping.

The woman pouted and crossed the rest of the way to her side. She reached out and gently wiped away Clarissa's tears. "Oh, my darling, you mustn't cry. You must conserve your fluids."

"I want my sister!" she moaned, unable to prevent the tears from flowing.

The woman sat on the edge of the bed and hugged Clarissa against her bosom, stroking her hair. She said something in a foreign language which Clarissa assumed was meant to be comforting. "Please do not fret, my darling. Emory and I, we are your family now. And you have many wonderful sisters awaiting your arrival upon Little Pearl."

GETTING RID OF THE BODY

GABE KNOCKED ON Cheery's door. It was past midnight and Digby wasn't in their room. He'd gone upstairs to Dig's usual smoke spot but hadn't seen him there, so he figured he must be staying over at Cheery's again.

He didn't want to interrupt them, but there was no sock on the door, so he assumed they were probably just sleeping or hanging out. He knocked quietly, heard nothing, then knocked a little harder, not wanting to wake any of their neighbors.

The door opened and Cheery peeked out, flipping down his eyepatch. "What is it?" The room was dark behind him. He blinked hard with his visible eye. "Gabe? What's the matter, honey? Your plan go to shit?"

"Everything's good, Cheery. I just..." He struggled to think how to explain that this was an emergency without giving away what was going on. "...I need Digby. Someone made a mess in the hold, and I need him to help clean up the mess."

Cheery frowned. "Can't it wait 'til morning?"

Gabe shook his head. "Not this time."

"All right," Cheery said with a sigh. "I'll get him. But we both know how hard it is to wake that man up. Gimme a hot minute."

He closed the door. Gabe waited anxiously in the hall. There was still plenty of time until morning, but getting Ernie Wallis up to the deck and tossing him overboard would be difficult while trying to remain unseen. It was possible they might need Cheery's help to run distraction in the security office.

"Raymond," Gabe heard Cheery say from behind the door. "Raymond, wake up."

After what seemed like forever, the door opened again and Digby stepped out, buttoning up a Hawaiian shirt. "What's up, Little Buddy?"

"Hey, Skip. Sorry to bug you guys an' all but there's a real big mess we gotta clean up before tomorrow morning. Figure it's probably smarter to tackle it tonight instead of right before we land."

Digby scowled. "What kinda mess?"

Glancing around Digby, Gabe saw Cheery dressed in a silky kimono, leaning forward to better overhear. "Can we talk in our room?" Gabe asked.

Digby tsked. "Cheery ain't gonna say nothin. Are ya, Puddin?"

"It's okay." Cheery waved him away. "Have your little chat, Raymond. I'll keep the bed warm."

Digby shrugged and stepped out.

"Goodnight, Gabriel," Cheery said in sing-song.

"Night, Cheery."

Digby followed Gabe across the hall to their room. "What's this all about, kid?"

"There's been… kind of an accident."

"What kind of accident? You two break a crate or somethin gettin up to no good down there?"

Gabe unlocked their door and stepped inside. He flicked on the lights and waited for Digby to follow him in, then closed the door behind him.

"Well?" Digby prodded. "What happened?"

"I need help—"

"That's why I'm here."

"I need help moving a body."

Digby opened his mouth to speak. Then he blinked and shook his head dramatically. "Say what now? What kinda shit you two get up to tonight?"

"It wasn't me. Well, it was and it wasn't."

"You're not making any sense."

Gabe wasn't and he knew it. Beating around the bush was getting him nowhere. "How much do you know about what goes on at Little Pearl, Dig?"

"What d'you mean? Like the luaus and shit?"

"No," Gabe said. He lowered his voice, "Like, super secret stuff with the VIPs. You know, the girls and stuff."

"What do you mean, girls and stuff?"

Gabe sighed, glad his partner didn't know about it, but anxious at having to explain it all. "Illegal stuff. With underage girls."

Digby's mouth opened again, then shut quickly. "*Underage girls?*" he said finally. "On Little Pearl? Who's been fillin your head with this stuff, kid?"

"It's true. The girl from the hold, Clarissa, her sister was in a crate down there. And she said there was more of em in the other crates. That's how come they were so heavy."

Digby stared at him a moment, then he laughed. "This is a prank, right? Girls in crates? C'mon, Little Buddy, you don't really expect me to believe this, do ya? I mean seriously."

"I ain't lyin."

"Well, shit then, if there's really girls in crates down there we oughta let em out, right? Before they suffocate or some shit?" He turned for the door. Gabe grabbed his shoulder.

"Dig—"

Digby fumed. "Kid, I'm tryin to be patient but I was havin a great post-coital sleep until you showed up at the door, now you're talkin all kinds of bullcrap about murderin some guy and underage girls in crates—if that's true, we gotta go get em out. And if it *ain't* true, I'm goin the fuck back to bed."

"We can't let them out, Skip."

"Well, why in the fuck not?"

"Because… they're *dangerous.*"

"The girls?"

"Clarissa's sister is one of em. She's the one who killed the guy I need you to help us move."

"Us, who? You and Clarissa?"

"Me and Abe. The old man. With the VH on his luggage?"

"Right, him. You two're hangin out with that old codger? Is that who got you two into this mess?"

"VH stands for *Van Helsing.*"

Digby shrugged. "Am I supposed to know that name?"

"Abraham Van Helsing. As in, the famous vampire hunter Abraham Van Helsing."

Digby barked a single laugh. "Jesus jumped-up Christ, kid. It's *vampires* now? What, sex traffickin underage girls wasn't good enough, now it's gotta be vampires, too?"

"The girls *are* vampires, that's what I'm tryna tell you. They keep em young forever. They sell em to rich perverts like Ernie

Wallis, the movie producer."

Digby's grin fell flat. "Is this some QAnon shit, kid? Are you on the 4chan?"

"I dunno what that is. Maybe? But I ain't *lyin*, Dig. How long've you known me? Just please, trust me, okay?"

His partner stared at him for a long moment. He crossed and uncrossed his arms, scratched his head in deliberation, pooching out his lower lip. Then he said, "Fine. But if this really is some pedo conspiracy, Cheery needs to know about it, too."

Gabe made to protest, but Digby was right. It wasn't fair to keep this a secret from Cheery, particularly after all the help he'd already provided tonight. He just hoped the man could keep a secret, and judging by his other life as a drag star which none of them knew about until recently, Gabe figured he probably could keep one better than any of them.

"Okay," he said. "Let's go tell him."

Cheery was easier to convince than Digby had been. He listened intently to Gabe's story about Clarissa and her little sister, questioned him about why Jackman would want to turn these girls into vampires if he knew they might end up killing the very men they were meant to service, like Ava had tonight, then simply said, "Well, I guess we'd better go toss the sick bastard overboard."

After Cheery got dressed, the three of them headed up to Abe's room. The old man was waiting for them, still sitting in his chair with his hands on the cane between his legs. He looked beyond tired, like he might just fall asleep at any minute and never wake up.

"I'd say it's a pleasure to meet you, sir," Cheery said, "but it's not really that kind of night, is it?"

Abe smiled. "No, indeed."

"Well," Digby said with a shrug. "I guess let's see it."

Reluctantly, Gabe opened the bathroom door. Digby and Cheery stepped in. "Careful of the trunk," Gabe told them.

Cheery took a deliberate step back from it, peering back over his shoulder with a nervous look. "That's her? Inside that trunk? Must be an itty bitty li'l thing."

Gabe nodded. "She's tiny but she's dangerous. You don't wanna wake her, believe me."

Digby drew the curtain and winced. A fly buzzed on the chewed-up face of the pallid corpse. "Jesus Christ on a cracker! She did all this?"

"I told ya."

"I was hopin this was gonna be some *Weekend at Bernie's*-style hijinks. How in the hell are we gonna get past the cameras with this raggedy ass stiff? Looks like someone ran him through a wood chipper."

"Well, I was a mortician in a former life," Cheery said. Gabe wasn't sure if he meant "former life" literally or figuratively, but considering everything he'd learned about the man this weekend, he wouldn't put either past him. "Let me scurry back downstairs and get my kit."

"Don't be long," Digby said.

"Won't be a minute." He pecked Digby on the lips and hurried out of the bathroom. A moment later, the door to the hall closed behind him, and Digby turned to Gabe.

"This is a real shitstorm you got yourself in, Little Buddy."

"I'm afraid this is my responsibility," Abe said from the chair. "Your colleague here was merely caught in the middle."

Digby stepped out. "So you're the famous vampire hunter, that right?"

"I once was. I'm afraid those days are far behind me."

"Comin out of retirement for one last job then, huh? I guess you're prob'ly lookin for someone to carry the mantle? Groomin my pal here for the job?"

"Nothing of the sort. I owe a debt. Once it is repaid, when I'm done with The Duke, the vampire scourge will no longer be my responsibility to fight."

"But there's still more out there, right? That aren't related to this Duke fella?"

The old man gave him a dark look. "Oh, yes. Far more than you can imagine."

"What's the pay like?"

"Excuse me? *Pay?*"

"Yeah, like how much a week?"

The old man smiled patiently. "The only compensation is the reward of knowing I've rid the world of another bloodsucking fiend."

"Huh," Digby said, giving this some thought. "Then why would someone like me, for instance, wanna step into the position? How've you survived for—" He looked at his watch. "—like a hundred and fifty years, workin a volunteer job?"

"Ah," the old man said, his smile turning sly. "There are certain benefits to exterminating high-profile elders. Many of them live quite extravagantly, much like our Mr. Jackman, and cannot bring their material wealth with them to Hell."

"So you rob them?"

"*Dig*," Gabe cut in. He'd been standing in the doorway watching their exchange in silence until he could no longer hold his peace.

Digby shrugged over his shoulder at him.

"I take only what is required to subsist upon," Abe told them. "But I do not do it for the money, I assure you."

"Well, if it *was* for the money, it'd be a decent salary—would you say that?"

The old man nodded. "It can be quite lucrative, yes."

"And when you're done with em, there's no bodies, right? Poof, and they just turn into a pile of ash? No evidence?"

"That's correct."

A grin spread across Digby's scruffy face. "You old scamp! This is some racket you got here, Abe!"

The old man laughed heartily. "Are you volunteering your services, Mr. Digby?"

Digby looked over his shoulder again at Gabe and shrugged. "Sure beat the hell outta haulin crates and luggage for Emory fuckin Jackman, wouldn't it, kid?"

"I dunno, Dig. They're real dangerous. Scary fast and teeth like vipers. And that's just the littluns. I ain't seen what an adult can do yet. Or an elder."

Digby got a twinkle in his eye he often got when discussing potential money-making schemes, which usually ended up being a product that was already on the market. "Sure, but *think of the money*, kid. Some of these scumfucks prob'ly got *Nazi gold* and all kinds of rich people shit socked away. We could get set up for life."

Gabe shrugged. "I'm not sayin no. Let's see how it goes with The Duke first, huh?"

"Listen to your friend," Abe said. "The life of a vampire hunter is not glitz and glamor. It is a solitary existence, defined by death and destruction. I have seen all of my friends perish"

"Well, okay then!" Digby clapped his hands happily. "Abe, I'm gonna give you a hand dealin with this Duke fella, if that's all right with you. If the two of us survive, I'm putting my hat in the ring to be your protégé. And if you wanna join me, Little Buddy, I'd be more'n happy to have a partner."

Gabe glanced at the trunk behind him, and the man in the tub. He swallowed hard. "I'll think about it, okay?"

Digby laughed, then spat in his hand and stuck it toward the old man. Abe looked at it with a slight grimace, then spat dryly in his own right hand and shook.

"Say, you got a strong grip for an old-timer. Must be handlin all them wooden stakes, huh?"

Abe gave him another patient smile. Gabe imagined the old man was thinking something Gabe's own grandmother used to say when he was little: *Beggars can't be choosers.* "Yes, I suppose it must be," the old man agreed.

A light knock on the door startled them. "Are you decent?" came Cheery's voice from the hall.

Digby leaned in toward Gabe with a conspiratorial look. "Don't say a word about this to Cheery," he whispered. "Let me talk to him first, okay?"

Gabe shrugged and nodded.

"C'mon in, Puddin."

Cheery came in with a brown leather doctor's bag clutched in his hands, and a silk print kimono draped over one arm. He looked at all three of them suspiciously before asking, "Were ya'll talkin about me?"

"Nah," Digby said. "We were just shootin the shit. Weren't we, fellas?"

Both Gabe and the old man nodded enthusiastically. It was obvious Cheery didn't buy it, but he said, "All right then. Let's make up the decedent and get him ready for his burial at sea."

It didn't take long for Cheery to make Ernie Wallis's corpse look presentable, using a fair amount of a wax-like substance he called "Plasto," and powder and makeup on top of it. Digby and Gabe dressed the dead man in the clean kimono from Cheery's wardrobe, which they weren't able to tie up due to the size of Wallis's stomach. When they were finished, the three of them looked him over and Cheery shrugged.

"We did what we could," he said.

"Close enough for cable," Digby said. When Gabe and Cheery turned to him for explanation he added, "That's what we used to say when I worked at WQRZ. We just gotta fool the camera into thinkin he's still breathin, right?"

"Good point," Cheery agreed. "I guess he is close enough for cable. Especially in the dark."

"But what if somebody finds him?" Gabe asked. "Won't the makeup and junk be suspicious?"

Cheery smirked. "Honey, in a few hours there won't be enough of him left to identify the body. Whatever the sharks don't take care of the water will."

Gabe shuddered, imagining the feeding frenzy out there in the dark water.

"Well," Cheery said with finality. "I guess we'd better get this belle to the ball, huh?"

"Any idea how you're gonna distract Blitz 'n' them?" Digby asked.

"I'll figure something out. I'm a student of the dramatic arts, Raymond," he said proudly. "The show must go on, and all that."

"If I may," the old man said from his chair. The three of them turned to him. Gabe had thought he'd fallen asleep, but he had both eyes open and looked refreshed and ready to go. "I'd like to be the one to distract our friends in the security office."

Gabe gave him an uncertain look. "You sure about that?"

"You gentlemen have been quite kind to have assisted me thus far. I'd like to put in some effort of my own. Besides, the last I spoke with Mr. Blitzen, I assured him I was Clarissa's grandfather. I'm curious what they might tell me when I inquire as to where she might have gotten to."

"All right," Gabe said. "But be careful. I don't trust that guy."

"He's a teacher's pet, that one," Cheery agreed with a nod. "He'll do just about anything to stay in Emory Jackman's good graces."

The old man pushed himself up with his cane. "I will be

cautious." He grinned, opening his vest to reveal an inner leather sheath holding three wooden stakes. "And I will be armed."

Cheery smiled and patted the old man on the shoulder. "Look at you! Big bad Abe, large and in charge!"

Abe grinned sheepishly. "Thank you, Charles. Now..." He clapped his wizened hands together and rubbed them vigorously with a dry sound like sandpaper. "Shall we begin?"

MEN OVERBOARD

WALKING AT A snail's pace with Ernie Wallis's arms slung over their shoulders like a four-legged race, Gabe and Digby tried their best to make his movements look natural as they carried him from Abe's room to the beach club deck. They'd tied his ankles to each of theirs, his right to Gabe's left and the left to Digby's right. Cheery walked ahead of them, scouting out the area to be sure the coast was clear. They'd made it all the way to the pool deck before running into someone, and it was only because the woman had been sitting in the dark on one of the loungers that they hadn't seen her before she spotted them.

"Hey, boys. Out for a nighttime stroll?"

They all startled, Gabe so badly he nearly let go of Ernie's arm and dropped him into the pool.

"You got it, honey," Cheery replied. "Just getting a breath of fresh air. Stargazing tonight?"

"Looking for shooting stars," the woman said. Gabe could just make out her face in the moonlight. She looked to be in her late fifties or early sixties, wore a bucket hat and had a pair of binoculars on a strap around her neck. "The Draconids meteor shower should be passing over later tonight."

"Well, make a wish for us, if you see one," Cheery told her.

Gabe and Digby began walking again.

"Your friend looks a little under the weather," the woman called.

"Shit," Digby muttered.

"That's why we're out here. Figured he could use a little sea air, and if he needs to be sick he can do it over the side."

The woman said nothing for a long moment, looking the three of them and their dead companion over. "Fair enough," she said finally. "Sea sickness gets the best of us. I've got scope patches in my room if he needs one."

"Thanks!" Cheery called back. "We'll be sure and let you know if he needs one."

"Good luck!" she said, then raised the binoculars to her face and watched the sky. "Ooh! That was a big one."

Gabe and Digby walked Ernie down the stairs carefully, one step at a time. They'd had a tough enough time getting him up the two flights from Abe's room, and going down these steps was even more difficult. Fortunately, there weren't a lot of them.

"That was a close call," Cheery said once they were far enough away.

Digby huffed. "You're tellin me. I just about shit a brick."

"Well, isn't that charming."

"Think she'll be a problem?"

"We'll go back through the beach club door."

"Isn't that usually locked this time of night?"

Cheery jingled his heavy key ring. "Pays to have friends in low places, doesn't it?"

Digby chuckled. They brought the dead man to the bottom of the steps. The water was black, the churn of the propellers dappled by white speckles and streaks of moonlight. The sky above them was awash with billions of stars. The stargazer would've been smarter to come down here, Gabe thought, but he was glad she hadn't. Probably nervous about taking a lounge off the deck, believing she'd get in trouble.

They carried the dead man to the end of the beach deck, then down the wide steps overlooking the water.

"Well, this is it," Cheery said. They had to talk loud enough to hear each other over the engine, and still hope they couldn't be overheard by the stargazer. "You ready?"

Digby's face looked deathly pale in the moonlight as he nodded. Cheery's skin looked gray. Gabe suspected he didn't appear much better. Because of the makeup, the corpse was the only one of them that looked like it had any life in it.

"Give it a three count?" Digby asked.

Gabe nodded.

"One..." Digby started counting. Then his eyes went wide. "Oh shit!"

"What?" Cheery said.

"Forgot to untie our legs."

"That'd woulda been unfortunate. Allow me." Cheery bent and untied both of their legs, then tossed the ropes aside. "Good to go, Raymond."

"Thanks, Puddin." Digby counted up again. On three, they launched Ernie Wallis into the sea.

"So long, chum!" Cheery called after the body.

"'Chum,'" Digby remarked. "That's a good—"

His comment was cut short as his legs swept out from under him and he hurtled over the edge of the deck, splashing into the water below. He was lost in the churn in an instant. Both Gabe and Cheery shouted his name. They saw him bob up a moment later, his arms flailing. Only one of the ropes lay at their feet. The other must have pulled Digby into the water after Ernie Wallis, like the white whale dragging Ahab into the sea.

"What do we do?" Gabe asked frantically.

Cheery reached for one of the lifebuoys, then stopped and turned to Gabe with a serious look. "I'm taking a boat and going after him."

Cheery hurried to the utility tenders hung from the mooring whips on the right side of the ship. "Send it down for me," he said, then jumped down into the boat. Gabe used the crank to lower it into the water. Cheery started the engine with two quick pulls of the rope. Its rumble was barely audible over the roar of the churning water. He peered up at Gabe with a despondent expression. "Whatever happens, henny, you stay safe!"

"You too! Please find him!"

"I will! You find your girl, too!"

Gabe nodded, though he doubted he'd be able to do much about finding her with only the old man to rely on. Cheery untied the boat, put the motor into forward, whipped around and began bounding over the chop left in the wake of the *Ceres*.

Gabe stood on the beach club deck watching until the boat disappeared into the dark.

The others had given Abraham a head start to doddle his way up to the security office. Once there, he rapped on the door and waited for someone to respond.

The door opened and a slim, attractive young woman in a

security guard uniform stood in the doorway. "Can I help you, sir?"

"I very much hope so, Ms. Terrell."

She frowned. "Misses. You can call me Journee though."

"Thank you. I'm searching for my granddaughter, Journee. Have you seen her?"

"Your granddaughter. She went missing?"

"Yes. I believe your colleague may have found her. A young girl with curly blonde hair—"

The woman blinked. "Wait. That's your *granddaughter*?"

"Yes. You see, I don't believe she was on the ship's manifest, and I think your colleague, Mr. Blitzen—"

"Blitz."

"Yes. I believe he may have mistaken her to be a stowaway."

"I see. That would be troubling."

"Indeed. You can imagine my surprise, I'm sure, when she did not return to our room this evening."

Journee glanced behind her into the office. "Could you come inside, Mister…"

He nearly slipped and said Van Helsing. "Coltrane."

"Like John Coltrane. A-N-E?"

"That's right." He followed her inside.

"Have a seat." She indicated a free chair in front of a desk. She sat with the array of security monitors at her side. Abraham eased into it with a groan. "You okay?"

"I'm quite old, as you can see."

"My mom's got arthritis, I know how it is." She slid a form in a clipboard across the table to her side, then grabbed a pen from her breast pocket and clicked it. "Now, could you please state your full name, for the record?"

He did. She scrawled it down.

"And your granddaughter's name?"

"Clarissa," he said, before remembering he'd told the behemoth her name was Wilhelmina. No matter. He supposed he could just say Wilhelmina was his daughter's name, and he'd gotten momentarily confused. Being elderly had its advantages.

"Is her last name Coltrane, too?"

"Yes, that's right."

"Now, sir—"

"Abraham, please."

"Abraham, why wasn't your granddaughter on the manifest? We don't get a lot of children on this ship. Matter of fact, I can't remember the last time I saw a kid on the *Ceres* who wasn't just taking a tour with one of our guests. This isn't really an all-ages trip, if you follow me."

"Yes, well—" Abraham glanced at the monitors and caught sight of Gabe and the others hauling the dead man up the stairs. He looked away quickly, pointing at the form in her hands. "Clarissa is with two Ss, not one."

Journee looked down at the sheet. "Oh, I'm sorry."

"No apology necessary. Now, as to your question. I was told when I was summoned by Mr. Jackman himself that I could bring a guest aboard. I can't speak to whether or not he told the captain, or whoever is in charge of the manifest—"

"That would be the ship's purser, Arlene."

"Yes, well, I can't speak to whether Arlene was given the corrected information before we departed, but I distinctly told Mr. Jackman I would be bringing my granddaughter, who is a minor and mustn't be left alone."

Journee looked up at this, concerned. "How old is Clarissa?"

"She's seventeen years old."

She tapped the pen anxiously on the form. "Seventeen."

"That's right. Is there a problem?"

She glanced at the walkie-talkie on the desk. "No... no problem. Let me just confer with my colleague for a minute. I'll be right back, okay?"

"Certainly."

The guard went to a door and entered the next room. He heard a blip, followed by Journee saying, "Blitz, it's Journee. Come in, please. Over."

Abraham watched for movement on the monitors. After a moment he saw Gabe and the others on the pool deck, their faces dappled by the rippling shimmer from the water. It looked like they were talking to someone unseen. He hoped they hadn't been found out.

"I have her grandfather right here in the office, looking for her," Journee said in a hushed tone. The man responded, but his voice was muffled over the walkie and behind the door. "Well, he says Mr. Jackman said he could bring a guest. Am I just supposed to call him a liar? Over."

While Gabe and the others left the pool deck, the man spoke again over the walkie. Abraham couldn't hear what he said but Journee's shock was evident. "Are you kidding me? What for? Fine. *I said yes*. Yes, *sir*. Right away, sir. Over."

A moment later, she returned with a dour look.

"Well," Abraham said. "This doesn't seem promising."

"I have to take you to the brig," she said glumly.

"Is that where Clarissa is?"

"Sir, I'm sorry, but until this is sorted out, you'll need to be detained."

"Well, this certainly is a turn of events, isn't it?"

Journee sighed as Abraham stood. "It certainly is, Abraham. It certainly is."

Feeling hopeless, exhausted and just about ready to give up on Abe and Clarissa and everything else, Gabe wandered back up the steps to the pool deck.

"Your friends go for a boat ride?"

The woman's voice nearly made him jump out of his skin. With all the commotion, he'd forgotten she was there. "Huh?"

"Your friends," the stargazer said from her lounger. "I saw a boat tear off just a minute ago through my binoculars."

"Yeah, they, uh… they were goin on ahead to Little Pearl. Get the dock ready for tomorrow."

"But they were going the other way."

"It's, uh… faster to go that way for small crafts. Too shallow for big boats like this."

"Oh." The answer seemed to appease her. "I made a wish for you, by the way."

"What'd you wish for?"

"I wished for a safe journey for you and all your friends."

Gabe thanked her for it, but he knew it was already too late. He returned to Abe's room and knocked. After nearly a minute with no answer, he used the key the old man gave him to get in. The room was empty, but it still smelled like blood and Abe's cologne. He sat in the old man's chair, staring through the bathroom door at the trunk with the initials VH engraved on the brass plate that started all of this, with the girl and her coffin dirt inside, until his eyes began to feel heavy. A half an hour passed without sign of Abe. Then an hour. A little while later, Gabe allowed his eyes to close.

He awoke early the next morning with the sun peeking in through a crack in the drapes over the porthole window. His gaze returned to the trunk, where the girl must have slept the entire night away in a food-induced coma. The sunlight didn't reach the bathroom. She was safe, for the moment.

Gabe left Abe's room and returned to his own. Digby wasn't there, and no one answered his knocks on Cheery's door across the hall. He wasn't in the cargo hold, nor were either of them in the staff galley when he shuffled in for a breakfast he didn't think he could stomach, but felt would be necessary, especially if he had to tackle the luggage and cargo himself once they reached shore.

He hoped Cheery had found Digby and managed to find land on an island or cay somewhere miles behind the ship. He hoped Abraham had found Clarissa, and they were together and safe, and that she hadn't been turned into a bloodsucking monster like her sister. He hoped these things but didn't believe them. There was more evil in the world than good, he'd learned that much over the past few days. Evil would find a way to creep into the most mundane or cheerful events. It was just the way of the world.

As he shoveled oatmeal absently into his mouth, Ava spoke again inside his mind for the first time since he'd released her from her crate, not from memory but directly, from the trunk in Abe's bathroom downstairs. *He's near*, she whispered, and before he could ask who, she added, *My daddy is very near*.

Gabe knew it wasn't Ava and Clarissa's parents awaiting them on Little Pearl. They were long dead, not turned like Ava but murdered at the hands of the vampire who'd kidnapped her. It was The Duke she meant, and realizing this sent a shudder through his tired body.

Certain he'd have to set foot on Little Pearl Island for the first time and confront the King of the Vampires if he wanted to save Ava and Clarissa and all of the other girls they'd turned into undead sex slaves, by himself if it came to it, Gabe powered down the last few spoonsful of oatmeal and started in on the heap of bacon piled on the plate beside it.

He'd need all the protein he could ingest, and drinking blood was clearly not an option.

PART 4

WELCOME TO LITTLE PEARL

HAPPY LANDINGS

THE *CERES* MOORED at Little Pearl Island's east dock at just past ten in the morning. Gabe reported Digby missing for duty to the chief steward as soon as she was at her post, who assigned a few of her crew to help carry the crates and luggage. The group of them managed to get everything out and onto the pier by twelve thirty without too much grumbling and complaining, and only one minor injury when a crate landing on a host's toe.

Gabe hefted Abraham's trunk downstairs with the help of Poppy, the steward he'd thought had recognized him when he'd played Mariah the night before. He'd told her that Abraham had left it with him for safe-keeping, since he was currently in the brig. "Feels like there's a dead body in here," she said as they dropped it off in his room. Despite his grim and exhausted state, Gabe had to struggle not to laugh out loud. "What's your friend in the brig for, anyway?" she asked as she left.

"Smuggling garlic on board. You believe that?"

Poppy laughed. "Fine, don't tell me. You just better not be ripping the poor guy off. If I hear about missing luggage, I won't hesitate to go straight to the German Tank," she said, using one of several nicknames the staff had given to Blitz.

"You won't," Gabe promised. Then he thanked her, and when she left and he closed the door behind her, he climbed up to the top bunk and stared down at the trunk in the middle of the floor, wondering what the hell he was supposed to do with the little vampire now that Abe was in jail.

Stewards went from door to door to make sure every last passenger had left their room with their carry-on items, as they did at the end of every trip. Only two people were unaccounted for, and one—Mags O'Keefe—had been reported missing by her fiancé the other day. The other was a high-profile guest, the film producer Ernie Wallis. His plus-one didn't appear to be all that concerned, more interested in the lack of bars on her cell phone as she and her little dog wandered off toward their cabana. The chief steward made a note to speak with Emory once the Jackmans were done with their little speeches. With the missing utility tender and two crew members gone AWOL, she thought it was likely they'd seen the film producer fall overboard and gone after him in the boat. Certainly, neither the porter nor the janitor had a record of bad behavior that would lead her to believe they'd kidnapped him. Or worse.

Emory and Erzsébet—known as Tess to the crowd gathered in the amphitheater—made a production out of their traditional welcome to the island, and while some believed the greeting violated unspoken rules about cultural appropriation, those who'd been to the island retreat before agreed Mrs. Jackman looked far more vibrant and youthful than the last time they'd seen her. "For those of you returning to Little Pearl, welcome back," Emory said at the end of his five-minute production. "For you new faces, I'm sure you'll all come to think of it as the jewel of the U.S. Virgin Islands as Tess and I do. Or at least the pearl." While the audience chuckled at his little joke, he put an arm around Erzsébet's waist and hugged her to him. Though the smile on her face might appear genuine to everyone in the audience, Emory felt her stiffen, and his thoughts returned to the knife blade she'd held at his neck, causing him to wonder if she'd let him live through the night.

While the new guests on Little Pearl were engaged by the Jackmans, Blitz drove their latest acquisition directly to the manor at the base of Mt. Elsinore, which was actually just a very large hill named after Emory's mother. The girl was alive, or so Blitz believed, but seemed to be only minimally functional. She wouldn't answer his questions yet followed instructions without dissent, like someone who'd accidentally worn too many scope patches.

Clarissa herself felt oddly at peace. The island was beautiful and the air smelled exquisite, a mixture of sea breeze, savory conifer and sweet flowers. The only thing she didn't like was having to wear a black hooded cloak, sunglasses and gloves to protect her skin from the sun. As she looked over her new surroundings, her thoughts traveled to the future. She hoped she would get an opportunity to see rest of the island, and that her new foster parents might take her on a tour after the sun set. She was eager to meet her new sisters, and hoped they were nice. She thought of how lucky she was to have found foster parents like Mr. and Mrs. Jackman, and was sure she'd grow to love living here on this beautiful island paradise.

While the new boss drove Clarissa to the manor, Journee and two of her colleagues used two of the Land Cruisers to bring the three detainees to the island jail, which had six cells as opposed to the two in the *Ceres*'s brig. Each detainee got his own, and with the man who was already there—awaiting transfer to a prison on the mainland—it left two cells empty. There were always one or two crimes committed on Little Pearl, beyond the ones sanctioned by its owners, and Journee figured they would likely need the space. Jasper Trip, one of the new hires, filled her in on the details of the guy in the far cell once they'd gotten settled. His crime was chilling, to say the least. Journee didn't even want to look at the guy, let alone have to deal with him until they were able to get him transferred off the island.

Abraham was tired as they placed him in his cell. He'd found sleep difficult on the small cot in the brig, especially since the other prisoners had been chatting throughout the night. Lacking a decent sleep, he doubted he'd be fully functional for several days. Still, he was happy to discover the cots here were slightly wider and more comfortable. He threw a pillow over his head and slept while Sven and the portly gentleman with the hangover spoke with the new fellow in the furthest cell.

Sven was eager to face the tribunal Blitz had promised. He hoped to testify in front of a jury of his peers about his proof that Emory Jackman and his wife were involved in sex trafficking minors to adult men on this island. Even if everyone in the courtroom were involved in the conspiracy, he felt that knowing that if he was able to uncover the truth, it would eventually surface elsewhere, with or without him, and knowing so would strike fear in their hearts. Perhaps one or more of them would swallow their pride and turn on their hosts for immunity or a lesser sentence. Stranger things had happened.

"What'd they get you for?" Tino asked.

Sven turned from watching the vampire hunter who'd joined

them in the brig late last night to the man who'd been here when they arrived. His maniacal eyes were sunken in deep dark pits, and his curly black hair was a haystack upon his crown. Smudges of soot streaked his face and stained his clothing. At the question from Sven's new acquaintance, the man looked up slowly with a grin spreading across his face like Anthony Perkins in *Psycho*.

"Arson," the detainee said, and left it at that.

"Arson?" Tino barked a laugh. "You bring any s'mores?"

"I set fire to a cabana," the man said, ignoring the sarcastic jab. "A man was inside. He's in the hospital recovering from third-degree burns."

"Did you… *know* there was anyone inside?" Sven asked.

"I knew. I was told he'd be there. I was told to burn him alive."

"Jeeeezus!" Tino said.

Sven was less impressed, having dealt with many criminals in his time as a journalist, a handful of them multiple murderers. "Shouldn't your co-conspirator be in here with us?"

"Yeah, where's your partner, Berkowitz?"

"Berkowitz?" Sven asked.

"Son of Sam," Tino said.

"Ah yes, of course. The serial murderer. I wrote an article about his claims to have been a part of a Satanic cult."

"*My liege!*" the arsonist exclaimed, so loud that Abraham awoke with a grumble and rolled onto his side. Sven felt his testicles climb into his abdomen at the sound of the man's voice. "They claim *he doesn't exist*! They say I *made him up*!"

"They said the same of Berkowitz," Sven said. "Why do they believe this man is a figment of your imagination?"

The man's grin widened. His teeth were speckled and stained with bits of black grime as if he'd eaten handfuls of ash from the fire he'd created. "He speaks to me in my mind," he told them, tapping his temple. "My Master's voice is *powerful*. When he speaks, *you do well to listen*!"

Tino turned to Sven with a roll of his eyes. "Yeah, sure thing, buddy."

"So I set the cabana on fire and watched the man burn, until they pulled me away laughing, and the volunteer firefighters put out the blaze."

Having already heard an equally unbelievable tale from the

vampire hunter, Sven was less skeptical. "Tell me, does your master have a name?"

The wild man stood abruptly and leaped at the bars, causing both Sven and Tino to sit up straight on their cots. "*My Master is The Unnamed! He is Evil Incarnate! He is the Prince of Darkness himself!*"

"Sounds like a bunch of names to me," Tino muttered.

Sven ignored him, focused on his thoughts. "Has your master ever gone by another name? The Duke, perhaps?"

The arsonist startled, letting go of the bars and taking several steps back. His eyes widened further and he pointed a gnarled finger toward Sven. "*Do not dare invoke him! He hears all! He SEES all!*"

Tino blew out a breath. "This guy's fuckin Looney Tunes."

"Perhaps," Sven said. "If I were to tell you something in confidence, Tino, would you swear never to repeat it?"

Tino huffed. "Cross my heart and hope to die," he said, making the sign of the cross. "You and me, we're practically brothers now. My word is my bond."

Sven watched the arsonist—who may or may not be The Duke's servant, or the vampire's *familiar*, he believed they were called—sit back on his cot and close his eyes, clasping his hands under his sharp chin as if in prayer. Then he said, "Perhaps I should start from the beginning…"

Gabe sat in the upper bunk staring down at Abraham's trunk, once again the last living person on the ship, although this time he had unwanted company. Aware of the incident from Gabe's past on an island much like this one—though unpopulated—the chief steward had confirmed with Mr. Jackman when Gabe was hired that he'd be allowed full run of the kitchen and premises while the others were ashore. Typically, he'd found this time away from others refreshing. Though he liked people, he was solitary by nature. He assumed he must've gotten used to being alone early because of the time he'd spent stranded on the island when he was three. The coast guard had never been able to tell him how long he'd been on the island, but judging by the state of his parents' bodies, it had likely been at least several days. All they knew for sure was that they had departed from Boothbay Harbor in Maine three weeks prior to Gabe's rescue. His parents had died several days before they'd found him, so it was assumed they'd been on the island for at least that, and possibly as long as a week. Even considering the unexpected cyclone that had apparently beached their boat, it would've taken them ten to eleven days to reach the island they'd been discovered on, depending on the wind.

Of course, no one could say how he'd managed to survive for even one or two days, a toddler alone on a deserted island. His parents, judging by their injuries, had been attacked by large bats, likely while searching for food in the cave in which their bodies were found. The strangest part was that the claw and bitemarks were quite larger than that of even the largest mammal endemic to the U.S. Virgin Islands, the fisherman bat. It was presumed that non-native flying foxes may have populated the island from a passing ship, though none had been seen by the coast guard during their search.

Maybe it was a vampire, Gabe thought, eyeing the trunk. *Wouldn't it be weird if my parents were killed by a vampire just like Clarissa and Ava's?* He let out a caustic laugh.

Not likely, he told himself. *First of all, the odds are pretty damn near astronomical. And second, if a vampire killed my parents why am I still alive?*

In the suddenly eerie silence, his thoughts returned to Clarissa. If she was on the island, whether or not they'd turned her into a vampire like Ava said, it meant she was in very real danger. He didn't want to think about it but she could be forced to have sex with men like Ernie Wallis if he didn't do something about it. Abraham wasn't around to help him. Poppy had told Gabe she'd seen him driven off by Journee and one of the other guards toward the island jail, along with the journalist and the music producer's son. He could wait around, hoping Digby and Cheery would manage to reach the island, but it was entirely possible they'd never make it here at all. Digby could have drowned, for all Gabe knew. And as nervous as she made him, Ava didn't need to be watched. She likely wouldn't wake again until the sun went down.

Knowing he couldn't sit around all day watching Abe's luggage, Gabe leaped down off the top bunk. He had to do something. He had to save Clarissa.

Which meant, no matter how nervous the idea of it made him,

he had to go ashore.

"Pull up your big-boy pants," he told himself. "Just this once and you never hafta set foot on another island again in your life. Do it for Abe. Do it for Clarissa. Do it for Mom and Dad."

As he opened the door to the hall, he thought he heard quiet laughter from behind him.

When he looked back trunk was still where they'd left it, latched and unmoved.

"I'll be back for you," he told Ava. Whether she was awake or not, she didn't respond. He left the room, locked the door and returned to the mooring platform. The stairs were still down. He trudged down them, heavy from the weight of knowing he'd be stepping off the end of the deck onto the island for the first time.

Little Pearl was lush and green, rising in the middle to the pointed apex of Mt. Elsinore, with a long white beach and guest cabanas to the north of the docks, and the main buildings to the south. Emory's observatory was just visible peeking up from the trees on the southwest of the island. The jail and security office were further inland, closer to the northwest shore. Gabe decided he'd go there first to check in on Abe. He knew it was unlikely, but he thought he'd try to convince Journee and them to let the old man go. The island was about two and a half miles at its widest, and the jail was about two-thirds of that distance. He considered taking one of the four-wheelers in the hangar, but figured it shouldn't take too long to walk.

Stopped at the foot of the ramp leading to the platform up on land, Gabe's stomach clenched with anxiety. This was as far as he'd ever gotten before. He'd never expected to feel the need to travel any further.

"This is it," he said, psyching himself for the final few steps. His right foot felt weighted down as he took the first. The left felt even heavier on the second. On the third, the weight began to lift. On the fourth and fifth, it was like he'd never felt it at all. Anxiety still gnawed at him, but physically he felt fine.

Maybe this won't be so bad after all, he thought. *Maybe I've been working this up in my head to be somethin bigger than it is for way too long. I probably shoulda done this years ago. Face my fears and all that.*

Thinking this, he stepped off the ramp onto the platform. Then he leaped down off the platform onto the soft white sand, and looked back at the ship in awe.

"I did it," he said aloud. "I'm on the island."

With a proud smile, he took off his shoes and socks, one at a time, and held them in one hand as he walked down to the water's edge, hot sand between his toes. He walked out until the water was up to his ankles. It felt amazing, immediately making him want to strip down to his skivvies and dive in. But he had business to take care of first. If things went well, then maybe he'd go in for a swim. Maybe Clarissa would, too.

My daddy is very near.

Ava's words from earlier echoed in his mind suddenly, causing him to shiver despite the warm sea breeze. He got out of the water and returned to the platform, where he wiped the sand off his feet and put his shoes and socks back on.

Gabe didn't know where The Duke might be hiding, but he had until sundown to do what needed to be done. He'd managed several voyages to Little Pearl without ever encountering the Vampire King, and no one on the staff had mentioned seeing a monster, nor had they ever mentioned anyone going missing.

He's gotta be feeding somehow. Not like he's gonna eat fish.

This brought a bitter laugh from Gabe, and he began his trek up the beach, then along the stone walkway between cabanas raised up on stilts. As he passed, he noticed one of the cabanas had been burned almost to the ground, only charred pieces of the frame still remaining.

Hope nobody was in it when that happened, he thought, and continued on from path toward the main road leading to the jail.

PRISONERS

THE MANOR HOUSE belonging to Mr. and Mrs. Jackman was empty when the massive security guard led Clarissa inside and down a flight of stairs to a darkened bedroom with no windows. Once there, he left the room and locked the door, allowing her to finally remove the hooded cloak and sunglasses he'd made her wear. She was hot and sweating, and wearing the shades inside made it difficult for her to see the beautiful surroundings in the rest of the house.

The bedroom he led her to was spacious, with lacy curtains drawn over a large four-poster bed of dark, ornately carved wood, a rolltop desk, a vanity and mirror inlaid with gold gilt, a plush carpet with an exotic-looking design. An impressionist painting of a young Victorian woman in a white dress having a picnic by the waterside hung on the wall beside the vanity. Lambs cavorted in the grass beyond the large tree she sat below. A bookcase stood beside a chaise lounge near the windows. She crossed to it and found it filled with old books with dusty cloth covers, from Brontë to Jules Verne, not a single paperback, and none of them recent.

Nothing here felt like home to her. It was all very nice to look at but impersonal, like a bed and breakfast from the 19th century. It lacked any sense of flair or personality, unlike what she'd managed to see in the upstairs rooms they'd passed through.

Filled with a sudden sense of despair, Clarissa opened all the drawers in the vanity and found them stuffed with new-looking underwear, socks, tops and pajamas. Many of them still had tags. She opened the wardrobe to discover dozens of hanging blouses and skirts and dresses. They all looked very nice and very adult but none of them felt like *hers*.

Studying herself in the vanity mirror, she noticed her face looked very sickly, with pale skin and deep bags under her eyes.

She hadn't seen the black velvet choker around her neck earlier, similar to the one Tess had been wearing the night before. Hers had a cameo made from mother of pearl, a bird in a cage carved into its iridescent material. Clarissa reached up to touch it when the door unlocked, startling her.

"Welcome, my darling," Tess said as she entered the room.

Clarissa turned, lowering her hand from her throat. "Where are my things?" she demanded, not wanting to sound accusatory but unable to feel otherwise.

A frown of confusion marred the woman's beautiful face. "Your… things?"

"My clothes." Clarissa shrugged. "I dunno. Shouldn't I have *things*?"

"There is new clothing in the wardrobe and vanity."

"I'm not talking about clothes. I mean… most people have *things*, right? Stuff they've collected, old toys, maybe, or books, or CDs—" She stopped suddenly, wondering why she'd mentioned CDs. Everything was on your phone now, wasn't it? She didn't think CDs were really a thing anymore but she was certain she'd seen one, even *listened* to one very recently. "Don't I have a phone, or anything? A purse? Where's my birth certificate? Where's my library card?"

"Your foster parents did not mention a… library card." Tess laid a comforting hand on her shoulder. For some reason, Clarissa had to fight from shrinking away from the woman's touch. "I am sorry, Clarissa. I would like for you to feel comfortable here in your new home, however when we came to collect you, you carried nothing. Your foster parents stated they would ship your things to the island, as we had to depart sooner than expected."

The explanation seemed to make sense but it didn't satisfy Clarissa's anxiety. She wouldn't have packed a small bag of stuff to carry with her? Not a purse or a single item of luggage?

None of this made any sense.

"I think I need to lie down," she said.

"Yes, that is very wise. You are likely suffering from the effects of your illness. Confusion is a common manifestation."

She helped Clarissa back to bed, drawing the curtains aside for her. Clarissa laid down against the springy pillows, beginning to hyperventilate. Tess brushed her hair from her forehead and smiled comfortingly.

"Let me fetch you a cool washcloth."

"No," Clarissa said, shaking her head. She didn't want a cool cloth. It would make her think of her mother, and it hurt too much to think of a woman whose face or even name she didn't remember. She thought she might cry, and Tess had said the night before she needed to conserve her bodily fluids because of her mystery disease.

"Very well," Tess said, and began to leave the room. "Rest now. I will introduce you to your sisters this evening."

The thought of meeting other girls her age made her feel slightly better, but something still troubled her. "Tess?"

The woman turned at the door. "Yes, my darling?"

"Is there… a cure?"

"A cure?" Tess clucked her tongue with a shake of her head. "No. But there are ways to stave off the worst of the symptoms. Your sisters and I will teach them to you tonight."

Clarissa stared at the door for a long time after Tess left the room. She didn't think she'd ever be able to sleep, with all of the thoughts circling her mind, but eventually the darkness of the large bedroom lulled her into a soporific state and her eyes drifted shut.

She slept.

With the road stretching over the lower part of Mt. Elsinore and twisting through the dry subtropical forest, it only took Gabe about forty minutes to reach the security office, but he was exhausted by the time he entered. He was glad to see Journee behind the desk, rather than any of her colleagues. Particularly Blitz.

"Gabe," she said with a smile. Then she gave him a curious look. "Don't you usually stay on the boat?"

"Yeah. But I needed to talk to you and I didn't get a chance before everyone debarked."

"I guess it must be real important then."

"It is. I think someone on the security team might have arrested my friend."

Journee glanced back into the monitor room. One of the other guards, a young beanpole of a guy named Jasper Tripp, who everyone on the crew called "Trip," or "Trippy" sometimes because he acted kind of braindead like he was constantly high, sat watching the monitors, eating a tuna sandwich judging by the look and smell. Journee stood and closed the door, leaving it open a crack, then stepped around the desk to speak with Gabe confidentially.

"Which one is he? The reporter, the old guy or the drunk yahoo from *Jersey Shore*? Please, just tell me he's not the guy who nearly killed Lewis Caspian burning down his cabana."

"The old guy," Gabe said. "Wait. Who tried to kill Caspian?"

Lewis Caspian was one of the only permanent residents on Little Pearl, a pharmaceutical genius worth somewhere around a hundred billion dollars. His company, before he'd walked away, had invented several so-called "wonder drugs," including a strong competitor to Viagra.

"Creepy white guy with hair like a young Albert Einstein," Journee replied, demonstrating what it might look like with her hands. "Looks like the kind of guy who'd prowl cemeteries at night looking for fresh graves, if you follow me."

"Did he say why?"

"Yeah." She squinched up her face in disgust. "But it's really strange."

"What did he say?"

Journee leaned in even further. Her perfume or skin cream smelled nicer than anything he'd smelled since he'd last been with Clarissa. "He said he was listening to the voice of his 'dark lord.'"

Gabe flinched, sure he knew who she meant but hoping he was wrong. "'Dark lord'? He said that?"

"Yeah. Like someone was talking in his head, I guess. Trip was here when it happened. He said the guy was ranting and raving about his 'dark lord and master,' when he led the guy away from the fire. He said he was *laughing*." She shivered. "I don't know about this 'dark lord' business but just knowing he's back there gives me the creeps."

"No doubt," Gabe said. "How come you guys arrested Abe? Am I allowed to ask that?"

"Abraham? Blitz insisted on it. He said he was 'aiding and abetting' that stowaway girl."

Gabe had to be careful about what he planned to ask next. One thing he'd learned from playing cards with Digby was not to show your hand, even if he didn't quite know how to put that advice into practice while actually playing cards. "There was a stowaway?" he asked innocently.

She glanced back at the cracked door to the monitor room. "This is just between you and me?"

"Of course."

"We caught the girl on the pool deck Saturday night. She was wearing a disguise. I didn't realize she was a girl at first until the hat blew off in the wind. Then she just started running. Blitz caught her and said we had to take her to Mr. Jackman."

"So she's not in the cells back there?"

Journee gave him a look of dismay. "No. And I'll be honest, I didn't like how everything went down in Jackman's quarters. I don't wanna tell tales out of school but I don't think everything's cool with those two. Him and his wife. I saw on the security monitors when Emory was bringing Tess back to their room. She was all hunched over and looked just about as old as time itself. I thought she must've gotten ALS or something since the last time I saw her. Now, she's practically glowing. And this guy with his dark lord talk, burning down Lewis Caspian's cabana. " She gave Gabe a dark look. "I dunno, but I've got a bad feeling. Something fishy is going on here on Little Pearl. Whatever it is, I think you were probably smarter than the rest of us staying on the boat."

"Sounds like it," Gabe said. He wanted to warn her but what could he say? That a two-hundred-year-old vampire was living somewhere on the island, whispering in people's mind to burn people alive? That his blood kin were having sex with old rich perverts for money? That Emory Jackman and his wife had turned Clarissa into one of them? And that the only one who could stop all of this from becoming a bloodbath, Abraham Van Helsing, was locked up in the back?

"Can I… talk with Abe? I promised I'd keep an eye on his stuff for him and I really need to talk to him."

Again, Journee glanced back at the cracked door. "Gimme a second," she said, then went back around behind the desk and opened the door. "Hey, Trip, you wanna take your break now? I'm gonna have lunch with Gabe but he's gotta take care of some porter duties first. I'll keep an eye on things."

"Sure thing, Jay," Trip said from behind the door. A moment later he stepped past her out of the monitor room with a brown paper lunch bag in one hand. "Hey, Gabe. Long time, no see. What brings you ashore?"

"Hey, Jasper. Figured it was about time I see what all the fuss is about."

"Yup. Do yourself a favor. Night swimming. It's *glorious*."

Journee raised an eyebrow. "Glorious, huh?"

"I said what I said. Hold down the fort for me, huh?"

"You got it."

The second Trip left the station, Journee peered into the monitor room and watched him saunter away on the camera above the door outside. Then she said, "Okay, Trip's probably gonna go out in the woods for a joint so you've got at least five minutes until he comes back. Blitz is due from the manor house any minute though, so if you hear the gate buzz you come back here as quick as you can, you follow me?"

"You got it," Gabe said with a nod.

"All right, I'm gonna buzz you in."

She pressed a button, causing a loud buzz and the *thunk* of a magnetic lock disengaging.

"Thanks, Journee."

"Don't mention it." As Gabe headed for the gate, she called after him. "You best not be trying to bust him out or I'll put you in the cell next to the dark lord's bestie!"

"I won't!" he called back, opening the gate wide enough to slip through, then closing it behind him. He followed a long hall with cinder block walls painted white down to the cells. In the closest cell on the left, a lanky man with red hair and thick-framed glasses sat cross-legged on his cot. In the next cell down, one of their repeat guests, Tino Bravo Jr., lay across his cot propping himself up with his hands behind his head. His shirt was unbuttoned and his round belly protruded, the color of a cooked lobster.

Abe was sleeping with a pillow over his head in the closest cell on the right, his polished shoes facing the door. Two cells down from him the wild-haired man Journee had mentioned stood gripping the bars, staring directly at Gabe.

"To what do we owe the pleasure?" the lanky ginger asked. He spoke with some kind of a European accent. Gabe guessed somewhere north, like Denmark or Switzerland.

Tino sat up and grinned. "Gabe! You come to bust us out, or

what?"

"Not this time, Tino." Gabe kicked the bars of Abe's cell. The man two cells down grinned so wide Gabe could see his blackened teeth, looking like he'd been chewing on hunks of burnt meat. Gabe did his best to ignore him. "Abe, wake up!" He kicked the bars again.

The old man groaned and raised the pillow from his face. He blinked several times before looking in Gabe's direction. "Gabriel," he said with a smile crinkling the flesh around his tired eyes. He sat up with a groan. "I'm very glad to see you."

"They got Clarissa," Gabe said hurriedly. "Blitz took her to Mr. Jackman and no one's seen her since."

The old man lowered his head. "Then it's true. She has become one of them."

Gabe knew it was likely but hadn't wanted to believe it. The statement came not as a dark revelation but as a validation of his fears. "Can we change her back?"

"We must vanquish the one whose blood courses through her veins. Only then will she return to life."

"*The Master will have his bride!*" the arsonist suddenly bellowed, rattling the bars of his cell, his wild eyes fixed on Gabe. "He awaits her in the shadow of the mountain!" The creep stretched a blackened hand through the bars, pointing at Gabe. "He waits for *you*! It's *your* blood he wants!"

"This fuckin guy," Tino said. "Shut up, over there! Can't you see people are tryna have a conversation?"

"Pay him no mind," the old man told Gabe. "He has been corrupted by The Duke, but he has no power over you."

"Oh, shoot!" Gabe said, clueing in. "He's Renfield!"

"The vampire's familiar," the redhaired man said. "A rather fitting comparison, I'd say. In fact, I believe I saw him eat what appeared to be a large green cockroach moments before you stepped in. However, Officer Terrell assures us his name is Stuart Smith."

"Stu," Tino huffed. "No better name for an asshole, you ask me."

"Are we okay to talk in front of him?" Gabe asked Abe, suddenly nervous that what they might say would make it back to The Duke.

Sven answered. "Ms. Terrell informed us he'll not be leaving that cell until the ship returns to Miami."

"Yeah, but..." Gabe stepped closer to the reporter's cell. "Can he hear us or see us *through* him? I feel like there's somethin like that with the really strong vampires. Like a deep psychic connection."

"Tell me, Stuart," the reporter said. "When you speak to your master, does he ever respond?"

"The Master hears all! He SEES all!"

"Yes, you've said that before." The reporter got up from his cot and approached the bars, closer to Gabe. "I don't believe this Duke fellow can truly see and hear all, despite what Mr. Smith claims. He speaks to him, but he does not respond."

"Gabe," the old man said, leaning forward and whispering hoarsely. "You must bring our little friend to the island after sundown. She will lead you to the others and then..." Abe paused, narrowing his eyes. "You will know what to do."

"I'll know what to do," Gabe said, worried that he was in way over his head, considering what he thought Abe meant was killing the Vampire King.

"Yes," the old man said. He opened his mouth to continue but the buzz of the cell block doors interrupted him.

Trip was back from his smoke break.

Or worse: Blitz was here.

"I gotta go," Gabe said. "I'll bring—" He almost said Ava in his rush to get going, but corrected himself just in case they were wrong about The Duke and the vampire was able to see and hear through his familiar. "I'll bring *our friend* tonight."

"Yes, and Gabe..."

"Yeah?"

"Take my kit with you."

Gabe remembered the rolled leather pouch was still on the table where he'd left it last night, containing half a dozen wooden stakes, a bottle of holy water, and the last of Abe's garlic pills. He felt like an idiot for having left it there and only brought one stake with him, tucked into the waistband of his cargo shorts. It'd been poking into his thigh and left a blood stain in his right pocket. Had he really been expecting to destroy the world's most powerful vampire with a single stake?

As Gabe said a quick goodbye to Abe, Tino and the reporter, the vampire's familiar never once took his eyes off of him. When he slipped through the gate and hurried back down the hall to beat whoever Journee had warned him about to the desk, the familiar's laughter chased him down the corridor.

THE VAMPYRE

CLARISSA AWOKE AS the last vestiges of sunlight sank below Mt. Elsinore, the large bedroom—she refused to think of it as *hers*, at least for now—as dark and silent as a tomb. It even smelled like dirt. The thought of this being her bedroom forever, or until they discovered a cure for her disease, made her more homesick than ever, even though she couldn't remember the home and foster family she pined for.

She climbed out of the large bed and went to the wardrobe. With a nice flower-print chiffon dress picked out, she untied the hospital gown, put on a pair of fresh underwear from the vanity, and slipped the dress over her shoulders. It fit well, though the hem went almost all the way to the floor. A dozen or so shoes were neatly laid out at the bottom of the wardrobe, and she chose a pair of flat sandals. She knew they didn't belong to her, at least not *before*, but like Cinderella's glass slipper, they fit perfectly. Either they'd asked her foster parents, or someone must've measured her feet while she was unconscious, and they'd one of the staff stock the closet for her.

She returned to the vanity and twisted back and forth in front of the mirror, lifting the hem of the dress as she twirled. Though the nap hadn't done anything for her complexion or the dark circles under her eyes, the outfit looked nice on her. The choker and cameo went well with the dress, so she didn't bother trying to remove it.

Ready to meet the rest of her new family, Clarissa crossed to the door. She turned the handle and pulled, but it wouldn't budge. She pushed and it wouldn't open that way either. She'd forgotten both Tess and Blitz had locked the door from the outside.

Clarissa reached up and touched the cameo on the choker around her neck, with the bird in its cage. She returned to the vanity and looked at herself, suddenly curious why they'd put the choker on her. She'd almost taken it off the first time she'd noticed it and would have if Tess hadn't interrupted her. Lifting her thick curls which had fallen lifelessly over her shoulders, she reached for the clasp. It took her a few tries to find it, then she fiddled with it for almost a minute before deciding she'd be better off trying to find a pair of scissors or a knife to cut it off. She started hunting through the rolltop desk, and though she found envelopes and paper and some old-looking pens, she couldn't find anything sharp to cut the velvet band around her neck.

Just when she was beginning to consider breaking the mirror and using a shard of glass to remove it, the door unlocked and Tess entered, wearing another stunning gown, this made of the same black velvet as the choker around Clarissa's throat. She saw Clarissa standing in the middle of the room, obviously looking frantic, and gave her a troubled look.

"My darling, what is the matter? You look positively vexed."

Clarissa pointed at the choker. "Who put this on me?"

"I did," Tess admitted.

"Can you take it off, please?"

"You do not like it? It belonged to my mother, the Baroness. It is quite valuable."

Clarissa tread carefully, not wanting to upset the woman. "It itches. Please, can you take it off for me?"

Tess gave her an aggrieved look. "I'm sorry, my darling. I have deceived you."

Clarissa's heartbeat quickened, expecting the woman to drop the bombshell: that she wasn't really her adoptive mother but a kidnapper desperate for a daughter of her own. There were no sisters. No Mr. Jackman. It was just the two of them.

"The choker covers quite a large gash across your throat from an emergency surgery due to your condition. I believed it would be too jarring for you to see such an ugly scar, marring your rare beauty, so I gave you the cameo from my own casket, which my dear departed mother gave to me."

Clarissa frowned, studying her reflection. "Shouldn't I have bandages?"

The woman clucked her tongue. "It is a very small scar."

"But bad enough I have to wear this," she said, touching the black velvet.

"Yes."

There was no logic to what the woman was saying, but Clarissa didn't think it was worth continuing to argue over, at least when there were more pressing questions on her mind. "When can I see my sisters?"

The woman smiled. Clarissa hadn't seen her smile since they were back on the ship, and she noticed now how sad it appeared. "I am happy you ask," Tess said, not looking very happy at all. "This is the reason I come to you now. To take you to your sisters."

"Really?" Excitement bloomed in Clarissa's heart for the first time since she'd awakened in the makeshift hospital bed. She was eager to see someone her own age, who might share her troubles.

Tess held out a hand for her. "Come. You look lovely."

"Thank you."

Clarissa took the woman's hand. She expected warmth, since her own hands felt so cold, but it was surprisingly even colder. Tess led her to the door, opened it, then ushered her out into the hall, locking the door behind them with a large brass key. The corridor stretched a long way to the left of the bedroom with no other doors nor windows, just paintings with dark scenarios and gaslit sconces along the walls between them. They walked that way, their footfalls echoing.

"Where are we?" Clarissa asked.

"We are in the basement beneath the manor."

Clarissa shivered, hugging herself. "Why is it so cold?"

"The manor was built upon subterranean caverns. The air may cause quite a chill if one is not properly attired. Fortunately, your sisters are in a different part of the manor."

They remained silent for some time after that, as Tess led her down one corridor and the next. Clarissa had too many questions to decide which to ask next and her hostess offered nothing further. They passed many imposing wooden doors like her own, and more dark pastoral paintings set between flickering wall sconces. She heard voices behind one of them, as well as familiar small squeaks and the clatter of wood on wood. Occasionally the corridor became colder, as if behind the doors the caverns led deeper underground. Eventually, they reached a door which surprised her by opening on a set of stairs leading further down rather than up. Sconces lit the way down.

Tess began her descent.

"Tess?"

"Yes, my darling?"

"Where are we going?"

The woman smiled back at her. "Do not fret. We are almost there."

Clarissa followed her down. After a time, the wooden walls and stairs gave way to bald stone, the sconces replaced by dripping candles inset within the rock. Cobwebs as thick as the curtains over the bed in her new room draped across the rough ceiling. Her breath plumed out in front of her.

Just when it seemed like it wasn't possible to go any further down, the stairwell ended in a large, dark chamber. It smelled horrid here, not just like damp earth and stone but sour, rancid animal feces and sickly sweet, rotting vegetation. Tess brushed away cobwebs and plucked a lit lantern from a recess in the wall. She held it aloft, illuminating the cave walls receding off to their sides, an area of smoothed stone floor from which stalagmites rose like jagged teeth, and a portion of the ceiling—about twenty feet above their heads—from which stalactites drooped like dripping candle wax. Dark shapes flittered back and forth within the light, wings flapping.

Bats, Clarissa thought, her entire body shuddering in the cold. "My sisters live down here?" she asked dubiously.

"No, my darling. Hold this, please?"

Tess held out the lamp. Clarissa took it and watched the woman remove a small switchblade from the sash on her gown. Tess drew it quickly across her own palm, wincing as the flesh split and her blood began to patter on the floor of the cave. She closed her hand into a fist and slipped the blade back into her sash just as quickly as it had emerged.

With the blood flow slowing, a serpentine hiss came from the darkness beyond the lamp's light. Clarissa turned to see two pearls of red shimmer like drops of blood beneath a full moon.

Eyes, she thought, horrified. Whatever animal they belonged to was at least as big as a man. She tried to turn and run but Tess caught her by the wrist and held her firm.

"Your sisters do not live here," the woman said, snatching the lamp from her and raising it. "*Your betrothed does.*"

Clarissa recoiled at the sight of the inhuman creature before them, though Tess prevented her from fleeing. Even curled up like a fetus against a grouping of stalagmites, it appeared impossibly tall, and although it was humanoid its legs looked more like a four-legged animal's, with clawed feet as long as a typical human shin. Its flesh was pale as milk, the network of black veins reminiscent of the gown Tess had worn earlier. Every rib was visible, yet its belly was distended. The lower half of its face and most of its chest were stained black as if it had been messily slurping from a bowl of oil. Its face was worse, something like the bats that still flittered above them, with its pug nose and fangs and large eyes as black as the stains on its chest, shimmering in the glow of the lamp. Pointed ears rose from the center of its face in lieu of eyebrows. Its hands hung loose at its sides, with long, clawed fingers webbed like fetal wings, and it reached out and grabbed protectively for something lying beside it, closer to the stalagmites. The shadows parted, revealing what looked like a desiccated human corpse clothed in rags. Bones—*human* bones—littered the ground around them.

"*What is that thing?*" Clarissa gasped, her breath pluming out in front of her.

"*He* is Duke Ștefan of Moldavia," Tess said. "He is the oldest living vampyre. And he is to be your husband."

"No! You can't make me!"

Tess gripped her firmly and pushed her two steps toward the creature. "Would you rather be eaten? I can arrange for that quite as easily."

Clarissa stared in panicked horror at the monster and its victim. She couldn't imagine how terrible being eaten by this thing would be, but being *married* to it—as if it were *human*?

Unfathomable.

As she began to weep, the creature uttered something which sounded like words, its wide animal lips not quite able to form them. Then they curled in a rictus grin, revealing dozens of fangs with extremely prominent canine teeth. The sound it made next was a hideous mix of laughter and growling.

"Come," Tess said harshly, pulling her away by the wrist, back toward the stairwell in the cave wall.

Clarissa glanced back over her shoulder to be certain the

monster wasn't creeping up behind them, but it remained in its nest, though as the lamplight retreated, she saw it drag the corpse onto its belly and bite into its throat.

They ascended the steps carved into the rock in a hurry, Tess dragging her along. As her tears subsided, Clarissa thought she finally understood what the creature had said. It was three simple words, but they chilled her to the bone.

"*We will feeeeeeed.*"

In one of the basement bedrooms, Emory used a crowbar to open the second last of the six crates Lionel had gifted them. Six crates for six girls. The lid pried off too easily, as if it had been opened multiple times before, and slammed against the floor behind it. At least one nail was missing and another had been bent flat against the underside of the lid. Back on the ship, he'd been relatively certain that someone had accidentally—*bad*—or intentionally—*worse*—released one of the girls, and here was the proof. He kicked himself for not having looked into it further on the voyage, but he hadn't wanted to run the risk of releasing all of them while looking to see which one had murdered the girl that he'd promised to Erzsébet. They'd have been sleeping during the day, but who knew what sort of damage they might do if disturbed? Especially if it had been more than one of them feeding on Mags O'Keefe.

"Fuck," he said.

Blitz leaned over him. "Fuck what, sir?"

Even the dirt level was much lower than the others had been. Emory gripped the stake in his hand tighter in anger. "This crate's been opened. More than once, by the look."

Blitz scowled. He reached into the dirt with hands that were already grimy from revealing the other girls who'd been sleeping within their beds of cool earth. He dug and dug but found nothing.

"*Fuuuuuuck,*" Emory said. "I *knew* we should have searched the ship when that dumb bitch model died!"

"I checked the crates, like you told me to. They seemed undisturbed." Blitz frowned and looked off, as if rethinking what he'd said. "Plus, we never informed the crew or guests about the stowaway."

"I didn't wanna cause any concern before the auction. Same reason we didn't alert people about the stowaway. If *anyone* suspected one of the girls had gotten free…"

The house of cards would come crashing down around us, he thought but didn't say.

"Head back to the *Ceres*," he told his security chief. "Search every fucking room. Every *corner*. I want this girl *found*, Blitz. If she gets to the others, there's no telling what the fuck might happen. Do you understand me?"

"Yes, sir. And bring her back here?"

"No. This one's had a taste of blood. She'll need to be taken care of."

"Understood," Blitz said. He stared down into the empty heap of dirt in the crate, his brow furrowed.

"*Fucking NOW, Blitz!*"

"Yes, sir," Blitz repeated. He turned stiffly and marched out of the room. The door slammed behind him.

Emory stood staring into the crate for a long time. This was supposed to be the little one, the youngest of his Little Pearls. Lionel had said he'd taken her when she was seven years old, according to the newspaper clippings he'd read about her kidnapping and the murder of her parents.

I bet she's tighter than a vice grip, Emory thought. Not that he was into preteens, but he'd had plenty of requests for them from his guests. He knew at least three who'd be disappointed to find she might no longer be available, especially the creep who'd won her in the auction.

Emory could only hope that Blitz would find her on the ship and she'd be reduced to a small pile of ash before nightfall.

God only knew what might happen if he didn't.

DINNER

SVEN DRIFTED BACK from a dreamless sleep in which he was being chased by a giant green cockroach through a warren of underground tunnels and discovered the very creature cavorting about on his chest. He flicked it off in distaste and rolled over, yawning and stretching. Abraham was asleep in the cell across from him. Tino snored in the next cell. The arsonist, Stuart Smith, was at his bars again—or *still*—gripping them and staring directly at Sven. Sven felt his scrotum shrivel as though he'd plunged into an ice bath. Even though the two of them were locked in separate cages, the arsonist made him nervous. If he truly was an emissary of the Vampire King, Sven suspected the familiar would do his utmost to get to each of them, be it physically or via psychic warfare. He'd already been doing his best to upset them with his talk of the "dark lord and master" hearing and seeing everything.

Sven sat up and stared back at the man, trying not to be the first to blink. After nearly thirty seconds his eyes hurt too much to keep them open any longer and he finally had to blink. He couldn't be certain, but he suspected the familiar hadn't shut his eyes even while his own were closed, and he imagined the man had been staring at him for quite some time before he'd awakened to find him that way.

"*Din jävla djävul*," Sven muttered, lying back down against the hard pillow and turning to face the wall to show the devil he wasn't afraid of him, though he was as frightened as a young child whose feet hung over the edge of his bed.

Another buzz sounded down the corridor, followed by the hard-soled footsteps Sven recognized as likely belonging to one of the guards. He sat up again and swung his legs off the edge of the cot just as the young female guard, Journee Terrell, entered the holding cell area.

"Sven?" she said, looking in his direction.

"Yes, ma'am."

The woman frowned. "You can call me Journee or guard or Mrs. Terrell, but never ma'am, are we clear?"

Sven smiled graciously. "My apologies, Journee."

"No trouble, Sven, just don't do it again. I'm here to escort you to the manor house. Mr. Jackman requested your presence."

Sven bristled. "Am I to face a tribunal?"

Journee opened the outer bars, then approached Sven's cell. "He didn't say that. He just said dinner."

"Dinner," he said dubiously.

"That's right." She used one of the keys on the keychain hung from her belt buckle to unlock his cell door. "Come with me, please."

"Hey, Sven! You show the big guy what's what, huh?"

Journee locked a pair of handcuffs on Sven's wrists. "Thank you, Tino. I hope your release is imminent."

"Safest place on the island right now, ain't it?"

"It may be, Tino. It may be."

The old man had sat up and raised his cane in farewell. "Godspeed, Mr. Olsen."

"Thank you, Abraham. And thank you again for confiding in me. I wish you good luck."

The old man gave him a single nod, and Journee led Sven out of the bullpen.

"Have you ever been invited for dinner at the Jackmans' manor, Journee?"

"Me?" Journee barked a laugh. "Not likely. I don't even think Blitz has." She walked him out into the main part of the security station. The man she'd called Trip sat in the room watching the monitors.

"Where is Blitz, at the moment?"

"Last I heard he was back on the boat."

"Last minute security checks?"

Journee gave him a suspicious sidelong glance. "Never you mind. Trip," she called at the open door to the monitor room, "I'll be back in a little bit. I'm just taking the reporter out to the manor house."

"Take your time, you're not missing anything here." He nodded at the CCTV screens.

Journee led Sven outside. The sun had begun to sink below the tree-lined top of the small mountain to the west of them. Shadows lurked in the jungle surrounding the station. Sven stopped suddenly, thinking back to what the familiar had said about his dark lord. *He awaits her in the shadow of the mountain.* Yes, that was it. Was The Duke's lair hidden somewhere on this side of Mt. Elsinore?

Journee opened a back door to one of the Land Cruisers they'd arrived in. "Get in, please."

Sven climbed in. She shut the door, went around the front, and got in behind the steering wheel. "Buckle your seatbelt," she said, clicking her own into place.

With his hands cuffed, Sven struggled with it but managed to get it locked in place as they pulled out of the small lot and started driving down the gravel road.

"Are there any caves on the island?" he asked.

Journee raised an eyebrow at him in the rearview mirror. "Caves? Not that I'm aware of. But I don't go exploring all that often. I'm more of a reading in a hammock on the beach type of girl."

"What do you read?"

"Oh, you know, Stephen King, Dean Koontz, Thomas Harris. Horror and thrillers, mostly."

Sven grinned. "Is that so? What are you reading at the moment?"

She smirked. "Promise you won't laugh?"

"I would never judge someone based on what they choose to read for pleasure, no matter the subject."

"The *Twilight* books," Journee said guiltily. "They're trash but they're addictive, you know what I mean?"

"Ah, yes. The sparkly vampires."

Journee smiled wistfully. "I just love stories about love conquering all, even after death. Maybe that makes me weird."

"I don't think it makes you weird at all. In fact, I think it makes you normal. Everyone loves a happy ending."

Her smile faltered. "Yeah, maybe. Look, I'm sorry we had to bust you. It doesn't really seem fair, you just doing your job and all."

"I committed a crime. Whether justly or not, I must be called to face the consequences."

"Well, I don't think it's right. In fact, between you and me, I'm pretty sure something strange is going on the island. Maybe even illegal."

"What makes you think so, Journee?"

"Just little things. And after the other day, taking that little stowaway girl up to see the Jackmans? I've decided I'll be handing in my resignation and taking the next trip back to Miami."

"I think that's a wise idea."

With a shrewd look, she said, "You know a lot more than you're telling me, don't you?"

"If I told you what I know, Journee, I don't think you would bother handing in your resignation. I think you would stop the vehicle right this moment, walk away, find the closest boat, and drive as far away as you can as swiftly as you are able."

"That bad, huh?"

"That bad."

She chuckled bitterly. "I guess I don't want to know then. At least not yet. I can't drive a boat, and I'm sure as hell not gonna row."

"I can drive a boat, Journee. I wrote an exposé on illegal fishing for *Sportsman Magazine*. The crew I was with taught me everything one might need to know about the open sea."

She locked eyes with him. "Ask me again after your dinner with the Jackmans. I don't wanna get fired before I can quit."

Sven nodded. He suspected he wouldn't last through his dinner with Emory and Tess, but he didn't push his luck. Instead, he hoped the vampire uprising might begin before the Jackmans could do anything to harm him. And if so, that the girls would see he was on their side, and spare his life.

After the reporter left with their jailor, the familiar began staring at Abraham through the bars two cells down, trying to intimidate him rather than their weaker cell mate. The New Jersian had fallen back to sleep again, snoring fitfully.

Prior to Sven's departure, Abraham had been trying to conserve his strength, getting as much sleep as he could despite the unfavorable circumstances. He'd slept through worse, during the World Wars, in particular the bombing raids when he'd lived in a flat in London, hunting several of The Duke's kin to find the whereabouts of the Vampire King himself. The apartment building he'd been living in had collapsed during the night, while he'd been out lurking the Blitz-ravaged streets. If he hadn't slept during the daytime—which still suffered its share of bombings, as well as many firefights in the air above the city—he'd have died along with many of his neighbors.

Or more likely, considering The Duke's blood coursing through his veins, he'd have survived but been severely injured, a walking, mangled corpse.

"Familiar," he said, addressing the man called Stuart Smith. "Where is your master? I'm here at his behest. Surely, he would like to address me himself."

The familiar grinned, displaying his blackened teeth. "Oh, he'll come for you, old man. When the time is nigh, he'll take what he's owed and more."

"It is he who owes. He took my family. He took my *life*."

"He *gave* you life. Just a drop of His blood made you immortal. What I wouldn't give to be like you…."

"Then you are a fool as well as a murderer. Your master's blood isn't a gift, it's a foul, loathsome thing, coursing through my tired body like the slowest-acting poison. Death is a *blessing*, familiar. I would *welcome* it as I would an old friend."

The familiar's grin spread almost impossibly wide. "You'll have your wish soon enough. Come moonrise, he will awaken. He'll set me free, his eternal servant, and he will make you *pray* you hadn't wished for death."

Abraham returned the man's grin, aware that Gabe would soon return to the island, bringing his hunting kit and the little vampire with him. "We shall see about that, familiar," he said. "We shall see."

Gabe had returned to the *Ceres*, made himself a quick sandwich even though he wasn't hungry, and returned to his room. He'd packed some clothes in a bag, just in case Clarissa might need something normal to wear, along with some snacks, two bottles of ice-cold water, and the Desert Island Disc his parents had brought with them on their final sailing trip, enclosed within its jewel case. Whether he made it off the island alive, wound up stranded there or worse, it felt fitting to have his only reminder of them close at hand. Not that he'd ever get a chance to play it.

He slung the bag over his shoulders and went upstairs to Abe's room. Even with the overwhelming sting of the bleach he could still smell Abe's cologne, the one that came in the white bottle with a ship on it, the earth from inside his trunk, and blood. He wondered if they'd ever be able to get rid of the stench of Ernie Wallis's bodily fluids, and supposed he'd be unlikely to find out himself. No matter what happened tonight, he was relatively certain he'd experienced his last voyage on the *Ceres*.

Waiting until the sun began to set, as the old man suggested, Gabe sat in Abe's chair reading the book he'd brought with him but hadn't had a chance to crack open previously. True-crime writer Martin Savage's first novel, *Witch Island*—which was sold as "autofiction," meaning part autobiography, part fiction—was pretty wild and Gabe was enjoying it so far. He'd signed it out from the Main Library, about a forty-five-minute walk from the marina, hoping to read it while everyone else was on shore. He also hoped he'd get a chance to see the movie based on the book that was apparently coming out in the next year or so—the book's cover boasted it was "SOON TO BE A MAJOR MOTION PICTURE," and he'd seen some "first look" photos of the old lady witches about a month ago—but he didn't expect he would.

Gaaaaaabe, Ava whispered in his mind.

He glanced up from the pages. "Sun ain't down yet. Get outta my head."

"*I can make you strong*," she said. This time her voice echoed from inside the trunk rather than within his mind. "*You just need to taste a drop of my blood and you'll be like me. Fly like me. Live forever.*"

"Who'd wanna live forever?"

"*My sister's already like me. If you were like us, she could love you.*"

"I don't need to cheat. If she likes me, she likes me. If she doesn't..." He shrugged, though the idea of her not even *liking* him hurt his heart to think about. "Well, I guess I'll have to get over it. Now leave me alone, I'm readin."

"*You'd have so much time to read if you were like us.*"

"Nice try."

Silence followed, long enough that he really started to think she'd leave him alone and let him read. Then she tried a different tactic: "*Wouldn't you carve her name into your flesh merely to feel her gentle caress upon your cheek?*"

The phrase shook him. Yes, he said he would do anything for Clarissa, and he was prepared to return to the island and possibly die tonight to save her from The Duke and all the sick perverts waiting on her transformation so they could do terrible things to her. But he wouldn't cut his flesh for either of them. The scent of blood would bring them running like ants to a picnic.

He stood angrily, slamming the book on the table. "Leave me alone, dammit! I wanna help your sister but I'm gonna leave you here to starve in that goddamn trunk if you don't stop hollerin at me!"

The little vampire didn't reply.

After a long stretch of silence, Gabe picked up his book and resumed reading. He was at the part where Martin Savage—a fictionalized version of the author—had just discovered his elderly, infirm mother was not quite as sickly as she appeared to be, when she danced the Charlston in the upstairs hall. The scene was effectively creepy, and when the heavy door to the stairwell slammed out in the hall, Gabe nearly threw the book across the room in alarm.

Instead, he closed the book carefully and placed it on the table beside Abe's chair, getting up as quietly as possible. He crept across the room to the door. A beep came from the hall, followed by a door being opened. His heart leapt at the thought that Digby and Cheery might've returned to the ship before he remembered he was on the wrong floor. When he reached the door, he leaned against it and peered out the peephole.

The door to a room directly across the hall, closest to the stairwell, stood open. Gabe held his breath and watched. After a long moment, Blitz stepped out of the room and closed the door behind him.

"Shit," Gabe whispered. *Why didn't you warn me?* he asked Ava in his mind, hoping she could hear him as he heard her.

You said you'd leave me here, Ava replied. *He's not gonna hurt you. He's looking for me.*

Out in the hall, Blitz went to the next door in line and opened it with his master keycard. It seemed like he was checking all the doors on the opposite side first, but Gabe didn't want to risk it. He had to let Ava out, but he wasn't sure he could trust her.

Gabe crossed quietly to the bathroom. *I'm gonna let you out, but you can't hurt anyone, okay? I want you to go into the ducts, like you did the other night. But follow me this time. Can you do that?*

He waited. When he didn't hear a reply after what seemed like a long enough time he asked, *Did you hear me?*

I nodded, she said.

Well, I can't hear you nod, can I? Just promise you won't hurt anyone, okay? And don't just nod. I need to hear it.

I promise, she said. He sensed the pout in her voice.

Okay. Gabe stepped into the bathroom and crept to the trunk. He undid both latches and raised the lid. He almost jumped when he saw Ava grinning up at him from the heaped dirt. "Jesus," he said out loud, then returned to his inner voice: *Okay, do you need me to get the vent off for you?*

Ava climbed out of the dirt and stood. The little dress she wore was filthy. He wished he had fresh clothes for her but she was too small. Nothing in his bag would fit her.

Across the hall, another door opened. Five doors on each side. Blitz had already checked three rooms. Depending on how long it took to search, he'd be at Abe's in less than five minutes.

Okay, go on then, Gabe told her in his mind.

Without hesitation, Ava leaped onto the wall, a blur of white and black. She scattered dirt on the floor and left black marks on the wall. Her fingernails worked impossibly fast, unscrewing the vent. It fell, and Gabe dashed to prevent it from hitting the floor. He caught it just as Ava disappeared into the rectangular hole.

Gabe worked swiftly then—though nowhere near as fast as if he'd taken up Ava's offer of a drop of blood—closing the trunk and leaving the bathroom, grabbing his bag and tucking Abe's leather bundle inside, then heading for the door.

He peered out the peephole just as the mountain of a man left the last room on the right and crossed the hall. Blitz used his key on that door, and stepped inside.

Gabe opened Abe's door as quietly as possible. He crept out into the hall and pulled the door shut gently. Its click made him wince.

He's coming, Ava said.

Gabe got moving. The stairwell door was heavier and would be much louder to open and shut. He just had to hope he had enough time before—

"Gabriel?"

Blitz's voice stopped him with his hand on the door. Gabe turned, trying his best to put on a calm expression. The big man was scowling. The door slammed shut behind him and Gabe couldn't help but flinch.

"Oh, hey, Blitz. How come you're back?"

"What are you doing up here, Gabriel?"

"I, uh… Guess I got off at the wrong floor."

He knows you're lying, Ava said.

You don't know that, he thought back. He smiled at Blitz, although he could tell it looked forced.

Blitz's frown deepened. "What have you got in your bag?"

In his fright, Gabe almost forgot he'd been holding it. "Just stuff. Snacks and whatnot."

"Then you wouldn't mind if I take a look."

"You don't trust me, Blitz?"

Blitz cracked his neck from one side to the other. "Let me see your bag."

Don't, Ava warned.

Gabe knew he was caught if Blitz got a look at what was inside the bag. The stakes alone would bust him. But his back was to the door. There was no way he could turn around, open it and start up the steps before Blitz would grab him by the scruff of his neck and check the bag with or without his permission.

Reluctantly, he removed the bag from one shoulder, then the next. He held it out for Blitz, who began lumbering down the hall to fetch it.

As Blitz's massive fingers gripped the shoulder strap, the vent above the middle door shot across the hall and slammed against the far wall.

Before Blitz could even turn, the little vampire leaped out of the ducts in a blur and landed on his back. He let go of the shoulder strap, and Gabe dropped the bag. Blitz reached up and grabbed at the girl's arms, wrapped around his neck. She sank her claws into his chest, tearing the fabric of his uniform. His name badge fell from his pocket and landed on the floor with a patter of blood.

The big man growled and flung the girl off of him. Ava struck the wall and dropped to the floor, then rolled into a crouch on all fours. She hissed up at him, baring fangs.

"What the hell?" Blitz said, breathing heavily, then turned to Gabe. "Stay back. I'll handle this."

"Uh, Blitz? I don't think you wanna—"

It was too late. Blitz kicked at Ava, intending to launch her back into the wall. His kick was perfectly placed and would have struck her if she hadn't already skittered up the wall, across the ceiling and leapt back down behind him before he even realized his foot hadn't made contact with anything. Blitz startled and turned, just as Ava sprung at his face.

Her claws and teeth tore at his flesh, peeling the shiny skin off the back of his head and tearing off his nose with a wet crunch. Ava dropped off his face like an insect and ate the chunk of flesh and cartilage as Blitz stumbled backward, bellowing in terror.

"*Mmmm*—much tastier than Milk," Ava said, and wiped her lips with the back of a hand.

"What the hell?" Blitz gasped, backed up against the door next to Abe's. Blood poured out of his exposed nasal openings as he stared at the creature at his feet. He turned to Gabe, his eyes white and brown spheres of terror. "*What the hell did you do, Gabriel?*"

Gabe picked up his backpack and slung it over his shoulders. "I told you not to mess with her. She's a lot stronger than she looks."

On all fours, Ava smiled up at the man, her face covered in his blood.

Gabe opened the door without turning. "Let's go, Ava."

"But I want *more*," she whined.

"And you'll *get* more on the island. I promise."

Ava pouted.

"He's not gonna try to hurt you anymore. Are you, Blitz?"

Blitz looked at the vampire in horror. He shook his head dumbly, tears spilling from his wide eyes, blood and snot oozing from the holes in his face. He sniffled, sucking it back into his sinuses. It was awe-inspiring, seeing this monster of a man reduced to a sniveling wimp by a child barely bigger than his chest.

"And you're not gonna follow us."

"*No*," Blitz said hurriedly.

"Good. It'll be safer here, but you prob'ly wanna go to your room and lock the door, just in case. And put somethin over your nose, before you bleed to death."

Blitz nodded again. He winced as he tried to cover the gaping holes with a hand.

"You ready?" Gabe asked Ava.

The girl stood and nodded. She held out a grimy, blood-streaked hand to him. Gabe took it.

"Let's go find your sister," he said. He led the way into the stairwell.

"*Wait*," she hissed.

"What?"

She pointed. "His walkie-talkie."

"Shoot, that's a good call." Gabe let go of her hand and approached Blitz. The guard reared back in fear. "I need to take your walkie-talkie, Blitz."

"W-what?"

Gabe snatched it off the man's belt. "Can't have you radioing ahead to spoil our plans."

"I'm done with all that! I promise!"

"Well, I guess I trust you just about as much as you trust me." Gabe fixed the walkie to his own belt, alongside the stake tucked into his waistband. He shrugged. "No hard feelins, big guy."

Blitz nodded again. It seemed to be just about the only thing he was capable of doing.

Gabe took the girl's hand again and led her up the stairs. At the top of the final stairwell, he opened the door a crack, making sure the sun had gone down fully, before letting Ava out into the fresh air on the deck.

He took a deep breath, smelling the sea and foliage, wanting to savor it, certain it would be his last night alive, one way or the other.

Then he led the child vampire onto Little Pearl Island, well aware that what he'd let her eat of Blitz had been a light snack, and that for her to be strong enough to help him free her sister, she'd have to feed again soon.

THE TRUTH

SVEN GOT OUT of the Land Cruiser when Journee opened the door for him, and regarded at the house nestled within the foliage at the base of Mt. Elsinore towering over it.

It looked like something out of a Southern Gothic novel, which Sven thought was fitting considering the Jackmans had slaves: a large white house with columns holding up the veranda and balcony stretching its entire length. Rather than ivy creeping up its walls like a house from a horror film, large vines hung from its rooftops, draping over it like the shaggy hair of a wild beast. With the sky above turned the deep purple of a bruise, it was every bit the imposing manse Sven had expected.

Journee shut the door behind Sven and led him up the walkway. As the crushed brick crunched under their feet, Sven couldn't help but think of this as a death row prisoner's last walk toward the execution chamber. The house looked charming enough and the scents wafting from within—redolent of fats and exotic spices—smelled heavenly, but he was sure this meal would be his last.

The Little Pearls *director was allowed to leave*, he reminded himself. *True,* his analytical mind countered, *but his memory was wiped clean somehow. Whether or not I live through the night, I think it quite unlikely I'll remember what brought me here in the first place.*

On the porch, Journee rapped loudly on the door using the extravagant brass door knocker Sven assumed from the beard, grapes and crown of laurels was meant to be Dionysus, the Greek god of wine, madness and orgiastic festivities. Fitting, if one considered what likely occurred within. He doubted the vampire girls would be permitted to visit cabanas in the dead of night, whether supervised or not. More likely their upscale clientele would visit the mansion, a house of ill repute with Tess Jackman as its madam and Emory its pimp. In his mid-twenties, Sven had written an article about a legal "ranch" in Nevada which housed as many as fifty women. They'd seemed happy, for the most part, though perhaps not of the Xaviera Hollander "Happy Hooker" sort. Many weren't highly educated and had gravitated toward prostitution as a way to make a quick buck, though a handful, like Hollander herself, were quite intelligent and found the profession both liberating and empowering. Granted, these were not women *sold* into sexual slavery like the girls on Little Pearl. Most if not all of them were there of their own free will. One woman had compared becoming what she'd called a "sexual companion" at a brothel versus turning tricks on the street to an army grunt taking a cushy desk job. Sven had found the comparison amusing. By comparison, the girls at the Jackman house had been drafted onto the front lines, essentially as cannon fodder. He assumed once they'd outlived their usefulness—using the term "lived" in its loosest sense—they would be let go with a stake to the heart.

The front doors opened and Emory smiled at them. "Sven!" he said with a bright smile, as if they were old friends. "So glad you could make it."

"I wasn't given much choice, was I?"

Emory chuckled. "No, I suppose you weren't. You can remove the handcuffs now, Journee. This is a friendly visit."

Journee gave Sven a brief look of concern, then unlocked his handcuffs and slipped them back into the pouch on her belt.

Emory held out a hand. Sven rubbed his sore wrists as he regarded it, like he might a predatory snake, then took it. As he had the first time they'd met face to face, Emory shook it in both hands. Looking into the man's gray eyes, Sven felt a bit of that same energy that had passed through him the last time. The sense that he and Emory were the last two people alive, the most important people on Earth. But he knew it was a parlor trick, some kind of low vampire magic, and he withdrew his hand quickly, to the chagrin of his host.

"Let's eat, shall we?" Emory said, gesturing toward his inner sanctum. "Thank you, Journee. We'll be fine from here."

"Yes, sir," Journee said. She gave Sven one last encouraging nod, then turned for the stairs.

Emory watched her go before shutting the doors behind them. "A fine woman, isn't she?"

"Quite." Sven stepped past him, into the foyer. A crystal chandelier hung from the vaulted ceiling high above their heads. The walls were decorated with all of the art Sven might have expected, both modern and classic, the furnishings in the rooms visible to him a tasteful combination in a similar vein. A curved, carpeted staircase led to a balcony on the second floor.

"You have a lovely home."

"Thank you, Sven. Tess does all the interior decorating. She's a bit of a wunderkind when it comes to that. I've got the culture of a warthog."

Sven offered a phony smile. "I sympathize with your plight. Tell me, Emory: I haven't been summoned here merely for supper and small talk, have I?"

Emory laughed. "I suppose I should've expected you not to bury the lede. Questions are your bread and butter, aren't they?"

"They are."

"I'm famished." The man put a hand on Sven's shoulder. It was all Sven could do not to cringe. "Let's eat while we talk."

"I'm quite hungry myself."

Emory led him to the closest room on the left, an elegant dining hall. The table appeared to seat at least twenty, though only three places were set at the farthest end, where Tess sat at its head, drinking red wine.

Or blood, Sven thought as she raised the glass in greeting.

"Mr. Olsen," she said cheerily. "So pleased to finally meet you."

"Charmed," Sven said as Emory led him toward his wife. "May I call you Tess?"

The woman's smile was positively vulpine. 'I'm afraid the press has labeled me incorrectly. Tess is Emory's pet name for me. You may call me Erzsébet."

"Erzsébet," Sven repeated. "Is that—?"

"Hungarian."

Emory pulled out the chair to her left and gestured for Sven to sit. Sven did, and Emory pushed in his chair until his bottom ribs were pressed tightly against the table. As his host leaned down and kissed Erzsébet gently on the forehead, her expression never changed, nor did her eyes—a mesmerizing deep brown—ever leave Sven's. With her ivory skin and black velvet gown, its sleeves long, its high neck and brooch fully covering her throat, she was every bit the elegant vision the tabloids made her out to be. And like her taste displayed in this home away from home, her ensemble was a mix of both modern and classic.

Erzsébet sipped her wine, studying him. Her husband took his seat at her right hand.

"Emory tells me you are an investigative reporter."

"Yes, that's correct. Freelance, mainly."

"And what compelled you to write an article about my husband?"

Sven smiled patiently. He saw no reason to "bury the lede," as Emory had put it. "I was informed that your husband, and perhaps you yourself, were trafficking in sexual misdeeds with underage girls."

Erzsébet swallowed a sip of wine hard and wiped her mouth with a long sleeve before cackling gleefully. "I am sorry," she said, setting down her glass. "My husband informed me you were... how do you say... *forthright*, but I did not expect such candor. Bravo, Mr. Olsen."

"We are all friends here. Please. Call me Sven."

Emory narrowed his gaze for the briefest of moments before smiling again. "He's quite the character, isn't he, my love?"

"Oh yes, quite. As to your... *accusation*, I believe I should be offended. That you could think something so heinous of my husband and I, who have been nothing but courteous to you—"

"I'd hesitate to call locking me in a jail cell courteous."

"Yes, of course. That was a mistake, for which I have thoroughly chastened my husband."

Emory offered a smile that didn't reach his eyes. "One of her many talents," he said, touching her shoulder. Erzsébet ignored him, and after a moment he let the hand fall back beneath the table. He picked up his wine glass with the other and gulped its contents, then offered the bottle to Sven. "Anyone for seconds?"

Rather than reply, Erzsébet said, "In regard to your rather crude accusation, I believe my husband has a proposition for you."

"What sort of proposition?"

"Well, Sven," Emory said, the bottle glugging as he filled his own glass. "It would appear, judging by what you've told my security staff, that there's a… let's say a 'witch hunt' against my wife and I. People are out for blood. I get it. Jealousy's a green-eyed bitch."

"I believe the expression is monster."

Emory chuckled. "Then you haven't met her. Sven, what I'm proposing is that you and I work together to clear my good name. I don't know where these accusations are coming from, but I find the very thought of them *repugnant*—"

"Emory, my I be frank?"

"I'd expect nothing less, my friend."

"I was privy to something I believe could prove lethal to your livelihood—your *freedom*, even. I saw the auction—"

Erzsébet glanced at her husband, her dark red lips curled in a frozen grin.

"—and I believe, no, I *am certain*, the allegations charged against you are without a doubt true. I am a journalist, Emory. I have spent time in Afghanistan, on several battlefields. I am prepared and willing to die for the truth. Whatever you offer me will not change my mind."

Emory's smile faded. "Well, I guess you've left me with no other choice. I know you've become friendly with our Mr. Coltrane. Earlier today my security team discovered evidence of an unknown young woman leading Ernie Wallis toward his room last night. We believe her to be the stowaway we discovered aboard the *Ceres*. You were witnessed causing a scene with Mr. Wallis and his guest the night before. And now, the respected studio head and philanthropist seems to have gone missing."

"What is it you're implying, Emory?"

"I'm *stating* that you, the old man and our young stowaway conspired to abduct and possibly *murder* one of my guests, and that I have the footage to put all three of you in prison for the rest of your natural lives. You may be prepared to die for the truth, Sven. But are you prepared to bet the truth against the lives of a bright young woman and a feeble old man with a loose grasp on sanity?"

Sven's hand shook as he raised his glass. He forced it steady and brought the glass to the center of the table. He was prepared to lose everything to bring Emory to justice—but he couldn't put the lives of a young woman and Abraham at risk, no matter how he felt about the truth. What he needed to do was buy them time. The porter and the young vampire would be here soon. As he had on the battlefield, Sven would play the rest by instinct.

"A toast," he said, forcing a smile. "To strange bedfellows."

His hosts gave each other a satisfied look, then raised their own glasses. The musical clink of all the three ringing together resonated throughout the dining hall.

The Duke rose from his slumber for the second time that day. The first had been when Erzsébet wakened him with blood to present him with the bride they had chosen for him. He'd been dozy, weakened from over a decade of living in this cave beneath the earth, provided barely enough sustenance to resist the ravages of time. He hadn't had the energy to properly introduce himself, for which he was regretful. Erzsébet and her pathetic husband had left him weak, and his children weaker. They needed to *feed*. He had made a mistake telling Erzsébet his secrets. But his fatal error had been to allow them to take his blood, particularly the worthless excuse of a man to which she'd hitched her wagon, who'd promised they would use it to extend his great lineage. Instead, they had created bastardized *Moroi* who did not know how truly powerful they could be, and were not even able hear his voice when he whispered to them in their sleep. Only the girl who had just arrived on the island was attuned enough to listen.

He awoke once more at moonrise, a surge of power rippling through his atrophied muscles and weary bones. It was not the disappearance of the sun which invigorated him but the blood of a live human consumed by the girl on the boat. This child of one of his lesser progeny—a pathetic excuse of a *Moroi* calling himself Lionel de La Haye—had somehow learned to feed on her own. He'd sensed her presence as the boat reached the island, just as he'd sensed the others, and in their joining of minds he'd gleaned that she was not like the rest, who'd been born and bred to service the sexual appetites of weak, pathetic human males. She had fed upon the blood of the innocent, and was eager to feed again—a desire she was able to satisfy moments before The Duke roused from his dormancy.

That mental link would soon bond with her sisters on the

island, and like the first spark of electricity The Duke had witnessed alighting the Avenue des Champs-Elysées in 1878, the lights in their minds would brighten and his misbegotten children would finally discover their true purpose in this world: to bring humanity to its knees and feed on its remnants.

The Duke reclined once more, his feeble body growing stronger as the bloodlust awakened in the minds of his daughters. He would need to be at his most powerful to rid this island of the human scourge. The time drew near to take his revenge upon his captors as well as his greatest foe, the tired old man locked in the same cells as his familiar.

His children would feed tonight, their first taste of blood.... but not their last.

They would feed until their bellies were full and their lifeless hearts contented.

And then The Duke would join them, his family spreading outward from Little Pearl Island to dominate and subjugate the living world.

THE STING

DINNER WAS QUITE delicious, for which Sven was glad, considering it was likely to be his last.

Staff rolled out cart after cart of more or less a *smörgåsbord* of silver platters and fine-bone china dishes filled with broths, crustaceans, vegetables, grains and meat. Sven, an avowed vegetarian to his dying breath, abstained from the latter. His hosts ate everything greedily, sopping up the animal's blood with bread, belying his assumption that the two of them—or at the very least Erzsébet—might be vampires themselves. Though he supposed it was possible vampire lore was inaccurate on the point of what could and could not be eaten. Abraham, who was surely an expert in the subject, seemed to be living proof that a human could drink a vampire's blood to acquire a modicum of their power. It was likely the Jackmans had done so themselves, feeding on the blood of this Duke Ştefan of Moldavia, whom Abraham suspected—and the familiar's rants seemed to verify—dwelled somewhere on Little Pearl Island.

In the shadow of the mountain, he thought, as Erzsébet led him upstairs after dinner. *This house is in its shadow, is it not? Perhaps The Duke has his own suite with adjoining bath? A vampire Airbnb.*

Whatever the truth was, Sven agreed to spend the night at the Jackman manor, not that he had much choice in the matter, and as Emory excused himself, Erzsébet led Sven to his room. He was a little tipsy from ingesting too much wine and felt logy from filling his belly. It would be nice to sleep it off in a large and comfortable bed, even knowing it was still likely, despite their Faustian bargain, an assassin could come in the night to dispatch him.

The house was much larger inside than he'd imagined when he first arrived, and the bedroom was on the second floor in a far wing of the manor. They passed at least four closed doors on their way to his room, and he guessed there were likely as many on the other side of the house. The hall was dimly lit, its walls adorned with dark, flocked velvet wallpaper and imposing, often grisly artwork, not the bright, stark white of the homes of other wealthy people he'd visited. While the main floor was an eclectic mix of modern and classical, in this wing at least, the style was decidedly old world, practically baroque.

Erzsébet unlocked the door to the last room on the left, stepped inside and flicked on the lights. They came on with a warm orange glow, two sconces above a large bed with a crimson silk satin bedspread and pillows heaped below a mahogany headboard. As Erzsébet stepped aside to allow him entry, Sven noticed the walls were made of padded brown leather. A stone fireplace took up much of one wall, with a door to the bathroom to the right of it. The large mirror directly across from the bed, practically wall-sized, had an ornately carved frame of gilded gold, with dozens of cherubic angels.

"Charming," he said.

"Thank you, Sven." The vulpine smile returned. "I will leave you to retire. While it was most agreeable to speak with you this evening, I'm sure it has been quite a long day for you, and you could use your rest."

"It has." Sven patted his stomach. "I haven't eaten so well in ages. I am quite stuffed and, I'll admit, shall probably sleep like the dead."

"Someone will rouse you for breakfast. Good night."

"*Jó éjszakát*," Sven said.

The woman seemed surprised. "You speak Hungarian?"

"No, I'm afraid. Just a few common phrases picked up while covering the Stop Soros movement in Twenty-Eighteen."

"I see. Well, *jó éjszakát*," she said, her pronunciation much better than his own. Erzsébet then stepped out and closed the door behind her.

Sven heard the sound of her key in the door. He tried the handle. It wouldn't turn. He knocked.

"Excuse me, Erzsébet?"

"Yes?" she said, her voice muffled behind the door.

"It appears you've locked me in my room."

"Yes. It is for your own safety, I'm afraid. My husband is afflicted with somnambulism, you see, and reacts violently to those who wake him. You will find all the amenities you require in the adjacent bath."

Sven glanced over his shoulder at the *en suite*. He doubted her "somnambulism" claim and didn't like the idea of being locked in the room, but supposed since he was at their mercy it wouldn't do to fight. "Thank you. Good night."

"Pleasant dreams," she countered. A moment later, he heard her footfalls retreat down the hallway.

Sven entered the en suite and began his pre-bed activities. He took a shower, using the little hotel soap and shampoo provided, dried himself with the plushest towel he'd ever used outside of a five-star hotel, found a fresh travel toothbrush and toothpaste still in their packaging, and brushed and flossed his teeth. While he did, he mulled over the events of the night and the past several days. He'd been surprised Emory and Erzsébet had admitted to every dirty deed during dinner aside from the vampire element of their enterprise, though he guessed they felt they had nothing to lose after he'd agreed to their deal. Even if he lived through the night, he would stay silent, for the protection of his new friend, Abraham, and the young stowaway. The three of them would be returned safely to the mainland in exchange for dropping the story, and though he did not fully trust either of his hosts, he was sure that if he survived the night, they would hold up their end of the deal. The director of *Little Pearls* had been allowed to return to the mainland, after all. Sven had to comfort himself with the fact that he had protected Abraham from the reprisal of The Duke, and the girl—Clarissa, they had called her—from sexual slavery.

Emory was nothing if not a shrewd businessman. Sven could see no reason for the man not to let them go, outside of spite, perhaps with their memories wiped clean. Erzsébet, on the other hand, he could not get a read on. Whatever beauty products she used made her expressions, aside from that vulpine smile of hers, quite inconclusive: a Botox poker face. Odder still were the moments where in certain light, such as when they had passed into the darkness between sconces in the outside corridor, she'd looked to be at least a hundred years old.

Sven dressed in a fresh pair of pajamas and slipped under the silk satin duvet. After a few minutes struggling with the top sheet rumpling under him, he climbed out of the bed, stripped it off and set it aside. Then he returned to bed, his bare feet slipping and sliding nicely against the silk, with only the smooth fitted sheet at his back. He flicked off the lights over the bed. In moments he began drifting off to sleep.

He awoke to the sound of the lock turning.

His instinct was leap out of bed, grab the fire poker from the mantle and await in the dark for his assassin. This same instinct caused him to duck when mortars fell or gunfire popped on the battlefield, or when a vehicle ahead of them in a convoy rolled over a roadside bomb.

Instead, he waited, calming his breath.

A small feminine figure entered the doorway, silhouetted by the light from the hall. Her hair fell in thick curls, and even in the dim light he could see it was the color of cornsilk. She entered the room quietly and closed the door. In the darkness that fell, he heard her tiptoe toward the bed.

Is this my assassin? They've sent one of their little vampires to kill me?

He saw her in a shaft of moonlight as she neared the opposite side of the bed. It was difficult to determine her age from the light but he guessed anywhere between sixteen and her early twenties. Whatever end of the scale she fell on, the fact that she'd crept into his room in the middle of the night—whether to kill him or with some other motive—made him uneasy. Laura would not approve in either case, surely.

What happens on Little Pearl... he thought, remembering what Tino had said the other night.

No. I mustn't.

The girl cautiously lifted the blanket and slipped in beside him. He felt her soft curls brush against his cheek as her smooth body slid up against his own. He shrank away from her, expecting to feel warmth, but instead found her flesh like ice. Even if she'd been warm, he couldn't allow this to happen. No matter what age she might be, no matter his feelings for Laura, he did not want to participate in transactional sex, particularly since it was non-consensual on both their parts.

"Please," he said. "I do not want this."

A chilly hand slid down his stomach and into his pajama bottoms. It found him involuntarily at half mast, and gripped him at the base of his shaft with cold fingers.

"*Let me please you*," the girl whispered into his ear.

He *didn't* want this, no matter what his stiffening penis might have to say about it. But the voice in his ear was seductive, almost overpowering. It seemed to echo within his mind, and her breath sent a tingle down his spine, like when he had researched for an article on the burgeoning field of Autonomous Sensory Meridian Response videos.

"Please," he said, taking her by the wrist and pulling her hand free from his pajamas. "I have a girlfriend."

"*I won't tell her if you won't...*"

Again, the voice sent shivers down his spine. It was breathy and husky at once. Whether it was the wine or the heavy dinner, or the fact that he'd been practically dreaming when she entered the room—*Maybe* this *is a dream*, he thought with very little hope—his head swam and the room began to spin. The hand slipped back under his waistband, grasping the head of his penis, already slick with pre-ejaculate. She kissed his neck, flicked her tongue into his ear and began stroking him.

No, he said. Or thought. He couldn't quite tell. Either he had said it in his mind or the girl hadn't heard, because she lifted the duvet and cast it aside. In the next moment, he felt her cold lips encircle the head of his member, an equally frigid tongue spiraling around it. He saw her curly hair rising and falling in the dim light.

Why is she so cold? he wondered, though his subconscious knew the truth. She was dead. One of Emory's Little Pearls. A *vampire*. Nascent or not, she held his manhood within her mouth. Her teeth worried him as much as anything else, but the pleasure was so intense there was no way he could stop her now.

"*Mmm...*" the girl moaned, and although his penis was still engorged within her mouth she somehow added, "*Give me your Milk.*" Maybe, as he had thought before, she truly was speaking directly into his mind. Some kind of vampire magic.

Whichever it was, he could hold back no longer and he ejaculated into her cold mouth, his body spasming, his mind crying out both in ecstasy and renunciation. The girl moaned with delight as she sucked every last drop from him. He fell back against the

Clarissa had no idea what the woman meant, but it wasn't the answer she was looking for. "Why would he want *me*?" she asked.

"Why would he not? You are a creature of rare beauty, my darling. The Duke desires none but the best."

"What about my sisters? Aren't they beautiful?"

"They are the most exquisite creatures on Earth."

"Well, then what makes *me* so special?"

Tess smiled back at her. "It is questions like these which make you special, my darling daughter."

Clarissa shuddered. The idea that this woman was now her mother was nearly as repugnant as the thought that The Duke would be her husband.

"Can I… see my sisters now?"

Tess gave her a sly look. "My husband will introduce them to you shortly."

After what seemed like an eternity, they reached Clarissa's room and Erzsébet left her, once again locking the bedroom door. Clarissa spent the next half hour going through the dusty old tomes on the bookshelf, trying to distract herself from thoughts of the monster beneath the house, when a knock came at the door.

"Yes?" she called.

"It's Emory," came a somewhat deep male voice. "Erzs—*Tess*, said you'd like to meet your sisters."

Clarissa stood immediately, eager to speak with someone other than her captors. "Yes," she said, crossing the room. "Just a second." She reached for the handle when she remembered the door was locked from the other side. "Tess locked it. She said something about sleepwalking?"

"Right. My sleepwalking." She heard keys jingle. A moment later the lock unlatched and a tanned, handsome man with silver hair opened the door. He looked fit, like he worked out a few times a week, and his smile—pearly white—appeared genuine. He held out a hand to her. "I'm Emory. Not sure if you remember me from when we picked you up from your foster home."

"Oh," she said. "Not really."

He shrugged. "You've had a difficult past few days. Are you ready?"

"Uh-huh."

"Please," Emory said, gesturing for her to join him.

Once Clarissa was out in the hall, Emory closed and locked the door behind her, slipping the keys back into the front pocket of his white linen pants. "You look healthy. Last time I saw you, you were pale as milk."

She'd still looked pale as she'd passed the vanity mirror, in her opinion. But she smiled and thanked him.

"We'll have you back in fighting shape in no time," Emory said, beginning down the hall in the opposite direction Tess had taken her earlier. "Tess tells me she introduced you to The Duke. He takes a bit of getting used to but you'll see he's just a little puppy dog."

"Why is he... *like* that?"

"He has the same disease as you, as a matter of fact. It's just progressed a lot faster because there was no treatment available until recently. In fact, he has the first known case. Our doctors considered calling it Ştefan syndrome, after him."

"Will I get like him?"

Emory frowned. "Oh, my dear, no. You see, we've created a vaccine to prevent the worst of its symptoms. That's what we gave you last night. It's not a cure but palliative, derived from The Duke's own blood."

"Does that mean... I have *his* blood in me?"

Emory chuckled as they rounded a corner. "Tess told me you were sharp. Yes, technically you have some of his blood in you. But it's in the form of albumin, a protein in plasma. Similar to a rabies vaccine. It's not like a transfusion or anything."

"Rabies," Clarissa repeated with a sneer of disgust. The monster in the cave had looked like a cross between a human and some kind of animal, a bat maybe. Was this disease of hers similar to rabies because he was some kind of werebeast?

"Does he know how old I am?"

Emory glanced back at her. "He does. But it's platonic, Clarissa. A marriage in name only." He used his keys to open a door at the far end of the hall, second from last on the left. Then he gestured for her to enter.

The room was dark. Clarissa expected another bedroom but instead it was narrow, with a small desk and a video camera set up on a tripod. A TV monitor hung from the far wall, displaying the image from the camera. The entire wall appeared to be glass, peering in on a bedroom similar to her own, lights on either side of the bed blazing. She stepped into the narrow room, and Emory followed, closing the door behind her.

"What is this?"

"The room we're looking at belongs to a man named Sven Olsen. He's a reporter from Sweden, currently based out of Miami. He's also a sexual predator."

Clarissa frowned. "I thought you were taking me to see my sisters."

"We are. Your sisters are doing important work, Clarissa. They're helping us root out the most vile scourge afflicting our nation today, in fact our world. The scourge of *sexual predation*. Men like Mr. Olsen prey on young girls like you and your sisters. What Tess and I and your sisters are doing here is a public service. We're *exposing* predators, or rather, facilitating these men to expose themselves."

Before Clarissa could ask him to elaborate, a pale-skinned man with ginger hair and glasses stepped out of the bathroom in plaid pajamas. He was flossing his teeth with a little plastic flosser as he crossed the room toward them. He stopped directly in front of Clarissa, and appeared to look directly at her for a moment. A chill ran through her body, but she sensed—in that way she seemed to sense things now—that he didn't see her. She took one step to her side and confirmed it. She was looking at him through a two-way mirror. After a moment flossing his teeth, staring at what was likely his reflection, he tossed the flosser into a trash bin and wandered back to the bed. He got in, had some trouble with the top sheet, which he eventually folded and laid on the floor beside the bed, then flicked off the lights.

While the bedroom remained dark, the image on the monitor switched to night vision, displaying the room in various shades of green. But Clarissa could also see what was in the room quite clearly through the mirror, despite the only light in the bedroom coming from a crack under the hallway door. Both her reflection and Emory's were visible on the glass.

"Emory?"

"Yes, my dear?"

"What's happening?"

He exhaled through his nostrils. "Have you ever seen the show

To Catch a Predator?"

Clarissa thought back to her life before but still couldn't remember anything prior to waking up in the makeshift hospital bed. She said, "I don't know."

"Of course, you don't. Clarissa, what we're doing here is called in the parlance of law enforcement a 'sting operation.' We're hoping to catch this bastard with his pants down, so to speak. In a few minutes one of your sisters will be entering the room. What happens will determine whether or not our Mr. Olsen is guilty or innocent."

They stood in silence, waiting. Despite the explanation, Clarissa still didn't quite understand what was happening, nor why she was being shown it. In the bedroom, the man finally settled and seemed to be falling asleep.

"Send in Lotte," Emory said. For a moment Clarissa thought he was talking to her, then the bedroom door opened with a shaft of light that made the green on the monitor go wild. Mr. Olsen's eyes opened wide immediately but he didn't move from under the covers. A figure about Clarissa's height stood in the doorway, her hair a wild tangle of thick curls. Her eyes, in the night vision, were pure white globes with small black dots.

She looks just like me, Clarissa thought.

The girl—Lotte—closed the door behind her and tiptoed across the room toward the bed.

"What is she—?" Clarissa began.

Emory shushed her with an index finger to his lips. "It's important that you watch this closely."

The girl who looked like her slipped into bed beside Mr. Olsen. He reared back from her, concern on his face and in his mind.

"Please," Mr. Olsen said. "I don't want this."

Lotte leaned in and whispered into his ear. He leaned back and allowed the movement under the duvet to continue, moaning slightly but as much out of discomfort than pleasure.

"Please," he said again, and the duvet rose further. "I have a girlfriend."

"He doesn't want this," Clarissa said.

Emory turned to her with a flat expression. "He will."

"But this isn't fair. You're tricking him."

She turned back to the bedroom, where the girl threw off the duvet and jerked down Mr. Olsen's pants. A moment later Lotte was putting the man's penis into her mouth.

"How old is she?"

"She's an adult. But he thinks she's *fourteen*, Clarissa. This is part of the game he paid for. The whole scenario, down to his protests."

Clarissa turned away. She heard their moans but refused to participate any further. Whether it was an illegal sex game he'd paid for as Emory suggested, or coercion and sexual assault against the man in the room, either way it was wrong, and she wanted no part in it.

"Don't you have enough?" she asked, feeling ill.

"Not yet. She hasn't finished."

Her foster sister appeared to be an enthusiastic participant. She moaned and stroked and sucked Mr. Olsen until his body went rigid and he cried out in pleasure, and Lotte made sloppy sucking sounds.

Then something strange happened. Not inside the bedroom but within Clarissa's mind. A bright spike of light pierced her brain and everything she'd ever experienced came back to her all at once. The Mall Monster murdering her parents and abducting her sister. The years spent at one foster home after another. The call to the ship from her sister—her *real* sister—the running, the hiding, the boy—Gabe—and the old man—Abraham—protecting her. The security guards capturing her, bringing her to Emory, who'd knocked her unconscious. Then waking again, finding herself upside down, as Emory smiled at her, having just cut her throat. The wretched old woman in the tub bathing in her blood as her life ebbed away. "Thank you for your sacrifice," she'd said, her voice and accent the same as Tess's.

A scream erupted from the man in the bedroom just as Clarissa screamed in fury and confusion inside of her own mind. *AM I DEAD? AM I A VAMPIRE?*

"Fuck! What the fuck!" Emory cried. "Blitz! *Goddammit, where the fuck are you?*"

Clarissa saw herself in the mirror, the choker with its cameo of the little bird in a cage. A surge of strength coursed through her and she tore the thing off her neck, revealing the slash Emory had made with his knife, already half healed. She turned to face her captor, her *murderer*, her jaws baring newly formed fangs, and opened her mouth to tear out his throat.

The killer was quicker by an instant. She felt a sharp sting in her shoulder and before she could do anything to fight back, Emory depressed the syringe's plunger and Clarissa tumbled back into oblivion.

PART 5

BLOODBATH

LITTLE PEARLS

IN THE SAME moment Ava tore Blitz's nose off of his face, a taste for blood awakened in each of The Duke's thirty-seven offspring on Little Pearl Island, setting off an unstoppable chain of events that would claim lives of nearly a hundred souls, both evil and innocent.

Sven's maiming, while excruciating, was nowhere near the worst to be suffered. After Lotte bit off his prick and sucked his blood from the open wound, he passed out quickly. Her feast was interrupted by Trip, who smashed down the door to prevent her from killing the man. Lotte leaped from the bed and pounced on the scrawny security guard. He staggered back until the two of them struck the wall, his mind reeling with thoughts of weed laced with psychedelics. Trip was certain he must be tripping. He reached for the Taser on his belt but with his sluggish reaction time the girl was much quicker, though she would've been even if he'd been a sober quickdraw. With her face and the upper half of her baby-blue satin negligee already dripping Sven's blood, she chomped down on Trip's wrist, causing him to drop the weapon. A shower of red spewed from his forearm, splattering like abstract expressionism across the wall. It made Lotte, who remembered her life before Little Pearl with total clarity in the same instant the others had, think of Spiderman. Her high-pitched laugh chilled Trip to his soul. The vampire tore out his throat and his scream filled her mouth along with his blood. He died in seconds, his small part in the events on the island over.

A few doors down the same hallway, Damien Evelyn Bulter, known professionally as Chef Amor, had been placing sushi on the nude, supine body of the young girl he'd won in the auction. The Japanese called it *nyotaimori*, but it was colloquially known as "body sushi." He gently laid two slivers of sashimi salmon over her nipples, and placed rolls of tuna and pickled daikon *makizushi* from her throat to her navel, which he'd filled with wasabi for dipping. Over her perfectly hairless pubis he placed a slice of grilled beef tongue, splashed with soy sauce. He always liked to cleanse his pallet with something cooked before diving into more raw flesh. He planned to eat this girl's pussy literally—as he'd eventually hoped to do to Shantelle, for ghosting him—shaving off thin sashimi slivers of her labia majora and minora and eating them and her nipples as he fucked her.

The girl didn't move a muscle. Her deep brown eyes stared at the ceiling without blinking. Her chest barely rose and fell, almost to the point that he thought he might be imagining it. It was like she was already dead.

He'd done body sushi many times, of course. There was etiquette involved. No talking to the model. No eating directly off the body, only ever using chopsticks. No harming the model. He would violate each of these rules tonight, starting with the first.

"Oh, Shannelle," he sighed. "You don't know how long I've wanted to *taste* you…"

He turned to get his sharpening steel and favorite knife for cutting raw meat. As he brought blade to high-carbon steel with a sharp *snick*, the sound of wet plops on the floor alerted him. He whipped around, knife and sharpener held in either hand, his gaze narrowing. Sushi littered the floor and table. Amor spun around twice but the girl was nowhere to be found.

"Where are you, little girl?"

The grilled beef tongue fell at his feet with a splat.

Amor looked up in the same moment the girl who looked like Shantelle dropped from the ceiling, literally scaring the shit out him.

As his bowels voided into his chef's whites, his body hit the floor. The knife and sharpener skittered away from him and the girl leaned into his face.

"*It's sushi time, baby,*" she growled.

She opened her mouth, showing him her brand-new fangs. Chef Amor screamed, and she grabbed his skull and lower jaw, prying his mouth open wide, then tore out his tongue with her teeth. It certainly wasn't the type of mouthfeel the chef had ever wanted to experience, and it was obvious he would never taste again, but in the next few minutes the girl would make certain he'd never breathe again, either.

From outside Amor's door came more screams. No one would find him for hours. No one would rescue him. The girl ate his tongue, then plunged her fists into his abdomen, punching through his weak flesh like stretched dough, painting his white uniform red. She pulled out his intestines, his stomach, spleen and liver, and took bites of each, savoring the various flavors and aromas, before casting them aside. Somehow, he managed to stay conscious for most of it, as his body became human sushi. To the girl—whose name was Hannah, not Shantelle—watching him suffer was the best part.

Tonight, the predators were on the menu. Their prey would dine well.

Dubstep thumped from speakers set up around the amphitheater as Gabe and Ava made their way toward the big house. Blue and red spotlights swung back and forth, shining as high as the low mantle of clouds that had appeared after sunset when they could find no dancing people or surrounding trees to paint with bright colors. Ava squinted at the lights, pausing as they neared. Gabe took her hand and led her along. The main buildings were close but the manor was probably another ten minutes' walk according to the map he'd studied on previous layovers. He wanted to get there and back to the ship as quickly as possible. From there, they would take one of the remaining utility tenders to the closest island, hopefully with Abraham in tow.

"*CALL 911 NOW!*" a woman screamed from the speakers right before the bass drop. DJ Safe-T spun records in his usual showy style, traffic cones and police tape decorating his booth, pumping a fist and twirling on his toes. "*Awright, you know what DJ Safe-T say*," his voice boomed. "*Stay hydrated, y'all! Drink that* H_2O*, yo!*" The crowd danced in an orgiastic frenzy, most of them young and pretty, glistening with sweat, clad in swim trunks and bikinis, though some wore white linen dresses or short-sleeved shirts and pants.

Gabe pictured himself leading Ava through the crowd like Blade entering the vampire dance club, but decided it would be easier to take her along the outskirts. Like at the pool the night before, he caught Poppy's eye again, this time as she worked the bar. She recognized him without his disguise, but her smile faltered when she saw the little girl. She said something Gabe couldn't hear that looked like, *What the fuck, Gabe?*

He couldn't waste time explaining, and didn't know how to communicate over the music and distance that he was protecting Ava. So he tapped his watch, hoping she understood he was in a hurry, and that she trusted him enough not to worry about Ava, and pulled her onward. Poppy watched them with a concerned look until they were back in the tree. Red spotlights cascaded over dark, gnarled branches, giving the forest a menacing vibe. With the sounds of the forest drowned out by the heavy beats blasting behind them, Gabe worried they'd get no warning if some predatory animal decided to attack them like whatever had slaughtered his parents on the island he'd been stranded on as a toddler, though he knew there weren't likely any large predators on Little Pearl.

Aside from sex fiends and vampires, he thought. *And we're headin right for em in the Jackmans' house.*

Ava stopped suddenly, causing Gabe to jerk to a halt in front of her, her grip strong. They'd been following Ava's senses toward Clarissa. The darkness closed in around them, giving Gabe a sudden sense of déjà vu—like he'd been in this exact place before.

"What's wrong?"

Her pale face flashed red with another shadowy sweep of the spotlight through the trees. "She's gone again."

"What do you mean 'gone'?"

"I don't feel her."

"But she's already dead, right?" Just saying it aloud made him feel sick. "She's already turned."

Ava nodded. "I don't know why. But she's gone."

Gabe turned in the direction he assumed their destination lay. "You can still find the others, right? The other girls?"

"Stronger than ever. They're like me now. They've tasted the blood."

"Then we need to keep going," Gabe said. "Whatever happened to Clarissa, we gotta find her. Then we hafta find The Duke and stab a stake through his heart."

He pulled at her hand but she refused to budge, and was far

stronger than him.

"Gabe?" She looked up at him with despair in her dark eyes.

"Yeah?"

"What's gonna happen to me?"

"If we make it out of this—" He almost said *alive*. "—we'll find Lionel and get rid of him, too. Now come on. We gotta find your sister before it's too late."

Ava came along willingly then, and with her direction they trudged through the dark forest toward the manor.

that was if he didn't come in his pants while spanking her.

She leaned over his legs. Kenneth willed himself not to come immediately, instead focusing on flipping her pleated skirt up over the back of her blouse and pulling her white cotton panties down over her healthy ass.

"You've been v-very bad," he hissed. Then he slapped her ass timidly, not even hard enough to leave a red mark.

"*Spank me harder, Principal Webster.*"

He did. This slap left a small red handprint on her left cheek. "Yeah, you've been a b-bad girl." He slapped her again. And again. She moaned each time, glancing back at him and licking the spherical lollipop. Kenneth fund himself getting more into it the more she moaned and licked.

When the first scream came from outside, he startled with his spanking hand raised. He tried to ignore it—*Who knows what kind of kinky stuff people are into on this island?*—and was about to bring the hand down again on her supple ass cheek, when the girl bit down hard on the lollipop, obliterating it in an instant. Since it was supposed to serve as an analog to his penis, this naturally unsettled him. He grew even more disturbed when her eyes began to blaze red, something that hadn't been in the fine print when he'd made his purchase.

The demon girl grinned up at him, baring teeth as sharp as razors. Before Kenneth could even consider standing up and casting her to the floor, she plunged the lollipop stick into his right eye, blinding him with searing pain. Warm fluid oozed down his cheek as she worked it back and forth in his ocular cavity until the injured eye popped free with a sucking sound and she brought it to her lips. Kenneth couldn't speak, with or without his nervous stammer. He couldn't even scream. With his uninjured eye he watched as Yvette bit down on his other eyeball, tearing it from the ocular nerve with a squelch, and chewed hungrily.

"*Mmm candy*," she said, then plunged the gooey stick into the remaining one.

Kenneth would never ogle another schoolgirl.

He'd endure several more hours of suffering to regret his purchase.

THE OLD MEN

AS HIS CHILDREN fed, The Duke felt true power for the first time in more than two decades, since he'd found himself stranded on this island with nothing to consume but vermin and bats. When Erzsébet and her lackey discovered the island—following directions from the "lost" journal of the couple who had hunted him here—they'd offered only enough human prey to subsist in his cold, cavernous prison, keeping him and his daughters weak. Now his body was repairing itself, its musculature rebuilding, his blood vessels thumping with the beat of his ancient heart. Soon, he might even be able to return to the form he'd taken in his youth.

Eventually, The Duke found the strength to stand.

He took his first weighted step away from the fetid place where he'd languished for over a decade, staggering like a seven-foot-tall newborn calf leaving its mother's womb. His next step felt lighter. On the third, his muscles shook off their torpor entirely. On the fourth and fifth, he stretched out his arms with wings fully formed, ready to carry him away from this dungeon.

Then he flew out the way he'd come in, through a shaft on the other side of the mountain, close to where he'd found himself washed ashore all those years ago.

In the same instant Abraham sensed the approach of his nemesis, The Duke's familiar grew agitated, shaking the bars and howling like an impounded lycanthrope.

"*He arrives! My Master nears!*"

"Yeah, yeah, keep it down," Tino muttered. "Hey, you got any idea when they're gonna bring us some chow? I'm starvin in here."

"*He comes for you, Strigoi!*" the familiar hissed, stretching a finger through the bars toward Abraham. "*He will take back the life he gave you!*"

"Let him come!" Abraham shouted back. "I'm counting on it!"

"Yeah, you tell him, Abe!"

"Thank you, Tino."

Abraham held the familiar's gaze, eager to show the man he wasn't scared, though in fact he was terrified. He'd lived longer than any man had a right to, wanting only to die for so long, but with his last moments ticking by he found himself wishing for more time. The familiar, unaware of the thoughts of mortality circling the mind of his master's nemesis, merely grinned back with blackened teeth.

Finally, the familiar blinked.

Abraham smiled proudly, having beaten the wretched man at his own game. In that same instant, the sound of the heavy exterior door striking the wall wiped the smile from his lips.

He was here. His greatest enemy had found him.

"You hear that?" Tino asked, as if anyone but the hardest of hearing could have missed it.

Shouts arose out in the security office, not from Journee or the man she'd called Trip, but a male voice Abraham hadn't heard before. The words were unclear but a loud crash came suddenly, which judging by the "Oof!" accompanying it was likely the man being thrown against something. A scream followed, and a zap of electricity. The overhead lights dimmed and brightened.

Tino stood abruptly. Abraham had never seen the man move so fast. "What the fuck was that?"

"I believe it would be our friend's 'dark lord.'"

"Oh, right," Tino said with a nod, realizing it was obvious. "My bad."

The silence stretched out as the imprisoned men looked at each other, wondering what was happening out front. Then a buzz echoed throughout the holding cells. The guard or The Duke himself had opened the gate.

"You think they got him?"

Abraham chuckled ruefully. "I very much doubt that, Tino."

With thumping footsteps, a giant, loathsome creature whose face was like a human bat slouched as it passed through the doorway. Its black eyes burned ferociously as it gazed upon Abraham, its pallid flesh splashed with crimson like warpaint. The animal lips curled in a smile, revealing rows of jagged, blood-pinked fangs.

Abraham had seen things like this before, *Moroi* so long removed from humanity they'd lost almost any resemblance to what they'd once been. The Duke had weakened significantly without blood, transforming him into the monster who stalked toward them.

"*My liege!*" the familiar cried, dropping to one knee in supplication.

"*SILENCE!*" the bloodsucker hissed.

His familiar fell backward onto his rump, clasping his hands together and squeezing his eyes shut in silent prayer.

The Duke opened the gate and approached Abraham's cell, his large paws thumping heavily on the hard tiles. Abraham's whole body quivered in terror, but he would not let the vampire know it. He kept his mind empty and grasped the head of his cane in both hands, steadying them.

"Abraham," the creature purred in his thick Moldavian accent. "My dearest and oldest friend. What has happened to you? You look positively ravaged by Father Time."

Abraham huffed. "Have you looked in a mirror lately? Oh, I'm so sorry. You can't, can you?"

"Because vampires can't see their reflection," Tino said with a laugh. "Good one, Abe!"

The Duke's batlike ears came together as his brow furrowed. "Who is this fat, pathetic vermin? This is the company you keep? My greatest nemesis?"

Abraham nodded toward the familiar, who muttered quietly to himself in the furthest cell. "And you? He's a far cry from the lovely young female familiars you'd surrounded yourself with back in London, yes?"

"Yes, well, the beggar cannot be particular with what he is provided."

Abraham pushed himself to his feet with his cane, gritting his teeth to suppress a groan. He wouldn't show his enemy weakness, not in the last moments of his life. He wouldn't give the creature the satisfaction. "Well, you've come here to kill me," he said, stepping up to the bars. "So why don't you have at it?"

The monstrous face looked as close to offended as possible

without eyebrows or a human mouth, spreading his winged arms out. "Abraham! My dear friend! I would do nothing of the sort!"

"Then why is it you have come?"

"Yeah," Tino said, plugging his nose. "If you're not here to kill us, at least take a freakin shower. You smell like a hamster cage."

The Duke flicked a clawed, long-fingered hand in Tino's direction, like swatting away a bothersome fly. Tino staggered backward involuntarily until he hit the back wall of his cell and plunked down on the cot, struck silent, his eyes wide.

"Where were we?" The Duke purred. "Ah, yes. I have come, my friend, to make you a solemn vow. My daughters and I will extinguish every last human life on this disgusting little island. Only then will I return… to take back the *gift* I gave you."

Abraham showed his teeth in a grin. "I'll be waiting."

The Duke stared at him a moment before his big black eyes blinked. Then he reared back his head and laughed. "You are quite the foe, old man! Courageous until the bitter end."

Abraham had nothing else to say, so he merely stood there, leaned against his cane, waiting for the Vampire King to leave.

The creature uttered a chuckle of amusement, then turned away from Abraham and strode with his long animal legs toward the last cell on the right.

"Jesus!" Tino laughed, pointing at him. "Lookit his little schlong! It's like a baby dick!"

The Duke paid Tino no mind, stalking past him to the cell of his familiar. "*RISE, PUNY MORTAL!*"

"Yes, my master!" The familiar got to his feet, brushing himself off despite being almost completely covered in soot.

The Duke grabbed the door to Stuart's cell in both paws. With very little effort he snapped the lock, tearing the whole thing off its hinges, and cast the door aside. It struck the floor with a reverberating clang.

"Thank you, Master! Thank you, thank you!" The familiar leaped off the floor and planted a kiss on the vampire's cheek.

"*NEVER DO THAT AGAIN!*" the creature roared.

The familiar shrank from his master's fury, throwing his arms over his head. "Yes, Master. Of course, Master."

"Now go," The Duke said. "Burn it all, Stuart. Leave nothing untouched by your flame."

The familiar bowed. "Yes, my liege!" He skittered off, shuffling his feet down the corridor and out through the gate.

"It's so hard to get good familiars these days," The Duke said, reaching through the bars of Abraham's cell. Abraham stood rigidly as the creature poked two vile claws into his mouth and spread his lips into a wide smile. The nails tasted of grave dirt and stale blood. "Cheer up, Abe!" The Duke said with a wolfish grin. "My presence here is a blessing. I shall return before sunrise to end your pathetic existence, as you wished."

The vampire retracted the horrible claws from Abraham's mouth. He remained silent as The Duke laughed once more, shook his grotesque head, and turned to stalk out of the bullpen.

"You know, I thought we were dead meat there for a hot minute," Tino said once they were alone again.

Abraham was also surprised The Duke hadn't murdered his cellmate. "He wants us to quiver in anticipation," he replied. "When he returns, don't give him the satisfaction."

"You got yards of guts for an old-timer, ya know that?"

"I've had plenty of practice, yes."

MASSACRE AT THE MANOR

WHILE THE DUKE released his familiar to burn the world, Gabe and Ava stepped out of the forest onto the immaculately groomed front lawn of the manor. The entire house blazed with light, from the spotlights shining up at its white façade to every single window on the first floor and several on the second and third. Most on the upper floors were lit red or dim yellow, while others flickered with candlelight. Gabe figured they must be the rooms where the winners of the auction stayed.

They'd followed the screams of terror and agony through the last half mile of trees and underbrush, and the howls of pain and cries for mercy still hadn't let up. Ava's "sisters," as she'd called them, seemed to take great pleasure in maiming and murdering these monsters, possibly more than draining them of their blood. While Gabe wasn't exactly a fan of vigilante justice, he couldn't honestly say he blamed them.

"Is Clarissa up there?" he asked.

The little vampire looked up at him, her face awash in yellow light. "I think so."

"Then let's get moving." Ava had told him Clarissa had been with the "Bad Man" when she'd lost their mental connection. If she'd meant Emory Jackman, Gabe didn't think they had much time to waste. Whatever Jackman had done to her, Gabe was sure he wouldn't let her join in the festivities.

He led Ava diagonally across the lawn and up the crushed brick walkway. It made him nervous, walking *toward* the sounds of terror and torment rather than running away from them, but with Ava at his side and a righteous purpose, he had to hope her vampire sisters would let him pass without tearing out his throat, or worse. He could only imagine the sort of atrocities that were going on in those bedrooms upstairs. Judging purely by the sound, murder might come as a blessing.

As they reached the porch steps, a second-floor window to their right shattered outward and a man came hurtling out, arms pinwheeling, legs kicking. Even half skinned and drenched in blood, Emory Jackman's idiot nephew, Colton, was easily identifiable by his doofus face. He struck the grass face first, his limbs crumpling and bones scrunching. He didn't scream or move, which likely meant he was already dead.

From the shattered window, a young girl with dark curls peered out, the curtains fluttering around her. Her skin was pale where it wasn't painted with Colton's glistening gore. She looked down at him, then turned her gaze toward Gabe and Ava. She smiled and waved for them to join her.

Ava looked longingly at the broken man in the grass.

"Later, okay?" Gabe said. "We don't got time for snacks."

Ava pouted. "*Fine*."

The door handle turned easily, and the door swung into the bright foyer. More glass shattered from inside, accompanied by thumps and echoed footfalls and the endless array of screams. Gabe drew the stake from the waistband of his shorts and held its point toward his feet, ready to swing in a downward arc if required. "Where was she last?"

Ava's dark eyes narrowed and she pointed toward the curved staircase leading up to the second floor.

Gabe didn't hesitate.

"Gabriel!" came a familiar voice from above them as they passed under the chandelier. "What a pleasant surprise!"

Gabe stopped in his tracks, Ava bumping into him from behind. It was Emory Jackman. He was glistening with sweat, panting, leaning over the second-floor railing. The sleeves of his white linen shirt were rolled up and his hair was damp and hung in his face. Splashes of red stained both his pants and shirt. He smiled at them, his eyes just about bugging out of his skull. He held what looked like a hypodermic syringe in his right hand, and the strap of a shoulder bag with the left.

"Aha!" he cried. "If it isn't our lost little scampire! I was wondering where you'd gotten to! Lo and behold, you were with my friend Gabriel all along."

"I'm not your friend, Mr. Jackman."

Emory scowled briefly. "Call me Emory, please."

"I don't think so. What happened to Clarissa?"

"Clarissa?" Something heavy and wooden smashed upstairs and Emory glanced anxiously to his right, then returned his manic gaze to Gabe. "Honestly, I have no idea who you're referring to, Gabriel, but it's nice to see you finally pay us a visit. Tess and I have been wondering if you'd ever work up the courage to step off the ship." He cast another glance down the opposite hall as a peal of high-pitched laughter arose. "Shame about the timing," he added with a dismissive shrug.

"Just tell us where Clarissa is. We only came for her."

"And I honestly wish I could help you. Unfortunately, things have gotten a little out of hand around here, and I need to get back to work."

"You had no idea what kind of Hell you were playin with here, did you?"

Emory laughed. "The best laid plans of mice and men, huh, kid?" He nodded brusquely. "Good luck. You're gonna need a helluva lot more than a wooden stake if you expect to make it off this island alive."

With that, he wandered off down the hall to the left.

Gabe hoped Emory and Tess would get their comeuppance but he wasn't the one to deliver it. He left the man to whatever he'd been doing and continued up the stairs, Ava following. The door to the hall Emory had entered slammed behind him.

"That way," Ava said, pointing to the door in the opposite direction.

Gabe headed for it, raising the stake above his head as he turned the handle, and opened the door toward him.

The dimly lit hallway was totally trashed. Wallpaper torn off with clawed gouges, paintings slashed and frames split, side tables smashed, sconces broken and bulbs shattered. Only one lamp still worked, at the far end of the hall. Many of the doors stood open, weeping and wails of anguish, as well as moans of pleasure and wet squelches Gabe felt no urge to identify, coming from within the rooms.

"Down there," Ava said.

The horrors they passed as the two of them headed down the hall would be etched in Gabe's mind for as long as he lived. To their right, a man had been strung up and strangled by his own intestines from a candelabra. His blood rained down on a teenage girl in what looked like a gore-soaked Little Bo Peep costume, judging by the staff lying nearby. She sat cross-legged below him, eating his severed toes one by one while muttering, "'*This little piggy went to market, this little piggy stayed home…*'"

To their left was somehow worse. An old man in an Oktoberfest getup lay dead on the floor with his erection jutting out from his zipper. On the bed, a girl in similar clothes was up to her shoulders in the torn-open stomach of an elderly woman whose heavy breasts sagged into her armpits. Her exposed larynx gurgled as slurping sounds rose from the girl in her belly. Gabe wasn't sure if she was still alive or if the movement in her innards was causing the gurgling from her throat. Either way, the old woman stared glass-eyed at the ceiling.

The next two rooms bore similar atrocities. Men and women torn to shreds, in various states of nudity. Ava's vampire sisters eating their fill, playing with the dead and dying bodies.

A man in blood-soaked pajamas, holding a crimson towel to his crotch, tiptoed out of the last room on the left. He looked shellshocked, his face deathly pale. Gabe recognized his ginger hair and glasses immediately.

"Sven?"

The blood-drenched man blinked blearily. "Gabriel?"

"Are you okay? What the heck happened?" The three of them met it the middle of the long hallway. Slurps and weeping came from the rooms to either side.

"I can't be sure," the reporter said. "Everything happened so fast, and I passed out. When I awakened, I found myself…" He swallowed hard before whispering, "…*emasculated.*"

Gabe glanced at the reporter's bloody hands holding the towel over his crotch, and shuddered. "You gonna be…?" He couldn't finish the sentence, unable to fathom the sheer agony the man must be feeling.

"I'll be fine, I am sure. I wrote an editorial on a choir of self-castrated sopranos for *Music Muse* magazine. One can still live quite a rewarding life lacking genitals."

It wasn't quite what Gabe had meant but he sighed heavily. "We're lookin for her sister. Have you seen her?"

Sven regarded the little girl. He didn't react to her presence as though he might fear her, though clearly one of her sisters had attacked him. Gabe didn't want to think too deeply on how he'd happened to get maimed in such a delicate place. He didn't want to think the reporter could be one of Them.

"The stowaway?" Sven rubbed the back of his head with a gore-streaked hand. "Sadly, I have not. Though to be frank, I cannot remember a single thing after going to sleep, and very little prior."

"Thanks, anyway. You should get medical attention," Gabe said as he began to walk past the reporter. "There's a medical hut back near—"

The walkie-talkie on Gabe's belt blipped. "*Blitz, this is Journee! Where are you? Over!*"

Gabe grabbed the walkie. He pressed the transmit button. "Journee? This is Gabe. You're alive!"

"*I'm hanging on.*" She sounded harried. "*Somebody killed Marcus and busted our arsonist out of his cell. Tore the dang door right off its hinges.*"

Gabe gave Sven an anxious look. The reporter frowned.

"Our vampire friend?" he whispered.

Gabe shrugged. "Did you talk to Abe? Did he say what happened?"

"*He was talking some nonsense about monsters, but I wasn't trying to hear that. Wait, how'd you get a radio*?"

"Long story. Journee, this is gonna sound weird, but what Abe told you, it's all true. You have to let him and Tino out of their cells and find that guy."

"*What? Gabe, I can't just let them out—*"

Ava tugged on his shorts. He looked down at her.

"My daddy wants him to burn the boat," she said.

Gabe's heart sank. He pressed the talk button. "You have to take Abe back to the boat, right now. I think the guy who busted out is gonna try to blow it up. He's gonna make it so we can't leave the island. Also, you need to send anyone else who's still alive to the big house. They gotta be armed. You'll need wooden stakes or spears. Tasers won't work."

"*Gabe, what the heck? Wooden stakes?*"

"Just trust me, okay? Stick with Abe. He's been doing this a long time."

"*Doing what, Gabe?*"

Gabe regarded the girl at his side, the sounds of murder assaulting his senses from every direction. "Killing vampires," he said. "Please, you have to trust me."

"*Okay, Gabe. Keep me posted.*"

"I will. Over and out." He hung the walkie back onto his belt. "Sven, you gotta get out of here."

"I would like to help, if I can."

"You're bleeding to death." What Gabe thought but didn't want to say was that the blood would make him a walking target, and they'd already have enough trouble if Clarissa wasn't in the room where Ava had last felt her presence.

"I'll be all right. Please." He gave them a grim smile. "I need to feel helpful."

Gabe nodded reluctantly. "Come on, then." He led the way back to where Sven had come from. As they neared the end of the hall, a teenage girl scurried out on all fours like an animal who'd been face-deep in a carcass. It was the girl they'd seen looking out the window when they'd approached the big house. Her eyes were wild, blazing red. She peered up at them and hissed with her fangs exposed. Then she galloped toward them, blood and spittle flying from her lips.

Ava raised a small hand, palm out. "*NO!*" she bellowed, using a deep, raspy voice Gabe would never have expected could come from such a small child.

Her sister stopped, skittering sideways on the carpet.

"*NOT FOOD!*" Ava shouted.

The girl cocked her head in curiosity. "*Not food?*" she grunted.

"*Not food. Friends.*"

The girl on the floor pointed at Sven. "*Friend?*"

Ava nodded firmly. "*Yes. Friend.*" In her own small voice she added, "Go now. Run far away into the woods and don't look back."

The other girl's eyes stopped glowing. She stood and walked past them, eyeing the stake gripped in Gabe's right hand. Her footfalls thumped down the hall behind them.

"That was a close call," Sven said.

"Too close," Gabe agreed. "Let's keep movin."

A cool breeze ruffled Gabe's hair as they passed another set of rooms. The curtains within the one to their right fluttered, broken glass littering the floor below. It was the room where the girl they'd just encountered had thrown Colton through the window. To their left, another of her sisters jumped up and down on the bed, causing the torso and severed head of the naked man lying on it, as well as the arms and legs she'd torn from his body, to bounce like the pieces in a game of *Perfection.*

"Charming," Sven said.

Ava stopped a few feet ahead of them. "Here," she said, pointing to a closed door next to the last door on the left. It was close enough to the next door that Gabe assumed it was probably a closet.

He raised the stake, prepared for a trap as he opened the door. The room inside was dark and narrow. Flicking on the lights, he saw a camera on a tripod, pointed toward a tinted-glass wall. The monitor next to it showed the inside of the room. Other than these and a desk with two folding chairs, the narrow room was empty. Gabe groaned in disappointment, shoulders sagging as he let the hand holding the weapon fall to his side.

"It looks like an observation room in a police station," Sven remarked. Somehow he looked even more pale than he had moments ago. His brow furrowed and he pointed at the camera. "I believe that's the bedroom Mrs. Jackman gave me."

"They were taping you," Gabe said. "I wonder why?"

Sven shrugged. "Blackmail, perhaps?"

"Whatever it was, nobody's here now. How in the hell are we gonna find her, Ava?"

"There is a sound system," Sven said. "In one of the rooms downstairs. Mrs. Jackman used it to summon the help. Perhaps we could use it to call for your friend?"

"Sven, if you weren't covered in blood I'd kiss you!"

The reporter's smile looked more like a grimace. "Let's find your friend before we get too excited."

The three of them headed back down the hall, Ava's small legs moving swiftly, carrying her ahead of them. He knew she could practically teleport down to the room where Sven had seen the sound system, but it wouldn't do any good without them, considering she wasn't likely to know how to use it.

"My goodness," Sven said, glancing into one of the rooms as they passed in the other direction.

"It's best not to look," Gabe said, trying to pretend he could ignore the horrible scents and sounds.

Ava waited at the door to the landing, turning back with barely contained enthusiasm. If not for the blood Gabe hadn't been able to entirely wipe off her face with his shirt, and the filth on her dress and skin, she might've looked like a normal little girl excited to see her sister. "Come on, come on!"

Sven chuckled. "She's quite the spirited little one, isn't she?"

Gabe shrugged. "She grows on ya."

When they reached her, she grabbed Gabe's shorts and tugged him along, hurrying through the doorway and out onto the second-floor landing. She stopped there suddenly, frozen at the top of the stairs, staring toward the black cathedral windows.

"What?" Gabe said, following her gaze. "What's wrong?"

The little vampire blinked. "He's here."

"*Who* is here?" Sven asked.

Ava looked back at them with fear in her dark eyes. "*My daddy*," she said.

DARK MAGIC

THE LARGE CATHEDRAL windows shattered as a giant winged monster hurtled through them. Glass pattered the floor far below, tinkling like wind chimes. The creature circled the chandelier, its massive wings beating with a leathery sound. The fleshy patagium between its long digits looked like a stretched scrotum, making Sven painfully aware of his missing manhood, numbed from shock and blood loss. He feared if he didn't get medical attention soon he would likely die, but he needed first to help Gabriel and the little girl find her sister. He wouldn't feel at all good about himself if he left them behind.

It was clear from Gabriel's expression, neither of them had been expecting the Vampire King to come crashing through the window, particularly in the form he inhabited, like some vile winged *draugr* from Norse folklore.

"How was he able to enter?" Sven wondered aloud, as the beast circled the ceiling like a humanoid bat trapped in a belfry. "I was under the impression vampires had to ask to be invited?"

"He did," Ava said.

Sven and Gabriel shared an anxious look. Had the creature spoken to the little vampire within her mind, and she answered in the affirmative? If that were so, how much longer would they be able to trust her?

The monster flapped its wings languidly as it descended to the floor below, where it landed on its hind legs with a heavy thud, its wings folding inward like hoisted sails. Sven realized there were five long-fingered claws on the ends of each arm, despite the bony structure of its wings, which meant it had more than ten fingers. He'd written an article on the native bats of the U.S. Virgin Islands for *Animal Kingdom*, and had learned quite a bit about their anatomy. This particular species had not been among them.

The Duke raised his pale pink pug-nosed face and blinked his oily black eyes in their direction. "Ava! My lovely daughter!" he said, his voice slightly slurred with a mouth full of sharp teeth. "It is you who blessed your sisters with a taste for blood. Come to me, dear child! Leave these puny men. The human scourge shall fall at our feet, begging to be spared. But we shall spare *no one*."

Gabriel grabbed Ava's hand, preventing her from rushing down the steps to meet her maker. She looked up at him.

"Ava, no," Gabriel said, shaking his head. "We have to find Clarissa. Your *real* sister."

She turned back to the monster downstairs, as he extended a long arm toward her.

The little girl tore her hand from Gabriel's grip.

Gabriel looked hurt. "Ava…"

"I'm going with my friends," she said defiantly, shocking both Sven and Gabriel equally. "We need to find my real sister. *Please*. Just let us go."

The Duke chuckled haughtily. "You *dare* defy *me*? Do not forget I made you who you are, darling daughter. If I wanted to, I could crush you like an insect. Your pathetic master is not here to save you, even if he *could* stand against me."

Ava shook her head. "And *you* better not forget, you'd still be lying in a cave if not for me."

Sven wasn't quite following everything, nor did it look like Gabriel was himself. He supposed Ava and The Duke shared a psychic bond which made her privy to information neither of them would be.

No matter the case, The Duke unfurled his wings and roared up at them, his black eyes blazing entirely red. "*UNGRATEFUL CHILD!* You have been spoiled by your contemptible master! I shall destroy him myself and *extinguish your life with a breath*!"

Ava stamped a foot. "Then do it, you big jerk! I'm helping my friends and finding my sister, and if you can't wait *five stupid minutes* for me to do that, just go ahead and *kill me*!"

The Duke blinked at her. Then he laughed. "You truly are your father's daughter, are you not? A jewel in my crown. Very well." He gestured with an arm for them to go. "You may go. But *do not linger*! Your sisters and I have much work to do ridding this island of *human scum*! I expect you would like to join us in feasting on their living flesh!"

Sven saw the flick of her tongue across her lips. She was clearly eager to satisfy her taste for blood, but she remained in place, and looked back at Gabriel expectantly. "Are you ready?"

Gabriel nodded.

Sven followed the two of them down the stairs. As they neared the Vampire King, he flashed his fangs at them. They were almost to the door below the staircase when The Duke bellowed, "*WAIT!*"

All three of them stopped in their tracks. Sven's body shook uncontrollably, though he imagined it was as much caused by his blood loss as fear.

"You! The young gentleman with the cap. What is your name?"

"Ga-Gabe?"

The Duke's eyes narrowed to black slits. "*Gabriel… yes…* It has been quite some time, has it not?"

"Some time since what?" Gabriel asked, his own eyes narrowed.

"Since you and I last met," The Duke said, his wide lips rising like the Cheshire Cat's shrew grin.

Gabriel shook his head. "I dunno what you're talkin about, but we don't got time for this."

"No? No time for the *Moroi* who saved your life?"

The young man frowned. "Come on, this guy's just wastin our—"

"*You were a small child* when we last met," The Duke said hurriedly, and Gabriel stopped abruptly, mere feet from the door. "Smaller even than my daughter, Ava."

Gabriel shivered. True or not, the Duke's words seemed to have gotten to him.

"You do not remember this, do you?"

He turned around violently, raising the stake in his fist. "I don't know you! I've never *seen* you before—"

"But you have," the vampire said. "You and your family washed ashore upon my island—*this* island."

The shock was apparent on the young man's face.

"I looked very different then," The Duke continued. Sven heard an air of wistfulness in the vampire's voice. "I had yet to lose my human physique. I was still… quite handsome, though that may be difficult for you to believe."

"No…" Gabriel said.

"*Yesssss*. It was I who protected you until you were saved by the men in the ship without sails…."

"No, that's not true…."

"*AND IT WAS I WHO TORE YOUR PARENTS LIMB FROM LIMB!*"

"You son of a—!"

Sven grabbed Gabriel's arm before he could get himself killed. "Gabriel. He's toying with you. Do not let him win."

"Yes, Gabriel," The Duke said, imitating a sullen tone. "We must not lose our temper. I am merely hoping to refresh your memory. Isn't that what you have always wanted? To remember the faces of your mother and father? To comprehend what was done to them on this island?"

"You're lying," Gabriel said softly, but it was clear he didn't believe it.

"Give me a taste of your blood and I will tell you *everything* you have ever wanted to know about your family. Why your mother and father traveled to *this* specific island. I assure you, Gabriel, it was not merely a storm which brought them here."

"Come on, Gabe," Ava said, tugging on his pocket.

"Just a single drop of blood and I will divulge *everything*."

Gabriel hesitated, seeming to contemplate The Duke's offer. Finally, he said, "Screw you."

"Screw *me*? You would be *dead* if not for me, boy! *I* saved your life, *not* the men in the ship!"

"*You liar!*" Gabriel shouted, tugging what looked like a crucifix on a chain from out of his shirt collar and holding it up as he took a single stride toward their enemy.

Rather than recoil like a vampire in a horror film, The Duke merely laughed. "Your god does not frighten me, boy!" He flicked a hand dismissively toward them, and though Gabriel was a good ten feet away from the creature's reach he flew backward, striking the wall beside the door with a thud. He slid down to the floor, shaking his head in a pained stupor. Sven hobbled over to him, picked the stake up from where it lay on the carpet, and handed it to the young man. Then he gave him his free hand, and helped him to his feet.

"You humans are all alike! You want to know the *truth*, but you cannot afford to pay the *price*! I will spare your lives until my daughter returns to me, as promised. And then you will *kneel* before me, and you will *beg* to drink of my blood!"

"You just try it!" Gabriel yelled, dusting himself off. "Come on, guys. Let's get movin."

"I'm right behind you," Sven said, eyeing the abhorrent creature cautiously as he followed the young man and the little vampire into the corridor below the balcony, and pulled the door shut behind them.

Stuart Smith, sometime arsonist, erstwhile prisoner and current familiar to the Vampire King, ran as fast as his legs could take him once his Master freed him from his cell.

He knew exactly where he was going. After he'd burned Lewis Caspian alive for reasons known only to his Master, he'd been told to go to the construction shed—but his fascination with the blaze had gotten him caught before he could do so. There was dynamite in the shed, leftover from when Emory and his workmen had cut through the rock for some of the more treacherous stretches of road, intended to eventually be used for the continuation of the underground passages across the island. Stuart knew this because he'd been in charge of the blasting.

It was his guess that Emory wanted the tunnels dug as an escape route should he ever need to flee from the authorities. The man and his wife were up to some sick stuff on this island, which Stuart had discovered far too late to back out of their contract. Some horrible, perverse stuff. Stuart didn't care much about that. What people wanted to do behind closed doors wasn't his business. His business was demolition, and his only interest was in what The Duke commanded of him. It was just a happy accident he happened to love blowing shit up. Or, he supposed, it was exactly why his Dark Lord had sought his assistance.

The shed lay in the middle of the island at the foot of the rocky hill called Mt. Elsinore. Stuart approached it cautiously. He'd bashed up his shins and torn his feet to shreds walking through the dark forest without a flashlight, following his memory when he was able to and The Duke's voice in his head when unsure. *Keep walking*, his Master said. *Turn right. Climb. Keep walking, pathetic mortal. It is so close now….*

Once there, he punched the code into the lock. It beeped angrily, flashing red. Someone must have changed it, and considering what he'd done to the pharmaceutical engineer, it made a fair amount of sense, even though Stuart's initial reaction was to curse God and punch the wall in frustration.

Fear not, The Duke cooed. *Do you truly believe I would send you all the way out here without knowing the code?*

"No!" he blurted out into the dark forest. His own voice startled him and he looked around himself to see if anyone had heard. The night was dark and silent but for the sound of crickets and the chirp of whistling coqui frogs. "Of course not, my liege."

Good. Then press these numbers.

Stuart listened. He pushed the numbers. When commanded to press Enter, he did.

The door rolled open, revealing the darkened interior of the wide construction shed. The crates of dynamite and blasting caps were stacked against the back wall. Stuart crossed to them, the cuts on the soles of his feet smearing blood on the polished concrete. In twenty minutes he'd loaded up enough dynamite into the mini dump truck to blow the *Ceres* sky high, and take out every single structure on the island if The Duke wished.

They may have changed the door code but some halfwit had left the key in the ignition. He turned it, and the big engine roared to life.

Stuart laughed gleefully.

For weeks the bars of his cell had separated him from his love of fire and destruction. He very much looked forward to their reunion.

The Duke *seethed.*

He had hoped testing Gabriel's eagerness to learn the truth of his family's l ineage would work in his favor, but he had apparently underestimated the boy's affection for the sister of his daughter, Ava. It was pathetic, the bonds humans held for each other. No mere mortal's life should be more important than one's own pleasure.

No matter. The boy would return with Ava and he and the red-haired columnist would meet their pitiable demises. His daughters had already gotten a taste of the reporter. The Duke was certain they would be eager for a second serving.

For now, there were more important matters to take care of. His daughters needed his guidance. They were rudderless ships on a stormy sea without him, and The Duke knew all about such things. He had been cast into the sea in a stone casket lined with silver on his way to America. When time had finally eroded his prison, he had swum ashore, discovering himself on an island without a single human inhabitant to feed upon. He had subsisted upon local bats, small birds and rodents, feeding like a scroungling *Moroi*, subsisting on the meager quantities of blood he had been able to suckle from their puny bodies, until the fragments of a small ship washed ashore, and the boy and his parents with them.

The moment the Duke determined who they were, he'd killed them in a blind rage before they could fight back, while their toddler wept. He had dashed the man's head on a rocky promontory and slit the woman's throat, her blood mingling with the surf. After he carried the bodies to his cave to drain their blood and have his way with the wife—who looked so much like his lost love he could not pass up the opportunity—he had hypnotized the child into forgetting what had been done to them, and fed him their flesh, claiming it belonged to an animal he had slaughtered. Over the following days, while the boy wept for his parents, he still continued to consume meat from their bones.

If The Duke had been stronger, if he had not conserved the blood of the boy's parents, worried he would be no further victims for quite some time, he might have attempted to slaughter the men from the ship without sails, and commandeer their vessel. Instead, he had been pleasuring himself with the mother's fetid corpse when they took the boy away, and The Duke had never expected to see him again. In the recent past, he had sensed Gabriel's presence nearby several times, though his weakened state had made it difficult to reach out to the boy using his *Moroi hangja*—the forceful voice. He had hoped to one day be reunited with the boy if only to share with him one last taste of human flesh. He'd only been able to reach his daughter on the ship because of her own mind, attuned to his by fresh blood.

Thwarted by the boy's base emotions, The Duke hoped to have another chance to test him, this time in the presence of the old man.

He had one last ace up his sleeve, and it was what Erzsébet's idiot American husband might call "a doozy."

The Duke ascended to the second floor. His limbs were far too long and ungainly for the shallow steps but his gait was becoming ever more graceful as his children fed. He suspected he would never entirely regain his youthful human form, though it was still possible. Ancient *Moroi*, especially those deprived of human blood for a long enough duration, often withered away to monstrous shapes. And while the fear it inspired in humans was quite delightful to behold, he much preferred being a wolf in sheep's clothing, moving undetected through crowds, seeking his next prey and seducing them with charm and beauty. His time spent with the Marquis and Marchioness de Sade had been many of the best nights of his life. Unfortunately, it was under their perverse tutelage that The Duke had sown the seeds of his own undoing.

The Duke sniffed the air. Beneath the pungent tang of blood and human waste, he smelled his target. The woman reeked so positively of corpse rot, it was a wonder her wretched husband could stand to be around her, let alone ply her with his feeble sexual ministrations. But her *glammer* was powerful. No one but a powerful *Moroi* such as The Duke himself could see—or *smell*—through its façade of human beauty. The hag was older than The Duke himself, only prevented from becoming dust by ancient magic and the blood sacrifice of the most radiant youths. His daughters had perished for Erzsébet's vanity and desire for immortality. It was a pact he had made in haste for the purpose of self-preservation, when Countess Báthory herself had discovered him on the island after more than one hundred years spent searching. The diary of the boy's parents, once lost, had directed her here.

The Duke sniffed her out, stalking to the door directly above the one his daughter and the boy had traipsed through moments ago. The hag was close. Her stink prickled his nostrils, far more effluvious than the corpses he had lain upon during the past decade, collecting bones like a dragon in a fairy tale. The scent was positively abominable. He followed it down a darkened, silent corridor, the sounds of his daughters feeding on the floors above dwindling the further he stalked from the great hall.

He stopped in front of a closed door. Her stink emanating powerfully from within, pouring up from under the door like invisible smoke. He nearly gagged, but managed to compose himself as he turned the handle.

The door was locked.

The Duke grinned. He stepped back and planted a solid kick to its middle. The door splintered, swinging wildly on its hinges, broken pieces clattering on the lavatory floor.

The desiccated creature that had once been a woman lay in a luxurious clawfoot tub filled with bubbles. Soap clung to her mummified flesh. Even masked by the lavender and rose of her bathwater her stench was atrocious. The beautiful form her dark magic created was only semi-visible to The Duke, layered over her corpse like a double-exposed photograph.

"Oh, my goodness!" the ancient woman cried.

"Ah!" The Duke said cheerfully. "The mistress of the house. So lovely to see you once again in the flesh. And a great deal of flesh at that, as withered and putrid as it is. No amount of lather will wash away such a foul odor, witch."

The woman-thing sneered at him with its rotten, fetid teeth. "You are one to talk," she said, covering her shriveled bosom with an arm like dried meat. "You come into my home looking like this? You should be ashamed!"

The Duke grinned. "The only shame I have is for my dealings with you and your weakling companion. Has he seen you like this? As you truly are?"

The truth enraged her. "*Get out!*" she bellowed, swatting at him, sending suds and water across the room. "*Get out of my house, vile thing!*"

The Duke crouched as he stepped into the lavatory, then stretched to his full height. The witch's cataract eyes widened in terror as she beheld him in all his glory. "*YOU HAVE NO POWER OVER ME, WITCH!*" he growled, using the *hangja*, shouting directly into her mind. "*I WILL REVEL AS THE LIFE EBBS FROM YOUR WITHERED CORPSE! I WILL DANCE AS MY DAUGHTERS DRINK YOUR BLOOD, YOU WRETCHED BITCH!*"

"Bring it," the corpse said. "You don't have the—"

The Duke flicked a hand in her direction, flinging the bag of bones from the tub in a spray of soap suds. She struck the wall, shattering plaster, and collapsed on the floor. The putrid thing raised herself up on decayed forearms and began to crawl miserably toward the adjoining bedroom door. With a grin, he reared back and kicked her in the face. Rotten teeth fell from her shriveled lips and clattered on the tiles and she moaned. He stepped on her pelvis, cracking both hips under his massive paw.

With his foot still holding her down, the Duke planted his hands on his hips and bellowed laughter. He summoned his children with the *hangja*. One by one they came to him, gathering at his feet in varying states of bedragglement and dress, their inquisitive eyes looking to him for guidance.

He picked the ancient hag up by her coarse hair and held her withered body aloft.

"*Please…*" she begged, her voice slurred.

The Duke slashed a single nail across her throat, then down her rotten chest to her abdomen. Her noxious innards spilled out over his daughters, bathing them in her blood as she had once bathed in theirs.

The Duke let her corpse fall to the floor in a ragged heap then, and as his daughters descended upon her, he set his senses upon the master of the house.

REUNIONS

WHILE THEY SEARCHED the back rooms of the manor for the sound system Sven had seen during his tour, Gabe tried his best not to mull over what The Duke had said about his parents, and what he'd claimed happened before the Coast Guard rescued him. No matter how hard he tried, his thoughts kept circling back to the man he remembered, who both his grandmother and the police had assured him was all in his imagination.

It was I who tore your parents limb from limb!

Gabe had always wondered how he'd survived so long on a deserted island without his parents. Was it possible what The Duke said was true?

He remembered what he'd told his grandmother years before her death, that a man had been on the island with him. He'd worn a black vest and a dirty white shirt with puffy sleeves and a ruffled collar like a pirate from a movie. His grandmother had assured him he'd imagined the man, and the men who'd searched the island for his parents had been unable to find any other inhabitant. But Gabe remembered the man's face quite clearly, even today. Clearer, in fact, than the faces of his own parents.

"*Eat this, boy*," the man had said, feeding him scraps of meat he'd cooked over a fire on the beach the night his parents entered the woods and never returned. "*Must not let you starve.*"

Gabe shuddered.

"Are you okay?" Sven asked, giving him a concerned look.

"Yeah. Just what he said back there. Shook me a little."

"I can only imagine." The reporter pointed. "I believe it was this room here."

Gabe held the stake aloft and opened the door. It was devoid of life, just as the others had been: the theater, the library, the conservatory. It appeared to be a sort of sitting room, with a carpeted sunken area where brown leather sofas, a marble coffee table and a few egg-shaped chairs stood. There was a stereo system along one wall, the old kind with wooden cabinets and speakers like the one his grandparents had. Shelves filled with records stood to either side. There was even a lava lamp bubbling beside the record player.

"Here we are," Sven said.

He crossed the room, following the reporter to the stereo, looking for something that resembled a radio or microphone.

Sven stepped aside and pressed a button on what appeared to be an intercom. It made a crackling thump, like the sound of a needle dropping on a record. "Care to do the honors?"

Gabe nodded and approached the man. "Clarissa, it's Gabe," he said, speaking clearly into the device. "Clarissa, if you can hear me, you have to wake up. Your sister's here. Ava. We need to get you out of here. *Please* wake up."

He turned to Ava. The little vampire shook her head.

Sven shrugged. "Perhaps she should try it?"

"Ava, that voice you used in my head—can you do that over the intercom?"

Ava seemed unsure, then nodded. "I think so."

Gabe stood aside as the little vampire wandered up. Even standing on her tiptoes she was too short to reach the intercom.

"Want me to pick you up?"

Ana nodded, already looking like she was losing the strength she'd gotten from biting off Blitz's nose. If she'd been stronger, Gabe figured she could probably just fly up. She held up her arms and Gabe grabbed her around the sides, hoisting her up to reach the speaker.

She turned to him inquisitively. "What do I say?"

"Tell her you love her," Gabe said, providing her with the words he'd wanted to say himself if he hadn't lacked the courage. "And you miss her. And you want her to come home with you."

Sven smiled and nodded. "I think that will do just fine."

Ava turned to face the intercom, and the reporter pressed the transmit button again. "*Rissa, it's Ava.*" The speaker whined with feedback from the intensity of her voice. Gabe felt it in the fillings in his back teeth. Sven winced. "*I love you and I miss you so much.*

Come home, please."

Sven took his thumb off the button. Ava looked back at Gabe for affirmation. He nodded. "That was real good, Ava. If that doesn't work, I don't know what will." He set her back down on her feet.

"I'm hungry," she moaned.

"We'll get you somethin to eat soon."

In the meantime, she stuck her thumb in her mouth. Little pearls of blood emerged from her fangs poking into the flesh, and she sucked on it like a kid eating her own scab.

They waited. After a few minutes, Gabe asked again if Ava heard or felt anything. "Or however it works," he added.

"Uh-uh," she said, shaking her head with her thumb still in her mouth.

"We mustn't wait here forever, Gabriel."

Gabe took off his hat and ran a hand through his sweaty hair. "I know." He looked around the room. There had to be some way to reach her....

His gaze fell on the stereo.

"I've got it!" He crossed to the device and looked over all of its components.

"Do you know how to use it?" Sven asked.

"My grandma had one like this. There has to be a—" He spotted it. "There!" He flung the backpack off his right shoulder, unzipped it and pulled out what he hoped would reach her when nothing else would.

"A CD?" Sven asked, looking dubious.

"This isn't just *any* CD," Gabe told him, pressing eject on the player. He pulled the writeable CD out of its jewel case. "It's my parents' Desert Island Disc."

Sven smiled. "Color me intrigued."

Gabe pushed the tray closed and waited while the machine loaded the CD. Then he skipped to the right song and pressed play.

Guitar strummed quietly from the speakers. Gabe turned up the volume as Rivers Cuomo sang, "*Hip-hip.*"

Sven's smile grew wider as he pressed and held the intercom button. "I rather like this song."

"It's my favorite," Gabe said. "Let's just hope it gets to her."

They listened for a moment in silence. The reporter broke it to ask, "What's the matter, little one?"

Gabe turned to see Ava had tears spilling down her ghostly pale cheeks. "Are you okay?"

Ava nodded. "I'm remembering," she said, wiping her tears with the back of a hand.

The girl roused in a familiar bedroom with no windows, and no idea how she'd arrived there or anything else. Her head ached, as if she'd been partying all night.

She ran her tongue across her teeth. Something in her mouth cut her tongue and she winced in pain. Music was playing from somewhere. It must've been what had woken her up. The song was familiar—a melancholic rock song about an island in the sun, which from its repetition she supposed could be its title—but she didn't know how she'd gotten here or even who she was. A black IV tube snaked from a needle taped to her wrist to an IV which was covered in a paper bag.

Something about the needle bothered her more than it should, and she tore it out of her arm. A pinkish fluid, rather than the blood she'd expected to see, spilled out of the small wound and dripped from the needle and butterfly clip hanging from the IV. A tendril of black smoke flittered up from the pinprick hole, as well as the drops on the floor.

More anxious than simply curious, the girl got out of bed and removed the paper bag covering the IV, revealing a clear plastic bag with the same clear pinkish fluid. A logo on the plastic said CASPIAN with a little green cartoon snake as the S, sticking out its red tongue.

She crossed to the vanity mirror and regarded her reflection, but couldn't recognize the frizzy-haired blonde girl in the airy flower-print dress staring back at her.

Where am I?

WHO am I?

"*Clarissa,*" came a young man's voice from somewhere nearby. At first the girl thought it was part of the song, but when the—*boy*—said it again, she followed the sound to a speaker in the wall, the source of the familiar song. "*Clarissa, please wake up.*"

The girl pressed a red button on the speaker. "Hello? Who is this?"

"*Clarissa! Holy crap, we've been lookin all over for you! Where are you?*"

She supposed she must be this Clarissa, since he seemed to recognize her voice. Looking around, she answered, "I don't know. I'm in a bedroom without any windows. Who are you?"

"*It's me: Gabe! Don't move, we're coming to get you.*"

"Who's we?"

"*Me and your sister.*"

The word *sister* made Clarissa's heart swell, but she still couldn't remember a thing.

Another man's voice added, "*And Sven Olsen.*"

"*We'll be right there, just stay put and if anyone but us comes to the door, don't let em in, okay?*"

Clarissa gave the door an anxious look. Were bad people coming to get her? "Okay," she said. Then she stepped back from the speaker, crossed her arms over her chest, and stared at the door, waiting.

After a while she decided if someone bad was coming for her she should be armed, so she made sure the door was locked, then scoured the room for something to hit or stab them with. There was nothing in the drawers, wardrobe, or on the shelves but clothing and books, none of which were heavy enough to really hurt someone, even the dusty old hardcovers. She settled on the hefty lamp on a table beside a comfy chair, and wrapped the cord around a hand, gripping the lamp tightly, waiting for her assassins or saviors, whichever came first.

As she stood there, the song ended and started over again. In her confusion and fear, she hadn't really been listening to it. Now that she had time to give it her full attention, she began to remember things. Sounds at first. The boy's voice, but not over the speaker. He was talking about his parents. *They* were talking about *their* parents, sitting on the top bunk in a small room that smelled like dirty socks. She remembered an earlier time: this same song coming on the car radio, and her parents turning it up to sing along to it, giving each other moony eyes while her dad drove. They were on their way somewhere and for some reason the name of that place—*Galaxy Galleria*—made her feel extremely sad.

My parents died there, she remembered. *And my sister, somebody kidnapped her. My name is Clarissa, and my sister is*

Ava. She was... on a boat. I heard her voice all the way from my foster home and came to rescue her.

Other pieces of the puzzle tumbled into place then, one piece linking to the next one after another, until it made a fuzzy picture of where she was and how she'd come to be here. She recalled the man who'd brought her here last: not the brute of a security guard but the handsome man with the wavy silver hair and chiseled jaw and his devious yet beautiful wife. *Emory and Tess Jackman.*

Clarissa touched her teeth with her tongue, certain what came to her next couldn't possibly be true. Their sharp ends drew blood. She lowered the lamp and stood in front of the mirror, looking at what appeared to be fangs in place of her canines.

"I'm a vampire…?"

It didn't make any sense but the evidence was right there in her face—although she was relatively certain vampires, at least in fiction, were supposed to have no reflection. Her memories, which seemed like they'd come from nightmares rather than real life, filled in the gaps. The corpse in the bathtub, bathing in her blood. The giant, pale monster in the cave.

A knock sounded, startling her so badly she nearly dropped her makeshift weapon. "Who is it?" she called.

"It's us!" came the same voice on the other side of the door.

"How do I know it's you?"

"Who else would it be?"

Clarissa tucked the lamp under an arm and tried the door handle. "You can't open it?"

"No," said the boy—Gabe was his name, she remembered. An orphan, like her and Ava. The song was from the Desert Island Disc his parents had brought to a literal desert island.

"It's locked on my side, too."

"Great. Well, hang on a second, I'll see if I can find—"

Before he could finish, a tiny fist smashed through one of the bottom panels of the door, sending little pieces of wood flying. Clarissa stepped back and watched as the hand retreated. Then a small face she recognized because it was once almost indistinguishable from her own when she was seven years old poked through the hole. Her sister—her *real* sister—smiled, revealing fangs of her own.

"Hi, Clarissa!"

Clarissa waved. "Hi, Ava!"

"Stand back, okay? I'm gonna punch the door *really really hard* and it's gonna go flying."

Ava's face disappeared from the hole in the door. While Clarissa doubted her statement, she stepped back just in case. In the next moment the entire thing came flying off the hinges with a loud *CRACK!* through the space she'd just occupied. A familiar-faced young man in a baseball cap stood beside Ava. Behind them was a very pale man with red hair, holding a blood-soaked towel over his crotch. She recognized him from the small observation room where Emory had stuck her with the needle. The sight and smell of his blood made her salivate, and a heart-pounding sort of desire overcame her.

If Ava hadn't come running into the room right then and hugged her around the waist, squeezing her cheek into her stomach, Clarissa didn't know what she would've done about Sven's blood. She thought, like her vampire sister upstairs, she might've tried to drink it right from the wound.

"It took us forever to find you," Ava said. "Were you here the whole time?"

"I was upstairs. Outside his—*Sven's*—room. I'm so sorry what happened."

"It's fine," Sven said. "Although I do feel I should probably lie down."

Gabe patted the man's shoulder. "Not until we get you to the medical hut." Clarissa noticed the little peach fuzz mustache he'd had when she'd first met him was gone.

"You shaved," she said, pointing to his face.

His cheeks flushed. "Yeah, uh… it's a long story."

"It's better," she said.

He gazed at his shoes, trying to cover a grin. "Th-thanks."

"Well, this was a pleasant reunion," Sven interrupted, "but if you wouldn't mind, I'd very much like to get to that medical hut before I bleed to death."

They all agreed, and returned to the ground floor the way Blitz had first brought her down, passing by the passage to the caverns where Tess had shown her the monster they'd intended her to marry. Clarissa shuddered at the thought of it, hoping she'd never have to see the terrible creature again.

The first floor was deathly silent. the foyer looking like it had been hit with a mortar. The chandelier lay on the floor in a confusion of crystal and brass. Every window was obliterated and both doors stood wide on the darkened front yard. The smell of blood and other human fluids were overwhelming, filling Clarissa with a powerful urge to ascend the curved staircase, where the smell seemed to be coming from, and feed until her belly was full. She took her sister's hand instead, hoping the two of them together would have the strength to resist it. Ava smiled up at her as the four of them navigated the debris.

"Looks like the coast is clear," Gabe said, having stepped out onto the porch. Each of the men held a stake in their free hands. Clarissa thought they both looked ridiculous and likely wouldn't have the ability to stop a small prancing deer, but if it made them feel safer, she left them to it. Little Ava had enough strength for all four of them, and Clarissa figured she likely wielded some of that same supernatural power herself, if she chose to use it.

Gabe pointed to one of the black SUVs, like the one Blitz had brought her to the house in, parked at the far end of the lawn near the trees.

"Let's take the Cruiser," he said.

The four of them left the manor, crossed the porch and started across the lawn. The cool grass felt wonderful on Clarissa's bare toes, and the stench of human misery soon gave way to more pleasant scents: flowers, grass, earth, sea breeze. She breathed it in deeply, but couldn't manage to shake the pungent tang of Sven's blood wafting back to her from where he staggered a few feet ahead, alongside Gabe.

Don't worry, Ava spoke quietly in her mind. *We'll feed soon. Daddy promised me.*

Clarissa didn't reply. An image of the tall creature standing in the foyer came to her when Ava said the word *daddy*. He'd escaped from his cold cavernous lair and was out there somewhere in the night, in the dark. *Feeding*. With her mind attuned to it through Ava, she felt his *hunger*. She felt the others, too—tearing flesh, snapping bones, gnashing at innards, gorging themselves on blood.

They climbed into the car. Ava sat in the front beside Gabe, Clarissa and Sven in the backseats. Luckily, the keys had been left in the ignition. Gabe started the engine and made a three-point turn to get the SUV facing the road. Then he popped the transmission into drive and said, "Buckle up."

He helped Ava with her seatbelt, then caught Clarissa's eye in the rearview. She tugged on her seatbelt to show him it was already locked.

"All right, let's get outta here," he said. The Land Cruiser rumbled forward into the darkened forest, where the monster and its children awaited.

"Clarissa…?"

Sven's voice was barely audible over the roar to the engine and the crunch of gravel under the tires. She turned to him. His wide eyes leaked tears, his skin so pale it was practically gray. "I didn't mean… didn't mean to…"

She took his hand, his blood slicking her fingers. She wanted so badly to taste it but she squeezed it harder instead, fighting the urge. "I know," she said. "It's okay."

"Will you tell them… I tried to break the story?"

"I will."

"You guys all right back there?" Gabe asked, glancing in the rearview.

Clarissa shook her head in despair. When she returned her attention to Sven, his fingers relaxed and his chest deflated as he exhaled his final breath in a sigh. His glazed eyes stared blankly past her, out her window, at the passing trees.

Clarissa raised his hand to her lips. She wasn't sure if she meant to kiss the back of it or something worse, but the smell of his blood was intoxicating. Without another thought she slipped the index finger into her mouth and sucked, savoring the taste of it, like a piece of semisweet chocolate. The horror of what she was doing struck her suddenly, and despite the overpowering urge to lick his fingers clean and bury her face in his open wound, she dropped his already cooling hand into his lap and glanced at the rearview, hoping Gabe hadn't seen. He was facing forward, concentrating on the dark road ahead of them with a scowl.

Ava had half-turned in her seat, her pale face smiling back at her in flickers of moonlight through the trees.

You see? Ava said in Clarissa's mind. *Now you're like me.*

Abraham sat in his cell, awaiting Death's return.

He had no brilliant plan to get the drop on the vampire in his final moments, no ace up his sleeve with which to cause the house to lose. The Duke would kill him where he stood. He merely had to make his peace with it.

He'd always suspected he would die on this island, but he'd hoped it would coincide with the death of the Vampire King. He'd imagined the stake in his hand undoing both The Duke with its sharpened edge and himself with the vampire's departure from this world. Those born of The Duke's blood would return to their former state as living human beings and the living beings cursed by his blood—*Strigoi* like Abraham himself—would breathe their last breath as The Duke's blood expired in their veins.

Abraham Van Helsing would die a hero, the first and last of his kind, the single greatest vampire hunter to have ever lived.

He'd extinguished as many as a hundred of The Duke's direct offspring in over a century hunting the fiend. He had hoped—he had *prayed*, when he'd still been a praying man—to be able to vanquish their sire before breathing his last breath, and to give these children back their former lives.

He'd pictured the girls wandering out of the forest, confused and hopeful, looking up at the sun for the first time in who knew how long as it rose above the surf, the vile things done to them and the things that they'd been forced to do erased from their memories, the future before them unknown but much brighter than their pasts.

This was his dream.

The Jackmans may have stripped the lives from these girls, but they no longer controlled them. Abraham was certain of that. With their first taste of blood still warm on their lips, The Duke would call each of them home. They would dine well tonight, on the blood of the innocent as well as the wicked. Perhaps they would find themselves vomiting a finger or an ear or some other scrap of flesh in the light of day, but they would never again be powerless to the allure of blood.

With The Duke and his children running free, the vampire scourge would probably overrun the island by morning, and with nothing to stop them, move on to the next, and the next. The Duke would spread his blood seed across the Virgin Islands, to Puerto Rico and the Dominican, to South and Central America and Cuba and the continental United States. The vampire plague would proliferate unchecked throughout the world, with no Van Helsing left to prevent it.

A door slammed out in the security office. Abraham sat up, locking eyes with the New Jersian. The man shrugged up his shoulders. "Well, it was fun while it lasted, huh?"

Abraham chuckled bitterly.

"What in the hell?" came a familiar woman's voice from out front. "Marcus, are you—? Oh my God…!"

"Guess we got a last-minute reprieve," Tino said.

"Mrs. Terrell!" Abraham called out, though his voice wasn't quite as loud as he'd hoped. In truth, he was exhausted. He doubted he'd be able to best the Vampire King even if he'd gotten the opportunity.

"Heyo, Journee!" Tino called, and began banging his metal cup against the bars.

"What's going on back there?" A moment later the woman herself appeared in the doorway. She saw the cell door on the floor and the arsonist's cell empty. "Oh, Lord. What happened, you two?"

"Would you believe an ancient all-powerful supernatural being broke your arsonist out of prison and promised to return to end us both?" Abraham asked.

"What in the world…?" She sucked her teeth. "No. Uh-uh. This is not happening."

"It's happenin, Jay," Tino said. "Fuckin thing was a *monster*. Tiny little ding-dong, though. Like a miniature Pinscher's."

Journee looked out of her depth, trying to comprehend what could have done this. "Okay, I am not trying to hear that right now, Tino. I'm in a lot of trouble here."

"So are we all if you don't bust us out."

"He's right, Mrs. Terrell. What is happening out there is beyond comprehension."

She blew out an uneasy breath. "Okay, you two just stay put. I need a minute to talk to my supervisor."

"We might not have a minute, Mrs. Terrell."

The guard had already turned her back on them and held up a finger to silence him. She removed her radio from her utility belt as she left the bullpen. "Blitz, this is Journee! Where are you?

Over!"

An excited male voice replied immediately, but Abraham couldn't hear what he'd said let alone determine who it was.

"I'm hanging on," Journee said, clearly harried. A moment later, an inner door slammed, muting the rest of the conversation.

"She'll let us out," Tino said. "She's a good gal. Smart."

"Smart is what I fear. She'll be far likelier to disbelieve. Let's just hope she's prudent, as well."

The two men waited, aware that every moment brought The Duke closer to them, and with him their demises. Journee would be just as vulnerable. A Taser and baton wouldn't stop the fiend. They needed stakes. Holy water. Silver. Garlic.

Journee came back with a sour look on her face, clipping the radio onto her belt. "Okay, here's the deal: I'm going to let the two of you out and the three of us are going back to the boat. But I don't want any funny business and no more talk about vampires. Are we clear?"

"We won't say peep, Jay."

"Clear as daybreak, Mrs. Terrell. Although, perhaps I could make a little modification—"

Journee scowled. "It doesn't seem like I was clear enough."

"My apologies. To the boat it is."

Journee gave them both a dubious look, then used her keys on Abraham's door. "Thank you," he said, leaning heavily on his cane to step out.

"Don't make me regret it."

Abraham smiled. The guard then crossed to Tino's cell and let him out. "You're a queen, Jay."

Journee huffed. "Please."

Tino laughed. "All right, let's blow this dump."

"Probably not the best choice of words," the woman said, "but I'll allow it. Follow me, boys."

The security office was a shambles when they stepped out to the front: the inner office destroyed, several of the monitors smashed and blacked out, the chair smashed against the far wall. Abraham peered over the desk and saw a guard he hadn't yet met crumpled on the floor in a bloody, broken mess.

"I'm sorry for the loss of your friend," he said.

Journee glanced back at Abraham as she opened the front

door. "He wasn't my friend, I just worked with him. But thanks." She led them to a Land Cruiser, parked close to the building, opened the closest back door and gestured for them to get in. Tino climbed in first, causing the vehicle to rock on its wheels. Abraham eased himself in with a groan and gripped his cane between his knees. Journee slammed the door and went around to the front, climbed in behind the wheel and started the engine.

"Hold on to your hats," she said. In moments they were heading back the way they'd come, the road and forest ahead illuminated by the vehicle's brights. Abraham held on to the door frame, bouncing from the bumpy and expedient—dangerously, he thought—drive.

In minutes they were driving past the amphitheater he'd seen earlier in the day, where people had gathered for their hosts to welcome them. At the moment it was filled with dancing people, and as they passed, slightly slower around a bend in the road, Abraham was sure he saw something large flying in the red and blue spotlights above. Loud drumbeats thumped, in pace to the increased rhythm of his heart.

"Mrs. Terrell?"

She frowned at him in the rearview. "What is it?"

Judging by her expression he knew no amount of begging would change her mind. If he wanted to help the people on the dancefloor, he'd have to open up his door and tuck and roll against the fall. He might have been able to do so a hundred years ago, when he'd been youthful and cars were decidedly slower. If he attempted it at his age, he feared he'd only end up breaking all of his brittle bones and lie in a ditch like roadkill until The Duke came to fetch him.

He just had to hope someone would notice the fiend circling above before his children descended upon the crowd. It was the only shot any of them had to survive, even if it was slim.

The vehicle rounded the corner and Abraham turned around to watch, but the amphitheater and its partygoers became obscured by a stand of dark trees. On the straightaway it was possible to see the beach through a break in the forest ahead. The *Ceres* stood like a black monolith on the edge of the moon-dappled surf. As Abraham regarded it, a ball of fire erupted from the stern.

"Holeeee *shit*!" Tino said, leaning over Abraham to get a better look.

"What in the Lord?" Journee muttered as the SUV rocked from the explosion. She slammed on the brakes, the vehicle skidding to a stop in the gravel road. "Oh, my God. Gabe… you were right."

"Now do you believe us, Mrs. Terrell?" Abraham asked.

She caught his eye in the rearview, flames flickering over her face. "I mean, I'm still not willing to believe there's an actual *vampire* out there, but I'm taking this a lot more seriously."

Another explosion rocked the vehicle, this second closer to the middle of the boat. The arsonist was setting off charges, probably watching from shore. Whoever he'd been before he met The Duke, he seemed to be adept at making things blow up.

If the fires spread, and Abraham supposed they quickly would, the boat would not just burn but sink into the sea, taking any chance of escape with it.

A SINGLE DROP OF BLOOD

GABE WIPED TEARS from his misty eyes with the back of a hand as he drove. Despite the evident blood loss, Sven's passing had still been unexpected. Gabe had naïvely hoped he'd be able to get the man to the medical hut before he bled out, but he'd had no idea just how much blood the girl who'd maimed him had sucked from his body.

He briefly considered stopping the SUV to bury the reporter, but they needed to keep moving. If they could make it to the boat before The Duke's familiar blew it up, they might have a chance to save some people, maybe most of them. If not, he supposed they'd have to find a radio to contact the Coast Guard. Although doing so without getting rid of The Duke would just give the vampires more potential victims, like the zombie police officer in *Return of the Living Dead* calling, "Send more cops." With no idea what they were walking into, they'd be massacred before they hit the beach.

Gabe had driven the girls almost to the amphitheater on the south road—running parallel to the north road Journee would've taken from the security office—when two sparkly figures ran out of the trees. He slammed on the brakes and the SUV careened a moment before stopping abruptly, sending everyone forward like ragdolls. Sven's head struck the backseat and his body slid to the side, slumping against his window. Gabe was just glad the airbags didn't deploy.

A man and woman in clothing fit for a movie premiere stood terrified in the headlights about ten feet from the car. Panting and wild eyed, panicked and weeping, they peered back into the dark woods they'd just emerged from. In the distance, Gabe heard shouting, cries for help, screams, all rising in a cacophony above a pounding drumbeat.

"Everyone all right?" he asked the girls.

"I'm good," Clarissa said, smiling flatly in the rearview.

Ava nodded, staring out at the fancy couple. As he followed her gaze, the duo in the road began waving frantically and approaching the vehicle.

"*Omigod why is this happeneeeeeng?!*" the woman yelped.

"*They're in the woods, they're fucking everywhere!*" cried the man.

Before Gabe could react, a slender shadow leaped out of the trees, clotheslining the two strangers. They struck the road with solid thumps, raising clouds of gravel dust. Wearing nothing but a masquerade mask and a black bra and panties, covered in shimmering gore from head to toe, the teenage vampire bit into the crying woman's neck. The woman's scream tore through the night as a geyser of blood erupted from her, hyper-red in the headlights, spattering her sequined dress. Her companion wailed and got to his knees but the girl grabbed him by the shoulders and tossed him skittering across the road. He struck the base of a bay rum tree and fell silent.

Gabe stared open mouthed at the woman being murdered before them, until the door chime started ringing, and Clarissa shouted his name.

"Huh?" he said, stunned by the sight before him. Coming on the heels of Sven's death, this was too much to handle.

Clarissa unlatched her seatbelt and opened her door.

Gabe turned to find Ava missing and her door wide open. He hadn't even heard her leave the vehicle. Hadn't even seen her move or the door open.

I think I'm in shock, he thought vaguely.

Clarissa leaped out. "Gabe, we have to go!"

He looked ahead again, expecting to find Ava had joined her vampire sister in feasting on the people in the road. But she was nowhere in sight. "Where is she?"

"She ran into the woods!" Clarissa slapped a palm against his door. "Let's go! Come on!"

Gabe left the keys in the ignition and stumbled out of the driver's seat. He had to consciously ignore the sounds of the vampire gorging on the screaming woman to push himself forward. Clarissa scurried down into the ditch. There was no time to help the woman or her companion, even if Gabe believed he could force himself to thrust a stake through the heart of a teenage girl, undead or not. Abe had told Gabe he was a natural hunter the night before, but he didn't feel like a hunter at all. He felt weak, witless, and scared out of his mind.

Why'd I think I could do this? I musta been nuts.

"She went this way," Clarissa called over her shoulder.

"Where's she goin?"

"To *him*!" she shouted, not even glancing back as she hurried into the trees.

Gabe dashed across the road, down into the ditch, and entered the dark woods. Unable to see a damn thing, he tripped over a root immediately, and would've fallen flat on his face if he hadn't caught a tree, wincing as he scraped up his palm on the bark. Even with the bright moon emerged from the clouds, the thick branches high above threw deep shadows over everything. He was lucky to be able to see Clarissa's shock of light hair moving swiftly ahead of him, and glanced back to see that the woods had already swallowed up the horrific scene in the road. The blood on his palm looked practically black against his skin in a shaft of moonlight.

"Dang it," he muttered, clenching his injured hand into a fist and pushing onward, certain it made him a walking target.

He tripped, stumbled, banged his shins and righted himself. Without the compass of Clarissa's bright form ahead of him, he would've been completely lost in seconds. Fortunately, she seemed to know where she was going. The mental link with her sister was strong, especially now.

I'm in love with a vampire, Gabe thought suddenly. Two days ago, just the idea of that would have made him laugh.

Clarissa disappeared in the darkness ahead.

He stopped dead, looking around himself anxiously, the dark closing in, his hear pounding in his ears to the rhythm of the distant drums. "Clarissa!" he called out. "Where are ya?"

The only sounds were the thump of music, the screams of panic and terror and rage.

"*Clarissa?*"

I'm here, came a voice inside his head, causing Gabe to just about leap in alarm.

Clarissa? he thought.

It's me, she said, her voice soothingly calm. *Follow my voice.*

Gabe started forward, following where her voice seemed to be projecting from. It was like listening to her from the television wearing headphones: even though the sound felt like it came from inside his head it also appeared to have placement in the real world. He stopped suddenly, an anxious feeling crawling up his spine. *Can she hear my thoughts?*

Clarissa didn't answer.

Can you hear my thoughts? he asked her pointedly.

I could, she said. *But I won't. Not unless you want me to.*

Please don't.

Okay, Gabe. I'm not far now. Just a little further and I'll get out of your head.

I don't think that's possible, he thought, and hoped she hadn't overheard.

He kept moving in the direction he'd been going, trudging carefully over roots and rocks and a large gumbo-limbo tree that had fallen right across the makeshift path. A screech from the trees ahead startled him, and he looked up to see a pair of forward-facing eyes glowing from the branches of a tree. Dark wings spread out and the creature—*Bird? Bat?*—hopped off the branch and flew directly at Gabe.

As the creature neared it locked eyes with him, unblinking, and *shrieked*. Panicked, fearing he'd stumbled upon a vampire who'd transformed into an animal, he ducked. The owl swooped over his head with a *woosh* of its wings.

Chuckling at his fear, he continued onward. *Musta seen my eyes and thought I was dinner.*

A few dozen feet further into the increasingly treacherous forest and he heard Clarissa speak aloud. "Here I am."

She stood in a gap between two narrow trees, waving at him. He approached her, glad to finally see her face again, despite barely being able to see at all. It was obvious she could see him perfectly. Like the owl, her vision was probably better at night.

"We're almost there," she said. "Come on."

Gabe could tell by the sound of the music and screams they were very close to the amphitheater. Less than a minute later they stepped out of the woods together, and what he saw nearly made him want to bolt right back into the trees.

Terrified people ran in all different directions, seemingly

without aim, many flailing their arms and screaming in terror. At their feet lay dozens of people who'd probably been running around just like them moments or minutes ago, no longer living. Several were being fed upon by the teenage vampires, while on the outer edges of the amphitheater, their sisters herded the intended victims back toward the carnage with screams of rage and menacing lunges. Few if any of the living dared to fight back. Some swung clutch purses or lobbed plastic water bottles, but it was a losing battle. The ones who made an actual physical attempt to breach the vampire offensive line were pounced upon and slaughtered. The thumping beat of some Katy Perry "Roar" dance remix from the empty DJ booth and the blue and red swinging spotlights turned the bloodbath into a bizarre mixture of bubblegum girl power and the macabre.

Amidst all of this, the Vampire King stood, his wings spread wide, grinning his feline grin as he reveled in the acts of violence and bloodshed his children wreaked upon the crowd.

"Hold my hand," Clarissa said, holding her left out to him.

Gabe looked at her, startled by the request.

"That medicine the Jackmans gave me," she said. "Whatever it is, I think it's wearing off. I need you to stop me from joining them."

Gabe swallowed hard and took her hand. It was cold within his own. She entwined her fingers with his and squeezed, turning to him with a sad smile. At least he didn't have to worry about his hand sweating with her freezing fingers to cool it down. It cold also numbed the pain from the cut he'd gotten in the woods. The fact it was caused by her being dead was troubling, but like his grandmother had often said, *It could always be worse.*

Clarissa started striding toward the massacre. Gabe stayed put, his arm stretching out until it stopped her.

"I can't just walk in there."

"Ava's there." She pointed with her free hand. The littlest vampire had buried her face in the crook of a young woman's neck very close to The Duke's hind legs. "They won't touch you with me. You're protected. *For now*," she added darkly.

Then she proceeded forward.

Reluctantly, Gabe followed.

Two girls on the outskirts of the dancefloor stepped aside,

allowing them passage. They hissed at Gabe as he and Clarissa moved cautiously between them. He turned to keep an eye on them as Clarissa led him toward her sister and The Duke, who appeared to be protecting his smallest daughter.

"Now!" the male model who lost his fiancée on the ship shouted to a middle-aged man who looked like Arab royalty, dressed in a sharp white suit and wearing a white-and-red keffiyeh. "Let's go!"

The two men made a break for it, running for the space Gabe and Clarissa had just passed through. They were just about through when the two girls attacked from either side. Gabe didn't see the rest as Clarissa tugged him along, but their screams were surprisingly high-pitched.

As Gabe and Clarissa neared The Duke and his favored daughter, Gabe recognized the woman Ava was feeding on. It was Marnie, the line cook Digby had his sights on before he'd gone off with Cheery. Gabe didn't know her much, but thinking of his best friend missing and possibly drowned weighed heavily on his heart.

It made him angry.

He focused that rage toward The Duke, who'd started all of this, intentionally or not.

"Clarissa, my lovely daughter," The Duke said. "And you've brought us a gift. How thoughtful."

"Keep your hands off him. We just want my sister, then we'll leave."

Ava looked up innocently from the line cook's throat, her face covered in blood. The vacant look of pleasure in her eyes hurt Gabe's soul to see. He'd hoped, in the short time he and Abraham had spent with her, that they'd impressed upon her the importance of choosing the *right* victims. Marnie wasn't evil, not like the men in the manor house. She didn't deserve to end up an entrée on the vampire's menu.

"Ava *wants* to stay," The Duke said. "Don't you, my child?"

Ava's eyes glowed red and she smiled, showing her fangs. "Stay with us, Clarissa. *Feed* with us."

"Ava, you have to—" Clarissa began, but her twin tucked her head back into the open wound and slurped.

The Duke chuckled. "You see? We could all be together, Clarissa. One large family, feasting together. Growing our number." The monster pointed at Gabe. "But you must first give up the boy."

Clarissa turned to Gabe, sadness in her eyes. Were The Duke's words getting to her? Was he losing her to this monster? He couldn't tell.

Until she let go of his hand.

She raised the hand he'd been holding in front of her face. His blood was smeared on her palm. She lifted it to her nose and sniffed.

"Clarissa, no," he said, his voice not much more than a whisper.

She licked her palm. Her eyelids fluttered in delight.

Gabe's heart sank. He'd lost her. She'd turned.

The Duke hissed suddenly, swinging one giant wing around his body as if to protect himself. "*Do not speak a word of what you know!*" he commanded.

Clarissa smiled, her lips painted crimson. "All this time, he was right here," she said to The Duke. "*She* was right here. She *left* you, you know. She knew the crew was planning to throw you overboard and she *let* them."

"*LIES!*" the Vampire King roared.

Gabe had no idea what the two of them were talking about, but it seemed he'd been wrong about Clarissa. Whatever she'd learned from his blood—*A single drop of blood and I will divulge everything*, the vampire had said—it made The Duke very angry, and, Gabe thought, even *afraid*.

"*You betray me! I should slaughter you where you stand!*"

"In front of my sister? My *sisters*?" she shouted, waving an arm at the carnage around them. "They know the truth now, just like you and me. What kind of *example* would that set? If they tell you the truth, you'll *kill* them for it?"

"It is *not* true!"

"*Blood doesn't lie*," Clarissa said. Her eyes blazed red as she held his evil gaze.

The Duke bared his fangs. "*Begone from my sight! Take your pathetic human and make haste! I will not give you another chance!*"

"Not without Ava!"

The Duke spread his wings and roared. For a single moment

the sounds of slaughter paused as every one of his daughters paused their feast to watch.

"Ava comes with us or I tell him right now."

"Tell me what?" Gabe asked.

"*TAKE HER!*"

"Tell me what, Clarissa?"

Clarissa ignored him. She held out a hand to her sister. "Ava," she said.

The little vampire cocked her head toward The Duke.

"*Go*," said the Vampire King.

Ava's face crumpled, as if she might cry.

"*Go, little one! Do not make me say it again!*"

Ava stood, her face and filthy little dress covered once again in gore. She stepped over the line cook's corpse and took Clarissa's hand reluctantly.

"*WHAT ARE YOU LOOKING AT?*" The Duke bellowed. "*FEED, MY DAUGHTERS! FEED TO YOUR HEARTS' CONTENT!*"

Unlike Clarissa, the other girls didn't need a second warning. The sounds of murder swiftly resumed, and The Duke watched powerlessly as Gabe and Clarissa and Ava moved past him, leaving their vampire sisters to their feast.

STRANDED

BY THE TIME Abraham and the others reached the beach, the *Ceres* was already sinking. Two more earth-shaking explosions had erupted on their way, taking out the engine room and the side of the boat holding the remaining utility tenders, both of which fell to the water below in burning bits of plastic and rubber.

The architect of this madness stood on the pier watching it burn, flames dancing in his wild eyes. The flesh had melted off of Stuart Smith's left arm and his pantleg on that side had burned away to ash. Half of his hair had caught fire and melted to little black nubs on his skin in the same blaze, struck by a blast of burning oil as he'd run from the explosion of the propane tanks in the kitchen. He'd barely managed to put himself out and flee before the final charge had gone off, blowing the hole in the bottom of the ship that was currently sinking it.

The moment the Cruiser stopped, Journee leaped out and hurried toward the arsonist, Taser at the ready. "Don't move!" she shouted as she neared him. Stuart Smith turned to them with a wild-eyed grin, put his hands behind his head and dropped to his knees. His work here was done. He'd started by burning the boathouse, and it was already a heap of smoldering cinders at the far end of the dock platform. No living person would escape from this island, unless they chose to swim. Even then, they wouldn't make it far.

Abraham pushed himself out of the Cruiser and watched the conflagration with a pit of despair forming in his stomach. He picked up the gnarled stick he'd snatched while Tino and Journee had struggled with the tree that had been pushed into the road to block their way, likely by the dump truck currently parked closer to the pier, and began to whittle with the small blade from the multi-tool in the head of his cane. It wasn't much of a knife but it would get the job done.

"Jesus!" Tino said, slipping out behind him. 'We're royally screwed, aren't we?"

"Yes, Tino." Abraham nodded. "I believe we are."

Down at the pier, Journee reached the vampire's familiar, holstered her Taser and took the cuffs off her belt. "Why would you do this, Stuart? Are you crazy?" Slapping the cuffs on his wrists and jerking him roughly to his feet, she answered her own question. "What am I saying? *Of course*, you are."

She shoved the arsonist forward, and he went willingly, only looking back to mutter, "My Master will consume you all. Your blood will sire *generations*."

"Good for him."

The two-way radio on her hip blipped. "*Journee, where are you right now? Over!*" It was Gabe.

She stopped her detainee and grabbed the radio off her belt. "Gabe," she said. "We're at the docks, but it's bad..."

"What do you mean 'bad'?"

"The boats are gone. All of them. We're stranded."

"*Stranded?*"

"I'm sorry, Gabe. We got here too late. We had to move a damn tree that was laying across the road, which I figure was the work of this fool," she added, shoving the arsonist forward. He stumbled and she righted him by yanking on the cuffs.

"We're almost there," Gabe said. "They'll be comin soon, so get ready."

"Now you're sounding like *him*. What's going on here, Gabe? We heard all kinds of screams coming from the amphitheater."

"You know what it is. Just be careful, okay?"

Journee still didn't believe all the stories about vampires, but he had been right about the boat. "All right, Gabe. Over and out."

Gabe didn't reply.

She shoved the detainee toward the Cruiser. Abraham was whittling a thick stick he must have found in the woods when she and Tino were moving the tree out of the road. "What are you making?"

Abraham looked up at her gloomily. "I'm making stakes, Mrs. Terrell. I suggest you find some driftwood and do the same."

"Okay then," she said, shoving Stuart Smith's head down and pushing him into the back of the Land Cruiser.

"*My Master and his brood will enslave the world!*" the man shouted at them. "*Your suffering will be the stuff of le—!*"

Journee slammed the door on him, cutting off whatever he'd been about to say. "I've had enough of his 'master' baloney." She scowled at Tino, who was taking off his shoes and socks. "What are *you* doing?"

"I'm gonna fuckin swim. It's what? A mile, maybe two to the next island? I'd rather take my chances out there than with that fuckin thing back at the station."

Journee sucked her teeth. "You are out of your mind, Tino. You'll run out of breath after two minutes. You just gonna float the rest of the way?"

"Maybe. I'd rather drown a hundred times than get my blood sucked by some three-hundred-year-old Eurotrash freakshow."

"Closer to two hundred, actually," Abraham said, looking up from his whittling. He brushed away little strips of wood, blew on the sharpened tip, and held it out to Journee. "I would feel much more comfortable if you held this."

Journee shook her head. "This is absolute lunacy."

"Please. Indulge me, Mrs. Terrell."

"Fine." She took the stake from him. "Now what do we—"

The words died in her throat as she caught sight of a thing that shouldn't be possible, something she wouldn't have believed even if she'd read it in one of her horror novels.

The silhouette of a giant, humanoid bird flew toward them from the dark forest, holding what looked like a man with its hind legs. A screaming, kicking and thrashing man. The massive creature and its prey were flying right toward them.

"Oh, my Lord..." Journee muttered. "Is that...?"

"It is, indeed, Mrs. Terrell," Abraham said.

"That's it for me," Tino said as he waded out into the surf. "Adios, amigos!" He waved at the two of them, then plunged headfirst into the sea.

Gabe was just about to end the radio transmission with Journee when something large rustled in the woods ahead of them. The three of them stopped dead. Ava hissed. Gabe and Clarissa raised their stakes.

"Who's there?" Gabe called out. "You better talk or you're gettin a stake!"

The bushes moved again and a man wrapped in reflective yellow DANGER tape scurried out, holding up his hands. He had a traffic cone on his head, wearing it like a wizard's hat. "Yo, don't kill me, cuz! It just be DJ Safe-T comin back at ya, remix Twenny-Twenny-Three, y'all!" He tittered nervous laughter. "You ain't one of them, is you? That shit was *buggin* back there, for real, though!"

Gabe sighed heavily. The last thing he wanted to deal with was some obnoxious, loudmouth DJ. But they couldn't exactly leave him out here to fend for himself, not when they could help him. Not when they'd already left so many others behind to die.

"Yo, can I roll wit your crew, homie? You know what DJ Safe-T say: they be safety in numbers, ya feel me?"

Gabe turned to Clarissa. She shrugged.

"All right, but you *gotta* be quiet," Gabe said. "And take off that stupid cone, you look like an idiot."

The DJ appeared confused, then reached up and grabbed the traffic cone in both hands. "Oh, shit, homie. I forgot I had this awn." He tittered again and tossed it into the woods, then pointed at the stake in Gabe's hand. "Yo, you got one a them big-ass toothpicks for me?"

"They're stakes," Clarissa said.

"I take mine medium rare, ya feel me?" Safe-T snickered behind a hand and snapped his fingers as if he'd gotten off a sick burn. Then his barber-slitted eyebrows furrowed. "Say, you look real familiar, my dude." He looked at Clarissa. "Matter fact, so do you."

Gabe's cheeks went red, remembering the last time he'd seen Safe-T he'd been in drag. He reached into his bag for a stake, and held it out. Safe-T grabbed for it, but Gabe retracted his hand before the DJ could take it. "No more yappin or hype-mannin or whatever it is you do from now on, you got it?" Gabe said.

Safe-T grinned. "Moms is the word, dawg. Cross my heart and hope to die, no cap, for real, fam." He bumped his chest with a fist and threw Gabe a peace sign.

Clenching his jaw in aggravation, Gabe handed over the stake.

Safe-T made him immediately regret it, tossing the stake into the air. The DJ spun around on the tips of his toes and caught it behind his back, then held it out with a flourish.

Ava clapped. "Again," she said.

"That was actually impressive," Clarissa said.

Safe-T smiled, showing off his metal grill. "You know what DJ Safe-T say—"

"*Nothin,*" Gabe said before the man could give them any further useless advice. "Because he *promised* he'd keep his mouth shut."

"Aw, shit, li'l man." The DJ held the tip of the stake to his lips. "My bad. I'll turn the tempo down to zero, ya feel me?"

Fuming, Gabe ignored the question and continued onward. Clarissa and Ava followed. Safe-T fell into line behind them, stumbling over something and righting himself. "I'm a'ight," he muttered to himself.

They trudged through the woods, following the firelight of the burning ship.

Ava peered up with sudden elation at the sound of wings flapping overhead. "Do you feel it, sister? Our father is near."

"He's *not* our father," Clarissa snapped. "He's a *monster*."

Ava just smiled and scurried ahead through the underbrush.

"Wait up, damn it!" Clarissa shouted after her.

The three of them ran after Ava, and in moments they emerged behind the main building, which housed the kitchen, the dining hall, the games rooms, the indoor theater, the gym and several other activity rooms. The kitchen faced them, gleaming white and chrome with all of the lights still on inside. Even over the stench of burning gasoline and plastic Gabe could smell whatever amazing food Chef Bialczyk and his crew had whipped up earlier, causing his stomach to rumble. His first instinct was to run inside and barricade the windows and doors. There would be plenty of knives and pots and pans to defend themselves with, as well as leftovers to scrounge. But Abe and Journee were waiting for them on the beach.

"It's all so empty," Clarissa said as they passed below the windows.

"Everyone who wasn't at the big house was probably at the amphitheater, I guess. Or hiding in their cabanas."

"Bet," Safe-T said. "We should too, ya feel me?"

Gabe shook his head. "We got friends at the beach."

"Shit, man, I fuck with that. Gotta stay true to family. I'ma hide in the kitchen though, my dude. I got the munchies, *for real*, yo."

"Stay safe," Gabe said as the DJ turned and headed for the back doors.

The DJ showed his shiny grill in a smile. "Safe is like, literally, my first name. Peace out, li'l homies."

Ahead of them, Ava scampered around the corner, heading for the beach. Clarissa hurried to catch up. Gabe followed them. Rounding the corner, he felt the heat from the blaze on his cheeks, warmer than the trade winds that sometimes blew over the decks of the *Ceres* when he'd stayed there alone. At the end of the pier, his home away from home sank lazily into the sea, creaking and groaning, wood splintering, plastic and other synthetic materials melting, gasoline pouring black smoke into the midnight blue sky. Flames flickering over his face, Gabe suddenly remembered they'd left Blitz Wagner on board after Ava had torn his nose off, and though he'd never much liked the man he hoped he'd managed to get out before the explosions. Burning alive was probably the worst death Gabe could imagine. Or it had been, before he'd met The Duke and his daughters.

Clarissa grabbed his hand, pulling him forward. "Come on!"

Ava was running on all fours across the beach, a small silhouette against fire-dappled waves. While they hurried after her, Gabe saw Abe and the others standing by a Cruiser parked closer to the shore. Tino whipped off his shirt and waded into the sea. Both Journee and Abe held what looked like makeshift stakes.

Between Ava and the others, The Duke swooped down from the sky, landing so hard his massive back paws raised plumes of sand. The man in white he'd been carrying sprawled on the beach beside the creature, then got to his hands and knees, trying desperately to scurry away. The Duke reached out a long winged arm and grabbed the man by the shirt collar, lifting him back up off his feet.

Ava reached the beast before Gabe and Clarissa could. She hugged his leg, and with the creature's free hand he lovingly patted her head.

As they neared, Clarissa still holding Gabe's hand in her cold grip, he realized who the man in white was, dangling from The Duke's claws, and he knew as surely as Ava had fallen to The Duke's sway, he was about to lose Clarissa, too.

It was the human monster, Emory Jackman.

BLOODLINES

CLARISSA RECOGNIZED THE face of the man who'd murdered her, the terrified expression he wore mirroring the look she'd had when his blade slashed her throat. She skidded to a stop in the sand, and Gabe, still holding her hand, stopped alongside her.

The Vampire King turned, his feline lips curling upwards in a monstrous smile as his black-eyed gaze fell upon her. "I have brought you a gift, my love."

"Clarissa…" Gabe said with a cautioning tone.

"I know." She stepped forward, letting go of his hand. The Duke wanted her to exact her revenge on the man who'd killed her. As much as she wanted to, as badly as she yearned to open his throat as he'd done to her and drink his vile blood while the life spilled out of him, she knew that if she took The Duke's "gift," she would do nothing more than further align herself with him. It was a trap. She might as well get on her knees and hug the creature's other leg like Ava.

Rather than respond to the offering, she addressed her sister. "You *called* me. I came to save you. I *died* to save you. This *thing*… is *not* our father. Our mom and dad—" Her voice caught in her throat as the image of her parents' blood splashing the car windows flashed before her eyes. "—our parents are dead. They're dead because of a monster just like him. Like *them*," she added, pointing a finger at Emory Jackman.

"I am *nothing* like him," The Duke hissed. "I *freed* your sisters from his heinous deeds. If not for me, they would still be *scrounglings*, subsisting on nothing but—"

"You're *exactly* like him! You're both bloodsuckers, stealing the lives of *children*!"

"*I GAVE YOU LIFE!*"

"*I* gave her life!" Emory shouted, dangling from the beast's claws. "You were a withered carcass when I got here, sucking blood out of bats and rats in a cave just to fucking survive! You are *nothing* without me!"

"And where would you be without me? Pathetic *Strigoi*. My blood gave you *everything*! My *glammers* made you rich beyond your wildest dreams!"

"I was rich before we ever met you!"

Clarissa grinned. Her words had done exactly what she'd wanted, providing Abraham with the distraction he needed to creep toward the quarreling monsters, readying his stake.

She gripped the stake in her own hand tightly, glancing back at Gabe. He nodded, understanding what needed to be done, and the two began creeping toward the monster themselves.

"Erzsébet was wealthy!" the vampire bellowed. "You were merely mouldable clay with the right connections, scarcely handsome and charming enough to suit her needs!"

"You're one to talk about looks, *Steve*!"

Ava looked up suddenly, her dark little eyes going wide as she spotted Abraham's cautious approach. "Daddy!" she cried.

Startled into action, Abraham lunged with his stake just as the Vampire King turned his attention toward him. The creature swung his right arm out to protect himself from the attack, and the thrusted stake plunged into Emory's chest. The rich man howled in agony, his feet trashing and arms flopping like someone having a seizure.

"*You fuck—*!" he cried. Then he gasped, and his limbs fell slack.

The Duke howled, tossing the dead man aside. "*YOU WILL PAY FOR THAT, OLD MAN!*"

The monster swiped at Abraham, claws slashing across the old man's chest. Clarissa heard his ribs crack, and fresh blood spilled from rips in his sweater.

"*No!*" Gabe cried.

The vampire hunter staggered forward, falling over his cane, uttering a weakened groan. Falling sideways, he sprawled in the sand beside Emory's rapidly aging corpse. She ran past The Duke and leaped over the dead man to Abraham's side. He looked up at her in despair. The meat of his chest was torn to ribbons, his cracked ribs exposed. "I'm… so sorry, my dear," he gasped with ragged breath. "I have... failed you…"

The Duke began to laugh, clapping his clawed hands together. "Wonderful! Simply wonderful! The last Van Helsing, reduced to a sniveling old man before the feet of his greatest nemesis." The Vampire King turned to Gabe. "Consume his flesh with me, boy. As you did your mother and father. *Eat his flesh and live forever.*"

"W-what?" Gabe muttered.

Clarissa blinked tears from her eyes. Gabe stood frozen where she'd left him, his mouth agape, the stake held at his side in a quivering hand.

She spoke directly into his mind: *Gabe. You have to kill him.*

"I can't," he said aloud.

"You *can*," The Duke said in a gentle voice, believing Gabe had been responding to him. "Your mother and father came to this island to destroy me. But they failed. As *Abraham* failed. As *you* will fail. Join me or die at his side!"

You can *destroy him*, Clarissa told Gabe. *The Duke never told you the whole truth about your parents. They came here to* find *him, Gabe. They crashed on the island but they were looking for* him.

"W-why?"

The Duke growled in frustration, returning his attention to Clarissa with a fang-toothed sneer. "You use the *Moroi hangja* to speak with the boy? There is much power in you, my daughter. Both you and your sister possess admirable strength and strong magic. Leave the old man." He stroked Ava's hair, holding out his free hand to Clarissa. "Let him die with the knowledge his bloodline ends here!"

Clarissa stood. "Except it doesn't, does it?"

The Duke hissed.

"What are you sayin, Clarissa?" Gabe asked.

"Abraham's niece, Wilhelmina—"

"*YOU DARE NOT SPEAK HER NAME!*"

"—she left with The Duke on a ship to America! But he never made it there!"

Abraham smiled up at her, tears glistening in his eyes. "Is this… true?"

Clarissa nodded.

"*I AM WARNING YOU, GIRL!*"

"She changed her mind, didn't she, Duke? She *told* the crew about you and they trapped you in a casket lined with silver and threw you into the sea!"

The Duke hissed, wrapping his wings around himself.

"Gabe, Wilhelmina Van Helsing is your *great-grandmother.* She married a man named Claus Zimmer, and they had your grandmother. Your mother is a *direct descendent* of Abraham Van Helsing. Your mom and dad were *looking* for The Duke!"

Abraham began to smile.

She spoke the rest directly into Gabe's mind: *That's why they were here, Gabe. That's why he murdered them! He killed them right in front of you and wiped your memory of what happened! That's why you don't remember anything! That's why your grandmother lied to you about him when you said you saw a man on the island. She was trying to keep you safe!*

Gabe just gaped at her, clearly unable to process what she'd told him.

"*ENOUGH OF THESE LIES!*" the creature growled. He stepped forward, raising a hand full of razor-sharp claws, ready to slash her the way he'd mortally wounded Abraham… But he froze suddenly, his snarl falling away as he looked down.

Ava still held his leg, wearing a fierce expression. It was clear she wouldn't let go.

"Little one…" The Duke said soothingly.

"*LEAVE MY SISTER ALONE!*" she bellowed, her voice loud enough to make the sand beneath Clarissa ripple and shudder.

The monster reared back in shock. Then he turned his rage upon Ava, who leaped away from him and skittered back on her butt in the sand.

"*Freeze*, you Volturi bastard!"

Clarissa turned toward the familiar voice. Journee Terrell had gotten close to them during the dispute and held a Taser pointed directly at The Duke. He roared at her, baring rows of fangs, clearly unafraid. Without hesitation, Journee pulled the trigger and the electrodes launched, sticking into the monster's chest. Electricity coursed through his pale, semitranslucent flesh, his body going rigid, his teeth chattering.

Gabe! Clarissa shouted in his mind. *You're a Van Helsing!*

Slaying vampires is in your blood! YOU HAVE TO HELP ME!

Gabe snapped out of it finally, mirroring her advance toward the Vampire King. They both raised their stakes at once, and the moment The Duke stopped seizing from the electricity, they plunged both weapons into his chest, Clarissa from the front, Gabe through the back.

The Duke howled. He raged. His head reared back and forth as he jerked from side to side, pivoting on the crux of the stakes piercing his evil heart. The stake began to burn Clarissa's fingers and she let go with a hiss of pain. Gabe let go of his own as both stakes burst into flames.

The Duke staggered forward, screaming at the sky. His arms and legs began to shrink, the bones crunching as they straightened. His sharp bat ears rounded, his lips curling inward, and his pug nose jutting outward as his face regained its human shape. All of this happened in the span of seconds. The two stakes still burned in the monster's chest, but the monster had transformed back into the human he'd been. Duke Ştefan of Moldavia, the Vampire King, uttered one final gasp and fell forward, his body turning to ash as it struck the beach, his remains all but indistinguishable from the blowing sand. Clarissa watched it whisper away, happy the nightmare was finally over, that her sister and herself and the others could go back to their lives, before the monsters, human and supernatural, had taken them away.

"Oh, my Lord..." Journee said. She held the Taser at her side, gripping the crucifix around her neck in her other hand.

Light-headedness struck Clarissa suddenly. She stumbled forward, and Gabe caught her in his slender arms. "It's over," he said with a relieved smile.

It was over, but not the way he hoped. Clarissa felt like she was dying all over again. She searched for her sister and found her little twin sprawled on the beach, her eyes closed.

"Gabe...?" Clarissa said, her voice small, echoing in her ears.

Then the darkness claimed her again.

SAVED

GABE RECOGNIZED THE face of the man who'd killed his parents the moment The Duke regained his human form—dark eyes, a mop of curly dark hair, sloped nose, square jaw—and in that instant the lost memories from those weeks spent stranded on the island came flooding back to him.

It was true. The Duke had saved his life and kept him alive with his strange, savory meat. Gabe had unknowingly consumed the flesh of his parents, and even though it technically made him a cannibal, he hadn't become a monster like The Duke. *He was a Van Helsing*. He felt it with every fiber of his being. Together with Clarissa, he'd slayed the Vampire King, and soon she would return to life just like the vampires in just about every book and movie on the subject.

Clarissa stumbled forward breathlessly and he caught her in his arms. "It's over," he told her.

She spoke his name, her voice sounding lost. Hopeless. Then her body went limp. Struggling to hold her on her feet, Gabe turned to find her sister sprawled on the beach.

"*No…*"

He eased Clarissa to the ground beside Abe. Like Emory Jackman's corpse, the old man had aged rapidly since his injury, his flesh sallow, gray and liver-spotted, his white hair falling out in clumps, his fingernails ridged and yellow. He was dying, if not already dead. No... Gabe saw his chest rise and fall, despite being slashed open, bloody and shattered. His eyelids fluttered. That was something, at least. None of this mattered if Clarissa and Ava were dead. If slaying the Vampire King didn't return them and their vampire sisters back to life, what good had they really done here?

"Wake up, Clarissa," he whispered, cradling her in his lap. He tapped her cheek lightly. Unlike Abe, her eyelids didn't move or flutter. She wasn't unconscious or dreaming. Her left arm slid off her lap and landed limply in the sand. "Wake up!" he shouted, his fear of losing her, of losing everyone he'd ever cared about—Digby, Abe, Clarissa, even little Ava, who'd grown on him—suddenly overwhelming him, brimming his eyes with tears.

"Gabriel," Abe breathed, his voice ragged.

He turned to the old man. Abe's eyes were milky, the irises and pupils like overcooked sunny-side-up eggs. He licked his split lips with a tongue dried up like jerky. "I'm… so very proud of you," he said. "Your mother and father… they would have been proud of you, too."

The old man reached out a withered hand and grasped Gabe's knee lightly. Gabe held it.

"I think… I always knew…" Abe's final words became a long, exhaled breath, the blood in his chest wound bubbling. His cataract eyes went wide, and his hand slid away from Gabe's, leaving a set of keys behind.

"I'm so sorry, Gabe," Journee said. She was crouched beside Ava, holding the little girl's wrist. She laid it over Ava's chest, clearly without finding a pulse.

Gabe regarded her with tears cascading down his cheeks. He didn't know what to say, so he said nothing, just returned his gaze to Clarissa and brushed the curls out of her face.

"I have to get my detainee back to his cell." Reluctantly, Journee headed off, back toward the man sitting in the back of the Cruiser, likely unaware of what he'd done to put him there.

"Gabe?"

He looked up.

"I'm sorry I didn't believe you," she said, looking back with a sad smile.

Gabe nodded, sniffling. "It's okay."

She returned the nod uncertainly, then left him alone with the dead. Gabe let his tears fall unashamedly then, hugging Clarissa's lifeless body in his arms. He held her while Journee drove off toward the road, until the burning remains of the *Ceres* extinguished as it sank into the sea, and the morning sun began to rise at the edge of the sea.

It was simultaneously the most beautiful and most terrifying sunrise he'd ever beheld.

Holding Clarissa closely, he expected her to turn to ash like The Duke or burn to cinders in his arms, and didn't care if he caught fire along with her, only wanted to keep her close. Peach rays of sunlight fell upon his face, warming him. As it touched Clarissa's skin, he flinched, awaiting destruction.

Instead, Clarissa sucked in a huge breath as if she'd just been underwater, and sat up abruptly in his lap.

She looked up at him, blinking rapidly until she was able to see him clearly. "Gabe?" she said. Not lost, like before. This time, her voice was steady and certain. She was *alive*.

Gabe hugged her fiercely. After a moment, Clarissa hugged him back. They stayed like that for a long moment, until a small voice spoke her name.

Clarissa gasped, breaking their embrace. "*Ava?*"

Her sister had sat up in the sand, rubbing her eyes like she'd just woken up from a bad dream, and Gabe supposed she had: an unimaginable, decade-long nightmare no child should ever be forced to endure.

Clarissa stood and hurried to her sister, swooping her up into her arms and spinning them around in a circle, laughing as she repeated her name over and over: "Ava, Ava, Ava..."

Gabe got to his feet, watching them, his heart filled with a joy he'd never experienced before. Or maybe not since The Duke had taken his parents away from him when he was three years old. Eventually Clarissa stopped spinning and looked at him, and through her tears she smiled, waving him over.

As Gabe neared, Ava looked up at him from her sister's arms. "Is he your boyfriend?" she asked.

Gabe turned to Clarissa. Had Ava forgotten everything? He hoped she had. The things that had been done to her, the things she'd been made to do... he wondered how anyone could come back from that. With luck it had all flittered away like The Duke's ashes, like the remnants of a dream, and she'd be able to live a life without ever knowing the horrors that had befallen her.

As much as Gabe wanted Clarissa to answer her sister, he was glad when she reached for him instead, saying nothing, just drawing him near. He hugged them both tighter than he'd ever remembered hugging anyone before, and they held each other as the sun rose above the horizon, the three of them laughing and crying as its light warmed the air.

Almost an hour later, Ava stood on the pier throwing flat stones into the water, trying to make them skip.

On the beach near the shore, Clarissa sat with Gabe, hugging her knees, her bare feet intermittently cooled by the surf. An awkward silence had fallen between them once Ava had run down to the water to find seashells. Clarissa remembered everything up until Emory Jackman had slit her throat above that horrible mummy woman in the tub, and she hoped her sister recalled nothing of her time as a vampire, either. Gabe had filled her in on the things she'd forgotten, or at least what he knew of them. Then they'd gone down to the water themselves and sat by the shore to watch Ava play.

"Must be weird seeing her like that," Gabe said finally. "Like a kid still. Fulla beans."

Clarissa smiled. "I never had a proper childhood. After I lost them, I never really let myself. It's good to see her have fun."

Gabe nodded. "Yeah," he said.

"Is it scary?"

"What?"

"Being stranded here again," she said. "After what happened to you and your parents."

"Yeah, kinda." He shrugged. "At least we've got all kinds of food and things to do while we wait for someone to rescue us. I bet they got a radio we could use to call the Coast Guard up in the activity building."

Clarissa nodded. That made sense. It wasn't like it was a true deserted island.

A voice called from the trees behind them. She turned and saw a girl wearing lederhosen, drenched in blood. Others joined her, both vampires and survivors. The spell had been lifted. Clarissa hoped the other survivors hadn't been part of Emory and Tess Jackman's perversions, but if they had, she hoped one day they'd pay for their crimes. She and Gabe would have to tell the girls what had happened to them, why they'd woken up from being taken by whichever of The Duke's offspring had turned them to find themselves on a strange island, as she and Ava had. For now, she just wanted to sit here with Gabe, watching her little twin sister play.

"Hey…" Gabe said.

She turned to him. "Yeah?"

"Do you, uh…" His cheeks turned red and she couldn't help but grin. "When we get back home, do you maybe wanna… I dunno… go to the movies or somethin?"

She smiled. "As long as it's not a *scary* movie."

Gabe huffed a laugh. "I doubt I'll be able to watch horror movies for a while."

Clarissa chuckled. Gabe squinted off at her sister, his expression darkening. Something was clearly weighing on him. With all they'd been through, she could understand, even if she couldn't truly remember much of it herself. He picked up a twig from the sand, snapped it in half, then tossed the pieces into the water.

"So, uh… when do you turn eighteen?" he asked finally.

"Next month," she said. "The eleventh. Why?"

Gabe shrugged, though it clearly pained him to have to say what was on his mind. "I was thinkin… maybe we should wait until then. You know, after everything that happened here. Just in case."

To be honest, she hadn't even considered his age. They were only a few years apart, but it clearly made Gabe uncomfortable enough to worry about it.

"You're probably right," she said. Smiling, she stuck out a hand. "Friends?"

Gabe took it and shook it, businesslike. "Friends," he said with a grin.

They both turned and watched Ava chase a seagull down the beach. After a little while, Clarissa thought she heard the sound of an engine over the crashing waves, and squinted toward it. A small dark object appeared to be moving toward them from far out in the water.

"What's that?"

Gabe held up a hand to shield his eyes from the sun. "It looks like a boat!" he cried, standing abruptly. He hurried toward the pier, where little Ava was now holding up a hand to look in the same direction. Clarrisa ran after him. They both started waving their arms and shouting as they reached the pier, and Ava joined them, laughing enthusiastically. None of it was necessary. The boat paused briefly, but appeared to be heading straight for the dock.

While other voices from the beach joined theirs, Gabe kept waving and shouting until they were able to make out the three men in the boat. "Holy Toledo!" he cried, smiling goofily. "It's Dig!"

"Dig?"

"My buddy, Digby! From the boat!" He hurried down to the end of the pier to meet them as the small boat neared.

Clarissa recognized two of the men as she followed him. The one in the back driving the boat was Cheery, the janitor she'd met on the first day, with his curly hair in a ponytail and a patch over one eye. She guessed the man in the middle seat, who she'd seen kissing Cheery in the hall the morning of the day she'd died, was Digby. She'd never seen the man sitting up front before, a round, sunburnt guy with no shirt and thick gold chains around his neck, glistening wet with damp hair.

"Gabe!" the sunburnt man shouted as the boat reached the dock. "Ain't you a sight for sore eyes!"

"Hey, Tino!" Gabe grabbed the front of the boat and pulled it by the rope so it thumped up sideways against the dock. "Skip, I can't believe you're alive!"

Digby grinned and squeezed Cheery's knee. "It was hairy there for a bit but he found me. How bout you? I thought for sure we'd be coming back to an island of dead people."

"We did okay," Gabe said, hauling his friend up onto the dock by the hand.

While Cheery leaped out and tied the back of the boat, Digby grinned at Clarissa.

"This your special girl, Little Buddy?"

Gabe looked like a rabbit caught in the headlights. "She's my—"

"That's right," Clarissa said for him, sticking out a hand. Digby shook it. "I'm Clarissa."

"Good to meet ya," Digby said. "Thanks for savin my pal's bacon."

"We saved each other," she said.

Gabe turned to her and smiled, his cheeks as red as apples.

The others arrived on the pier then, DJ Safe-T and some crew members who seemed to know Digby and Cheery and Gabe, and more than two dozen girls drenched in the blood of their oppressors.

The Coast Guard and local police would find more survivors over the coming days, some of them raving about teen vampires, others wondering where they were and how they'd gotten there, asking for their moms and dads. All in all, thirty-three girls would be reunited with their families, their parents and siblings finally able to wake from a nightmare that had gone on far too long.

"We're gonna need a bigger boat," Digby said as the crowd approached.

"Clever quip like that got you pulled into the sea last time," Cheery said with a grin.

Digby grinned back. "But you saved me."

"We saved each other," Cheery said, slipping an arm around Digby's waist. "Folks!" he said, addressing the crowd. "We're gonna take the first bunch over to the big island, then we'll make sure the Coast Guard comes back for the rest of y'all! You can count on Cheery!"

SLAYERS

IT TOOK TWO years for the fund from the Jackmans' estate to pay out their victims. All told, two hundred and forty-three million dollars was divvied up between those who'd accepted the offer. Several families rejected a settlement, planning to sue for more. Gabe couldn't say he blamed them.

The whole "teen vampire" story was roundly rejected by the mainstream media, who claimed those who'd died had been victims of the migration of unusually large feral bats. Those who'd told the press what they'd experienced were dismissed by so-called experts as having succumbed to mass delusion, and those speaking the truth on several social media platforms were banned. Still, rumors of the "Teen Vampires of Little Pearl" continued to circulate elsewhere, on podcasts and the dark corners of the internet to this day. Gabe had even heard one of his favorite true crime writers, Martin Savage—whose book he'd been reading on the *Ceres*, which had likely gone down with the ship—was writing a novel about it. Most people said it was in poor taste. Gabe figured Sven Olsen might have said, *If it bleeds it leads*. Not like the news didn't make a gagillion dollars out of their own versions of the truth, anyway.

On the subject of books, Gabe had found an interesting one in Abe's cramped apartment above an amazing hole-in-the-wall Cuban restaurant in Liberty City. It was a journal, similar to the one Clarissa had been reading the day she'd died, although this one outlined the best ways to dispatch vampires, listing several dozen leads on potential "elders" and "hives."

Gabe, Digby and Clarissa stood outside one such place on this sunny November morning: an abandoned railway station in Florida City, its doors boarded and its windows covered with sheets of plywood and old newspapers. They were dressed all in black and wore infrared goggles to be able to see in the dark hive like their prey. They each held a silver stake dipped in garlic juice, so that even if they happened to miss the hearts, they would still do quite a lot of damage.

"You two ready?" Digby asked.

Gabe turned to Clarissa. She nodded, and he nodded back. This was their third time clearing a large hive. The previous two had been "hairy," as Digby liked to say, but they'd managed to come out practically unscathed. They'd already crossed several big names off of Abe's list. Today's was likely to be one of the biggest.

"Remember," Clarissa said, "we find the elder and take them out first. The less we have to kill, the better."

"Amen to that," Digby said.

Clarissa took Gabe's hand. He squeezed hers and returned her smile. They'd become close in the time between Little Pearl and now, sharing Abe's old apartment with Ava in the spare bedroom, even though they could afford more with the money and items they'd acquired. All told, they'd slain four elders and freed twenty-seven of their blood kin, possibly more if any of them had already left their hives. As far as Gabe could tell, the elders they'd slain so far had yet to free generations of young vampires, only their small enclaves. And Lionel de La Haye, Clarissa's Mall Monster, was still out there somewhere. But The Duke hadn't been the only Vampire King around, at least not according to Abe's journal. There were even a few Queens out there in the night, stalking victims and turning others to strengthen their number. Some ate flesh to survive and others merely drank blood, finding the consumption of flesh too close to cannibalism for their taste. Abe had written about entire clans who refused to consume anything human—his journal called them "scrounglings," or "scavengers"—subsisting instead on stray pets and wild animals. Even harder to find were those who'd merely consumed *Moroi* blood, which Abe's notes called *Strigoi*. They often held positions of power and walked during the daylight, like the Jackmans and Abe himself. They didn't *require* blood to survive, but many still chose to consume it to maintain their limited powers. Some bathed in it, like Tess Jackman. However these *Moroi* and *Strigoi* chose to survive, word had spread among them about a new brand of slayers, who used technology as well as cunning to stalk their prey.

They were *scared.*

"*Looks like there's three of em, sleeping in the office right behind the front desk,*" Cheery said over their headsets. He was in the van looking at a laptop with a drone camera view from the inside. Vampires tended to sleep so soundly during the day the small buzz of its propellers never seemed to wake them. "*Four more in the waiting area for the other tracks.*"

"Copy that," Digby said. He tried the door handle and unsurprisingly found it locked.

Gabe got the can of compressed air from his backpack and sprayed it on the handle until it looked good and frozen, at which point Digby struck it with a hammer. The handle came off, pinging on the concrete at their feet, and Digby pushed open the creaking door on the dark, dusty interior.

"We good, Puddin?" Digby asked.

"*No movement, clear for entry,*" Cheery said. "*Slay, sisters!*"

With their stakes at the ready, Gabe, Clarissa and Digby burst through the doorway.

A NOTE FROM THE AUTHOR

You might be surprised to know that an early draft of this book was a lot darker than what you've just read.

Then again, considering the title, you might not.

I conceived this novel as a splatterpunk satire, and took it to some dark places, particularly in the middle. This was partly due to my attempt to get "canceled," or at least drum up some controversy. I was being, in the words of some of my critics, a bit of an "edgelord." To be fair, I felt I was channeling '80s and early-'90s Clive Barker with these scenes, but they didn't help move the story forward in any way or provide any extra depth. They did paint two evil characters as even more monstrous, which I don't think was necessary considering what I *did* leave in. Upon reading them over, I also felt like they didn't really fit with the rest of the book and decided to cut them. I generally write first drafts in a whirlwind, possessed by the "muse." Sometimes it takes me places I don't want to go—okay, *often*—and sometimes the places it takes me aren't necessary to tell the story.

I decided instead to play up the vampire aspect a lot more with tweaks on mythology and lore, and tone down some of the "sexual" stuff. It's still there, as you've seen—you can't write a book called *Pedo Island Bloodbath* and not have some sex and violence—but it's a lot less mean toward the victims. Which I think, considering all they've been through, even as fictional characters, is for the best.

The end product isn't an extreme horror novel, I don't think, and may not even be splatterpunk. I feel like it's a mostly mainstream horror novel with a few somewhat over-the-top deaths and sex scenes. Like the horror I enjoyed from the '80s to the '90s.

Anyway, as usual, the thank yous. This time around my wife needs to be thanked more than ever, for suffering through the early draft with the terrible stuff intact and helping to make the end product much better. Thanks to Danika Meyerson for convincing me I needed to write it based on the title alone. And thank you to early readers Shannon Marie, Frank Spinney, John Lynch, Warn Iverson and Stephanie LaFever for your thoughts and catching issues. I'd also like to thank the authors who paved the way for this story, including but not limited to: Sheridan Le Fanu, Bram Stoker, Richard Matheson, Stephen King, Anne Rice, Ray Garton, Richard Laymon, Poppy Z. Brite, John Ajvide Lindqvist, Gary Raisor, Seth Grahame-Smith, Charlaine Harris, and despite how I feel about the novels, even Stephanie Meyer.

And of course, thank you as always to those of you who chose to pick up this book. I greatly appreciate your support and reviews, whether through word of mouth on social media, or on sites such as Amazon and Goodreads.

This is a heavy topic, and I'd be remiss if I didn't leave with some words about it. The numbers vary depending on who you listen to but the International Labour Organization estimates that approximately 6.3 million people are currently being forced into sexual exploitation worldwide. Of them, 4.9 million are women and girls. Almost 20% of those victims are children.

Whatever side of the political spectrum we belong on, this is clearly unacceptable. There are plenty of reputable charities worth donating to, if you feel moved to do so.

And for the record: Epstein didn't kill himself.

Until next time, keep it creepy!

D.R.
Oct, 2023

For more delicious dark fiction,
visit **www.DuncanRalston.com** and
www.ShadowWorkPublishing.com.

SHADOW WORK
- publishing -

Printed in the USA
CPSIA information can be obtained
at www.ICGtesting.com
LVHW040834230324
775330LV00033B/549

9 781988 819426